ALSO BY SUSAN COLL

karlmarx.com

Rockville Pike

A SUBURBAN COMEDY OF MANNERS

~

Susan Coll

SIMON & SCHUSTER

New York   London   Toronto   Sydney

Simon & Schuster
Rockefeller Center
1230 Avenue of the Americas
New York, NY 10020

For information about special discounts for bulk purchases,
please contact Simon & Schuster Special Sales:
1-800-456-6798 or business@simonandschuster.com.

Manufactured in the United States of America

1 3 5 7 9 10 8 6 4 2

Library of Congress Cataloging-in-Publication Data
Coll, Susan.
Rockville Pike : a novel / Susan Coll.
p. cm.
1. Housewives—Fiction. 2. Married women—Fiction. I. Title.
PS3553.O474622R63 2005
813'.6—dc22   2004052485

ISBN 0-7432-4477-X

For my father, Joseph Keselenko

ROCKVILLE PIKE

Part One

What Gloria hoped in the tenebrous depths of her soul, what she expected that great gift of money to bring about, is difficult to imagine. She was being bent by her environment into a grotesque similitude of a housewife.

The Beautiful and Damned, F. SCOTT FITZGERALD

~

1

MY HUSBAND accused me of embezzlement just before lunchtime on a Tuesday in early September. His aged and partially deaf Uncle Seymour sat at the sales desk a few feet away, straightening a stack of credit card brochures and reorganizing a jar of pens.

"You are robbing us blindly," Leon said. He held a sheaf of papers that might have been the most recent bank statement. He waved his arm maniacally. "Almost two thousand dollars are missing . . . it is like you are embezzling from your own family. Stealing from yourself, even!"

Delia, the patio furniture buyer, stood loyally by his side clutching a notebook. Her porcelain skin seemed to mock my own ruddy complexion. A middle-aged customer in a sleeveless orange dress pretended not to notice that an incident—still vague in nature but clearly not congenial—was unfolding before her, blocking her way as she studied the price tag for a queen-size sofa-bed. An aria intended to enhance her retail experience poured from the ceiling.

"You're totally exaggerating," I protested. "We had huge bills last month. I can explain each one of them." There were many other, more private things I longed to say. Leon and I were long overdue for a somber conversation, for some sort of major marital reckoning. We had just muddled through the worst summer in the history of our seventeen-year marriage, struggling to keep our troubles private in an effort to give our son the illusion of a happy, or at least stable, family life. We had never before let our personal problems spill into the workplace. Maybe this was really it, the beginning of the end of us, at last.

Or maybe it was just the heat. The entire region had been teetering on edge for weeks. The very ground under our feet showed signs of distress; the parched landscape around the store had been subject to a series of underground tremors thought to be related to the record-breaking temperatures. Manhole covers kept exploding off the street, injuring passersby, causing electrical failures, and baffling teams of experts recruited by the local utilities. It was an unfamiliar sort of atmosphere for Washington: hot and dry, with a sharp flammable breeze, not unlike the Santa Ana winds that blow through Los Angeles, sending the murder rate soaring in detective novels.

Instead of looking Leon in the eye as I spoke, I stared down at my new sandals, purchased just the day before. They were an unnecessary splurge, equivalent to the amount of money I had saved by bringing my lunch to work each day for a month, according to my rough calculations. This retail therapy increasingly required a bit of creative financing as our resources dwindled. My toenails poked through the top strap, advertising the need for polish.

Our personal bank statements were usually about $1,000 in the red, and had been for years. This past month was only slightly worse than usual and there were legitimate reasons for the expenditures. The more alarming financial problems, in my view, had to do with the store. Not only were we just skirting bankruptcy, but money kept disappearing from the cash register. Twenty dollars here, thirty dollars there. Small amounts that were beginning to add up. I had no desire to discuss this in front of Uncle Seymour, Delia, and the middle-aged customer in the sleeveless orange dress, so I turned, without speaking, and left the store. I realized only after I had made my dramatic exit that I had forgotten to grab either my pocketbook or the keys to the van. A crumpled wad of cash in my pocket amounted to ten dollars, which, for better or worse, limited the possibility of permanent escape.

I had been seeking refuge at the graveyard for years. I went there to eat in silence, sometimes walking a block in the wrong direction to the sanctioned crosswalk, other times dashing impatiently across nine lanes of midday traffic—my private flirtation with suburban suicide. Pedestrians were few, leaving the sidewalks weirdly empty. Only the disenfranchised walked, and then it was only to the side of the road to wait for the bus. There were of course the sandwich-board men, a couple of whom I had gotten to know in a casual way, fellow pavement dwellers who crossed my path at roughly the same time each day. I had gone so far as to exchange first names with the man in a wheelchair, an African American in his late fifties with thick-rimmed glasses, named TeeJay. He had spent a year between placards advertising tropical fish for Aquarium World, two blocks north of the graveyard. He put in an eight-hour day, he said, and thought it was not bad work: he was outdoors, and could listen to music on his Walkman. The other guy who claimed the same territory advertised half-price CDs for a shop run out of the back of a truck. He remained elusive, less cheerful about his work. We acknowledged each other most days with somewhat suspicious nods. He was probably a front for something else entirely.

Approaching from the south, the graveyard appeared to be a traffic island, with water-stained tombstones dropped at the intersection of two wildly busy thoroughfares. There were so many twisting, bifurcating, angry lanes of traffic that the road itself seemed an optical illusion, the tiny church off to the right a mirage.

I have stood at the edge of the graveyard, staring at the sea of cars, trying to understand the flow: lights timed to precision; cars crisscrossing, veering, and merging effortlessly, almost magically, without collision. It was a wonder, as mind-boggling as a sunrise. I imagined this as the work of men at drafting tables with long sheets of paper that arrive on bulky rolls. I saw them using T-squares and drawing ornate diagrams.

The cemetery's sole flaw was the noise on its periphery. If you closed your eyes, if you stopped protesting and simply gave in, it was possible to hear the drone of traffic as the churning of a sea. The illusion was easily spoiled by a honking horn, or rap blaring from jacked-up woofers, but this was my summer vacation, the closest I was going to get to any beach this year.

The Fitzgeralds' tombstone was mildly eroded, with an accumulation of moss. Its sleek surface suggested coolness, but positioned horizontally, it actually absorbed the full impact of the midday sun. It was warm and inviting and vaguely medicinal. I couldn't help but wonder what Scott and Zelda would make of their current surroundings. *And so we beat on, boats against the current, borne back ceaselessly into the past.* The last line of *The Great Gatsby,* now an epitaph.

I felt a presence here sometimes. Once, when I lay splayed atop the tombstone like Christ on the cross, and not yet like a madwoman fleeing charges of embezzlement, I sensed the coolness of a shadow overhead, and sat up with a start. I looked around but saw nothing. Moments later I thought I heard a rustle in the bushes but again saw no one. I looked down and noticed an empty jar just below my feet, still bearing the Ragu sauce label. Inside was a bunch of blue hydrangeas. Perhaps it was there before I began to doze, although surely I would have noticed this particularly vivid bunch, so unlike the drab, pinkish ones in my own overgrown garden. Flowers frequently appeared, like garlands for Hindu gods, even though I never actually saw anyone visit.

That day it appeared that their grave had been the site of a party the night before: a candle had been melted down to a puddle of blue wax, and an empty bottle of champagne leaned against the stone, balanced precariously. Under the champagne, blue hyacinth. The hyacinth had been there all summer, supple despite the drought, apparently sprouting from a single bulb. Blue hyacinth, blue hydrangea, blue candle wax. Azure. The color of vacations we once took, in happier times.

From the graveyard I had a panoramic view, and just enough ironic distance, to stare back at the mammoth piece of real estate that had brought me here. Kramer's Discount Furniture Depot, so romantically named by my father-in-law during the late 1950s, when Rockville Pike thickened to four lanes to accommodate the phenomenal surge in retail stores and people had a greater appreciation of no-nonsense furniture.

Having grown up during the 1970s in a succession of cities overseas, all about as far from Rockville Pike as one can get both geographically and spiritually, I had at first perceived a certain splendor here. I was delighted by the specialty stores with names like ancient fiefdoms: Bagel City, Appliance Land, Tile and Carpet World, Lara's Plus-Size Universe. The road had once been a dusty Indian trail. It was later packed with ten-inch-deep flint rock in a process known as "piking." The Great Road, as it was called for a time, was plagued by traffic problems even back in the days of the stagecoach, when James Polk and Andrew Jackson were among the travelers who stopped at local inns along the way, heading north.

The only child of a financially strapped aid worker and an emotionally unstable poet, I viewed my parents as tiresomely principled. My family engaged in endless good deeds and meal-times brimmed with urgent intellectual chatter. Salon-style dinner parties with visiting diplomats and journalists and local writers followed one upon the other, from Delhi to Jakarta to Johannesburg. We lugged hundreds of books around the world, feigning indifference when they began to reek of the leaky vessels that transported the likes of us—people without the means to pay for international moving companies or spring for air transport. I met Nelson Mandela once, and while I understood intellectually that this was an honor, what I really longed for was the life of comfort I saw at my cousin's house on Long Island on the few occasions we had visited the States: cartoons on a color television set, a pool table in the basement, and membership at a swank country club, where kids tooled around on golf carts, unsupervised. The cousin had disappeared many years ago, just weeks before graduating with some sort of impressive physics degree from Cal Tech. For a while I thought he was the Unabomber, and was privately disappointed when it turned out that he was not.

I met Leon a couple of years after I graduated from college, shortly after my parents' car plunged off a winding road with my mother at the wheel. The police report said suicide, and it was hard to argue with that determination given her acutely messy mind.

I had found Leon dazzling with his Slavic good looks, his faintly accented voice that reminded me of a dozen different cities at once. Although he was born in this country and held degrees from some of our finest institutions of higher learning, his immigrant parents spoke Ukrainian and Yiddish at home, hence his command of English could be idiosyncratic, particularly when it came to adverbs. But this did not get in the way of his promising future as a high-yield bond trader. When we met he was already one of the most successful young MBAs Drexel Burnham had ever seen. Leon was not only willing to offset the losses I had incurred with my multiple student loans, but he encouraged me to give up my dead-end temp job and apply to graduate school.

We met in New York, in a furniture store, of all places. I had stepped into the musty, cramped shop on Amsterdam Avenue to buy a futon for my equally dingy apartment, and he was there just checking things out. He had gone to great lengths to flee the furniture business, but clearly it was in his blood. Of course I didn't know that at the time, although I did mistake him for a salesman, and he gave me good advice. We continued our conversation over dinner that night. I never bought the futon.

I found him generous and kind, and devastatingly attractive. But I think what attracted me to him above all was the prospect of instant family. I thought it quaint that his parents owned a furniture store, sweet that he was willing to take a leave of absence when his father had a heart attack, to roll up his sleeves and sweat a sale on a hundred-dollar coffee table.

That I might one day be fleeing to a graveyard to escape all this was unimaginable.

In the past I had worked only while Justin was in school, taking the summers off. But this was the year of belt tightening. The store once paid the colossal mortgage on our house, bought us cars, allowed us a few extravagant European vacations. Now it was struggling, and my extra hours on the sales floor were part of the conservation scheme.

One reason the store was failing seemed obvious enough to me: our furniture was ugly. Reasonably priced, yes, even *cheap*. But tasteless and out of style. I had expressed this view on several occasions, even imploring Leon and his father to accompany me to Crate and Barrel and Pottery Barn to show them current trends in popular furniture. The one time they'd acquiesced, my father-in-law had scoffed. *Who would pay $1,499 for a leather armchair that looked like it had been through battle in World War II?*, he'd asked, kicking the wooden leg, offended. *Plus another $600 for the ottoman!* I understood his incredulity, but tried to explain that people were indeed spending such ridiculous sums on "distressed" furniture. This look was "in." That and the sleek contemporary furniture that had been popular in the 1950s— "mid-century modern," they called it. He'd looked at me, raising an eyebrow, as if all this was my very own bad idea.

By that point Leon had wandered off to Starbucks and ordered a frappuccino with too much whipped cream, so he had not been able to verbalize the argument that what people really want are more leather giraffes to stick next to their affordably priced neoclassical TV/DVD stands with Corinthian columns for legs. And hey, who was I to judge? They had built their empire long before I stumbled onto the scene.

Yet the store bled money and our personal bills mounted. Justin's already exorbitant private-school tuition had just increased by fifteen percent, and we owed our lawyer thousands of dollars. Forgoing a summer vacation, pitching in at the store, bringing tuna-fish sandwiches in brown paper bags, and trying to limit recreational shopping were my paltry contributions to the cause. The sluggish economy was partly to blame, but the bulk of our problems stemmed from the just-completed, overly ambitious expansion of the store. Leon hired an expensive financial consultant he knew from business school who wore Hawaiian print shirts and spent hours poring over spreadsheets. But he offered an analysis no more sophisticated than my own observation that we were headed toward financial ruin.

· · ·

Over the past couple of years our marriage had begun to wither for a variety of reasons, some obvious (accruing debt, legal problems, middle-age malaise), some painfully ambiguous (thwarted dreams, possibly); I had begun to long for more: more passion, more intellectual stimulation, more consumer goods to numb my want.

To this end, I had recently decided to launch my own business. Well, it *could* be a business: I had business cards, anyway, and made an initial investment in materials. If I was able to stick to the monthly earning schedule proposed by the parent company, I would be on track to win a free cruise someday. There was also the possibility of winning a car down the line, not to mention a trip to the company's world headquarters, as well as a new house and a million-dollar bonus. Fabulous incentives aside, I was ready to do something creative and needed space, a break from beloved Uncle Seymour and my father-in-law and my husband, who—since we hardly spoke at home anymore— was prone to asking me in front of customers if I had remembered to pick up his dry cleaning; if the car insurance had been paid; if I knew the whereabouts of our son, who had just turned sixteen and was enjoying great success with his recently formed Goth band and therefore was absent much of the time. Still, it was the monthly questions about our bank statements that I had come to fear the most. One had arrived a week earlier, and I had stuffed it, unopened, underneath a pile of junk mail. Evidently Leon had found it that morning.

One storm was followed by another. "Delia has had a brainstorm," Leon said, after he'd paged me over the loudspeaker. *Janie to Mr. Kramer's office. Janie to Mr. Kramer's office.* The nickname was a term of endearment from long ago, now used out of

habit. The formality of "Mr. Kramer" was meant to impress customers, I supposed. I didn't like being paged. It made me feel
submissive. Perhaps I had just grown unsentimental from too
many years spent talking people into gratuitous furniture purchases, into opening lines of credit sure to haunt them for years
to come, but I couldn't help but wonder: would *I* be the one
paging people should Mr. Kramer go away? At times our problems seemed so emotionally and financially complex that I
imagined the best solution was for one of us to simply disappear.
I wasn't quite ready to contemplate divorce, still felt too tender
toward Leon to actively fantasize about his demise. Although
given the amount of weight he had put on these past few years
and the history of heart disease in his family, a coronary episode
seemed a legitimate concern. (Leon's overeating was possibly
proportionate to the debt we accumulated.) Then again, should
he somehow happen to not show up one day, I would probably
dump the store sooner than you could say "liquidation sale." I
knew it was irrational to turn my personal frustration into a rage
directed at a furniture store, but this awareness did little to help.

Delia's brainstorm occurred when she saw the invoice for a
couple of Ernest Hemingway Cherry Grandfather Clocks,
$2,749 apiece, retail. Why not take advantage of our location, she
asked?

Delia had only been around for a few months. She did not
actually work at the store: she was a patio furniture saleswoman,
a representative of a company based in Pittsburgh. But she
seemed to take a special interest in Kramer's, or at least it could
be said that she spent a lot of time at the store. In that short
period she had proven to be a genius, according to Leon. In the
forty-eight-year history of Kramer's Discount Furniture Depot,
the store had never stocked patio furniture, not until Delia
walked in with her briefcase full of catalogs. She had pointed out

that while there were something like five furniture stores per square mile along Rockville Pike, there were no patio furniture outlets for two miles in either direction from Kramer's. And on this crowded strip of commercial paradise, she said, that was practically the equivalent of an entire state, dry. Leon appeared to believe this was the insight that would finally pull Kramer's from its slump.

I wasn't sure where Delia was going with all this. I had looked at her blankly, without judgment, envious of her enthusiasm. Envious of everything about her, really. It was not that I had any desire to have long ceramic nails like hers. Nor was I interested in the plastic surgery I suspected was responsible for her remarkably large breasts. But I was envious, truly, of anyone who could care that much. In striving to earn enough in sales commissions to drive a silver Lexus, she exuded a lust for life. Brava for caring, I thought privately. I couldn't help but suspect that my husband's newfound enthusiasm for patio furniture had something to do with Delia herself. She was oddly mesmerizing. She was not especially young—close to my own age, I guessed. Nor was she especially beautiful. She was, in fact, a rather large woman, but she moved gracefully and with absolute confidence, as if she were a Ford model. How could she be so confident when her role in life was to sell patio furniture to the likes of Kramer's Discount Furniture Depot? I found this, too, somewhat enviable. Although I had never had a private conversation with Delia, I knew this much about her: she was not the sort of woman who would flee to graveyards when the bank statement arrived. Not the sort of woman who drove a minivan grimy with the accumulated debris of carting her son and his friends around to school and sports events and, lately, even to clubs in the wrong parts of town for Goth gigs. She was not a woman in a rut. I understood instinctively how that made Delia attractive to my husband, even if she was really too tall, even if she could stand to lose a few pounds, even if her lipstick was, objectively, a shade too bright.

But it was not until that day when Leon had summoned me to his office that I decided they were lovers. I could see, or I thought I could see, that this idea of hers, this incredibly exploitative—but not necessarily bad—idea, had been first suggested in bed.

And so the idea was born that we develop a line of patio furniture based on the general *aura* of the Fitzgeralds. Kramer's was not in the manufacturing business, and yet Leon was ready to take the plunge. He was ready to diversify, he said. (With what money? I didn't ask.) And I was being invited to participate in this scheme. Flattering, but it was a confusing mandate.

"Did the Fitzgeralds have any special connection to patio furniture?" I asked Delia, still thinking this might be a joke.

"Had Hemingway anything to do with grandfather clocks?" she replied.

As she spoke, I was fixating on her low, sultry voice, imagining her rolling over in bed, after making love to my husband, her long body wrapped in a white sheet, a varnished nail tracing a line down his chest. Admittedly I had been given to occasional fits of hallucinatory jealousy since Delia first appeared in the store this past spring practically bursting out of her clingy strapless dress. Still, this new stab of pain was fierce, primordial.

"I don't know. Did he?"

"No! Of course not. The whole line of furniture was based on his aura, his machismo, the idea of what sort of furniture he might be, incarnate."

"Anthropomorphism," I replied. "But with furniture."

I believe it was because of my sudden, clairvoyant vision of Delia, which included her blowing smoke rings in bed, that I lied. I wanted her on my side, needed to stay on her team, if only to keep the lines of communication open in order to know what it was she wanted with my husband. So I said that it was a brilliant idea. I said I would be happy to participate. I said that Fitzgerald and Hemingway had always had a complicated, competitive relationship. Indeed, why not follow this to a new arena: competition in furniture sales?

"It's a fucking great idea," said Leon, leaning back in the swivel chair that groaned beneath his weight. "This is the perfect thing for you to work on, Janic. Right up your alley."

Delia smiled so sweetly that for a moment I set aside my theory of infidelity and thought I detected something like genuine warmth.

2

I CAN'T say whether I was seduced into starting my own little business by the lure of gadgetry or by the prospect of financial independence. Maybe it was the free cruise. It didn't matter: the closer I came to satiating my desire for amusing work-related contraptions, the farther away drifted my hopes for building a liberating nest egg.

Tiffany Fleisher first told me about her job as a memory consultant as I sat in my minivan while Justin played soccer in the rain. It had been my first visit to the new Soccerplex just a few miles north of Kramer's, where 655 acres of farmland had been converted into twenty-four identical, manicured playing fields. A stadium with bleachers was still under construction, as was a BMX bicycle course, an archery range, tennis courts, and an indoor arena with a snack bar. Something for everyone, except for the anti-sprawl advocates. Theirs was a lost cause from the start: soccer fields trumped farmland every time, with minimal debate.

Although I didn't know it at the time, it was to be Justin's last season on the team. On that day the construction equipment sat idle, perhaps on weekend furlough or in surrender to the heavy rains. A giant crane loomed, suspended midair, as my son pranced around in fluorescent green, chasing a ball. I had the eerie sensation that I had just landed my minivan on another planet comprised of nothing but soccer fields, where even the mud was not quite the color or consistency of earth mud, but was chemically engineered. Soccerplex muck looked like coagulated henna, and permanently stained the floors of my van. A lovely old farmhouse stood proudly, defiantly, in the middle distance.

I was spooked by Tiffany's light tapping on my window. At first I figured she had come to inform me of a change in schedule, or was taking up a collection for a gift for the coach. Perhaps I had forgotten it was my turn to bring water, or the team snack. I was already reaching for my diary to see if I had committed this suburban infraction when she handed me a soggy business card along with an invitation to an introductory memory workshop at her house.

After she left, I began to think I might be having some sort of religious epiphany, there in the rain, in my Taffeta White Honda Odyssey. Perhaps Tiffany Fleisher, whom I couldn't claim to really know, despite the fact that we had been soccer moms together for close to a decade, was a messiah with a business card, sent to help me remember all the things I was having trouble keeping straight. How did she know I was suffering? I was routinely misplacing car keys, running back to restaurants to retrieve sunglasses left on tables, unable to recall simple facts, like capitals of states or names of acquaintances. Globules of information stubbornly refused to adhere, gliding off my brain surface like the raindrops on my windshield that had made it difficult to watch the game that day.

It was a Tupperware sort of thing, as it happened, but with pictures. "Bring five to seven family photographs," she advised, already poised to move on to the next vehicle. "Pick a theme and bring your checkbook," she added. "Or you can pay now. It's twenty dollars to participate in the workshop, more if you decide to purchase supplies."

More if I decide to purchase supplies? This was what I did best as of late—purchase supplies. And what good timing! That same day I had been invited to secure further supply-purchasing power by way of a pre-approved credit line of $10,000. A Platinum Plus Visa card with no annual fee. I would earn five thousand bonus gold points after using the account for the very first time. Several exclamation points (as well as asterisks referring me to some fine-print disclaimers) followed that portion of the announcement. With my bonus points, evidently, I could earn free appetizers and desserts, as well as hotel stays, car rentals, and merchandise for my home and garden.

Normally I would have thanked Tiffany politely and then crumpled the invitation on the spot. This sort of thing did not appeal to me: it was too social, for one thing; too sentimental, for another. I saved what little socializing I did for obligatory business events, which were generally tedious enough to scare me off wanting to go out at all. But I felt a curious draw toward this scrapbooking thing, which may have had something to do with the dozens of shoe boxes in my basement closet stuffed with family pictures, waiting to be sorted. I had all of my parents' photos down there as well, and had taken cursory passes at these, but the task invariably proved too painful. So here was the chance to get organized. But I didn't stop there: part of this strange feeling I had, this quasi-religious epiphany or possible nervous breakdown, was the thought that maybe I, too, could go into this business, whatever it was, and walk up and down the soccer field, handing out business cards and collecting twenty-dollar bills.

Like the neighbor who once showed me her garage stockpiled with canned beans and bottled water meant to sustain her in the event of blizzard or nuclear war, I collected contingency plans should my current life collapse. After securing a leave of absence from graduate school, I had taken a number of preliminary steps toward new careers over the years, including learning to design web pages and attending a prep course for the LSAT. When Justin was younger, I had considered becoming a Discovery Toy representative and had ordered an expensive cache of sample products before determining I would never be any good at sales, an assessment confirmed by my poor track record in the furniture business. Most recently I had begun to compulsively read employment ads so that I would always be armed with a job possibility should Leon and I finally split, should Kramer's go bust, should I find it within myself to walk away and begin a new life. The safety net was of course illusory; the jobs I qualified for would barely put food on the table, never mind support my increasingly extravagant shopping habits. Still, each week I sat with a red pen and the latest issue of the *Gazette,* circling jobs. Pickings were admittedly slim for middle-aged former English majors who had failed to complete their graduate work.

Scrapbooking sounded good to me. No commuting on the Beltway, for one thing. And I was flattered to be included, having come to think of myself as something of an outsider. Although most of our boys had played on the same team since elementary school and I had faithfully come to every game, I hardly knew these women, who all seemed to know each other. I sometimes wondered if I had missed out on some soccer rite of passage, or was oblivious to a certain form of etiquette. Each week they would spread their blankets side by side and produce thermoses of coffee. Others brought impressively engineered chairs that folded up like the slim umbrellas they set up to block the sun. Even that day, in the rain, they had gathered together under the shelter of the rear door hatches of a couple of minivans, parked side by side, backed into spots to face the field. They knew the names of one another's spouses and seemed to share an easy confidence. They understood what an off-sides foul was—something I still didn't get despite all my hours logged on the field—and expressed outrage when the referee made an unfair call. I would join them sometimes as a sort of social experiment, acting nonchalant, simply inserting myself as if I belonged. No one was ever rude, but then, no one offered me a swig of coffee, either. Over time I came to feel conspicuous, as much of an outsider as the foreign families who appeared on the team periodically, usually during short-lived diplomatic tours or World Bank stints. These were people who didn't fret about their inability to fit in: they weren't supposed to, and they would soon be gone anyway.

It was of course possible that the fault was mine: I was something of a misfit, accustomed to feeling displaced. I also spent so many hours working in the store that I might have missed out on some crucial bonding time. The Kramer's controversy was another possible factor in my sense of soccer-field alienation.

My very first encounter with Tiffany had taken place in the marbled front lobby of our children's school many years ago. "The thing I love about this school," she had said to me, "is that I can dress like *this,* and you can dress like *that,* and we both feel comfortable." Tiffany was dressed in a navy blue suit with a neat scarf around her neck and a Coach briefcase hanging from her shoulder, on her way to her important job as a federal prosecutor. I was on my way to the gym, wearing sweatpants and a T-shirt, with my hair pulled up into a ponytail that sprayed sloppily on top of my head. Part of the fabric on my right sneaker was worn through, gym clothes being one of the few areas of spending in which I skimped, and I remember concentrating hard on my footwear as she spoke. My socks were neon orange, a color that suddenly seemed absurd, unnatural, too bright to be brandished in the sedate entranceway of Rockville Preparatory School with its subdued colonial color scheme and oil paintings of stern-looking headmasters from the late 1800s. I had felt acutely uncomfortable, and had wished that my son went to a school where we were all schlubby housewives, or indentured servants in family furniture stores, and that mothers clad in designer wear with important jobs would be required by law to educate their children elsewhere.

At the soccer field, those of us who dressed as though we were going to watch our kids play a ball game, wearing old jeans, anticipating mud and grass stains, were in the minority. Mostly people looked as though they shopped for these events in the weekend sportswear departments of preppy boutiques. Once fall set in, some of the especially style-conscious parents began to dress in tweed ensembles, as if they were setting off not for a soccer game but for a fox hunt, one on a grand country estate where they would drive their SUVs on rugged back roads, then drink tea and smoke pipes while servants cleaned their guns.

If only my discomfort had been limited to feelings of social awkwardness, to differences in clothing styles. Then I might have dismissed it as a sign of mild neurosis—simpler to live with this self-diagnosis than with the thought that perhaps other people genuinely did not like me, that maybe many of my soccer-parent peers really did regard me with suspicion, if not outright contempt. And if they did keep their distance, it all had to do with the store. Everything always had to do with the store. The recently completed expansion of Kramer's had drawn even more public opposition than this Soccerplex, and there was still public resentment as well as ongoing litigation in various stages of appeal surrounding legal technicalities of our project. Adjectives such as "hideous" and "monstrous" were routinely used in the press to describe Kramer's new metallic façade, even though we had hired an award-winning architect to draw up the plans. He had been a finalist in the bid to design the Guggenheim Museum in Bilbao, or so he claimed.

Occasionally I fretted that the chill I felt on the soccer field had nothing at all to do with Kramer's, or with me, but rather with my son. Was he disliked, a bad influence? Doing drugs or having sex? At the time this had seemed impossible, but maybe these parents sensed something I did not. By the end of that season he had acquired the first of many facial piercings, and then he quit the team.

Goth was a phase he would surely outgrow. Justin was a nice boy, although admittedly a bit withdrawn as of late. I kept a close eye on his moods, and tried to remain positive. He had a few bleak tendencies, but was not entirely uncommunicative. And he was a very good musician. Our neighbors did not always agree, and the police had been summoned on more than one occasion when his band practiced in our garage. But he did well in school, and had never once missed placement on the honor roll. He was also the only member of our family who did not protest when it was time to have his teeth cleaned every six months, and the dentist said he was a model flosser.

I was too old to care about the opinions of these women, I told myself. It was okay that I had simply failed to integrate myself as a soccer mom, even though I could think of no better way to spend the day than to watch my son run up and down the field, exuding good health and a surprising athleticism, especially given his parents' static tendencies. I had grown resigned to sitting alone in my van, as Tiffany had found me that day.

I remember giving Tiffany's invitation one last glance before setting it aside as Justin clamored into the van. He was wet. A scab had torn off his knee and the wound was swathed in blood and dirt. His cleats were encrusted with that peculiar orangey mud. Maybe I would go to Tiffany's workshop, and maybe I would not. It seemed to be of no great consequence. It was just a little thing, a new activity, a change in the old routine. But sometimes when a life is grinding gears, the small adjustments make a difference.

3

THE NEW improved Kramer's looked more like a spaceship than a discount furniture store, and there were those who wished it would actually lift off for some other galaxy. I confess to seeing a strange beauty in the redesign. With its boxy contour and jutting annexes it was ungainly, yes, but it also had a boldness of spirit, like a woman with fat thighs who is not afraid to wear a miniskirt. It was especially striking in the late afternoon, when the sun bounced off the metallic façade refracting the light like a giant disco ball, although there were occasional complaints from motorists who claimed they were temporarily blinded as they approached the Pike, heading west.

Until the scaffolding went up and more than 200,000 square feet of furniture store materialized, swallowing the adjacent buildings and felling a few trees in the process, Kramer's had sat inoffensively at the north end of a strip mall near the town center of Rockville. Samuel, my father-in-law, had purchased the property in the late 1950s, and leased the contiguous parcel of land to tenants that had most recently included a Korean grocery store, a manicure boutique, an optician, and a Vietnamese noodle shop. A shrewd businessman, he turned what he had begun as a mom-and-pop operation specializing in reclining chairs into one of the Washington region's most successful small businesses.

Even back when I first visited Kramer's after Leon and I became engaged, the store was bulging with inventory, so over-stuffed that it was difficult to walk through the showroom without stumbling into an ottoman or tripping over the cord of a haphazardly placed light fixture. Occasional visits from the fire department threatened to bring fines and permit revocations if aisles remained clogged and access to the back door was not liberated. Samuel always managed to finesse these situations without rectifying a single thing, relying solely on the charm and business acumen that must have contributed to his overall success. The same charm and acumen, I suppose, that must have conveyed from father to son, and had helped Leon win me over without effort.

Leon had been advising his father for many years that it was time for change. Kramer's had long been profitable, and Leon urged him to open a second store, or relocate to a larger property. The idea to expand on the existing lot had never been considered, possibly because it would have meant the demolition of the adjacent properties. While that was legally within his rights, it was something outside the realm of Samuel's way of thinking. Samuel was full of old-country superstition. He couldn't believe his own good fortune and did not want to tempt fate by appearing too greedy. His family had escaped the pogroms of Ukraine when he was a boy, then had settled in Germany before finally fleeing to the United States. Samuel met his future wife, Esther, in Berlin. She was also from a family of displaced Russians, and it sometimes seemed to me that was all they had in common. He sent for her once he had settled, and they bought an unassuming brick rambler just blocks from the store.

Samuel quickly became a local legend. He was honored by the Rockville Chamber of Commerce as Businessman of the Year three times, and his picture hung on the wall at the local chapter of the Rotary Club and in the front lobby of the Jaycees.

Leon continued to press, and Samuel finally relented. He agreed that if Leon would come home from New York and put his expensive MBA to work for his family instead of helping the rich get richer, then perhaps they could turn Kramer's into something remarkable.

We had been married less than a year when the summons came from Rockville. Samuel had collapsed on the sales floor while clearing space for a new shipment of teak end tables. A customer administered CPR while they waited for an ambulance. The next day, Samuel underwent open-heart surgery.

Leon took a temporary leave from his job, and I confess to having been privately relieved by this ready-made excuse to take a break from graduate school. I was headed nowhere, really, working on an MFA in creative writing but ambivalent about my work, and fearful of winding up like my mother. Besides, I was three months pregnant, and it seemed like a good time for a spell outside New York.

And those first few months in the store were fun! It felt like we were playing house. Or rather, playing furniture store. Samuel was at home, recovering from his surgery, with Esther by his side. Apart from Uncle Seymour and some part-time salespeople who came and went on an irregular schedule I could never quite follow, we had the store mostly to ourselves. There was a nice, easy rhythm to the days. Leon was in his element; he loved schmoozing with the customers and seemed cheerful and relaxed. Sometimes I would find him lounging in his father's favorite plaid reclining chair, dispensing investment advice to family friends as well as random shoppers. Later, after our troubles began and Leon slipped into a state of permanent anger, this once tranquil husband was hard to recall.

For much of this period I was desk-bound with swollen feet, assigned to paperwork, which I enjoyed. Furniture store tasks had a nice finality to them that graduate school did not. Invoices were put in envelopes and stuck in the mail, for example, and then they were gone. Or they were put in filing cabinets, with drawers that clicked shut. They did not sit around and taunt, like the unfinished stories I was meant to write for class.

Often after closing, Leon and I would lock ourselves inside the showroom. Our short-term studio apartment was so tiny that we found it more comfortable to spend leisure time at the store, even if those quarters were only slightly less cramped. Sometimes we stretched out on a plush sofa and watched the small television Samuel kept in the back office. Leon would get us take-out food from the noodle shop next door and we spread out paper plates at a dining-room table and talked for hours, scheming about the future, as well as about furniture. We had a silly game we'd invented that involved betting on which items would be the next to sell.

Once Justin was born, we no longer fit into the apartment we had rented just south of the Mid-Pike Plaza, so we signed a year-long lease on a townhouse. We didn't particularly like its location, in a planned community where all the streets were named after racehorses, but there was lots of space. From the corner of Secretariat Lane and Alysheba Court, where our white brick house sat at the end of a small cluster of identical white brick houses, we heard cars rushing about the Beltway, despite sound-proofing walls cleverly disguised by berry bushes. The mailboxes were all identical thatched birdhouses, and covenants proscribed such blemishes as metal fences and basketball hoops, inappropriately colored garbage cans, or anything else the seemingly clandestine neighborhood association deemed likely to erode property values.

Leon and I were still on the same page back then. This was a pleasant interlude, but he didn't really want to stay in Rockville, and we told Samuel that we would be moving on once he regained his health. Leon had been helping out on the sales floor since third grade, often doing his homework in the back office. He had even manned the cash register as a college student, commuting to classes at Georgetown. He was enormously proud of his parents' success, grateful for the opportunities Kramer's had enabled him to enjoy, but he had worked hard in school precisely to escape this life, and had no intention of taking over the family business. Neither did his evangelical Christian sister Elaine, an emergency-room physician who had recently moved to Oregon and was suspiciously on-call during most family crises.

Back then the phone still rang with exciting offers—one caller urged Leon to apply for an opening in a London brokerage—but Samuel's condition had not yet stabilized. Brief consideration was given to letting Uncle Seymour take charge, but this was not really a viable option. Seymour had never been the brightest crayon in the box, as my father-in-law put it. He had suffered multiple learning disabilities as a child and was unable to read beyond a fifth-grade level. His thinking process was excruciatingly slow; his brain seemed to operate like an old computer trying to download too much information.

Uncle Seymour had always been my favorite member of the extended Kramer family. His love was unconditional. He was constantly following me around the showroom, close on my heels, dripping with affection. Later, when Justin was old enough to spend time in the store, Seymour would entertain him with corny jokes and magic tricks. His pockets were always stuffed with sweets.

Regardless of whether he was any good at his job, he did seem to love it. He was widely praised within the family for his superior salesmanship, but this was a conspired lie. Most customers seemed either annoyed or spooked by his attentions, although he did have a few loyal patrons who always asked for him by name. While no one dared keep tabs, he likely chased away more sales than he snagged. But Seymour was family. And this was a family business.

Then, just as it became clear that Samuel would make a full recovery, Esther was diagnosed with breast cancer. The tumors had been growing for a year, and she acknowledged that she had felt them, but her distrust of doctors—her own daughter evidently included—was such that she refused to visit one. Leon was shattered, which surprised me more than it should have. He'd always had a difficult relationship with his mother. They fought constantly. She still nagged him about his wardrobe, his haircut, his shabby shoes, his choice of wife. We all privately believed that she was at least partly responsible for Samuel's heart attack, having aggravated him to the point of coronary protest. Of course, this was not entirely fair: At the time he had weighed nearly 250 pounds and smoked a pack of cigarettes a day. The Kramer men, otherwise disarmingly handsome, tended to yo-yo dramatically in their weight.

Esther had not liked me from the get-go, but I tried not to take it too personally. I don't think she would have liked any woman Leon brought home. The night before she died, she rose from the coma in which she had lain for three days, went into the kitchen, and prepared an imaginary meat loaf. Samuel found her at 2 A.M., standing in the dark wearing an apron and oven mitts. When he asked her what she was doing, she explained that she was making dinner for Leon because I wasn't feeding him properly. This had always struck me as a piece of information that Samuel might have chosen to keep to himself.

We stayed, of course. And things were not all bad. Times were good in the furniture business in the late 1980s, and we were getting rich. Although not as rich as a high-yield bond trader might get, and certainly without the glamour.

After about a year, Leon felt it was a good time to venture into real estate. He landed us in a frighteningly large house with a fountain in the front yard, pink shutters, curly faux New Orleans iron trim, and complicated window dressings that looked like they ought to be torn down and made into prom dresses. The marble floors refracted sound, crazily bouncing our voices around. The house was like a mausoleum, not unlike the sort of place Jay Gatsby might have built had he elected to live in suburban Maryland, without the parties and the expensive shimmer of the Long Island Sound.

I had lobbied against the house, but Leon said it was a good investment, a quick sale by a Middle Eastern oil executive being transferred back home, with minimal haggling over details. Distracted by the baby, and in a hormonal, sleep-deprived fog, I was content to let Leon worry about things like shelter. Truly, I didn't care where we lived because I was sure things were temporary. My family had never stayed in one place for more than three years; it had never really occurred to me that other people unpacked their suitcases and stayed somewhere forever.

Perhaps I should have been paying closer attention, because this was about the time things began to change. Leon, for example, insisted on furnishing the new house not just with Kramer's furniture, but with Kramer's *rejects:* chairs with subtle rips in the fabric, tables with wobbly legs, rugs with flawed patterns or mismatched tassels. The runner in our front hallway had a cigarette burn in the corner, which I tried to disguise by placing the leg of the hall table over it. This required an angling of objects. Our entranceway looked, and was, slightly askew. I began to dream about quality furniture, sneaking catalogs into bed at night, reading them clandestinely, like pornography.

Later, we discussed such home improvements as ripping out

the trim, painting the shutters, and razing the fountain, maybe replacing it with a basketball court, but we never did. The fountain broke after a year, and it was too costly to bother fixing. The stagnant water grew green, then black, with algae, and that was only one indication that our lives were moving in the wrong direction.

There was admittedly something unhealthy about the way we overspent in the early days of our relationship. Leon had once whisked me off to Nice for the weekend, spur of the moment. Another time he bought me a showy diamond ring that I hardly ever wore. Amassing large sums of money was not something either of us aspired to, but for a while we happened to have a lot of it. We liked to believe that what set us apart from the rest of the decadence on Wall Street in those days was that we never lost our sense of perspective. We *knew* it was ridiculous to spend $300 on dinner for two, particularly when we weren't even people who could taste the difference between the food at a hot new five-star restaurant and Sizzler Steak House. I suppose we were both engaged in private rebellions, the manifestations of which involved throwing money around in a manner that would have appalled both our sets of parents. I had gone and found myself a true capitalist, the very antithesis of my socialist do-good father. All Leon had to do to rebel was stay away from Kramer's Discount Furniture Depot.

Anyway, those heady days were officially over, as indicated by Leon's sudden imposition of a household budget. He insisted the point was not to constrain our spending, but rather to make the most efficient use of our resources. He based his numbers on the collection of a month's worth of household receipts, then assigned prescribed sums to categories such as groceries, clothing, and entertainment. I believe that my penchant for so-called embezzlement may have begun at this time.

Leon did not bother to adjust his figures to account for inflation and cost-of-living expenses, or even for the more general changes in our family lifestyle over the years. At first I stuck to fiddling with the sums in ways that I considered fair: squeezing extra money out of the grocery budget by buying store brands and using coupons, then taking any surplus cash and using it to supplement the clothing budget. Other methods were more creative, such as using reimbursement checks from doctor's visits for the occasional personal splurge. Over time I gave up and chose to simply *ignore* the budget. Not a month went by without some sort of extraordinary expense: braces for Justin's teeth, hip surgery for the dog, and endless expenses related to our house. We never spoke of these transgressions directly. There was nothing to discuss back then, really, because we could afford the overages and besides, these were mostly unavoidable expenses, except for the dog—the surgery failed, and he eventually had to be put to sleep, with no refund for the botched $4,000 hip, a financial fiasco that Leon had trouble putting behind him.

Seasons changed, marked by the steady accumulation of controversial bank statements and different-colored soccer jerseys. I was afraid to do the math, dared not contemplate the number of lost balls, outgrown cleats, or half-empty water bottles left behind at fields that gauged the passage of time. Justin grew, boxes of schoolwork accumulated in the garage, years blurred together, marital harmony waxed and waned as did jealousies and fleeting flirtations, and before I quite realized what was happening I was sitting in a law office above a dry cleaner on Rockville Pike, signing my name to a five-million-dollar construction loan. A loan that threatened everything from the little bit of money we had set aside for Justin's tuition to the new winter coat I'd been eyeing all month.

This last-minute change in the terms of our loan agreement was yet another bad sign. The financing was not supposed to affect our personal assets, yet we had been forced to throw our house and savings in as collateral, lending analysts having determined that there was, contrary to Leon's own learned insistence, a finite amount of growth that any single furniture store could realize in a given year. The bank people thought Leon's numbers were unrealistic, that Kramer's could never hope to turn over the amount of inventory he planned to stock in the new mega-store he envisioned, notwithstanding his concept of turning the place into something like a furniture theme park, with a café serving fancy coffees and a staffed child-care center with bilingual minders and a constant rotation of toys.

I had a bad feeling about this, but it was hard to separate my premonitions of financial ruin from my own increasing desire to flee. This was when the fights began in earnest. Leon said we were forced to expand the business because we could not afford to live on our current income. I said—somewhat unfairly and irrationally given that I had been passively floating along, letting Leon make all of the financial decisions—that our expenses were the result of living the wrong sort of life in the first place. Who needed a crumbling mini-mansion in one of the most expensive neighborhoods in the country? Who needed to send their son to private school? This was not how I had grown up.

What did I want to do then, Leon asked. Should we pack up and move to Bolivia? Did I really think my own childhood had been so glamorous? And look how well things had turned out for my mother! Not to mention my father. If I had wanted to live a different sort of life, maybe I should have thought about that before I'd dropped out of graduate school and wasted $30,000.

I was speechless. Was this not the beauty of marriage? Knowing how to most efficiently paralyze your prey?

And so I would take a deep breath, scold myself for not having done anything more productive with my life, for not finishing graduate school, for being unable to follow through on a single plan, for spending the prime years of my life selling furniture. Then, like clockwork, the guilt would follow: I should be more grateful to Leon for providing me with this comfortable life. I'd muddle on with resolutions to find a hobby, or make some friends, maybe join a book club. At the very least, I could try a little harder to sell a few sticks of furniture.

Leon said that my negativity was contagious. Tensions ran so high it was impossible to get Justin off to school without a blowup over something as minor as a perceived sense of idleness in his morning search for his sneakers or his backpack, one or the other of which would invariably make him miss the bus. I felt frazzled all the time, had one eye on the clock as Justin would begin to recite the details of a long, convoluted dream while I made him breakfast, calculating whether I'd have time to jump in the shower before opening the store, wondering when I could squeeze in a trip to get groceries. One day, I knew, my life would be too quiet and I'd long for this constant buzz of activity, this demand for my attention. But to have it all at once, every single morning, was almost more than I could bear, particularly when it was accompanied by Leon and me snapping at one another all the time. We had begun to fight quite freely in front of Justin, possibly in subconscious attempts to appeal for his support, something we had vowed to avoid back in our more naïve days of thinking it was possible to conscribe family behavior.

Just as my relationship with Leon was dangerously unraveling, I bonded with Uncle Seymour. I hung out with him in the store when it was quiet, took him to lunch sometimes, and even invited him over for tea in the afternoon. Leon thought this was strange behavior on my part: Uncle Seymour had been a constant, needy fixture in his life. A beloved family member to be sure, but more burden than companion. To Leon, Seymour was the slightly daft bachelor uncle who had lived just down the street when he was growing up, who came over once a week for dinner, and who needed practical guidance at every turn. Seymour would become flummoxed to the point of tears by something as routine as a notice in the mail that it was time to take his car in for an emissions test, and we'd all have to talk him through it.

I missed having a father, someone to love me unconditionally. Seymour filled that role in a way that Samuel did not. Samuel and I got along fine, and I was sure that he loved me in his own way, but he treated me more as a welcome guest than as a member of the family, for reasons I was pretty sure had to do with religion.

I tried not to let the fact that Seymour would love *anyone* unconditionally interfere with my gratification. Besides, talking to Seymour was cathartic, and he was the perfect person to have as a confessor. I knew that he could not hear much of what I said, although he did occasionally blurt out something trite but profound: *Smile and the whole world smiles with you* was something he liked to say a lot, a quote from either the Bible or a happy musical, and I thought this might be true. If only I were more the smiling type, maybe I could find out.

Seymour had always been a prolific doodler, and sometimes when we were cleaning up at the end of a day we would find sketches he had made of furniture. One series in particular was remarkable in its prescience. He had drawn a line of reclining chairs that resembled the bulkhead seats on airplanes, with tray tables that lifted up from the armrests and sported giant cup holders on the side. One chair had space underneath for a mini refrigerator, intended to keep a six-pack of beer cold, he said. Both to encourage Seymour's creativity and to test-market what seemed to me a possibly successful product line, I talked Samuel into developing a few prototypes of these chairs. In the end we had a dozen of these accessorized recliners—Superbowl Specials, we called them—but we never sold a single one.

• • •

It would be easy to suggest that this troubled period was all about money. Most things were, in the end. But it was also about who we were, how we saw ourselves, and how we stood in the community—the sorts of things I had not given much thought to until we began to bleed outside the lines of who I imagined us to be. Until we became the subject of newspaper stories and were forced to turn over a substantial chunk of our monthly income to retain a lawyer with the unfortunate name of Chandler Chandling, whom I neither liked nor had much faith in. He was Leon's best friend from high school, and the two of them played golf and went on occasional fishing trips. The fact of their great friendship didn't stop Chandler from gouging us financially, however. My other gripe about Chandler was that Leon regressed when they were together—they'd drink too much beer and make lewd comments about women. This was as curious as it was mortifying. Although I had met Leon when he was already twenty-seven, there was nothing in his manner to suggest he'd ever behaved like a drunk fraternity boy. Sometimes I worried that he was maturing in reverse. He had been so responsible as a child and young adult that in his mid-forties, he was first experiencing male adolescence. And this was possibly where Delia fit in—a young man's dream with her brash femininity, even if the appeal was somehow over-the-top to the rest of us.

Opposition to Kramer's expansion plans came as a surprise. It was not as if we were proposing to open a hazardous waste site, or an adult video store, or even a Hooters, which was in fact just down the street. Admittedly I felt some solidarity with our opponents at first, whoever they were—just a collection of names on a petition. I didn't want to expand the store, either, and I thought that their objections might help my cause. I didn't understand at the time how high the personal stakes were. I figured that Leon would acknowledge that this was not a good idea, after all, and then we would move on. Instead, it had just the opposite effect: it made him fiercely determined to succeed. This land belonged to the Kramer family! This was America! He could do whatever he damn well pleased! The thought of some bureaucratic planning commission reviewing his blueprints, passing judgment on his floor plans, made him irate.

The initial phase of hearings made front-page headlines for months. In fairness to Leon, we were victims of bad timing, and I could understand how the seemingly arbitrary nature of the controversy irked him. The same week we applied for our construction permit, two major national retail chains sought approval to open franchises within a mile of Kramer's, also generating news stories. An emergency meeting of the traffic planning committee was convened, and it ran twelve hours straight after a prominent council member proposed diverting funds from the school budget to build a new road to accommodate the flow of cars that the three major retailers would attract. This resulted in an emergency meeting of the school board, and the rumors of layoffs and cuts in teacher pay drew a slew of protestors, including flag-waving children from a nearby elementary school. The historic preservation people checked in with a last-minute concern that the original Kramer's building was a landmark and therefore could not be torn down, which was laughable given the condition of the ancient one-story storefront with mold growing beneath the floorboards and rat infestation in the cellar. Then, in a final assault, a group of Vietnamese waiters appeared, asserting that Kramer's proposed demolition of the adjacent noodle shop would put them, and dozens of others, out of work. Leon suspected that they had been put up to this, but in a show of his magnanimity he offered to hire all of the displaced employees to work for him at double the pay they were currently receiving. None of them took him up on his offer, which had not been entirely insincere: back then we could afford more help. Kramer's was finally given the go-ahead in a nod toward encouraging "containable" business growth in the region. Besides, we already existed, we owned the land, and there was evidently no precedent to prohibit us from building on our own property. The two national retailers, however, were told to resubmit their plans in three years.

If only Leon had been able to leave well enough alone. The renovation was nearly completed, the press had grown bored with the story, and public attention had finally turned to a much larger, more egregious development project, one that involved mowing down dozens of homes and two patches of parkland in order to build an inter-county highway. But Leon got an idea stuck in his head. Since the contractors were already there, he said, and since the original project had come in slightly under budget (which was not saying much given the outrageously inflated original estimate), why not tear down the old barn behind the store and turn it into an office?

This made no sense. We had just built one of the largest free-standing furniture stores in the state, and it contained plenty of office space, surely more than we would ever need. To Leon, however, the calculation was entirely about costs and benefits. If we waited until a later date, we would have to start over, find a new contractor, and then it would be much more expensive. As it was, our current contractor was willing to do this on the cheap since he had an extra couple of weeks to kill before beginning his next job. The fact that we didn't need additional office space any more than we needed a bowling alley didn't seem to factor into his thinking.

While Leon and I argued over this, the contractor went ahead and filed the new round of paperwork. Given the initial wave of controversy, he said, he wanted to do everything by the book, and he applied for a demolition permit even though it was not obvious that one was technically required given the small dimensions of the barn and the negligible parameters of the project. The permit was granted quickly without incident, but the day that the bulldozer arrived, so did Anna Berger, the loose-cannon chairwoman of the Historic Preservation Commission. In an unhappy coincidence, Anna Berger was the aunt of one of the boys on the soccer team. This was a city of more than 47,000 people, a county of close to a million, and yet there was little anonymity when it came to our store. Our world seemed to consist of a minuscule cast of characters, all of whom knew each other, and every one of them seemed to know our business.

Anna pleaded with Leon to spare the barn until her people had a chance to assess whether it qualified as a historic property. She did not have any legal papers, or even a convincing argument about why he should listen to her. Leon laughed. He laughed loudly, and his laughter grew wilder, thicker, maniacal, rising up across the field to the second story of the store, where it found me. I was standing behind a yellow armchair at the time, reaching for the price tag that was affixed to the back, and then, with a felt-tip marker, reducing it by 30 percent.

I went to the window to see what the laughter was about and saw Leon point to the demolition permit affixed to a tree beside the barn.

"You people are a bunch of fucking lunatics," I heard my husband yell, at which point I decided my presence was required. By the time I reached them he was breathing heavily, and his face was growing purple. I immediately recalled that during an argument with a meter maid over a ticket she was writing, Leon's uncle Bernie collapsed on a Brooklyn sidewalk, dead. For his uncle Ralph, it was standing on the shoulder of the Van Wyck Expressway, arguing over a fender bender.

"I can't believe you'd have the nerve to come here!" Leon railed. "The store has been determined to be of no historic value whatsoever, so who gives a flying fuck about this termite-ridden barn?"

Anna was a soft-spoken woman in her mid-fifties with shoulder-length gray hair and enormous tortoise-shell glasses. She spoke very slowly, with a saccharine earnestness that made her words grate. I had met Anna on several occasions, but she never seemed to remember who I was. In addition to chairing the historic preservation committee for the past ten years, she had launched an unsuccessful bid for Congress in the last election and was currently hosting fundraisers presumably aimed at another run. She was an outspoken feminist who was said to have ghost-written a few of Hillary Clinton's speeches. But Anna had always struck me as the type of feminist who did not like women very much, or at least not women who were insufficiently powerful, like me. Perhaps key to my fear of Anna Berger was the fact that she was also a practicing psychotherapist. We had never had a prolonged conversation, in part because I sensed that she could sum me up if I dared to open my mouth and give her fodder for analysis.

Anna told Leon that she had been doing research about runaway slaves and had learned that many of them traveled parallel to Rockville Pike as they made their way north. Often they were taken into hiding by sympathetic farmers. It was possible the barn had once housed fugitive slaves, she said, and it would therefore be of historic interest not just to the community, but to the entire country.

"Oh, please!" Leon replied. He picked up an axe that was lying in the back of the contractor's pickup truck and took a swing at the barn. An entire side panel collapsed, and we all stared at it, not sure whether to be impressed by his strength or surprised by the flimsiness of the structure.

Anna Berger came back a week later with a lawyer and a legal order granting her access to the property. She was accompanied by a bunch of unsmiling colleagues, all wearing boots and wielding shovels. By then the walls of the barn were already gone and the framing for the new office was partially constructed, but they dug anyway. Within an hour, they had produced three bones.

There were hoots of celebration, much merriment and raucous cheering that seemed more befitting a home-team victory than the discovery of human remains. Leon resumed shouting with Anna. Actually, Anna didn't really shout—she just replied tersely—but Leon's loud volume sufficed for them both. I approached the sight of the excavation and picked up what looked like a piece of jawbone. I held it up in the air and turned it around, inconclusively. But Leon was more certain.

"It's a fucking cow," I believe were his exact words. "This was a fucking barn. That is a fucking cow. There are probably dead animal carcasses all over the place."

"I've been doing my homework," said Anna, quietly. "I'm quite willing to wager that those are the bones of a young slave girl."

We all looked at her, astonished by this deductive leap.

One of Anna's colleagues suddenly recalled that a string of murders had occurred in the region in the early 1970s. Three college students had disappeared, he said knowledgeably, all of them last seen in Rockville. He speculated—a bit too enthusiastically, it seemed to me—that perhaps these were the bones of dead coeds.

Whosoever bones they were, they were eventually bundled into plastic bags and taken away in the back of a police cruiser, where they were meant to be transported to a forensics lab. But something went wrong en route, and the bones never reached their destination. They went missing, just like the dead coeds had more than thirty years before.

The discovery of the bones and their subsequent disappearance also made headlines, and it was at about that time that the neighbor behind us, who had called the police on at least two occasions when Justin's band practiced in our garage, put a billboard on his front lawn, opposing our expansion. I did not point out to him that he was too late—the store was already rebuilt by then and open for business. In a heartwarming footnote, the neighbor to our right, who happened to be the highest-ranking Cuban official in the United States, dropped by with his wife and son and gave us a box of cigars to offer his personal, though explicitly unofficial, support.

I wish I could say that I mustered a more worthy display of conjugal solidarity. Publicly I stood by Leon's side, but privately I agreed with the people who worried that our building design was inappropriate for the neighborhood, and that the traffic such a mega-store was likely to attract would overwhelm the existing road infrastructure, notwithstanding the approval of our request for a traffic signal with a left-turn arrow. I suspected above all else that the lending analysts were on to something in their projections of financial doom. And I still couldn't think of a single logical reason to build an office behind the store. So I began to think of illogical reasons. And then about bones. Thoughts that didn't add up to much, but were disturbing all the same.

It was in the midst of all this that we lost our dog. I had always been ambivalent about Patch—so named by Justin for the splotch over his left eye—yet found myself completely inconsolable when he had to be put to sleep. These things happen —marriages hit rough spots, dogs die, bones might even mysteriously appear beneath barns—and people bounce back. But I was having trouble on the rebound.

Someone later told me this was just a crisis of normal life. I liked the cadence of that phrase. It lent a mild literary air to my otherwise mundane collapse in the suburbs.

4

A CUSTOMER once told me about the little experiments she liked to conduct at home with her furniture. She was a petite woman in a floral housedress, nondescript except for the wild look in her eyes. Each day she would make one change, she said. She'd move a reading chair, or maybe switch the rugs around. Sometimes the changes were slight: she would swap the desk lamp with the one on a bedside table, or she'd move the toaster, putting it where the coffeemaker usually sat. When she was feeling particularly hostile, she confessed, she would ask a neighbor to come over and help her drag the television set from one end of the family room to the other, then rearrange the sofas accordingly. This was all in an effort to get her husband to talk to her, even if it was only to complain that the cable no longer reached the TV. This seemed a sad story, especially because she was telling it to me, a virtual stranger. It was surprising how many people broke down and offered confessions over the sales counter. It probably had something to do with the cleansing effect of shopping: they were purging themselves of money and secrets.

Or maybe Leon was right. His theory was that most women were nuts.

·   ·   ·

The first time I visited Tiffany Fleisher's house was after that soggy soccer game. She lived in a brand-new seven-bedroom McMansion erected atop what had until recently been a working chicken farm. This might have been the henhouse, I thought, looking around the massive dining room. The house smelled of paint and freshly sanded wood.

Tiffany made small talk as she led me toward the dining room and invited me to settle into a spot at the end of the table, but I was barely listening. I was busy appraising her furniture. The table was a reproduction Chippendale with a matching sideboard and china cabinet. It was a nice copy, not quite the real thing but not cheap, either. *Bloomingdale's? Maybe Macy's? $1,599? Were those winged armchairs part of a special promotion?* A low-hanging four-arm colonial revival chandelier was similar to a knockoff version that we carried in the store. I could tell that Tiffany's light fixture was several grades above ours. We didn't have much luck when it came to electrical goods. We constantly fielded complaints from customers about appliances that didn't work, or worse, blew fuses or caused fires.

She had thrown together a hodgepodge of styles. Her Turkish rugs were gorgeous; the Hepplewhite Early American sideboard possibly antique; the funky-looking Moroccan table in the corner was probably from the new import shop in Potomac. I was encouraged at first by the coincidence of the chintz curtain fabric, which had recently been featured in Kramer's window as enhancement for a cozy family room scene we had created in an attempt to subliminally increase sales of sectional sofas. But upon closer inspection I could tell that her fabric was of a far better quality than ours. A French import, perhaps. I wished I could stop noticing these things. Too often I found it difficult to form an overall impression of a house as I was involuntarily assigning price tags, but in this case I couldn't help but notice that her ensemble worked: Tiffany's house looked like a home.

This was more than I could say for my own opulent piece of real estate, the interior of which more closely resembled the abandoned palace of a third-world despot.

"I love what you've done with the house," I said. "Did you do it yourself, or did you use a decorator?"

"You must be joking!" said Tiffany. "We're having an estate sale next week—all this stuff is going. This house was the model for the development, and it came with the furniture. But it's not me at all. This is all too stuffy. I'm more of an . . . I don't know . . . more of a Fjorki-type person. More modern. More European. I'm originally from California," she said as if this sufficed as an explanation.

There were seven of us at the table, which constituted about half of the mothers from the soccer team. While there were several soccer parents with whom I had become at least superficially friendly over the years, this group was part of a batch of newcomers I did not know at all. I guessed that most of them had joined the team sometime after I had begun to do my spectating from inside my minivan. Two of the women were German; one had just arrived from Lesotho. The other three seemed to be very quiet Americans. I wondered if any of them found Tiffany's pronouncement pretentious, or if they knew what a Fjorki-type person was; the Germans were usually pretty cutting-edge on matters of design.

Either no one else knew what Fjorki was, or everyone was too intimidated by Tiffany to speak freely. She was daunting in her lawyer clothes, her brown hair pulled into a severe bun. She looked ready to prosecute. She had to be at work in three hours, she apologized, interviewing witnesses in an ongoing case involving a Colombian drug dealer and possible police corruption. In her spare time, besides raising three perfect children, she ran these workshops, held office in the PTA, and took her standard poodle—who was currently locked in the basement, emitting occasional high-pitched protests—for three-mile runs along the canal.

My plan had been to sit back and simply absorb Tiffany Fleisher, to see as a sort of psychological experiment whether my envy would mutate into hate or self-loathing. I was on the lookout for flaws in the seemingly perfect façade. Perhaps she did not really bring home-baked goods to school functions. But then, neither did I.

Tiffany offered us all iced tea, but this seemed a polite formality we were encouraged to decline: the tumblers might spill, she warned, ruining our photos. Before beginning, she walked over to a cabinet in the corner and pushed a switch. A Brahms cello concerto flooded the room. It was one of my favorite pieces of classical music, and yet I did not find it soothing. It was not just that I was frightened by Tiffany; I did not fully trust her. I had the vague feeling that I was in for something much stranger than an introductory scrapbooking session; maybe this was like something out of a science-fiction movie and I was going to be brainwashed or converted and would agree to wear white robes and write her large checks.

"Ladies," she said, clapping her hands to get our attention, an unnecessary gesture since we were all silent, awaiting her command. "You might think this introductory memory workshop is simply about pasting photos in a scrapbook. But there is much more to it. Memories, Inc. has been the U.S. leader in memory technology for more than ten years. We are represented in forty-nine states and in three countries. There is a reason for our success. And that has to do with the company's manifesto. *Happy memories equal happy families.* Your job is to *create* happy memories. Think about it: what will your children, and their children, remember about last week's birthday party in twenty years? Will they remember that little Tommy and Lilly had a fight? Or that they didn't like a certain birthday present? Probably not. What they will remember is what you choose to put in the photo album. So choose happy photographs. It is up to you to inspire hope for future generations. This is an enormous responsibility."

She walked around the table, handing each of us a single empty page from a scrapbook. I was not sure I was up to the task. What was memory technology? I didn't want Tiffany mucking around with my mind or my family memories. Was I the only cynic in the room? I looked at the woman from Lesotho and at the Germans, wondering if their command of English was sufficient to grasp how weird this was. My throat was dry and I debated whether it would be rude to ask for that iced tea, after all. Perhaps I had been right in thinking there was some sort of religious thing going on here.

I raised my hand boldly, planning to ask Tiffany to elaborate on the issue of memory technology, but a more timid question spilled from my lips.

"Why only forty-nine states?" I asked.

She looked at me for a minute. Her speech must have been rattled off so many times that she barely remembered its content. "Oh," she said at last. "We don't have any representatives in Oklahoma."

Another hand went up. One of the German women asked a complicated question having to do with digital photography and the downloading of family videos onto the home computer and some scrapbooking CD-ROM she had just seen at Staples. Her question seemed to imply the possibility that this old cut-and-paste method of scrapbooking would soon be obsolete.

Tiffany shot her a cross look and said that was not an area of memory technology that she was familiar with.

There were no further questions, so she returned to the recitation of maxims having to do with preserving the past and enhancing the future and enjoying the moment that sounded as if they were lifted from one of those Chicken Soup for the Soul books. My photos were hardly up to such a mission: I had grabbed a somewhat random batch of pictures that morning, including a few from Justin's most recent birthday, as well as a couple of shots from his last season of soccer. These I had chosen deliberately, thinking it might make me seem a more integrated member of this particular group—an involved soccer mom. This was part of a spontaneous self-improvement campaign. I had decided just that morning as I dressed for the event, even donning a string of beads in a rare attempt to accessorize, that I wanted to become a different sort of person. I wanted to be more fun. To fight the inertia and social awkwardness that had taken hold of me like some kind of tree-rotting disease.

To this end I had left the pictures of my mother behind, and this was definitely a critical step toward the creation of happy family memories because sometime before she veered her car off the road she had attacked the family photo album with a pair of scissors, exorcising her face. Enough of her high forehead and her long black hair remained in some of the snapshots to remind me of how beautiful she had been.

I looked down at my photos—there was Justin sopping wet, cleat poised midair. I recalled that the downpour had begun just moments into the first half of the soccer game, and I had privately wished for an electrical storm, the prospect of a lightning strike being the only way to persuade the overly zealous referee to call the game.

As I stared at my empty page, then back at my array of photographs, I didn't know where to begin. The other women were already working intently, cropping their pictures and jockeying for the supplies set out in the middle of the table. Tiffany saw that I was struggling and tried to help me by producing a magazine: *Scrapbooking Today,* in which her own work was featured. I gathered from the amount of enthusiasm generated in the room that this was sort of the scrapbooking equivalent of getting a short story accepted at the *New Yorker*. The layout was from a journal she had made for her husband for Father's Day, she explained, and the theme of this particular award-winning spread was "fishing." There was her daughter, Cassie, sitting on the edge of the dock, rod in hand. There was her son Edward, Justin's teammate, with an enormous trout dangling from a hook. There was her youngest boy, Aaron, playing with the standard poodle, whom he had chased into the lake. None of this was especially remarkable; it was the accompanying artwork that made it distinguishable from, say, my own albums, which I got around to assembling every few years, sticking pictures from a box in the basement behind sheets of plastic purchased from the likes of K-Mart. If you looked closely at Tiffany's spread, the background paper was composed of . . . teeny tiny fish! And the photos were not your standard 5x7 rectangular jobs, but rather each was cut into a perfect fish shape. The page was annotated with bubble writing, vaguely fishy in style. A vignette accompanied each photo.

So, Tiffany explained, this was not about warehousing photos in an album. Anyone could do that. People had been doing that for decades, using improper materials that actually caused the photos to age, to slowly self-destruct. Our goal was to be historians, storytellers, creators of nuance and complexity, coaxing layers of meaning from a single photo. Whatever we were in our non-scrapbooking lives—housewives, soccer moms, part-time prosecutors, reluctant employees in a dying family business—at this job we were art directors, curators of family, writers of memoir.

I did not feel compelled to tease our lives into aquatically themed albums, and yet this still had surprising appeal. I was flooded with images, mostly sepia-toned and artfully blurred, of a beautiful happy family, of Leon and me taking long walks along the ocean, sipping wine at sunset, diving recklessly off cliffs along the Mediterranean, like kids. Of a deliciously chubby toddler waddling on the beach with a pail and shovel. As I let my mind drift, these images began to involve my family posed against the backdrop of places we had never been. I imagined myself young and tanned, lying on a raft in some exotic-sounding sea. And there was Leon . . . except that it was not really Leon at all but some impressionistic, dazzlingly fit *über*-man there on the raft, talking about things not involving furniture.

To be most effective, I heard Tiffany say, we needed to become familiar with the tools (all available for purchase). There were numerous gadgets to round edges of photos, turn rectangles into ovals, eliminate superfluous objects, and get rid of strangers lurking in the background. There were scissors with ridges of the sort one might use to scallop vegetables, as well as a variety of templates designed to enable flawless circle cutting. And there was much more—many hundreds of dollars' worth more, including special adhesives, pens with a wide variety of points, colorful triangles of acid-free construction paper, a multitude of stickers, an array of blades, holiday borders, page protectors, sheets of scenic landscapes, mounting corners, books of scrapbooking ideas, tote bags, file folders.

I wanted them all, immediately, and was disappointed to learn that it would take as long as two weeks for my order to arrive since Tiffany was low on stock. Listening to her speak, seeing her perfect page in the magazine, I felt something like shame, accompanied by the onset of panic. My own family life seemed suddenly spare, possibly nonexistent. Where was my kid's first days of school? Lodged in my memory, but what would happen when that faded? Soon my family would be gone forever. Those summer lemonade stands Justin used to hold at the foot of our driveway? Nothing more than a blur. The lemon rinds in the sink, the sticky trail from the kitchen to the front door? The wasps that had descended on the pitcher, sending Justin to the hospital? What happened to these moments that were not recorded? Had they really even existed? I was feeling treacly.

Tiffany had a bit more to say about our responsibility to preserve the past, a few more instructions and tips about our one-page assignment. I kept reminding myself that I had come here to see how I might make money from this racket, but I was still getting sucked in by the craft. By the end of the two-hour session, I had finished my page but could not really say whether I had preserved the past or reinvented it. There were pictures of Justin and his teammates, cut into ovals, resplendent in their soccer jerseys set against ridged pale blue borders. As I lay the pictures on the page, I could suddenly see all sorts of possibilities. *Happy memories equal happy families.* Perhaps that season had not been so dreary as I recalled. I cut a yellow circle and drew a smiling face on it, utilizing the jewel-tone fine-tip pens. There was something undeniably therapeutic about this. Here was Mr. Sun! Never mind the endless rain that spring, the wet uniforms, the gray clouds, the mud on soccer cleats, the roof on our house that had sprung a leak and had eventually required replacement for just over $6,000, the damage incurred when small drops of water squeezed through the shingles into the attic, then later through the floorboards and into Justin's bedroom. A few more thousand. None of that polluted the page I created.

Tiffany came by and looked over our shoulders while we worked. She paused and studied my page and nodded with approval. She said I was a natural. Buoyed by this praise, I took an old picture of my husband, which I guessed was from about four years earlier, before he had put on an extra forty pounds. He was standing in front of the store, leaning on a putter. Chandler was behind him, waiting for him to get into the car.

Leon never came to soccer games. He was always working on

Saturdays, which were of course busy retail days. On the very rare occasion that he took a weekend afternoon off, it was not to watch Justin, but to play golf. I pointed this out once and it led to a rather ugly fight. We were incapable of small fights, it seemed, because there was so much pent-up hostility on both sides that even a wet towel on the floor or a slightly shocking American Express bill got blown out of proportion by whoever was doing the accusing. We later kissed and made up, but the underlying issue was left unresolved.

Of course, this was not the way we would want our son to remember things and besides, there was a speck, or some sort of blurred object, in the background of the photo. I used Tiffany's miraculous little paper cutter to simply snip out Chandler and the offending smudge that seemed to hover just above him. I then took some extraneous background that I had just cut from another picture and pasted Leon on top of a clump of grass. There! Now he was on the soccer field, cheering just behind the goal, as long as you didn't nitpick, take a magnifying glass to the photo, for example, and ask why part of his shoulder was missing.

Then there were the photos of Justin's most recent birthday. These were not memories I especially wanted to preserve. He had pierced his cheek just the day before, forging my permission on the release form provided by the store at the mall, and his face was raw and puffy. It would in fact begin to show signs of infection within a week, requiring antibiotics and minor surgery to remove the stud, but this would not deter him from acquiring several more piercings over the course of the summer. An earlier photo would do just as well. And me? A trick of the shading pen: any blemishes on my face erased, my skin translucent, pale as the proverbial English rose. Pale as Delia.

.   .   .

After the session I tried to corner Tiffany to ask her a few questions about how her business operated, but she told me to call her later; she was running late for court. She did say she had a lot of overflow work and suggested I might be able to subcontract from her. All I had to do was fill out an application and write a check for $500. I said I'd think about it, and in the meantime I handed her a check for $20 to cover the cost of the session. Then I wrote a second check for $387.50, for supplies. I had a lot of history to correct.

Yet by the time I got home later that day, after a typical but aggravating stint at the store (an angry customer wanted to return a set of six dining-room chairs that she had bought four years earlier because she claimed the wood was rotting), I had pretty much lost my enthusiasm. When the box of scrapbooking tools arrived it went straight into the basement closet unopened, next to the box of photographs and alongside the samples of Discovery Toys, which rested beside supplies for some of the other hobbies I had briefly entertained, such as knitting, needlepoint, oil painting, and mosaic tiling. Tiffany called and left multiple messages to which I did not respond.

That I was drifting through life rudderless was a fact I had come to accept.

Five months elapsed before I ran into Tiffany at the grocery store. I didn't recognize her at first—she was out of context in casual clothes, behind a shopping trolley. Also confusing was the fact that she had become a blonde. We talked briefly about her daughter. She had just left for college, and Tiffany said her house felt empty even though she still had two kids at home. I studied her groceries as she unloaded them onto the conveyor belt, hoping to glimpse something I could hold against her:

gallon-size sodas loaded with caffeine and sugar, perhaps, or processed foods heavy in preservatives, maybe even a tabloid newspaper. But there were only fresh fruits and vegetables for the Fleisher family, organic juice, yogurt-covered raisins evidently sufficing as snack food.

She asked if I was still interested in scrapbooking. I lied, and made no reference to her unreturned phone calls. I said I had used up all the materials I'd ordered from her, guiltily unloading my less healthy stash from my cart. Leon had recently developed a hankering for sheet cakes. I bought him one each week, always feeling slightly embarrassed when I declined the baker's offer to have a free, personalized "Happy Birthday" greeting inscribed in icing. I embellished my lie and said I had created a few super journals—I actually used the word *super*—and had been meaning to call her to order more materials and discuss possible subcontracting opportunities.

She said this was incredibly fortuitous, this meeting here at Giant Foods, because she was currently overwhelmed. She had just been assigned another huge case at work, something I didn't quite follow. The project would require her to work more than her usual thirty-five hours a week. The memory consulting business was good just now, demand overwhelming. She had begun this as a hobby, never imagining it would catch on as quickly as it had. She was looking for a recruit, she said. There were a couple of sessions coming up next month. She produced a pocket diary and read me the dates. Was I interested? Did I still have the application? Did I remember there was a $500 initiation fee?

Her neediness made me suspicious. But then, when was the last time someone had really wanted me to work for them? About sixteen years earlier, when I'd first set foot in Kramer's, was the only answer I could come up with.

Maybe she could sense my hesitation, because she sweetened the deal. "The application is really just a formality," she said. "It's not like you are going to be rejected or anything. And you can take your time with the $500. Whenever you get it to me is fine. Memories, Inc. also has a special promotion going right now. They will match your sales with cruise incentive points. Say you sell $400 worth of goods this month, you can count that as 800 points toward a free cruise."

"A cruise?" That got my attention. "How many points do you need for the cruise?"

"I think about 500,000. But I'd have to check."

That was a lot of points.

"You could have my points," she said. "I don't really like cruises."

Neither did I, actually. But that didn't stop me from picturing myself on deck, wearing nautical clothing and sipping a strawberry daiquiri. I had only been on a cruise once and had not enjoyed it in the least. Samuel and Esther had taken the whole family on a Disney cruise to celebrate their thirtieth wedding anniversary and it had given me a week-long headache, with the endless music and the rowdy inebriated people gorging on round-the-clock buffets. I didn't like cruises, didn't like daiquiris, didn't like rowdy inebriated people, and yet this offer still had surprising appeal. I imagined myself stepping onto the shores of some tropical island, discarding my daiquiri in the first available trash can, and then disappearing into the horizon of a fiery sunset.

I mumbled a hesitant "maybe" to Tiffany but then said I didn't have my checkbook with me.

She seemed pleased, and somehow winning her approval—which I suspected was not an easy thing to do—was satisfying. "What I'm going to do is call you when I get home to confirm the dates," she said. "In the meantime, I'm going to go ahead and order you a bunch of business cards." This struck me as a bit aggressive, but I didn't protest. I'd never had a business card before.

"I'll also drop off another copy of the application and some additional material about Memories, Inc., how it all works. In fact," she said, pausing while fishing around in her shoulder bag, "I have the entire packet right here. Always prepared!" she quipped, and I didn't doubt it.

I pulled out a wad of coupons while glancing at the brochure. It was an impressively designed piece of literature, as of course it should have been given that the very point was seductive presentation.

After a reminder that Memories, Inc. had been the U.S. leader in memory technology for more than a decade, there was a picture of the Memories, Inc. Ladder, with a list of ranks, categories of seeming non sequiturs. There were eleven possible rungs, beginning with being a Freshman Memory Consultant. Princess Memory Consultant, Tiffany's current status, was a stop pretty far along the road to becoming a double Ambassador Memory Consultant. Double Ambassadors got a $1 million bonus check for achieving this status, as well as a free car, an all-expense-paid trip to World Company Headquarters in Salt Lake City, a private dinner with Mrs. Sheri Turk, founder of Memories Inc., and qualification for the Home Incentive Program, where, according to the brochure, the company would build you a new home and assume your mortgage.

There, on page five of *Memories, Inc.* magazine, which had been included in the packet Tiffany gave to me (you earned a free subscription when you qualified as a Senior Memory Consultant, I learned), was a woman named Joy Kern. Joy was able to build her dream house—a seven-million-dollar extravaganza on a cliff in Malibu next door to Johnny Carson—after just five years in the business. She had earned the free car, a Mercedes, and had her picture taken at the Salt Lake City World Headquarters compound with Mrs. Turk. They were arm in arm, both smiling brightly. Mrs. Turk's teeth were a shade too bright, as if something had gone wrong either with the photo processing or with the bleaching trays at the dentist's office. I looked more closely: Joy Kern was holding a check for a million dollars.

I felt a gentle tap on my shoulder. When I turned to see what the customer in line behind me wanted, she pointed her finger toward the checker, a striking young Indian woman with an arm draped in bangles. She had evidently been trying to ask me an important question ever since Tiffany had left.

After we clarified the matter of paper or plastic, Malika had another question: "Cash or credit?" Malika was obviously a new employee.

"Credit!" I replied, perhaps too enthusiastically. As if I ever paid cash for groceries. As if I looked like the sort of person who might have cash on hand.

I turned my attention back to the brochure. Sprinkled freely throughout, always in bold print and surrounded by a sea of asterisks, were the words "★★★★Unlimited Earning Potential.★★★★" I felt that old, familiar surge of enthusiasm, that same buzz of possibility I had that day on the soccer field. I could do this! I was going to climb that ladder all the way to the top! I would earn more money than any memory consultant in history! That there was something suspect in all this didn't really dampen my enthusiasm. So what if the words "pyramid scheme" were running through my brain like a news flash at the bottom of a television screen?

5

THE STORE'S exterior may have been fantastically modern, but inside things ran largely the same as they had since 1957, or so I imagined. Leon had masterminded the renovation almost entirely on his own, yet he still felt oddly, or perhaps just dutifully, compelled to consult his father over the most minor details. There was a family dynamic at work that I didn't quite understand but had to negotiate daily. When I offered suggestions—switching manufacturers, exploring new advertising schemes, rearranging the showroom—I was deemed overly critical. When I backed off, withheld opinions, I was accused of indifference. It was of course possible that I stood guilty as charged: there might have been something in my attitude that projected a certain hostility even when I was trying to be pleasant. There were certain things one could not help, like wincing when a bee stings.

So it took me by surprise when Leon announced his decision to jump-start this particularly sluggish season with an unprecedented post–Labor Day sale. Samuel was in Kiev visiting relatives, and I could only surmise that Leon must have spoken to him on the phone.

My own theory of retail—such as it was, having been an English major—was that too many sales had a cheapening effect. We didn't want to turn into one of the many Oriental rug shops along the Pike, the ones perpetually liquidating their stock.

I said this politely. Leon and I were always polite to one another in the store, or at least we had been until this week.

At home, we passed each other in the halls like ghosts, not even bothering to fight anymore apart from the occasional morning tussle mostly involving getting Justin out the door. When we did speak it was usually in acid tones, full of barely suppressed contempt. It was only recently that Leon had become enamored of the word "fuck." Its entry into his lexicon can be traced roughly to the previous spring, when Anna Berger found the bones beneath the barn. At times the offending word made an appearance in appropriately angry sentences, such as "Did you pay the *fucking* water bill?" But sometimes it was more benign, as in, "it's fucking nice outside." He made it into an adverb once, announcing that it was *fuckingly* hot upstairs, and when I tried to correct his grammar he responded, more appropriately, "Fuck you." While the word itself may have had a neutral connotation, the frequency with which it appeared in our conversations seemed to me indicative of other, larger issues.

The Anna Berger bones incident seemed to have brought our marital problems to the boiling point. Even if the newspapers were not actively documenting our little domestic squabbles, the effect was the same—our private life felt public. And all the bad things were related: a question like whether the leaking faucet in the master bathroom needed repair took on added significance in light of the fact that we could barely afford a plumber after paying Chandler Chandling and assuming the new mortgage on the store. The tension sent Leon feasting his way toward the accrual of an additional twenty pounds, thereby tipping the balance from him being just another man with an unsightly beer belly to one who was officially, unhealthily, fat. For my part, I went shopping.

The bad place that Leon and I had arrived at was just barely inhabitable. Yet I did not really want to *leave* Leon; I just wanted things to be different. I did not want to be divorced, or widowed, or otherwise abandoned. The only thing I knew for sure was that I did not want to end my days dealing discount furniture. And while I may have grown pretty disagreeable, I did not feel spiteful: I did not want to destroy Leon's hard earned happiness, although whether he was really happy was a different question altogether. Since there seemed no way to reconcile all this, it seemed best that I simply get out of the way. The only problem, of course, was that I had nowhere to go.

Anyway, our estrangement was not quite complete. We may have barely been on speaking terms, yet we were still physically intimate in ways that seemed worthy of a nature documentary. (*So strong is the need of the human species for physical contact that even partners who are repelled by one another can sometimes be found, during deep REM cycles, curled together like gerbils . . .*) We still shared the same bed. This was part habit, part animal weakness, and perhaps the tacit understanding that to do otherwise would herald a profound change in the status quo, one that might require a prolonged conversation. Maybe because it was our only form of honest communication, sex was no longer a tender affair; our lovemaking was more like a brawl, both aggressive and needy, and it was not all bad.

It was possible that our troubles at home improved our office relations. We put up a good front, I thought, not unlike the families you read about in the newspaper, where the husband bludgeons his wife to death and the neighbors gather outside the home to tell reporters about their shock, what a happy family they had been, what nice children they had. That was us, assuming our neighbors had not overly focused on the occasional morning shouting match. Or the Goth thing. Or the bones.

Delia did get my heart racing. Did I harbor feelings of love for my husband that were embedded so deeply into my psyche that even I couldn't see them? Or was this purely sexual jealousy on my part? Or was it possibly wrapped up with some sort of perverse resentment having to do with patio furniture? Why was Leon so excited about *her* ideas, when I had been lobbing my own at him for years?

Leon prevailed on the sale, and I didn't put up much of a fight. While business was always slow in the late summer, it was even worse this year. Part of it was just the flailing economy, the daily high-tech layoffs, the local dot-com busts. But we were also affected by the most recent manhole explosion, which had closed a half-mile stretch of Wisconsin Avenue only two miles south of the store. This meant traffic was even worse than usual. Anyway, who cared? What possible danger could there really be in cheapening the brand name? Our stuff *was* cheap. That was the point! Cheap furniture, cheaper.

The marquee went out Tuesday morning, stretched across the mammoth striped awning fronting the store. Ads were scheduled to air all week on WZOP radio (official station of the Washington Redskins), where Kramer's had been advertising since the 1960s. Special hours. Open 'til midnight. I suspected that meant I would be working special hours, myself. Bonus savings! *Take an additional ten percent off every purchase when you apply for Kramer's low-interest financing and defer payment until February.* Cash rebates, on a sliding scale. Spend $1,000, get $100 cash back. Spend $500, get $50. That was a new one. We had never been quite that desperate before. There was another glut of sofas that we were trying to unload. Italian leather sofas, chenille sofas, microfiber sofas, velvet sofas with mahogany-stained block feet. A second promotion was scheduled to begin Wednesday: an entire living-room set, love seat, sofas, coffee tables—the works —just $2,999.99. That was another thing: I had been arguing against these strings of 9's for as long as I'd been married. Also cheapening. People were simply not that stupid. Just round it up! Whenever I made this suggestion, Leon would look at me as if I was an idiot—and maybe I was, about sale decimals, anyway.

Since the subject of my so-called embezzlement had not come up again, I figured we were free to move on to a new fiscal month, to begin with a clean slate, marred only by a lower net worth. But then the other issue—that of the leaky cash register—reared its head. One hundred dollars had gone missing in less than twenty-four hours, Leon informed me.

I had not taken money from the cash register. I may have been guilty of other money-related sins, but pilfering from the till was beneath my dignity. The store was too frail. Stealing from it would have been like snatching a purse from an old lady. To his credit, Leon did not actually suggest that I was to blame. He was really just alerting me to the problem, and we agreed to keep a closer eye on the registers.

But we were right back where we started, yelling at each other on the sales floor about my spending. I told him that it was impossible to live within our budget, and he told me that I didn't even try. What I didn't tell him was that some of the debits on that last statement had been expenses incurred after my most recent encounter with Tiffany. She had called to tell me that the business cards were ready, and then she sent me a bill for $200, which I had not expected. She had also talked me into buying a $300 "starter kit" which she insisted I would need once I began to run my own sessions, the dates of which were now in flux. None of that was taking into account the very large check that I still needed to write and which I would have to hand in with my application in order to become an official Memories, Inc. franchisee.

In the meantime, just out of curiosity, I had stopped into one of the crafting stores along Rockville Pike to see what sorts of materials were available through other venues, and to see how prices compared. The amount of accessories available for purchase was staggering, and the store itself was big enough to park a couple of jumbo jets, wing to wing. This whole scrapbooking thing seemed to have mass appeal, and Memories, Inc. was just a corner of it. How was it that I'd missed it all? I paused to admire a drafting table, as well as a $367 tote bag on wheels. I also found myself coveting a Xyron Pro, model 2500, priced at $1,499. With this I could produce stickers, laminate things, make magnets. It occurred to me that this could come in handy at the store, and the words "Corporate American Express" flashed through my mind. But I did not succumb to that impulse.

It was only about noon, far too early to despair, but so far our radio ads seemed to be having no effect. I had spent the morning on the sales floor, and only two customers had crossed our threshold. Neither one had wanted my assistance. Uncle Seymour, God bless him, couldn't help himself. He came from the school of salesmanship that recommended harassing the customer like a shopkeeper in an old city bazaar. Annoy them sufficiently, he seemed to think, and they will eventually buy something if only to get away from you. "You like? I make it only ten rupees," I half-expected him to say, as he chased a customer around the store, pointing out the special attributes of computer tables. He called all women "doll." He could not hear either my occasional gentle admonitions or a customer's response. "Bugger off," someone had yelled just that morning, in a charming cockney accent, as she'd stormed out the door. I'd watched him adjust his hearing aid, perplexed.

As an indication of how slow things were, Leon suggested we alternate shifts—a skeletal staffing plan usually unheard of during a sale. Would I mind if he took the next few hours off? He'd come back around three, then I could leave so I'd be home in time to meet Justin after school.

That was fine, I replied. I didn't bother to remind him that Justin rarely came home directly from school these days. "If it's still quiet, you can help out with the books, also maybe follow up on that lamp order," Leon said.

He meant I could help transfer some fifty years of paperwork onto the computer that the financial analyst had talked Leon into buying to update our antiquated system of bookkeeping. The man in the Hawaiian shirt had laughed out loud when Samuel produced boxes full of dusty ledgers, figures almost illegible with decades-old pencil smudge. There were so many oddities at work here, and I could only suppose every one of them had to do with family. Leon had been one of the youngest and most productive bond traders his department had ever seen. Yet here in the store it was as if he caved in on himself. We hired this clod in the Hawaiian shirt, half as smart as Leon, to look at our books. I had heard others say that this happened to them, as well: no matter how old they were, how successful and functional, when they went home they regressed. Without living parents, I had to dredge for other excuses for my own periods of immaturity.

"I'm just going to slip in here for a minute if you don't mind," Leon said, moving farther into the back office. We were standing just inside the door, on the threshold of a larger room with three other desks meant for support staff we could not afford. And if our legal problems ever went away, if the bones were ever found and determined to be of animal origin (although preferably not of some interesting variety, like dinosaur), or if a judge decided to just let us move forward with the project, soon we'd have a whole barn's worth of office space for even more would-be employees.

"I need to change clothes," he explained. He was wearing khaki pants and a sweat-drenched white shirt and I supposed he was going to change into a dry version of the same. His thick head of dark hair was also matted with perspiration. At age forty-five, his hairline had not receded an inch, and I wondered if anyone had ever thought to study the correlation between sheet-cake ingestion and hair retention. I stared at him for a moment, taking stock. For whatever reason, I was feeling a pang of tenderness, thinking that he looked inexplicably sexy in this sweaty condition, even if he was overweight, even if I spent most of my time wishing for a life without him. But sometimes, such as at that moment, I remembered that we had been best friends before we had become wary opponents, before our relationship had been reduced to a montage of bank overdrafts and ugly furniture, of mounds of cellulite and credit card debt.

"I'll be right out," he said, looking at me strangely. Then I realized that he needed me to actually step out of the way so he could shut the door.

I was slow in moving, and continued to stare. Why was he changing clothes, and anyway, why did he need privacy from his wife? We may have been out of synch on almost every level, but we still saw each other naked.

"I'm just going out for a jog," he said defensively. "I brought a change of clothes and thought I'll just slip in here rather than go home . . . to save time. Do me a favor and keep an eye on the sales floor while I change."

He was going out for a jog. *He was going out for a jog?* Why did this otherwise innocent sentence so completely enrage me? This was a good thing! I wanted Leon to be fit again—not because I was a snob about weight, but because every time I looked at his enormous girth I felt an awful, guilty responsibility. Even if I privately blamed Anna Berger for pushing him over the brink, his weight gain seemed a deliberate declaration to the world that I made him unhappy. Last month he had had to have his wedding band removed with a frightening-looking metal contraption because it was cutting off his circulation. What did it mean that he had made no effort to replace it?

The significance of this jog was too much for me to process, so I shrugged my shoulders noncommittally and headed out to the floor. Seymour was standing at the register, putting the final touches on the correction notice that he was about to hang in the main entranceway. There had been a typographical error in that morning's newspaper advertisement. A French country kitchen ensemble—pine table, six wooden chairs, accompanying dry sink and chopping block—had all erroneously been advertised at $199.00. We'd lost a "9" somewhere along the way. Even at just under $2,000 this was a steal, but we seemed to attract an inordinate number of hard-core bargain hunters who showed up brandishing their ad copy, then claimed to have driven all the way from Trenton, New Jersey, in an effort to finagle the entire set for $200. This was in part why we could not leave Seymour alone in the store today. He was not capable of fending off the vultures. Personally I thought his unwillingness to do so was a sign of his inner genius—he was smart enough to realize that it was worth every penny of the lost $1,800 plus tax not to have to argue with these people.

Seymour pulled out a roll of tape and began to affix his cheerful correction notice (he had inexplicably drawn hearts and balloons around the borders) to a piece of poster board just as Delia appeared, a sight to behold with a Kate Spade purse the size of a laundry hamper. The purse suddenly began to broadcast a loud Japanese-sounding techno-pop tune that went on far too long. She reached into the bag with sharpened pink nails like daggers and retrieved a cell phone. Delia was such a frenetic whirl of activity that it took me a moment to realize she, too, was wearing jogging clothes.

"Hi, honey!" she said, running in place. Although her eyes were trained on me, I couldn't tell whether I was the intended target of this endearment.

"Hang on . . . I've got another call," she said, glancing quickly at the screen on the phone and then depressing another button. "Yes?" she said, addressing this caller in a somewhat more subdued voice. "Right . . . Of course . . . forty wrought-iron benches . . . yes. I've been meaning to call you. Listen, I'm in the middle of a business meeting. Can I call you later?" She hit another button and was presumably transferred back to the first party. "Hi. Sorry. Important business call. Listen, honey, I'm in the middle of a business meeting . . . yes. . . . No . . . Listen, I've got three clients here and I'm about to close on a big deal. Let me call you later. You're a real sweetheart. Yes, chicken is fine. Ciao!"

She dropped the phone back in her bag and dashed past, explaining she was going to leave her stuff in the back office and would I keep an eye on her things while she went for a run. I felt almost giddy watching her, idiotically flattered to be put in charge of the personal goods of this busy professional woman. Seconds later she and Leon appeared together, jogging in place, synchronizing their watches, and mumbling goodbyes. She was the same height as Leon, but somewhat more svelte. She wore large, pink Pumas. Her heavy breasts bounced in a sports bra. She blew me another kiss by way of goodbye.

"If anyone calls for me just tell them I'm in a meeting," she said.

I watched them jog out the door, struggling to feign indifference.

Possibly a vestige of the days when men hunted and women gathered, one of my chief strengths seemed to lie in the collecting of objects, an activity sometimes disparagingly referred to as shopping. To this end, I had purchased the complete works of F. Scott Fitzgerald and piled them high on the desk in the back office. I had read most of the books before, back in high school and college, but had decided to take Delia up on her invitation to determine what sort of patio furniture Fitzgerald might have sat on, assuming he ever had a patio. I had no real interest in participating in this project, which I thought was absurd and, if not technically immoral, was certainly in bad taste. Mostly I was doing this for my own edification, and, I supposed, to play along.

I might not remember where I parked my car at the grocery store some days, but I did recall that Fitzgerald supposedly used some 450 words in *Gatsby* that referred to the concept of time. In fact, I remembered all sorts of obscure details about *Gatsby:* that Myrtle Wilson had wide hips, that Daisy's voice was full of money, that Jordan Baker was incurably dishonest. What I did not remember was a single stick of patio furniture.

And for good reason. While I found multiple mentions of couches and tables in *The Great Gatsby,* there were no lawn chairs or umbrella tables, which was surprising, given the novel's aquatic setting (". . . the white palaces of fashionable East Egg glittered along the water . . ." and "the lawn started at the beach and ran toward the front door . . . ," etc., etc.). So where was all the outdoor furniture? All I had been able to find was one wicker settee, mentioned twice. Or were they two separate wicker settees? An interesting question, as both settees made appearances at homes occupied by Daisy—one presumably in her childhood residence, where Gatsby and Daisy first kissed; the other at her marital West Egg home, where Nick and Daisy sat. Was it possible that this settee was of such sentimental importance to Daisy that she had kept it over the years? Did Fitzgerald mean for us to note the coincidence of the wicker settees, or was he just oblivious to its multiple appearances?

I set the book aside and stared at Delia's stripy bag, which was resting on the credenza and had begun to vibrate, causing the bag to jump a little, before broadcasting its jarring tune. Should

I answer her phone? Per Leon's instructions, I was already on the phone, on hold, following up on that lost shipment of floor lamps from China. I recalled Delia's instructions to say that she was in a business meeting if anyone called. I stretched the phone cord across the desk, knocking my pile of Fitzgerald books to the floor, and retrieved her bag. By the time I located the phone and figured out which key to punch, it had stopped ringing. The screen display said, simply, "missed call."

But there I was, my hand already inside her bag for perfectly legitimate reasons and, with a mind of its own, this hand began to sift through her belongings. Depraved jealousy seemed to win out easily over the shame of what I had become: a wife reduced to rifling through another woman's purse, pretending to be busy in the back office while my spouse, the least health-conscious person I knew, was out *jogging* with that other woman. I was unaware that he even owned a pair of sneakers. But now that I thought about it, there had indeed been small changes in Leon's behavior, and it seemed possible that his waistline had begun to shrink ever so slightly. Just the day before I had found the remains of a perfectly edible bit of sheet cake in the trash, and had also noticed a pint of some zero-calorie tofu confection in the freezer. I hadn't given it much thought at the time, but now this all seemed to point toward a shocking betrayal. We had been together for nearly two decades, and in that time I had never known Leon to throw away dessert food or set foot inside a grocery store.

Still grazing inside the bag, my hand retrieved, really almost *accidentally,* a wallet. And without quite meaning to, tucking the store phone under my chin, I undid the magnetic catch and peered at Delia's driver's license.

But something was wrong. Could it have been that I had the wrong bag? Or that Delia had the wrong bag? Or possibly I had grabbed the wrong wallet within the bag, because the driver's license peeking through the plastic window did not belong to Delia-whatever-her-last-name-was of some suburb outside Pittsburgh but rather one Andrew Ryder, born 1961, organ donor, corrective lenses required. Maybe this was her husband? It had never even occurred to me that she might have been married. She didn't wear a ring, didn't give off married vibrations, even if she had been contemplating consuming some chicken with whomever she'd been talking to on the phone.

A voice came on at last to inform me that the lamps shipped from their New York warehouse two weeks ago, and should arrive any day now. That I was given this same information more than two months earlier failed to impress this person, but I didn't really care; they were shoddy floor lamps anyway.

I hung up the phone and examined this person in the photo and thought I saw a resemblance to our Delia. The fact that this man looked an awful lot like Delia did not necessarily negate the husband theory: like was often drawn to like. The phone rang, but I let it go.

Andrew Ryder had the usual stuff in his wallet. Visa, American Express, a library card, a picture of a young boy. But it was otherwise spare in clues. There was no additional photo ID. The wallet must have belonged to her husband, although, frankly, it seemed to me rather feminine in style. So she was married and had a son. Big deal. There was a lot I didn't know about this woman, after all. We had never had a proper conversation, other than the one about patio furniture.

But why couldn't I find another wallet in this bag? Possibly because it was a bottomless pit. Inside it fit a change of clothes, for after her jog. A sophisticated-looking silk blouse from Ann Taylor, a matching silk chemise, a pleated size-16 skirt, a C-cup bra—she *was* a large woman, but she carried it well, was undeniably sexy, and I looked down at my shriveling breasts. Leon was a large man. Perhaps what he needed was a large woman.

Digging deeper I produced a makeup bag, a hairbrush, keys, sunglasses, an electronic organizer, a month-old issue of *People* magazine, but no second wallet. I pulled out the license again and stared. Did this fellow look like Delia, or was I imagining this? A host of improbable theories raced through my head, among them the possibility that Delia had robbed Andrew Ryder, whoever he was. Robbed and killed him and kept his wallet as a trophy. That Delia was a criminal might help explain the missing money from the till. Why did I think such awful thoughts? It was shameful of me to be so suspicious, and yet ever since the discovery of the bones, all new revelations seemed potentially criminal. I found myself wondering about the missing coeds sometimes, wondering what Leon might have known about them, even though that was absurd. He would have been a boy of about thirteen the year they disappeared, hardly the age for striking out as a serial killer. I tried to push these twisted thoughts from my mind, but equally horrifying ones quickly took their place, rushing to fill the void like weeds in my neglected flower beds.

The telephone was ringing again. I picked it up.

"Kramer's Discount Furniture Depot," I said in my most faux cheerful voice.

"Yes, may I speak to Mr. or Mrs. Kramer, please?" A personal request for the owner usually meant a grievance. But something about this voice sounded more sympathetic, not combative. *French?*

"Who is calling, please?" I asked, giving Delia's purse one last going-through, opening her flamingo-covered makeup bag, pulling out a small bottle of Marc Jacobs perfume (this Delia had a lot of money for a patio furniture saleswoman). I sprayed a bit on my wrist and sniffed. Not bad. Then I retrieved a tube of bright orange MAC lipstick. I turned the dial and examined the stick of color closely. I smelled it, put a streak of orangey-red on the back of my hand. Inconclusive. I put the lipstick back in the little plastic bird-speckled pouch and was about to drop it back in her purse when, instead, I stuck it in my pocket. Why did I do this? I didn't know.

"This is Jean Michaels calling from Rockville Preparatory School," the voice explained in accented English. "Is this Mrs. Kramer?"

"It is," I replied, alarmed. I returned the Kate Spade to the spot on the credenza where I'd first found it. "Is something wrong?"

"It's about Pablo. I am his guidance counselor. Not to panic, this is nothing major, but there's just been a small accident in which he was involved and while I wanted to notify you, I also thought that we should arrange to speak in person. Is this possible?"

"Pablo?" I repeated, relieved. "You have the wrong parent. My son is Justin."

He laughed. Even this sounded somehow French. "My apologies, Madame Kramer. I am Justin's counselor but I am also his Spanish instructor. In that class he has chosen for himself the name Pablo."

"But you sound . . . French," I said hesitantly.

"Yes. This is of course very confusing. I teach French and Spanish and I am his guidance counselor as well."

"What do you mean, an accident?" I asked.

"No one was injured. Pablo was with another one of our students, perhaps you know him . . . Mike Stahl."

"Of course I know Mike," I said, barely able to disguise my hostility. Mike was the sort of kid you felt you should not have to put up with when you were paying $21,000 a year in tuition.

Now the other telephone line was ringing, annoyingly, and Delia's phone had again begun to whine from the credenza.

"They were in Mike's car just a short while ago during lunch hour—and as you must recall from our rule book, which all parents were required to sign, only seniors have permission to leave school grounds during lunch, and then only with parental permission. They had a minor collision on Rockville Pike. We still don't have all the details, but the important thing is that no one was injured."

"Jane?" Seymour began shouting my name loudly, over the intercom. He had never grasped the concept that the intercom system amplified volume all on its own. I ignored him even though the sound of my name was deafening.

"They were only half a block from school," the French and Spanish teacher *cum* guidance counselor continued. "It is not even clear whether it was Mike's fault, but they collided with an elderly woman, and she has made quite a fuss. Filed a police report, I'm afraid. Said she was hit by a couple of devil worshipers and that this was the work of Satan . . ."

"Oh Good Lord," I exclaimed, both to Jean Michaels and to Uncle Seymour, who had found me at last but was nonetheless still shouting my name.

"Jane! You have a phone call on line two."

I put my hand over the receiver and asked Seymour to take a message.

Jean continued: "While I don't see this becoming quite the outrageous incident this woman makes it out to be, I do think it appropriate that we take some sort of action against Pablo for leaving school grounds without permission. Pablo is . . . *was* . . . one of our finest students, and this is . . . well really *was* . . . would have been . . . really anomalous behavior on his part. So what we need to do, I think, is suspend him for the equivalent of one week, at least . . . Do you suppose that you or Mr. Kramer could come to school to collect him?"

"I'll be right over," I said, trembling. "But what else has been going on? Obviously you are suggesting there are problems."

"Nothing terrible. Please do not overreact. We can talk about it when we meet. There have just been a couple of minor incidents at school."

"Like what?" I shrieked.

"There was a small fight in the biology lab, and he walked out of class . . . but it will be much better to discuss this in person. I have been a guidance counselor for many years and in my experience this is the age of experimentation, of pushing limits. This is not as awful as it sounds."

It sounded pretty awful to me. Instantly I put myself on trial. Had I been too lenient? Too passive in tolerating this Goth thing? Had I been giving him too much freedom? But Justin had always been largely self-sufficient. I was only trying to give him room. For years I had rushed home every single day to meet him at the bus and give him a snack—I was quite possibly the only mother left in the world who actually greeted her kid with milk and cookies after school. But now Justin worked three days a week at Rockville Music. The other two days his band usually gathered in our garage for practice. I gave the band milk and cookies, which they seemed to appreciate even if Justin was mortified, but otherwise I tried to stay away.

I wondered if I had been ignoring obvious danger signs. I sometimes thought I detected in Justin's drift something more than an age-appropriate pull toward independence, but I worked hard to not overreact. What did I know about teenage boys? Sometimes he seemed to me brooding, a little bit sad. But then, who didn't feel that way once in a while?

Mr. Michaels heard the worry in my voice and repeated that this was not a big deal. Lots of kids left the campus without permission for lunch. No one had ever bothered to enforce the rule, or so he understood, being relatively new to this particular school.

"Still," he said, "I think it might be appropriate that we meet to discuss the situation. I like to get to know all of my parents anyway. Sometimes I find, Madame Kramer—and I hope you will not take this the wrong way—that these problems can be reflective of things going on at home. I don't want to ask any personal questions, but you might want to think about whether he might be picking up on any family issues."

Defensive, I heard myself make the absurd claim that Justin had been somewhat depressed since his dog died, failing to mention that was more than two years earlier.

"Yes, that makes perfect sense," he said, but I suspected he was just being polite.

After some back-and-forth about dates, we arranged to meet at lunchtime on the following Monday. Mr. Michaels concluded by saying that he looked forward to seeing me again.

Again? I had no memory of this man. "We met at back-to-school night last year," he added, sensing my hesitation. "I am easy to spot, the only African man at the school," he said with what might have been a laugh.

If I didn't remember him, I couldn't imagine him possibly remembering *me*. I was just another middle-aged white woman, unremarkable in every respect. No one ever remembered me. Neither my dentist nor my OBGYN, both of whom I had been seeing at least twice a year for sixteen years, ever seemed to know who I was when I showed up for my regularly scheduled appointments.

"You were so funny! You made me laugh," he added.

That made me laugh. Then we both laughed awkwardly. I wondered what I might have said that was funny. Maybe he was just easily amused.

"I also remember you because you look different from the other mothers."

"Different?" There it was again, another backhanded compliment. Along the lines of *I can dress like this, and you can dress like that* . . . This was an exclusive school, after all, the sort where most mothers—and even the nannies and the glamorous young au pairs—got dressed up to collect their children, to sit behind the wheels of their Mercedes SUVs and their sporty little Jaguars and even a Hummer or two in the carpool line. I had drawn more than a few stares over the years sitting in my Honda Odyssey wearing a baseball cap, blasting alternative radio through the open windows.

But really, who knew what little thing about me he might have recalled? A person could live her life carefully, trying to remain even-tempered in front of customers, polite to other mothers on the soccer field, courteous in dealings with teachers, and then be remembered for the one time she finally lost her composure. It was easy to be remembered for the wrong thing. There was a house on our block where I once noticed an empty carton of José Cuervo set out with the trash, for example. Now I couldn't help but think of those neighbors as heavy drinkers, even though I knew perfectly well that the carton might have been used to innocently transport cabbage from a farm stand, or it could have been left over from a party, one we were not invited to.

"I have also seen your picture in the newspaper," he said, which was surely intended as an innocent observation but really landed hard, like a one-two punch. Was there anyone in the entire tri-state area who did not know about our problems?

"I hope I wasn't wearing pinstripes," I said idiotically.

He laughed again. "See! You are so funny! This is what I was talking about. I will see you next week, then. I will send Pablo to wait for you now in the reception area with his belongings. And not to worry, he is being sent home with a week's worth of work, so he won't fall behind."

"Thanks," I said, not quite sure for what I should be thankful.

Should I wait for Leon? Glancing at my watch, I figured that he would not be back for at least half an hour, though of course that was just a guess. I had no idea how far he was capable of jogging, especially given the heat.

It was best to go up to school on my own right away, I decided. Leon had zero tolerance for Goth, never mind its latest mutation—Industrial Goth—so it would probably be wise to vet the situation before involving him. Surely Seymour could handle things in the store for a short time.

On my way to the door I was intercepted by Uncle Seymour, who handed me the phone. I didn't understand at first, but then realized that someone was on the line for me. I tried to signal to Seymour that I didn't want to take the call, scribbling in the air with an imaginary pen that he should take a message, but he didn't respond.

"Jane Kramer," I said at last, putting the phone to my ear while jangling the car keys impatiently.

"Jane! Good grief, I've been holding on for about ten minutes. I was about to give up but I'm desperate. I really hope you can help me out."

It was Tiffany Fleisher.

"Hi, Tiffany," I said, signaling again to Uncle Seymour, who was standing still, staring at me blankly. I was trying to tell him that there was a customer behind him.

The woman looked haggard. She was less than thirty years old, I guessed, but had four children in tow. She was standing by the accursed French country kitchen ensemble that was advertised in that morning's paper and she set an infant down on the pine table itself, where it seemed entirely possible that she would change its diaper. Yes, that was clearly her intention. She began to undress her baby, holding its chunky little legs in the air while she slipped the dirty diaper out from underneath, and, judging by her diaper-changing bravado, I had little doubt about what was going to transpire next: this was going to translate into an ugly scene about the typo. She was going to mention the words "lawyer" and "better business bureau" and "Morton's Furniture Warehouse" (our biggest competitor), and I was suddenly quite relieved to be rushing off to my delinquent son.

I glanced at my watch, listening impatiently to Tiffany. ". . . an emergency hearing," she said. "Just scheduled for tomorrow morning." She needed to be in court, but had a Power Scrapping Session scheduled. Could I fill in?

The words *unlimited earning potential* once again collided in my mind with the words *pyramid scheme* and triumphed. Still, there were complications. My son had just been suspended from school for a week and I didn't know what I would do with him if I filled in for Tiffany. Instantly I felt simpatico with all the working mothers whose dilemmas I had read about ad nauseum in popular magazines. Somehow, working in the family business never really felt like *working* to me. Our place of employment was merely a secondary location in which we hashed out the same set of problems. Sure, Justin was old enough to stay home alone, but given the problems he was having, this did not seem wise. It would be best if I could supervise.

"You can have the session anywhere you want," Tiffany said preemptively. "At your house? At your store? Anywhere that's convenient."

I would be far too embarrassed to have these women set foot in my house with its horrible furniture and overgrown garden. It would be even worse to have them in the store. I could just imagine Delia jogging in and out with her cell phone, Uncle Seymour wandering by every few minutes asking questions.

"You could even have it at my house, if you want."

"Your house?" I repeated.

"Great. I'll tell everyone. Ten A.M. I'll call you tomorrow morning with some last-minute instructions because I've actually got to run. Thanks. You're a lifesaver. By the way, since you are doing me such a big favor what I'll do here is rather than have you subcontract—usually you need to give me back twenty percent of your earnings—you can keep the entire fee on this one, which is twenty dollars per participant, plus the commission from the products you sell. And of course you can count the sales toward the cruise. I'm guessing there will be about six women, maybe seven, so that's at least a base of a hundred-twenty dollars."

I was on the slow road to financial independence. Before I got the chance to protest that I didn't actually know what a Power Scrapping Session was, Tiffany had already thanked me and said she had a few other things coming up next week that she might need some help on as well.

Between Justin and Delia and this Jean person who thought I was somehow *different,* I felt like I was about to combust. Or perhaps that was just the heat, and my $120, already burning a hole in my pocket.

6

I RACED to the front door and scooped up the furniture catalog as it dropped through the mail slot, pretending not to notice the thick stack of bills that came cascading through with it. At first I thought that the catalog was just one of the regular batch—we got at least three furniture catalogs a week. They all professed to have different themes, their own unique styles, although it seemed to me the contents were mostly indistinguishable.

Yet the picture of the sofa on the front page of this catalog was somehow mesmerizing. Bolstered by a gleaming metallic frame and oversize, plump cushions in a nearly blinding shade of pinkish red, there was something enchanting about this sofa, something forbidden and delicious, like a heap of too-rich frosting on one of Leon's sheet cakes. I couldn't take my eyes off the woman standing behind it. She was about my age, roughly my size, sporting my same nondescript hairstyle. She looked a lot like me, actually. We locked eyes for a minute, me and the woman who was not me, and I thought she was trying to tell me something as she hoisted a glass of wine in the air, leaning against the couch, smiling. Maybe that was it: she was telling me to lighten up, to have a drink and smile.

I leafed through the rest of the catalog in a semi-trance. What made this furniture so appealing? Was it simply that it was not from Kramer's? Surely that was part of it, but really it seemed there was something more complex, something slightly sinister at work here, as if some evil advertising genius had determined through illegal medical research and illicit zip code sorting that women my age, in my income bracket, could be subliminally manipulated into thinking that they actually needed splashy new living-room ensembles every couple of years. I flipped back to the front page to see what the catalog was called, where it came from. Fjorki.

Fjorki? Wasn't that what Tiffany had been talking about? And here it was, at last, my own long-awaited invitation to some Icelandic-sounding secret furniture society. Why was I always the last to know these things? By now the whole Fjorki thing, whatever it was, had probably ended. I flipped the catalog over to the back page and was surprised to see that it had been addressed by hand, in someone's loopy cursive. The ink was slightly smeared. Who had ever heard of addressing a catalog by hand? There was no return address, just a toll-free phone number for placing orders.

I opened it again, thinking perhaps an address was printed inside, and got stuck for a few minutes lusting after an Ava chaise on page twelve. The Ava chaise in Erin scarlet rested on Sadie driftwood. I would have liked to have named a baby Ava. I stared at it longingly for a while and then noticed it, like the couch on the cover, was on wheels. I'd never seen a chaise on wheels before. I began to flip back through the pages and then realized that all of the furniture was on wheels. Even the bed. In tiny print, on the back page, was the sentence: *Fjorki: Simply Transporting.*

Still, it was the model who intrigued me most. She stood in the background of just about every page, her hand poised midair, always holding the same glass of wine while smiling at other people just out of sight. She did not seem burdened by a marriage hanging by threads. Certainly she had never received alarming phone calls from her son's high school guidance counselor, or been troubled by the discovery of bones behind her furniture store. In one spread her smile was slightly saucy, as though she was speaking to her husband, or her lover, on the next page. You could imagine him exactly, reclining on one of the chairs with appropriately masculine names—the Churchill leather wing chair, the Jules recliner.

I stared at the furniture and stared at the woman and wondered if there was any connection between the two. Could she be so happy simply because she had Fjorki furniture? Could I be unhappy simply because I did not? This seemed possible, because there were moments, increasing in frequency, when I felt I was slipping off the edge of midlife without even a decent piece of furniture to prop me up.

Justin had tried to explain his drift toward Goth (I still thought of it as a drift, not a full-fledged conversion) by saying that it couldn't really be explained. Unsurprisingly, I had not found this very illuminating. When I pushed him further, all I heard was what Goth was *not*. It was not a cult. It was not a gang. It was not Satanism, contrary to the opinion of the old lady with whom he and Mike Stahl had collided that afternoon on Rockville Pike. And it was definitely not about anything along the lines of Columbine. It was, for Justin at least, just about the music. Or so he said.

Industrial Goth, he called it. A bit like punk. I tried to keep an open mind by listening to his music, which was not as much of a stretch as it probably should have been. My tastes had failed to grow refined with age. I listened to age-inappropriate radio stations, their advertisements for condoms and skateboards constant reminders that I was not part of the target demographic.

But I was still pretty far from grasping the appeal of Goth. I said I liked Green Day, but that made Justin roll his eyes.

I had gone onto a Goth website and found a primer for parents. It offered this sage advice: "If your kid has turned Goth, try to ride it out. It won't make him/her build pipe bombs. If your kid stays Goth, s/he can still have a career and family."

It could always be worse: He could have joined the Taliban. Which was not to say that Leon agreed. Leon had been nearly apoplectic when Justin came home with his first facial piercing and had ranted for a week when the band debuted in our garage. Justin had tried to appease him by comparing Goth to a subculture not unlike Orthodox Judaism, which only enraged Leon further. It also set Leon off in an altogether different direction: he suddenly got it in his head that Justin would someday inherit Kramer's, and began to talk about that incessantly. He would begin random sentences with *"When Justin takes over the store . . ."* For his part, Justin had begun to demonstrate an interest in home décor by painting his room black and sketching a vampire on the wall. He had also wrapped his Redskins beanbag chair— a present for his twelfth birthday—with mosquito netting that he had dyed black.

But it really *could* have been worse, or so I had thought until the phone call from school. Justin was, in all other respects, a model child. It was hard to be displeased when he brought home his perfect report cards and demonstrated a willingness to perform all manner of household chores. He didn't spend excessive time online, as I'd heard most kids his age did, and he wasn't even interested in video games, choosing instead to concentrate most of his energy on music. He was also gainfully employed. My occasional spot checks of his room and backpack turned up no evidence of drugs. And he still communicated.

Or rather, he *had* communicated. He seemed to have less to say to me these last few months. And the fact that he always had the headphones for his iPOD stuck in his ears meant that he missed at least half the things I said to him. One evening I stood in Justin's doorway urging him to come with me to Seymour's apartment to help set up the computer a cousin had given to him when she'd upgraded her own. It seemed unlikely Seymour would make much use of the Internet—he had trouble understanding the basic concept of cyberspace, never mind search engines and e-mail—but he was fascinated by computer solitaire. He loved choosing new decks, and was thrilled when the cards danced when he won. I got angry with Justin when he did not respond, then went off on a tangential lecture about how he had not been spending enough time with the family, growing even more agitated when he didn't reply. Then he swiveled around in his chair and smiled sweetly. He removed an earphone and asked, "Were you talking to me, Mom?"

It all seemed within the realm of normal teenage behavior. Even if strangers seemed afraid of him, to me he was a little boy, with big cheeks and a spray of freckles, who just happened to have a small assortment of metal studs and rings on his face and who lately had begun to wear dark eyeliner. He had also grown about eight inches in the last two years.

My attempts at broad-mindedness came up short of accepting Mike Stahl, however. Why did Justin have to hang out with him? Because Mike was an unparalleled bass player, was the inevitable response. That he was an amazing musician was inarguable. Mike was the pride of Rockville Prep's music department; he had once played at the Kennedy Center with the National Symphony Orchestra after winning a county youth competition, and I had taken Justin to see him. That was just prior to Justin's drift, before my subtle dislike of Mike had turned to dread. He had even looked respectable in a tuxedo, black nail polish notwithstanding.

Mike's family had been unable to attend his performance—a

lapse I viewed as instructive. His father traveled frequently; he had founded a local biotech company that had been the first to clone a rat. The company had gone public five years earlier, and the Stahl family joined the ranks of the new billionaires without a clue about tasteful spending. Roger Stahl purchased three adjacent houses in Potomac, one of which had formerly belonged to Mike Tyson, and hired a contractor to link them together. The result was a compound that looked something like an airport, with terminals connected by covered walkways. I had never actually been invited inside, even though I had driven Mike home at least a dozen times before he got his license and felt like a surrogate mother. Mike and his brother shared a house with the butler, a dazzling young Caribbean man named Lord. My impression was that Mike Stahl was raising himself, and he was not doing a great job of it.

Anyway, I *felt* like I'd been inside the house as I'd seen countless pictures, as had most newspaper readers in the Washington region. When Roger Stahl was forced to tear down the fence he built without a permit, he sued the county zoning board, and the story led the evening news on and off for a couple of months. He had also been made to halt construction on an in-ground swimming pool, which was situated illegally on the side of one of the homes. A county regulation only permitted pools *behind* a house, and the Stahls' backyard was inconveniently occupied by the Potomac River. I was surprised they hadn't yet launched a drive to have the river diverted.

Rita Stahl was an alcoholic agoraphobic who had not left her wing of the middle house since she moved in. Mike was seventeen, but was still in the tenth grade, having stayed back a year in school. Mike's parents compensated for their absenteeism by indulgence: he had a bank card with instant access to cash, and he was given a BMW for his sixteenth birthday. I had seen it in the school parking lot when I'd picked the boys up an hour earlier. There was a dent on the driver's side, and the front bumper was hanging off.

The last thing I wanted to do was bring Mike Stahl home with us; I wanted to get Justin alone and hear his version of events, but I was listed as the emergency contact on Mike's school form, and no one else was available. His father was in Geneva at a biotech conference, the school secretary told me, rolling her eyes in a manner that suggested she, too, had had her fill of dealing with the Stahls. She didn't even bother to mention Mike's mother. Her sad story was pretty much known by all.

It was only about one o'clock; Mike and Justin shared a ridiculously early 11:30 lunch period, and in a sense I could sympathize with their inclination to cruise Rockville Pike rather than eat cafeteria slop at that hour of the day. The two boys dropped their backpacks in the front hallway and headed straight to the garage, and as I sorted through the rest of the mail I could hear their music wafting up through the floorboards. Because it was just the two of them—sans their noisy drummer Brett and their alarming lead singer Zondra (although her euphonious name seemed worthy of a chaise in the Fjorki catalog, with her wan pallor and emaciated frame she looked like a heroin addict and her voice sounded like the screeching brakes on a semi truck about to collide with a freight train), their music this afternoon was surprisingly . . . *musical.* I had almost forgotten that we'd spent thousands of dollars on classical guitar lessons for Justin. The music he typically performed consisted of three dissonant chords that even I could probably manage.

He was unplugged, and he and Mike were playing a quite remarkable acoustic duet, vaguely Spanish in style, that bathed the house with warmth, filling me with hope. Boys that could play music like this could not be all bad. *Ergo,* a house in which music like that was being performed by two teenage boys could not be in the state of crisis one might suppose given that nestled in that day's pile of mail was a final notice from the telephone company.

We had three days in which to pay our delinquent bill before being disconnected, the notice informed me in bold red type. I kept meaning to take care of that. It was a large bill, the sort that grew larger every day with its assorted penalties. In just three months' time it had blossomed into nearly three hundred dollars' worth of phone bill. I suppose I had been hoping for some miraculous change in the state of things, some surprise influx of funds. I quickly tucked the notice into the pile of mail, hoping that it would cause me less angst if I couldn't see it, and resolved to call the telephone company later in the day.

We seemed to get an inordinate amount of junk mail at our house—another consequence of staying in one place too long. There was something to be said for moving on from time to time, leaving behind the unsolicited garden catalogs and the magazines that no one ever read, along with the uneasy relations with certain neighbors and kids like Mike Stahl.

And yet this music from the garage was so soulful that it seemed wrong, ungrateful, to fret about things like unpaid bills, about living in a place I didn't really want to be. Buoyed by the music, I began to drift through the house making beds, collecting laundry, sweeping large dust balls from behind doors, cleaning windows and mirrors. Which brought me face to face with myself. Staring at my reflection, I wondered why I didn't look more like that woman in the Fjorki catalog. I leaned a hand on the railing of the bed and pretended to hold a wine glass in the air, but there was no transformation. I couldn't help but think that I looked a bit like a Kramer's reject, an occupational hazard. The upholstery was still salvageable, but frayed and sagging, in need of repair. I struck another pose, then I smiled. I still looked like me.

A bit of color couldn't hurt, I thought, remembering Delia's makeup bag in my pocket. I studied a small but expensive compact with a trio of eye shadows and decided to give it a try. A bit of silver, some of the sparkly stuff. This looked like something a fourteen-year-old girl might wear. What was Delia thinking, buying this stuff? I put the powder on my eyelids—a different color on each, just to see which looked better. Then I applied her mascara. There was also some powder blush, which I brushed on somewhat sloppily. Then I stared at myself. Something was still missing. I reached back into the pouch and retrieved Delia's sleek phallic tube of Merry Mango. The color was certainly as bright as the name. Smeared on my lips, the effect was curious. Did it make me look like Delia? No, for better or worse, I looked nothing like Delia *or* the woman in the catalog, although I did look a bit like a clown.

A radio began to blare from the street, growing louder as it moved toward the house. I couldn't quite make out the song, but it sounded like a Muzak-y version of something familiar, possibly a Beatles song. A glance out the window confirmed my worst fear: it was Delia's silver Lexus pulling into our driveway, with Leon behind the wheel. Letting someone drive your car, never mind your silver Lexus, seemed to me to indicate a pretty high level of intimacy. My pulse quickened as Leon opened the door. Delia's long leg emerged from the passenger side and I could hear them talking but could not make out the words. Her calves were tanned and well toned, muscled, powerful-looking. From my second-story vantage point I couldn't tell whether they were clean-shaven, but I sensed they were. Of course they were. Probably waxed at a fine salon. The most expensive one in Pittsburgh.

Leon went around to the rear of the car and opened the trunk, where he retrieved something that appeared to be a suit bag. That was strange. Had they gone shopping? Had he gone shopping without consulting the budget? And what were they doing here? Had they been planning an afternoon tryst? My emotions gushed like blood from a slit vein, like hormones through the system of a peri-menopausal woman, morphing within seconds from anger to jealousy. Before I knew it, I was actually crying.

Their chatter was still mostly inaudible as they approached the house and the key turned in the door. I heard footsteps, the sounds of keys clanking onto the hall table, of Leon rifling through the stack of mail. I could make out Delia complaining that her sneakers were too tight and were giving her blisters.

"Janie?" Leon's voice boomed, echoing up the staircase. I pretended not to hear, but of course I did hear—the house had become completely still when Justin and Mike ceased playing just seconds before the car pulled into the driveway. "Janie?" he called again, sounding puzzled.

"That's odd," he said to Delia. "She must be here, somewhere. Her van is in the driveway. Why doesn't she listen to me? I told her to stay in the store until I got back."

I didn't much like his tone. He'd told me to *stay,* like he was issuing commands to a dog. Stay, Janie! Sit! Now I wondered, had he asked me to stay to mind the store, or to stay as in stay away from the house so he and Delia could have it to themselves?

"Janie!" he called once more, now insistent. His voice grew louder as he neared the bottom of the staircase.

"Maybe she's working in the garden," Delia offered.

They had to know I was somewhere on the premises, and I was trying to stem the flow of tears and pull myself together to greet them when I heard Leon's sarcastic, "Ha! Janie in the garden? I don't think she knows where the garden is!"

Granted, that was not an unreasonable thing to say; I might have made the same quip myself in response to any suggestion that I was outside pulling weeds. But there was no need for that mocking tone, no need to say such a thing in front of Delia. Just then the musicians in the garage began to play again and I could imagine the baffled look on Leon's face. I knew the exact spot where a dimple emerged on his left cheek when he scrunched his face into the thinking position, the way his forehead furrowed when distressed.

"What the . . . ?"

His voice trailed off as he walked through the kitchen and down the back stairs, toward the garage.

This was bound to be ugly. The only mature thing to do was just plunge forward and enter the fray. I had to protect Justin from his father, because Leon was surely going to go ballistic. I raced down the stairs, through the kitchen and into the garage, arriving just seconds after Leon and Delia. The scene in the garage reminded me of a western movie in the tense, silent seconds before everyone draws their guns and starts shooting. Mike stood at his bass, his bow hovering just an inch from the strings, frozen by Leon's icy glare.

"Dad . . ."

"Cutting school, are you?" Leon boomed before Justin could finish speaking. "Where's your mother? Does she allow this? Does she *condone* this? How long has this been going on? What, does she let you stay home every day so you can practice your . . . your . . . your *music*?"

Leon took a handkerchief from his pocket and dabbed at his brow. The heat in the garage was oppressive. Perhaps *this* would prove to be the end of him. I was about to cut him off, but Delia beat me to it.

"Leon, Leon, take it easy, hon . . . ," she said, laying that neatly polished hand on his shoulder. She rubbed his upper back in circles with her palm. "I'm sure these boys have an explanation."

"Yes, they do," I interrupted, and four pairs of astonished eyes turned in my direction. I wished I hadn't said that, because I realized that the explanation I had to offer on their behalf was not really very helpful. They were not *cutting* school. They had been *suspended* for cutting school. "I picked them up," I explained, "after speaking to Justin's guidance counselor . . . Leon, I think this is sort of a private matter that we ought to discuss later. Alone."

Delia's phone began to ring. How was that possible? So far as I knew, she'd left her bag at the store, with the phone inside. But she reached into the pocket of her shorts and pulled out another phone. This one was pink, like her nails. It reminded me that my own phone had been missing for more than a week, and that I really ought to call and be sure no one else was using it, running up another bill that we couldn't afford to pay.

"Oh, hi!" she said, her voice pitching an octave higher. "Listen, honey . . . uh huh . . . uh huh . . ." She tapped her foot impatiently.

The rest of us stood silently, but it seemed everyone was staring at me. Why were they staring at me? Delia was the one speaking. After a few minutes she extracted herself from the call, tucked the phone back in her pocket, and then began to stare at me, too.

"What?" I finally asked.

"Mrs. Kramer," Mike ventured, "Your face is kind of messed up. Are you okay?"

"Have you been crying, hon?" Delia asked perceptively. "I'm guessing that your makeup is just smeared from rubbing your eyes?"

I rolled my head, neither yes nor no, hoping that she didn't recognize her hodgepodge of beauty products on my face.

"I don't think I've seen you wear makeup before. It's good . . . it's a big improvement, don't you think, Leon? But that lipstick, it's too bright for you. You need a more neutral color. Something to blend, to complement your natural coloring, which is fabulous, don't get me wrong . . ." By now she was standing next to me, running her fingers through my hair like a stylist. "I'd say you are not really an orange-type person." She took a step back, studying me. "I'd go with something slightly more pink in tone. Were you getting ready for tonight? What color is your dress?"

"Tonight?"

"Yes. What are you wearing? I'm so jealous! I wish I could go, too."

"What am I wearing where?"

"Oh for fuck's sake," said Leon. "Don't tell me you forgot."

"Don't swear in front of the kids," I snapped.

"The WZOP dinner. It's tonight. Black Tie. I put the invitation on your desk a month ago."

"I would have seen it if you did!" I snarled unattractively.

"Look, why argue?" asked Delia reasonably. Except that it was unreasonable that she was standing in my garage in skimpy jogging clothes, participating in our marital drama.

"Why don't you just take *her*?" I asked. "She said she wants to go." My suggestion, though born of bitterness, was not entirely disingenuous. As a patio furniture saleswoman, Delia might find networking at the WZOP dinner useful. At the last dinner party I had been to, a political fundraiser about a year earlier that Samuel had insisted we attend, I'd been seated at the same table as Anna Berger. I had not spoken a single word the entire night. I came home feeling vaguely depressed. I performed poorly at these dinners, generally. So why not let Delia go in my place? Since I sort of assumed they were having an affair, I sort of assumed they assumed I assumed so.

"Because Delia was not invited," Leon said reasonably. "The

invitation was for Mr. and Mrs. Leon Kramer. Last I checked, that was *you*."

Although he said this sarcastically, it was still oddly touching. I had this sudden irrational thought that maybe if I just put on a nice dress and went out on the town with my husband, all of our problems might melt away. This was just a phase. A bad phase, nothing more. Someday we'd laugh about it. (Remember when we almost declared bankruptcy? When Justin went Goth? When I thought you were having an affair with that tacky patio furniture saleswoman? What a rough time we had!)

Leon suddenly noticed there was a coffin in the garage, and he took a step back. "My God, Justin . . . *Why do you have a coffin? Is someone dead?*"

"Leon, I think we really ought to talk about this privately," I tried again. The coffin had been there for a couple of weeks, and I'd been trying to think of a gentle way to explain its presence to him.

Delia raised her hand, like the smart kid in class. "I'll bet this coffin is for their band," she said. "I'll bet they have a number in which someone, probably the lead singer, pops out of the coffin."

"How did you know that?" Mike asked, deflated.

"Honey," she said, "I've been to a gig or two in my life."

The boys exchanged weary looks.

None of this seemed to be having a calming effect on Leon, however.

"I've had just about enough of this Goth crap," he boomed. We all stared at him worriedly. Leon about to explode was never a pretty sight. *"This is it. I don't want you hanging around like this unsupervised,"* he shouted, darting an accusing look in my direction. "I want to know where you are after school. I want you . . . in the store. Yes, that's it. In the store. Working." He began to relate the familiar story of how he used to do his homework in

the back office while helping his father at the store, how his family didn't even own a car for their first five years in America, how his mother had struggled to learn English. It would have been moving (a) had it been relevant and (b) had we not heard it many, many times before. Even Mike Stahl could probably recite the saga from memory, were it not for the fact that the details grew more dramatic with each recitation.

"First of all, I already have a job," Justin boldly interrupted. "And secondly, I know that when you were my age you worked in the store every day, but that was different . . ."

Justin stopped mid-sentence and waved through the side window of the garage to Enrique, the little Cuban boy next door. I had watched Enrique a couple of times, when his parents were stuck for a baby-sitter. He was a sweet, curly-haired eight-year-old kid carrying an instrument in a case that was nearly as big as he was. He was smiling. He was always smiling. He waved back, showing his crooked pre-orthodontic grin, and then everyone in our group waved. We all froze for a moment until he was out of sight.

"Listen, Leon, honey," Delia said, "I think you need a time-out. Just cool off for an hour. Go have a nice shower. Or go out back and hit a few golf balls. Maybe drink a cup of nice herbal tea. Iced tea would be even better. Janie, would you mind running upstairs to make Leon some tea? I find that calms him down."

I was on the verge of saying something I'd surely regret, but then her cell phone rang again and she fished it out of her pocket and began chattering away.

"Hi, honey!" she said. "No, no, not a problem. You caught me at a great time. I'm just coming out of an important business meeting . . . hang on." She put her palm over the receiver and looked at me. "I'm gonna run now. Ciao!"

"Ciao," Leon and I said at the same time.

We watched her walk out the side door, in silence. I was thinking that I wanted to somehow eliminate this strangely predatory patio furniture saleswoman with the disconcerting mystery in her wallet. I didn't really want to know what Leon was thinking, although I could certainly venture a guess.

7

KRAMER'S had been hawking furniture on WZOP radio since 1963, which gave us special status as the second-longest-running advertiser in station history. An initial, three-year promotional package was secured by Samuel, who, with negotiating skills worthy of a union arbitrator, managed to parlay the deal into decades.

Only Roger Josephs Jr., a personal-injury lawyer with offices a few blocks from the White House, could boast more continuous air time. (*"Marjorie was left with three kids under the age of five when her husband, Larry, was impaled by a steel beam while working on a construction site,"* began one Roger Josephs Jr. classic. *"Fortunately she had the presence of mind to call me— Roger Josephs Jr. Now, she has a housekeeper and drives a Mercedes . . ."*) His print ads hailed him as the "The King of the Litigation Bar," but it was never clear to me whether this was in any way an official title or something he had thought up himself.

Samuel and Esther had delighted in attending the dinners WZOP threw each year to fete its big spenders. Back in the station's fledgling days, before it had been taken over by a national network and acquired NFL broadcasting rights, the Kramers had been treated like royalty. They were seated at the head table with the station manager, honored with champagne toasts, given WZOP hats and coffee mugs and T-shirts and even occasional trophies, which still sat on their mantelpiece. Surely most of the attendees regarded these dinners as a nuisance—an annual festival of chewy roast beef and overcooked vegetables, ghastly music, and painful small talk tolerated solely for the purpose of preserving business relations. But Esther anticipated these events eagerly. Each year she would begin fussing as soon as the engraved invitation arrived. Weeks were devoted to searching for the perfect dress and shoes. Hair was done up specially, manicures and pedicures procured. Then, for as many weeks afterward, she would reminisce about the crystal wineglasses, the elegant ballroom of whatever out-of-the-way hotel it had been held in that year, the charming station manager who treated her like a queen, or at least like the wife of the second-longest advertiser in station history.

Kramer's still had a historic relationship to boast about, but we were no longer key players at WZOP. Anyone who tuned in to 1650 AM, however briefly, could testify that commercial breaks these days were dominated by ads for Viagra and a variety of other performance-enhancing remedies that, with their frank discussions of premature ejaculation and vaginal dryness, actually made Roger Josephs Jr.'s ads sound like poetry. The only time slots we could afford were between midnight and 5 A.M. As with so much else to do with the business, I believed that we needed to rethink our advertising strategy—our customers were primarily young families in need of affordable furniture, and a large percentage of them were recent immigrants, non–English speakers unable to fully comprehend the terms of our credit agreement. These were probably not the people listening to all-news radio in the wee hours of the night, but Samuel was resistant to change. He had been advertising on WZOP for more than forty years, and my suggestions were considered further evidence of heresy.

Although these dinners were annual events, I had never been

to one before. It had never occurred to me to *want* to go. There were many social obligations that came with being the owner of a small business, and I was generally happy to let Leon and Samuel carry the flag. My days were long, getting up early with Justin and then working in the store, so I relished any weeknight opportunity to forgo feeding Leon, instead sneaking into bed early to read. I knew it was not terribly progressive of me, but I still felt some wifely obligation to fix Leon dinner each night, to keep him well nourished, like a prized farm animal. I thought I did a good job of feeding my family, even if my mother-in-law had disagreed. My sense of kitchen duty was probably rooted in maternal rebellion: my own mother had never taken care of anyone, including herself. I was on the phone once with Leon's sister when I heard his keys turn in the door. I told her I had to go and turn on the oven. "To cook dinner?" she asked, "or to stick your head in it?" This did not strike me as a very Christian question.

After Delia walked out of the garage, Leon and I continued to argue pointlessly about whether he had left the invitation on my desk several weeks earlier. He had known that Samuel would be away, he said, and he was quite certain he had put it in an obvious place where I would see it. I refused to concede the possibility that he was right, even after conjuring some dim memory of a fancy card amidst the stacks of bills.

A quick mental inventory of my closet left me blank. It had been years since I'd donned a fancy dress. The last formal event I could recall attending was Leon's cousin's daughter's bat mitzvah in Minneapolis—a winter affair to which I had worn a long-sleeved black velvet gown that would be entirely inappropriate for this still oppressively hot September evening.

Of course Leon and I had gone out more recently than that—

just not to anything requiring formalwear. It was not so very long ago that we had done normal couple things like acknowledge anniversaries. On our fourteenth, Leon had surprised me with a reservation at Nora's. It had been a wonderful evening, a distant memory by now. Although Leon liked to eat, we had long ago stopped splurging on expensive dinners, especially ones that consisted of lettuce leaves with names he could not pronounce and organic cuisine with portions too small to satisfy his super-size appetite. If he was going to spend good money on a meal these days, he wanted a big, juicy steak, he said. I later learned that he was given the meal gratis as barter for furniture for Nora's cleaning lady, but I did not begrudge him the arrangement, which had led to one of the last truly romantic nights I could recall; the last time we had made love, as opposed to simply filling the gaping hole in our lives with angry sex.

The thought of going out with Leon to a dress-up event had a sobering effect. We may have been mired in dysfunction these last few years, but at the most basic level, we were still in this together. We were owners of a small business, with obligations to fulfill. The only thing to do was to make ourselves presentable and press forward. Our streak of bad luck was bound to come to an end soon. And in the spirit of looking ahead, I made a bold decision. I would not pull out my credit card and buy a new outfit. We lived in a house of many closets; surely one of them contained a dress.

"Lies, lies, lies. All anyone in this town wants to hear are lies," Leon said, punching the button on the radio irritably. I tossed an empty liter of Coke and an open bag of Fritos into the back as I climbed in the car, stuffing the taffeta train of the dress into the passenger seat.

"What lies?"

"It doesn't matter *what* lies, Janie. Everything is a lie. And tonight will be more lies. The whole point of this dinner is to sit at a table and tell each other lies. 'Oh, Leon, Kramer's is our most highly prized account,' some ad salesman is going to say. 'And because we value your business so highly, we've got a special package for you, special rates . . .'"

I wondered what he had been listening to that had set him off. It could have been anything, really. Even a weather report. It didn't take much to get him going these days. "Why don't you tell me a lie, Leon," I said, trying to lighten his mood. "Tell me I look nice."

He turned and glanced in my direction before throwing the car into reverse and backing out of the driveway. "You do look nice," he said, softening. A half-hearted compliment seemed the best he could do. We hadn't yet left our neighborhood and already I felt deflated; it was hard to remember that fleeting moment in the garage when I had supposed we could gloss over our difficulties just by getting dressed up and going out on a pseudo-date.

Now that we had finished conversing he turned on the radio again, with its lying broadcasters, and punched in WZOP just in time for the traffic report. At least *they* weren't lying. Their report of trouble on the Beltway was unfortunately completely true.

Leon was clearly in a funk, and it occurred to me that perhaps he was still upset about the scene in the garage that afternoon. I leaned over and turned down the volume on the radio. "Leon, we need to talk about Justin. The reason he was home, in the garage with Mike . . . I got a call from his guidance counselor and he seems to think . . ."

"Holy Fucking Cow . . . What's going on here?" he interrupted. Traffic came to a standstill as we approached the entrance to the Beltway. A couple of vehicles were actually making U-turns off the ramp. The air was beginning to choke with thick black smoke that had a vaguely toxic aftertaste. A green Jeep suddenly came barreling off the ramp in reverse, motioning for people to roll up their windows; it nearly collided with a police car making a pitiful attempt to cut through the gridlock. Leon turned the volume back up on the radio, but they were back to broadcasting commercials.

We were afforded a strange vantage point sitting motionless on the entrance ramp; a view not meant to be, like looking down on the earth from a plane suspended midair. The setting sun glinted off the surfaces of cars, casting searing streaks of light. The signs all looked too big. I had never noticed the dying bushes or the tangled clump of vines off to the side. This was an eight-lane, sixty-four-mile circle of asphalt best glimpsed in passing, at no less than fifty-five miles per hour, although in reality traffic was frequently so choked it was hard to get up to speed.

Another car reversed off the ramp; the man in the passenger seat held a Terrapins cap over his face to block the smoke and shouted that a truck hauling hazardous chemicals had just caught fire.

As Leon began to back up, too, nearly taking out a small swath of parched shrubbery and muttering expletives under his breath, I cringed, thinking that we were possibly the only people in America who still had recalled Firestone tires on their Ford Explorer. Out of the side-view mirror, I saw a large vehicle. A truck. It was trying to creep around the side of us, angling to cut in front.

"Look out!" I shouted as our Explorer scraped the side of the pickup.

"I know how to drive, Janie," he said condescendingly, getting out of the car to survey the damage. The driver of the truck got out, as well. He was roughly the same size as Leon and even looked a bit like him, but was bearded, and not wearing a tuxedo. They shouted at each other, exchanging the word "fuck" several times, gesticulating wildly. This was definitely not the evening I had envisioned.

"Leon," I called to him, "let it go! It's not that big of a deal." The old Leon, the one I had fallen in love with, would have laughed it off. That Leon had a sense of humor, was easygoing to a fault, could wade through the chaos with his eye trained on the big picture. Unfortunately, I'd only had a brief glimpse of that particular Leon before he morphed into who he was possibly meant to be—a short-tempered overweight man with a genetic predisposition to die while arguing over a minor traffic incident. There was barely a scrape on either vehicle and anyway, our car was hardly in mint condition to begin with.

"This is crazy," I said when he returned to the car, still cursing.

"I agree," he said.

So we agreed on something. We managed to extricate ourselves from the traffic without further incident and headed toward another Beltway entrance that would allow us to bypass the accident. We didn't speak again until we were nearly there. I had no interest in starting up with Leon just before going into this party—being in a real fight was worse than being vaguely estranged—but I couldn't help it. Perhaps *this* would be the end of us, here, on the Beltway. I contemplated flinging myself dramatically out of our slowly moving vehicle and beginning a new life on the inner loop, stumbling away awkwardly, tripping in my too-high heels.

"What do you mean, Leon?" I asked, possibly sounding too combative. "What is it exactly that you agree with?"

"I don't remember what we were talking about."

"We're stuck, don't you think?" There. I had said it aloud.

This was possibly the most audacious statement I had ever made about our marriage.

"Yeah, it's pretty bad, but I think it's clearing up ahead. Just past this next exit . . ."

"That's not what I mean, Leon. I mean in life. We're stuck in life."

"We're just having some money problems, that's all. We just need some cash to jump-start things. I think this patio furniture idea is going to turn us around, Janie. We may need to borrow a little money to get it going. As soon as this lawsuit goes away we'll be fine. Chandler thinks I could counter-sue, maybe get punitive damages . . ."

Was this all that was on his mind? Why did I always leapfrog to solutions involving death or divorce, when really everything could be fixed by simply robbing a bank?

"Chandler is an idiot," I said. "And anyway, we can't borrow any more money. We're already totally overextended. As it is, we're going to have to take out another loan to finish paying for Justin's high school. Then there's college to start worrying about. We're in no position to expand the business. If anything, we should be trying to downsize."

"We'd just borrow a little bit, Janie. Just a bit to get started. This Fitzgerald thing is brilliant. It's the ticket. I can feel it in my bones," he said as we pulled into the parking lot of the New Carrollton Ramada Inn.

"Please don't say that word."

"What word?" He looked confused, as he hadn't uttered the "F" word for at least sixty seconds.

"*Bones.* I think those bones out back are a curse of some sort."

"Oh, come on, Janie. Don't be so sensitive," he said, softening, rubbing my shoulder. "Look, these have been bad times. I know that. And this evening didn't get off to a good start. I'm sorry for whatever fucking thing it is I said or did. I don't even remember, it's so goddamned hot. The traffic really aggravates me. Let's just get this dinner over with and go home," he said.

"While we're on the subject of offensive words, could you not say 'fuck' quite so often?" I asked, sensing his conciliatory mood.

"Sure, honey. Anything you want," he replied, giving my shoulder a pat. "Let's just get this over with," he repeated, squeezing himself out the door.

We were among the first to arrive, even though we were more than an hour late. The entire metropolitan region was suffering ripple effects of what was now a confirmed toxic chemical spill resulting in a fire that still burned. A five-mile stretch of the Beltway remained closed in both directions. One beleaguered guest said she had sat in traffic as far away as Baltimore, where she'd been a chaperone on a bus full of eighth graders on a field trip, one of whom had vomited in her lap. Leon took a step back as she spoke. Guests continued to stagger in stupefied, looking as if they had just gotten off a roller coaster.

After hearing the appalling traffic conditions described at least six times from as many different people, I left for the refuge of the ladies' room. A quick glance around the ballroom confirmed that I had erred quite severely in my dress selection. I was the only woman in the room who had taken the words "black tie" seriously. Perhaps because it was a weeknight, perhaps because we were in a Ramada Inn ballroom in New Carrollton, Maryland, perhaps because every other woman in the room left her house—or at least her discount furniture store—more frequently than I did and therefore did not overreact, fashion-wise, to an evening out, nearly all of them were clad in what I would have technically considered business attire, not black tie.

Alone in my house, in front of a mirror, the dress I had selected seemed subdued, tasteful, even elegant. It had been a bridesmaid's dress from the wedding of a college friend I had not spoken to in years. Now it seemed a bit much, and frankly even a little bit slutty. I hoped we would soon be seated; that way I could at least pull the top of the dress down tight to try and keep my bosom, such as it was, from spilling out of the skimpy bodice. And I could tuck the ruffle-work at the bottom, the five layers of lace and chiffon and taffeta, under the table.

On my way to the ladies' room I accidentally bumped into a man the size of an armoire, knocking the drink out of his hand. We exchanged apologies, and I tried to wipe his jumbo pant leg with a tiny cocktail napkin. The dress made loud swishing sounds as I moved away, making an effort to glide more quietly. As I headed back toward Leon I noticed a table full of cards. Seating placements, presumably. There were two Kramer envelopes. One for Mrs. Leon Kramer. One for Mr. Leon Kramer. Never a good sign. This suggested we would be seated at separate tables, which meant that I would be required to actually *speak*.

Leon was standing with a small group of people, and I inserted myself beside him and handed him his envelope. A tiny woman in a yellow dress was still talking about the traffic on the Beltway—"backed up in both directions all the way to Waldorf!" she reported almost gleefully. She seemed intoxicated. Leon nodded politely and leaned over to whisper in my ear.

"Do you know who you just bumped into over there?" he asked.

"No idea. But I made him spill wine all over himself. It was very embarrassing."

"You *should* be embarrassed—that was Trey Cleveland! A.K.A. 'The Jackhammer.'"

"Who?"

"Trey Cleveland? The Jackhammer?" Leon repeated, clearly astonished that I did not know who Trey Cleveland The Jackhammer was. As if Trey Cleveland The Jackhammer carried equal name recognition as, say, Saddam Hussein the Evil Dictator. "Cleveland's the best linebacker in the NFL!"

"A linebacker!" I tried to sound excited. "What team does he play on?"

The woman in yellow was now staring at me, incredulous. Her dress was the color of egg yolk. Was her skin yellow, too, or was that just the reflection of the dress?

"You don't know who Trey Cleveland is?" she asked.

"I grew up overseas," I replied. While that answer got me out of a lot of jams, in this case it didn't actually work as an excuse. Still, I was hoping it would at least serve to change the subject.

"Remember the last Super Bowl? Trey Cleveland broke the collarbone of the Giants quarterback in the fourth quarter," she explained.

"Oh! Of course! *That* Trey Cleveland!" I was tired of talking; my claim of recognition seemed to work. Maybe Leon was right: all anyone wanted to hear were lies, anyway. "What do you suppose he's doing here?"

Leon leaned in close and whispered in my ear that all of the Redskins players were present, on account of the fact that WZOP was their official radio station. I gathered that this was something I ought to have figured out, myself.

"What a beautiful dress! Wherever did you get that? It's so fresh. So . . . youthful!" exclaimed the woman in yellow.

I was spared having to answer because just then, a woman with short spiky hair and massive loopy earrings tapped her on the shoulder and they stepped aside to discuss something in private.

Leon and I just stood awkwardly for a few moments, fake smiles plastered on our faces. I looked around the room feeling queasy. I was terrified by the thought of sitting at a table of complete strangers, making small talk, or worse, talking about important things—world events, advertising strategies on local radio stations, or even football. I wished I was home in bed.

Just then a dinner bell rang and we were urged to find our tables. "I wish I was home in bed," said Leon, and I smiled at the thought that perhaps our marriage was based on some deep common bond, after all: we were at least united in our alienation.

My seat was at the far end of the table, next to a Mr. Thor Johnson. Was that name Icelandic? Might he possibly know something about Fjorki? (I had tried to call Fjorki to inquire about the price of a spectacular bed that looked almost as if it was floating, but a recording informed me that the number had been changed and I was unable to get a new listing from directory assistance.) On the other side of Thor was meant to be a Mr. Phillip Toffley III. Why was that name familiar? Perhaps he owned something, or had endowed something. I walked around the table trying to be inconspicuous as I studied the other place cards. There was only one name that I recognized: Roger Josephs Jr. This seemed incredible. Roger Josephs Jr. had been the butt of jokes in our house for so many years that I had never actually thought of him as a real person. I feared that when I finally met him, I might burst out laughing or say something completely inappropriate. I contemplated dashing over to Leon's table to tell him the news, but did not especially want to flaunt my dress now that I had the opportunity to tuck the absurd train beneath a tablecloth. Or I would, if my tablemates ever showed up, enabling me to sit down.

An overly tanned, almost crispy-looking woman with a too-tight face—Botox?—approached wearing a bright sequined affair that looked like something better suited for a flapper party. It was impossible to guess her age, other than that it was probably much older than she wanted us to think. The dress was so

heavy with beads it looked capable of standing up on its own—
which was more than could be said for the woman encased in it,
who looked as if she might collapse without the dress to immo-
bilize her spine. As she continued toward my table, I could see
that she was wearing matching sequin earrings. I was working
up a compliment, but she walked right past me to table 14.

I continued to stand behind my chair, smiling nervously.
Now a man approached. Tall, blond, bespectacled, neatly coiffed
moustache. Nordic Thor? No. He, too, walked past to table 14.
Why wasn't I at table 14? That table was filling up, and everyone
looked quite merry. A waiter was already pouring wine into their
glasses and they were toasting one another, clinking glasses.

People at a couple of other tables began to take their seats,
bodies sinking into chairs with the synchronicity of collapsing
card houses. I could see Leon chatting with the woman next to
him, but I couldn't glimpse her face. I hoped she wasn't beautiful.

I had been standing alone for only a couple of minutes, but
it felt like an eternity. What was the proper etiquette? Should I
just sit down and begin picking at my salad? Wasn't that better
than standing alone, drawing attention to myself? Fortunately, I
was relieved of this earth-shattering decision when three men
approached the table. They all seemed to know each other. They
all seemed to know *me*.

"Jane Kramer?" said a humongous man with odd tufts of hair
on his face who looked like he would be more at home on the
World Wrestling circuit than at a WZOP dinner party. "I'm Thor
Johnson," he continued, extending his hand. I couldn't tell if
those patches of hair on his face were a fashion statement or the
result of some sort of pituitary gland condition. "Sorry to leave
you stranded here alone. We all found each other earlier and
went out to have a smoke . . . well, I was out having a smoke, and
they joined me. We're all from . . ."

"Iceland?"

He looked confused. "From the station . . . we're all colleagues at WZOP and are honored to have you—one of our most important advertisers!—at our table. But Iceland is close. My grandmother was from Norway. But close enough, Jane, close enough!" Thor put a beefy hand on my shoulder and began to introduce me to his colleagues.

"This is Rajiv Kumar, our deputy advertising manager, and Phillip Toffley, our afternoon news anchor . . ."

"Oh, that's it! Phillip Toffley III," I interjected. "From the radio!"

"Indeed," offered Toffley III, extending a hand to shake.

"I'm not sure where our other guests are. You are supposed to be seated across from Giddeon Gordon, you know, the new Redskins quarterback and, let's see . . . that's Jerry Radnor, over there. He's the new features editor at *Washington!* magazine. And next to you is . . . ," he said, straining to read the tiny print on the card . . . "Roger Josephs Junior. He's a lawyer. Big player at the station. And wide receiver Jonny Moser will be sitting right there. Speaking of the devil . . ."

Wide receiver Jonny Moser appeared, his tuxedo at least two sizes too small, and everyone shook hands excitedly and slapped one another on the back.

The sequined lady returned just as we began to settle into our seats. She appeared to be making the rounds at each table and she also, mysteriously, seemed to know me. "Jane . . . Lana Linden . . . events coordinator for WZOP. I was so looking forward to meeting you. Let me explain something," she said. She spoke very quickly, and I had to listen carefully to keep up. "Weactuallyranoutofwomen," she said in a whisper, cupping her hand to her mouth, presumably so others wouldn't hear. "We were going for the boy-girl-boy-girlseatingarrangementplusjustmixingpeople upwiththeirprofessionsandwhatnot"—she stopped for breath and then slowed down for a minute—"but we ran out of girls!" She paused again before saying something I couldn't quite make out but included the words "Kramer'sbeingoneofourmostloyal customers . . ." I wished she would go away.

"Besides," she continued, "who wouldn't want to sit with this handsome group of men?" She half winked when she said this, but her eye would not fully close, probably the result of too much Botox. "Surely you've met Thor Johnson . . . our Assistant Special Events Coordinator. The Chief Special Events Coordinator couldn't make it. Busy time of year!" she said cheerfully. I tried to smile as widely as Lana, which was easy to do because my skin was still elastic, and I do believe I managed to say something, although I'm not sure what. The word "flattered" possibly spilled from my lips somewhere in an otherwise incoherent string of words, but by then someone who identified himself as the Deputy Station Manager was clanking a spoon to a glass and loudly clearing his throat to get our attention. I glanced over to Leon's table and decided that if there was a shortage of women at my table it was possibly because there was no shortage at his, where there were only two men to six women. Perhaps Lana Linden had trouble with the whole matching pairs thing.

"So, Jane," Thor said, digging into his salad. "What do *you* do?"

This was always my least favorite subject. It didn't matter who asked it or in what context—whether on tax forms or at dinner parties, the question always made me cringe. I felt like I was on the witness stand, defending my life, justifying my existence. What *did* I do? Well, obviously I was a co-owner of Kramer's Discount Furniture Depot. That was why I was here at this fabulous dinner party, after all. So wasn't that good enough? Why didn't it *feel* good enough? I was about to answer when I was mercifully interrupted by what appeared to be Jerry Radnor, who turned out to be not the glamorous magazine editor I had imagined, suave and JFK Jr.–like, but rather an older, slightly disheveled man with thick white hair and a matching mustachio in need of a trim, wearing wire-rimmed glasses held together at the side with a small safety pin. I had read about him recently in a gossip column but I couldn't quite remember the specifics, only that it had to do with some sort of disgrace that had cost him a lateral position at *Los Angeles!* magazine, which was owned by the same parent company. He had been transferred to Washington, land of ignominy, to begin anew. "Sorry I'm late. The traffic . . . you wouldn't believe it . . . Must have been an accident or something . . ."

"Chemical spill on the Beltway," three people reported simultaneously without looking up from their salads.

Jerry shook everyone's hand at the table before sliding into his chair and picking up his glass of wine, which he drained in one long sip.

"So, Mrs. Leon Kramer," he said, reading my name off the place card. "What do you do?"

"Please, call me Jane," I offered.

"Jane. Pleasure to meet you. So what do you do?"

"I am a memory consultant," I heard myself say. That was not quite what I'd meant to say. I'd meant to say something about Kramer's Discount Furniture Depot, but I couldn't seem to get the words out of my mouth.

So I tried again. "I'm also designing patio furniture," I offered. "For the store. Kramer's . . . store . . . furniture . . . in Rockville . . ." I was having trouble speaking, even though I'd only had one glass of wine. Perhaps what I needed was another, but the waiter was nowhere in sight. I reached over and took Roger Joseph Junior's glass, which was full and awaiting his arrival.

"A memory consultant!" said Phillip Toffley III, as if this was indeed the most fascinating thing he had heard in weeks. "Do you help people with memory problems? 'Cause let me tell you, I'm having a few of those myself. Just yesterday we were up in Chopper 4 over the beltway and I was about to do my four o'clock . . ."

"I heard you!" said the *Washington!* editor. "You were saying something about the drought, but you got it wrong. You said it was the worst drought since 1998, but you must have forgot about 2000!" I stared at him, wishing I could remember what bad thing he had done to land himself here and why he would have that particular piece of weather trivia lodged in his brain.

Phillip's face reddened. "Actually, I was going to say I was up in the chopper about to do my four o'clock when I realized I forgot to tell my wife that the baby-sitter had called that morning to say she couldn't pick up our daughter at school . . ."

"Oh," Thor said, cutting him off. "So is that what you do, Jane? Help people remember things like that? Conveying messages and such?"

"No, no," I laughed, as if I was used to having people misinterpret my line of work. "It's a small business, actually. I help people preserve their family memories."

"Oh!" Several people answered at once.

"So you . . . preserve family memories!" Thor said politely.

"Exactly." I was eager to change the subject. "What happened to your daughter?" Now everyone looked at me, confused.

"When you forgot to tell your wife the baby-sitter couldn't come." I had this terrible image of a little girl standing alone on a street corner, waiting to be abducted.

"Oh, right. Sarah. The school hung on to her until my wife could get there. She's fine!"

I was desperate to keep the conversation steered away from me and my occupation, so I offered up a series of horrifyingly stupid questions about football instead.

After downing the second glass of wine I believe I may have

asked the wide receiver what position he played, which caused a loud round of guffaws. Was I the only one in the world who didn't know? I thought it was more of a size thing, being wide—like being husky or petite—but the more I tried to explain my confusion, the louder everyone laughed.

"So tell us about your furniture designing," said Jerry Radnor, by which time I was glad to return to a subject I knew something about. Well, more than football, anyway. But since I had not designed any furniture, and had no intention of designing any furniture, the conversation went less smoothly than it might otherwise have.

"We're always looking for local people to profile," Jerry continued. "Creative people. People who are not politicians or policy wonks, anyway."

When in Washington, *lie*. Technically this was New Carrollton, Maryland, but the mantra was the same all over the region. The practice was infectious and would soon spread to innocent border states like Delaware. "Well, I'm still in the planning stages," I said, slightly tipsy, "but I've had this idea, given the location of the store, to develop a line of patio furniture based on the works, or really more the aura, of F. Scott Fitzgerald. Capitalize on our location, you know. We are across the street from the graveyard where the Fitzgeralds are buried."

"Hey, doesn't Hemingway have a line of furniture?" Rajiv asked.

"Yes, he does," I replied, surprised anyone not in the furniture business would know such a thing. "His whole line of furniture is based on his aura. His machismo. The idea of what sort of furniture he might be. Incarnate." This sounded familiar. I thought for a moment and then realized it was exactly what Delia had said to me in her initial sales pitch. Had I just chosen her words exactly? I thought of Delia's lipstick in my pocketbook, on my lips, in fact, and wondered if I was somehow channeling her.

"F. Scott Fitzgerald is buried on Rockville Pike?" Jerry Radnor asked.

"Well, not *on* the Pike, but just off it. I mean, you can actually see the grave from the Pike. There are flags up and stuff . . ."

"He was buried in a different graveyard first," said Rajiv. "They moved his body so that he could be with the rest of his family in 1975. A minor point of interest, Jane: Did you know Fitzgerald's father was a failed wicker furniture salesman?"

"No, I did not!" I said, astonished. "You must be joking. Why do you know such a thing?" I asked.

"I have a Ph.D. in American Literature. I wrote a little biography of Fitzgerald after finishing graduate school but was unable to get it published. The field was flooded, all the publishers said."

"That's too bad. Maybe you could try again. There seems to have been a resurgence of interest in him the last few years."

"Well, you know, I'm settled in, selling advertising for WZOP, actually," he said. "I also do some of the in-house promotions. You know the jingle, 'All News, All the Time'?"

"Sure. Of course."

"I wrote that," he said, proudly.

"That's so clever."

"This is a great local story," said Jerry Radnor, handing me a business card. "I'd love to come out and talk to you, if you wouldn't mind. What did you say the name of that furniture store is?"

"Kramer's Discount Furniture Depot," I said, sitting up straight, forcing myself to enunciate. It seemed problematic to me that a local features editor did not know Fitzgerald was buried in Rockville. Or that he had never heard of our godforsaken store. We were a local institution in our own right.

"Oh, hey, aren't you the guys with the dead bodies in your store?" asked wide receiver Jonny Moser.

Everyone stared at me, worriedly.

"They were bones," I clarified, "old bones. And they were not actually *in* the store."

"I remember when those girls first disappeared," said Phillip Toffley III. "I was just a kid, and one of those girls lived around the block from me when I was growing up. Who would have thought her bones would wash up on Rockville Pike? I would've bet money they'd find her down by the canal, or in the woods or something."

"They have no idea whose bones those were," I insisted. "They could well have been cow bones!"

"Freaky how they disappeared," said Jonny Moser. "The bones, I mean. Not the girls. Although that was freaky too. The whole story is freaky."

There was an uncomfortable silence, as it seemed to occur to everyone belatedly that there was no way for me to not take this personally. Perhaps this would have been a good time to ask Jerry Radnor what had brought him to Washington.

"So do you have a card?" Jerry asked me, thankfully changing the subject.

I was about to say "no" when I realized that, actually, I did. I opened my evening bag and pulled out one of my memory consultant cards and handed it to him. I don't know if it was because I was nervous or because I had now downed two glasses of wine, but as much as I dreaded getting up from the table in my ridiculous dress, I had to visit the ladies' room.

The most direct route to the restrooms took me right past Leon's table. Until the subject of the bones had come up, I was almost enjoying myself, almost thinking that this dinner-party stuff wasn't so bad after all. Now I wanted to leave; surely Leon could be persuaded to duck out early. He was no longer chatting with the woman beside him but had actually pulled his chair away from the table and was quite rudely engaged in conversation on his cell phone. I knew at once that he was talking to Delia. He saw me and covered the receiver; he must have sensed that I knew, because he said something apologetic about how Delia was having a patio furniture crisis of some sort and was just seeking his advice. I said "oh," as if I didn't care, and kept on walking.

When I returned to the table, brightened with a false smile enhanced by a dash of Merry Mango, a surprisingly attractive man had taken the seat beside me.

"What a gorgeous dress," he said in a delightful southern accent. "Now why don't women bother to dress like that anymore . . . you look so young, so refreshing. You look almost like you were going off to your prom!"

I shuddered to think about any girl going off to a prom in a dress this revealing but was a sucker for a compliment. I decided at once this was the most delightful man I had ever met until he introduced himself. "Roger Josephs Jr.," he said. "Pleasure to meet you. And you are?"

"Roger Josephs Jr.!"

"No, darling, that's me. And you are?"

"I've been hearing your name for so many years. You have no idea. I've heard your commercials . . . I'm Jane Kramer. Of Kramer's Discount Furniture Depot."

"What a pleasure!" he replied. I found myself staring at him. His face was craggy yet handsome. I'd seen his picture in the paper, arms akimbo, looking laughably like a caricature of a tough litigator. In the flesh, however, he was almost regal, worthy of his King of the Litigation bar moniker. Or was I just drunk?

"I've been listening to *your* commercials for years," he said. "I've met your mother and father any number of times . . . A pity about those bones. You know, what you really need is a good lawyer." I had thought that last bit was a joke, but he actually pulled out his wallet and gave me his business card.

"Those are my in-laws," I quickly corrected as a waiter removed our salad plates and replaced them with some sort of creamy chicken concoction. "My mother-in-law is dead," I added, perhaps too abruptly. It was not that I was happy about her being dead; I was just anxious to dispel any notion that we shared the same blood.

"Well, your father-in-law is quite a man," he began, but he suddenly stopped speaking and stared at something behind me.

I turned around and saw Leon, red-faced. I had no idea how long he'd been standing there. He leaned over and whispered in my ear. "We're going," he said, sounding angry.

"But Leon, I haven't eaten yet," I whispered back. I glanced at the chicken thing on my plate and had to admit I could walk away from it without much regret.

He leaned closer and seemed to be gritting his teeth as he whispered. "Say the baby-sitter has to leave."

"What baby-sitter?" I said aloud.

Leon glared at me. "Say the baby-sitter just called on my cell and she's having an emergency," he whispered again.

"Oh, you mean like a patio furniture emergency?"

Then I stopped myself. There seemed no alternative without causing a scene. "Gotta go, everyone," I said dutifully. "Baby-sitter problems."

My tablemates smiled politely. Jerry Radnor actually ventured aloud that he'd call me, confirming that he had my number, and Roger Josephs Jr. urged me to call him. These innocent solicitations did seem to give Leon a moment of pause. This warmed my heart ever so slightly. It had not occurred to me that he might care.

As we walked out of the ballroom I had one more pang of regret. "I forgot to ask Thor about Fjorki," I said aloud.

"You forgot to ask who about what?" Leon asked. "What are you talking about?"

"Nothing," I replied. "Just furniture."

8

THE SURPRISING thing about Nancy Reisman was not that she'd been falling apart for at least a decade, but that she was still hanging together at all. I hadn't thought about her since Justin quit soccer, and was somewhat startled when I opened the door and saw her standing on Tiffany's front porch wearing all red, from the tip of her baseball cap to the laces on her Converse sneakers. The only thing that was not red was an incongruously gaudy diamond bumblebee brooch affixed to her T-shirt. She was half an hour early for the Power Scrapping Session. Clutched to her chest was a photo album; the other hand held a tote bag stuffed with what appeared to be scrapbooking accessories and photographs. Despite a forced smile, it was obvious she'd been crying.

We had all tiptoed uneasily around Nancy since the strange episode in which her husband, John, had decided to become the soccer coach. This had happened many years ago, when Justin was in elementary school and I was still making attempts to be a friendly sort of soccer mom who interacted with her peers. What made John's efforts peculiar was that we already had a coach, and the services of a new coach were neither required nor desired. Martin Walker had put the team together when the boys were all in first grade, and he had been a steady and reliable coach, even tempered, adored by the players and their parents alike. The team was good, but not great, and this was fine with everyone except, evidently, John Reisman.

No conversation, informal or otherwise, ever took place between the regular coach and John. On his own initiative—prompted by demons or by God—John began to call team members, all then about ten years old, to lecture them at length about their inadequate performances. He stood on the sidelines at the games and confused the referees by issuing instructions, blowing a whistle to substitute players, juggling the field line-up, pulling boys aside as they came off the field and barking instructions, reducing them to tears. He scheduled impromptu practices and no one was ever sure whether to show up for these or not, because it was not clear which coach had initiated the phone tree designed to pass along such information.

Our official coach tried the kind-but-firm approach first, explaining that the situation was confusing to the players. If John wanted to be his assistant that would be great, but they should talk about it and be clear about the chain of command. John nodded his head agreeably, but it did not seem to register. Nothing changed.

It was then decided that Martin's wife, Carolyn, should approach Nancy Reisman to see whether the wife could straighten out the husband. Carolyn, a former trial lawyer, was said to have good people skills.

But this, too, went poorly. Nancy broke down and cried. She was unhappy, she said. She didn't really love her husband, she had never wanted a dog, and her kids were selfish. She was terribly unsympathetic even as a broken-down housewife because much of her unhappiness seemed to stem from her belief that she should have been dealt a better hand in life. She wanted a bigger house and a better car; she felt she deserved it. She should have gone to medical school instead of getting married.

John was not a very good husband, she added. He did nothing around the house to help out and he had forgotten her last birthday.

Carolyn quickly retreated. Someone on the team called the conference coordinator to see if he could enlighten John Reisman about his status as a non-coach, which he did, but that had no effect either. There was some discussion about calling the police, but it was hard to figure out how that would help, whether there was anything remotely illegal about pretending to be the coach of a recreational soccer team.

By the time the next season rolled around, John had stopped coming to the games. No explanation was ever offered about his delusional behavior.

Tiffany had been quite specific in her instructions. She told me what time to light the gas grill (twelve o'clock sharp), when to start cooking the chicken kebabs (12:20), and precisely when to serve lunch (12:45). The kabobs were already prepared, she said, and could be found marinating in a blue Pyrex dish on the second shelf of the refrigerator.

"You'll find the ingredients to make a Caesar salad in the vegetable bin in the fridge," she added. "The kabobs will cook pretty quickly, so I'd say make the salad first, then throw the meat on the grill. Fruit for dessert (also in a blue Pyrex dish on the *third* shelf of the refrigerator), coffee is all set to go—you don't even have to turn it on, 'cause I've set the timer for twelve fifty-five. You should have everyone back at the table working by about 1:10 and then you can do the dishes while they are wrapping up. The session runs until two. But there are always malingerers. Some of them will stay all day if you let them, so try and get them out the door.

"And FYI, Aaron, my twelve-year-old, gets home from school

around three, so if you don't mind, maybe you could just wait for him, make sure he doesn't need anything. Edward won't be coming home after school because he's got football practice *and* Spanish Honor's Society plus a student government meeting, poor kid. And Cassie, of course, is off at Yale."

As she spoke I thought I heard clicking in the background, and imagined Tiffany multi-tasking, issuing my orders while composing a closing argument seeking someone's death by lethal injection.

What had I signed up for here? A Power Scrapping Session, although I still didn't know quite what that was. She had not mentioned anything about cooking lunch for eight people and then cleaning up and baby-sitting.

"Oh, Jane, if you don't mind, one more thing. Before you leave, could you take the dog for a quick walk?"

At least I had no particular gripe with dogs. I even missed our dog. Until his hip had given out for good, he used to follow me around the house, trailing me from room to room. Now that he was gone, no one seemed to care much about my comings and goings, unless it involved locking or unlocking the front door of the store. When he was eight, Justin had launched a vigorous campaign for a puppy that lasted more than a year and in addition to nonstop whining, it consisted of plastering pictures of dogs all over the house—on the insides of closets, on bathroom mirrors, even once inside the oven, which caught fire when I made the mistake of preheating it without first glancing inside. We finally gave in and adopted Patch from an ad in the newspaper.

Tiffany had also given me complicated instructions about turning off the alarm when I first arrived, and I had to accomplish this task while her dog stood beside me, growling menacingly, failing to perceive my neutrality. I couldn't really blame the dog entirely—I was an intruder, after all, and it was just protecting its turf. I needed to concentrate. Three minutes to disarm the alarm. I felt like I was on some sort of game show in which the loser would be arrested for breaking and entering and possibly be mauled by an angry poodle and the winner would get to host a Power Scrapping Session and have a shot at earning bonus points toward a free cruise. With all of twenty seconds left to spare, I managed to punch in the code.

The dog followed me to the dining room, still barking, still eyeing me suspiciously, a sign of its inner genius perhaps, because even if I had been legitimately invited onto these premises, in spirit I was an intruder, strangely accustomed to feeling like I didn't belong. Growing up overseas I was always on the outside, had always felt like I never fully grasped what was going on around me. Even back in my own country, I never quite got it right. I was not as whacked as the wanna-be soccer coach, but I felt as though I'd blown some sort of mental fuse, possibly the result of having seen so much genuine suffering that I could never fully engage in the problems of suburban life. It hardly seemed I belonged in my own house, never mind on the sales floor of the Kramer family furniture store.

But hosting a Power Scrapping Session at Tiffany Fleisher's home was almost certainly the farthest I had strayed in life to date. Sure, I had derived some short-lived pleasure from the scrapbooking workshop I'd attended at Tiffany's a few months earlier, but now it seemed that had just been a fluke, or maybe the whole scrapbooking thing had tapped into my own troubled relations with family photographs and succeeded in briefly seducing me. I didn't really understand the idea of getting in your car and driving to someone else's house in order to perform an act that struck me as personal, as something you could do at home in your pajamas, for free.

And yet I saw easy money, a chance to sail away from a life that had hit a brick wall. I also saw a chance to make repairs. I was not proud of our delinquent utility bills. I was not proud of the fact that we no longer had a newspaper subscription. Even though we always paid that bill, it was often a few weeks late; the delivery man must have considered us a liability, because he eventually dropped us from his route.

Tiffany's house seemed entirely different from the place I had last visited. A self-guided tour confirmed that she had completely redecorated. She had transformed it from the cozy colonial furnishings I had admired to sleek modernism. Everything about it was subliminally suggestive of ice—the granite surfaces, the marble floors, or maybe it was just the light fixture that actually looked like clusters of icicles. In a small sitting room off the kitchen were two wafer-thin metal chairs with filigree supports. They looked lightweight, aerodynamic, almost like gliders. I thought hopefully for a minute that they might be Fjorki—I was desperate to see an actual piece of Fjorki furniture, to put my hand on the back of a Fjorki chair and see if I wasn't somehow transformed—but a quick inspection revealed the absence of wheels. Still, it was a close cousin, from what I could tell. Everything was seamless, modular, and cool. It was hard to imagine it could get hot inside or stay warm in winter. And it was just as hard to imagine people living here, children bounding through the door with muddy shoes, or doing homework at the kitchen table.

I had trouble locating the refrigerator at first, but then realized it was hiding behind panels painted David Hockney blue. Locating some sort of protrusion, or secret indentation, anything at all to grip in order to actually open the refrigerator, presented another challenge. I finally swung the door open and felt an irrational sense of accomplishment. The kebabs were actively marinating according to plan. Coffee was poised to commence dripping at 12:55 in a contraption that looked like it could launch a nuclear warhead.

I continued my inspection. This was not snooping; it was familiarizing myself with my work environment. Tiffany's house was immaculate. Even the laundry room off the kitchen was spotless, no stray bits of lint between the washer and dryer. I paused in the powder room to admire the paint—a sort of silvery white with matching soaps that smelled and felt vaguely spalike. I wondered if Tiffany had designed this all herself, or had hired someone. The answer seemed fairly obvious, and I could imagine her rattling off instructions to a decorator while composing a motion for summary judgment and dicing vegetables for a difficult recipe that involved hours of preparation and dashes of exotic spices.

A spot check in the medicine cabinet turned up small cosmetic items, the sorts of samples one gets as a free gifts during special promotions. There was also a small bottle of perfume from Tiffany's. How cute: Tiffany's for Tiffany! I meant to put just a dab on my wrist, but the liquid came gushing out and I was overwhelmed by the flowery scent.

A glimpse of myself in the mirror as I attempted to rinse off the fragrance confirmed that I looked as hung over as I felt after my radical two-and-a-half glasses of wine at the WZOP dinner, but at least my face was made cheery by Delia's lipstick, which I had taken to wearing. And now I reeked of Tiffany's perfume. What was wrong with me, anyway? There was a clinical name for this, no doubt. Or at least a fairly obvious condition—desire to be someone other than oneself.

The doorbell rang, which sent the dog into a paroxysm of barking, and I followed it down the hall. That was when Nancy Reisman arrived, in her cheerful red ensemble.

"Hello, Buffy!" She dropped to her knees to nuzzle the dog, who in turn was licking her face. "And hello, Jane," she said, back on her feet. She hesitated, unsure of whether to give me a peck on the cheek. I was equally unsure but was suddenly overcome with an odd burst of hospitality, of confidence, of affection, which possibly stemmed from my spiritual fusion with Tiffany's house, or the physical absorption of her scent, and I gave her a kiss. We were old friends. Or at least longtime comrades on the soccer field.

"Tiffany told me you'd be covering for her. I know I'm a bit early, but I just dropped the kids at school and went straight to the dry cleaner and pharmacy and, well, I figured if I went home first then by the time I got back here . . ."

"Not to worry," I said, leading her into the dining room. I hadn't noticed until then that Tiffany had clipped little tiny trash receptacles emblazoned with the Memories, Inc. logo around the table. They hung with neat plastic bags from the table edge like the portable booster seat we had when Justin was little. Each participant would have her own trash bin. These had not been featured at the introductory scrapbooking session I'd been invited to, and I wondered if they were new inventions, or atmospheric perks earned by stepping up a grade to the more intimidating-sounding Power Scrapping Session.

Nancy settled herself into a chair and began to assemble her materials like a student preparing to take an exam. The scrapbook itself was placed directly in front of her. Just above it, to the right, she arranged a color-coordinated fan of about two dozen pens that she pulled individually from her tote. Four different pairs of scissors came next, placed just below the pens, set in descending order of size. I didn't realize I was staring at her until she looked up me, quizzically.

"Sorry," I offered. "I'm kind of new at this. I'm just watching how it's done."

"This isn't how it's done. It's just how I do it," she said frostily. Then she immediately burst into tears.

"I'm sorry," I replied, rubbing her shoulder awkwardly. This was not the best way to inaugurate my new career. "Did I say something wrong?"

"No, *I'm* sorry," she said, blowing her nose. "I've got to stop doing this. It's just so awful."

"What's so awful?" I asked, hesitantly. I wasn't sure I really had the resources to deal with Nancy's problems, which I had every reason to believe cut pretty deep.

"My therapist says I need to be more composed. She said I need to stop telling my problems to strangers. Not that you're a stranger of course . . . ," she added apologetically.

I wasn't sure how to respond to this, so I offered her coffee. This seemed the sort of thing the British were always doing—rushing to put the kettle on for tea when bad things happened, like when picnics were rained out or relatives were maimed in train wrecks. I was privately relieved when Nancy declined, concerned about having to decommission the coffeemaker.

"I'll be honest," she said, ignoring me. "It's not just the traffic that brought me here early. Seeing as we've known each other for years, and you are hardly a stranger, do you mind if I tell you something personal?" The dog was now lying peacefully at her feet, which I found vaguely insulting given that I considered myself the marginally more mentally balanced role model for a dog.

"Personal?" I asked, wearily, wishing the doorbell would ring again. I really didn't want to get into this with her. Two acquaintances had sought me out in crisis over the last few years, and I couldn't help but feel I had failed them both, even though I knew there was nothing I really could have done for them. First, there had been Fiona, a former neighbor whom I barely knew, who had begun to show up in her bathrobe each morning weeping. I invited her in once, and her visits then turned into a daily ritual. She and her husband were having sexual problems (he could get an erection, she said, but had trouble ejaculating) and since I was too meek to do anything other than nod as she spoke, she evidently took this as a sign of interest and presented me with frequent updates that were increasingly graphic—he could come when she did *this,* but not when she did *that,* and should she take this personally? When they divorced and sold the house I couldn't help but feel somehow responsible. Then, another neighbor told me she was having an affair with a father on her son's football team. After it ended she had a breakdown of some sort. She was also a regular visitor for a while, until she just stopped showing up one day. Where she went I never knew. I asked her husband once and he said that she had moved out, but I sometimes wondered if she wasn't really buried in the basement. Or maybe those were *her* bones below the barn. Eventually, a much younger woman moved into the house.

I had mused aloud one night about whether there was some fundamental horror of suburban life that was eroding the well-being of these women, myself included. Or was it more of an approaching-middle-age phenomenon, a hormonal thing? Or possibly something environmental: pesticides or fluoride or radioactive rays emanating from our microwaves that was causing everyone, including myself, to suffer severe mood swings? Leon had a simple explanation for this, the same one he had offered to explain the behavior of the customer who rearranged her furniture each day. "It's women," he said. "Women are nuts."

I glanced at my watch and skimmed Tiffany's note as Nancy began her recitation. Tiffany had instructed me to check the supply closet in the office just off the dining room. Evidently it was full of extra merchandise, which I was encouraged to sell. She even offered a few supposedly subtle sales pitches, such as *"That page would look beautiful with some gingham borders . . . would you like to see them? I think I just got a shipment in!"* She had a lot of stock—pens, adhesive tapes, journals, paper cutters, and a list of about ten additional items. I scanned the price list and remembered why I was there. Had I been a cartoon figure, my eyeballs would have morphed into dollar signs.

"The thing is," Nancy began at last, blowing her nose again, loudly, "I've really done something awful."

"What's that?" I asked. I feared she was about to confide to having poisoned her husband or burned down her house. Actually, I was only somewhat off the mark.

She opened her scrapbook to a two-page spread that was, eerily, nothing but cars. Well, one car, actually, an SUV, posed in front of a variety of settings and captured from a wide range of angles. There was even an aerial view. Another batch of pictures featured John, her husband, washing, polishing, and driving the car. Nancy appeared in one photo sitting in the passenger seat, waving out the window although not looking especially happy.

"Your problem has something to do with the car?" I tried.

Then her tears turned into loud, wracking, shoulder-heaving sobs. I really was not very good at this job, I reflected. "John bought it for himself. For his fortieth birthday."

"It's very nice." I said. "Shiny and big!"

"It cost a fortune and it made me angry. It doesn't even fit into the garage. And we can't really afford the payments. I'm still driving a ten-year-old piece-of-crap Volvo. *I'm* the one who needed the new car! But he loved it. I think he loves that car more than he loves his family."

"That's absurd," I said. "You know that's not true."

"He's going to kill me."

"Why? What happened?"

"I did something awful."

"What? When?"

"I had too much to drink. Two nights ago. I haven't told him. He's in Chicago on business. He's going to kill me."

"Nancy, it can't be that bad. What did you do?"

"I smashed it up a little bit."

"What does that mean?"

"I got a little angry. I took it out on the car."

"You didn't mean it, whatever it was, right? It was just an accident."

She stopped speaking and then reached into her pile of photographs and asked if I had any scalloped scissors. It took me a minute to absorb this transition. "Sure," I said, "I'll just go look. But Nancy, whatever you did, I'm sure it can be fixed."

"Don't be so sure," she said. "I was pretty wasted. The spray paint won't wash off. And the windows are all broken."

I stole another glance at my instructions, hoping that Tiffany might have offered some advice about what to do with Nancy Reisman. (Call her psychiatrist? Make a pot of herbal tea with special calming properties? Find Xanax in the top shelf of the kitchen cabinet?) Funny, in all those years on the soccer field Nancy had barely spoken to me, and now she was pouring out this random, frightening, confession. Did it have to do with my position of authority as a memory consultant? Had I achieved instant status as a seer of some sort? A goddess of memories? Why would she want to make a scrapbook commemorating a vehicle she had just vandalized? But my job was not to deconstruct her motivation; I was only supposed to enable the process by supplying the so-called technology.

I was grateful to hear the doorbell ring. It was the rest of the group, who had evidently all traveled together in one red minivan. There was Carolyn, who continued to dress like a trial lawyer, with conservative pumps and a skirt and blazer, even though she had retired seven years ago to be home with her kids. It was hard to imagine Carolyn even riding in the same minivan as Rita, who was still a hippie at forty-something. She had long blond hair tinged with gray, a few strands of which were braided and adorned with beads, and she was always splattered with paint even though I didn't know exactly why. I had asked her once, years ago, what she painted. She had said, simply, "forms."

In addition to painting forms, Rita was a regular on the protest circuit— pro-choice, anti-guns, pro-peace . . . I forgot her position on cloning, affirmative action, and health care reform. I had never understood what Rita was doing in the suburbs or how it was that she seemed so content, and suspected she might have been a fugitive of some sort, perhaps a former member of the Simbionese Liberation Army, now masquerading as a scrapbooking, form-painting soccer mom.

And Liza. How intimidating! I hadn't realized she was coming. Liza was a former chef at a well-known French restaurant in Georgetown who was always talking about recipes. She was now home with three-year-old twins, reportedly still breast-feeding them and hand-mashing organic baby food. I was not thrilled by the prospect of preparing her lunch. Also present were Madeline and Elly, cliquish mothers of two cliquish girls, subject of rumors for many years that perhaps they were lesbian lovers, which was doubtful but would have been refreshingly different if true. I'd had awkward relations with Elly ever since an incident about ten years ago, when her son had come to our house to play with Justin and had then gone home and reported that we had a naked man on our refrigerator. Elly called me that evening, extremely agitated. I explained that the naked man in question was a magnet reproduction of Michelangelo's *David*. Although he came with clothes, he happened to have been disrobed that day, his pants and leather jacket having drifted over to the freezer compartment. I expected her to laugh at her mistake, or at least apologize for implying that I was somehow a corrupting influence on her kid, but she had not. That episode and its lack of a resolution still nagged at me.

Women in their forties aged at such different paces, I couldn't help but observe. Nancy Reisman looked much younger than her peers despite her ever-present air of distress. I wondered if her ongoing breakdown was not somehow restorative. She let it all out, perhaps purging herself of the stress that aged the rest of us. People I had known for years sometimes appeared old all at once. One long night tossing and turning, or one particularly virulent fight with your spouse, and the next thing you knew you had crossed the line to old. I once noticed this with a father on the soccer field, who looked like he had aged ten years in the course of a week all because of one freshly sprouted white chest hair that poked up through the neck of his T-shirt like a periscope and moved about distractingly as he spoke.

Some of this group were already dowdy, appearing at least ten years older than they probably were. One especially matronly looking woman present was Anna Berger's sister, Joyce, who, like Anna, had gone prematurely gray. I could not quite believe she was there, although I should have anticipated her presence, given her affiliation with the soccer team.

Still, Joyce Berger at a scrapbooking workshop? She seemed too busy and self-important to sit around with the likes of us. She rarely showed up at the soccer games, usually sending her nanny instead. Like her sister, she was a therapist who dabbled in local politics, which seemed to automatically place her in the anti-Kramer's camp. That said, there did not actually appear to be any *pro*-Kramer's camp: even the pro-growth politicians seemed loath to take our side since the bones debacle began. I had seen Joyce at that same scarring dinner party the year before, the Democratic fundraiser where Anna was present. Like her sister, human warmth was not high on her list of personal attributes.

We all feigned joy at seeing one another, our greetings really borderline shrieks punctuated by disingenuous remarks such as "You look great!" and "What a nice surprise!" and "Someone smells so good!"

The women made their way into the dining room and began

to spread out their materials without any help from me, and I could see that my presence was incidental. I was suddenly grateful for Tiffany's punch list, for my orders to slip into the kitchen, where I could stay out of sight until it was time to collect my money and go home. I heard a couple of people compliment Nancy on her red outfit.

While tossing the salad, I was summoned from the kitchen to fetch razor-tipped pastel pens, a combination pack of page borders, and special photo adhesive tape. No sooner had I located these items than three more requests were made, and I had to step back in to get a pen and write it all down. Someone needed a circle maker. Someone else needed a square maker. Someone wanted a dozen Memories, Inc. refrigerator magnet frames. I didn't even have to consult the price list to determine that I had already made about a hundred dollars, and this was just the very beginning. The requests were infectious. Everyone was reminded of something else she needed and there seemed to be no end to the ingenious product line, which included a Memories, Inc. golf umbrella as well as a set of six coffee mugs.

The session passed quickly. I busied myself in Tiffany's kitchen, successfully lit the grill and made kebobs without incident, and was periodically sent to the supply closet for more goods. I was also summoned once or twice to join in on conversations about real estate, the gist of which was that prices had skyrocketed out of control—tear-downs were going for over $800,000 in Liza's neighborhood—and that we would all be smart to sell our houses and move, although no one knew where we should go. I heard someone say that Tiffany had already drawn up plans to pop the roof off her house and add another floor with a larger master-bedroom suite.

Joyce Berger snidely opined that Tiffany had some sort of nesting disorder akin to anorexia—like women who never thought themselves thin enough, Tiffany could not be satisfied that her house had enough square footage or was sufficiently well-appointed. Joyce said she'd been seeing a lot of that lately among her patients, and thought it was becoming so prevalent as to warrant classification as a new syndrome.

Then the conversation moved on to the question of whether it was better for our kids to get an "A" in an honors class or a "B" in an AP class. These sorts of discussions made me nervous. I felt the long dormant patch of eczema behind my ear begin to burn. I slithered back into the kitchen but was quickly summoned by Rita, who wanted to know whether Justin was in Algebra 2 or Calculus, and whether he would be taking AP Spanish junior year. I scratched at my ear and drew blood. How could I possibly know what he would take next year? It was only September of his sophomore year. I seemed to be the only mother not actively plotting college admission strategies. I suspected I was also the only mother in the room unsure of how she would finish paying for her child's high school education.

"John bought himself a new car for his fortieth birthday," Nancy offered, apropos of nothing. The room became silent but for the sound of several pairs of scissors cutting purposefully through mounting paper, of acid-free journal pages being turned, of bits of photographic debris falling into cute tiny trash bins. I wondered if everyone else already knew this story.

"He bought a Lincoln Navigator," she said.

Still, no one spoke. No one ever seemed to know what to say to Nancy, and everyone was fearful of setting her off. After a few uncomfortable moments, Rita gamely ventured that she'd recently seen one. "Those things are huge!"

"Yes, well, that's the point. It makes him feel like his penis is bigger," she said.

Again, no one dared reply. No one even snickered. The only

positive thing to be said was that Nancy was not crying. I retreated to the kitchen, never more delighted to wash dishes.

I had always considered it wrong to measure happiness in relative terms. Thinking you were happy only because you were less unhappy than someone like Nancy Reisman seemed like selling short the essence of happiness in a way that would displease philosophers. And yet I couldn't help but wonder if things with Leon and me were possibly less bad than they seemed. I was not talking about his penis in public. I had not trashed his car, although if I did, he would probably thank me for doing him a favor.

"Jane?" I heard again, from the other room. I was definitely feeling like a maidservant, albeit one who was racking up a lot of cash and bonus points. I recognized Joyce's voice, and I felt my body tense. Perhaps she just wanted something from me—a cup of coffee or a Memories, Inc. storage box for her photographic negatives. But I wouldn't have put it past her to whip out a subpoena, and was just paranoid enough to think that this entire Power Scrapping Session had been organized by a clever process server. Still, we had been together for close to three hours and she had not mentioned anything about our store.

I came scurrying back in, wiping my hands on the apron.

"Rita tells me that you own Kramer's."

"Guilty as charged," I said. She didn't laugh, didn't even smile. I tried to not be offended by the fact that even though our kids had played soccer together for more than a decade, she never seemed to know who I was. But then, I was getting used to that.

She handed me an envelope and I thought for a minute that maybe my paranoia had not really been misplaced, that maybe it *was* a subpoena, but it only contained pictures. This, too, felt like a trap, but even if it was, there was nothing to do but walk into it.

I looked at each photograph hesitantly. They were snapshots of the store. Given who her sister was, I would have expected grainy photos from the 1950s, ones that would have quaint historic street signs or antique gas lamps, something to make a not-so-subtle point about historic preservation. But they were more recent than that. They were from only about three years ago, probably taken about the time we had filed for our initial construction permit.

"Why do you have these?" I asked, trying not to sound suspicious.

"They were just in my mix of photos that I brought. I'm putting together a booklet for the Historic Preservation Society as a favor for my sister. Anna Berger? I think maybe you've met? She said she knew you. She said you'd met at your store once. And when I heard about this workshop, I thought it would help motivate me to finally sit down and do it. You can keep those. I think your family is in some of those shots."

My family *was* in some of the shots, in fact, and I felt strangely violated. Clearly we had not been the deliberate subjects of the photographs, but there we were in the background, all the same. I knew from just the limited information provided by one of the photos—Justin's ratty old backpack and the hound's-tooth skirt I was in love with that fall—that that had been the beginning of bad times. It was the year of the dead dog and the year of exhaustion. The year that I once went to pick up Justin at the wrong practice field and sat for half an hour as it grew dark, wondering where he was.

There was a speck in the background of a couple of the photographs and I stared at it, brought it closer to my face. I wondered if there were any magnifying glasses in the Memories, Inc. supply kit. Was that just a speck of dirt, or was it a blurred figure? Whatever it was, it looked as if it was floating off the ground, hovering just above the old neon sign. The bulb behind the "K" had burnt out, so the sign actually read "RAMER'S." I looked more closely, wondering what it could be. Hadn't I seen a similar sort of speck in another batch of photos? There must have been a scratch on the lens of the camera. That was the only explanation that made sense. But then, it made no sense. The photos were not from the same camera, since these were from Joyce Berger. Maybe it was time for reading glasses.

Thanking Joyce, I took the pictures and put them in my purse before returning to the kitchen to continue cleaning up. By two o'clock I had done everything on Tiffany's checklist except successfully send everyone away, and I was desperate to leave. Justin was at home with instructions to stay put until I picked him up, which was supposed to be right about now. Then we planned to head into the store for an afternoon shift. Leon and I had barely spoken on the way home from the WZOP dinner. We had slept facing opposite directions, and the only words exchanged in the morning had to do with sorting out the details of our work schedule. I had deliberately not told him about the Power Scrapping Session to avoid being mocked, and had simply volunteered to mind the store in the afternoon. Now it was the afternoon, and I wondered what I was supposed to do, exactly, to get everyone out of here.

I paced between the kitchen and dining room, my heels making loud clomping noises on the slate floor, but no one seemed to notice. I then made my way around the table, peering at everyone's scrapbooks and offering praise. I probably sounded like a first grade teacher, commending each woman on her ability to color inside the lines, but really my admiration was genuine. Each scrapbook was a small masterpiece. Even Nancy Reisman had succeeded in creating the illusion of an enviable family life. She had turned the car page and was now arranging photos from what appeared to have been a trip to Paris. There was a fairly recent picture of her and John holding hands and smiling against the backdrop of the Eiffel Tower. What a lucky, handsome couple, one might think, with the means to jet off to Paris for a romantic getaway, although if you looked more closely there was a sour look on Nancy's face. Still, it seemed like the sort of thing future generations would hardly notice.

Nancy caught me eyeing her picture. "It was a business trip last year," she said. "I *hate* France. Everyone speaks French. But all the spouses had to go. Our hotel room was unbelievably tiny."

"Really? You look so happy in these pictures. Look at you there . . . ," I said, pointing to one of the couple in front of a bistro. "You guys look like you're on your honeymoon."

"We do?"

"Did you eat at that restaurant?" I asked.

She giggled. "We did, but we didn't know what we were ordering. We just pointed to things on the menu. I think I ate ostrich or something! But the wine was good. We knew how to order that, at least."

"That sounds like fun," I said, and Nancy smiled.

"I guess it wasn't so bad."

"Maybe you should try to write down a few of the good things that happened," I suggested, thinking back to that first session at Tiffany's house. "Like, write about the dinner. That way you'll remember the wine and the ostrich long after you've forgotten the tiny hotel room. I can go get you a pack of journaling cards—you can stick them in your purse and then you'll have them handy to jot down thoughts whenever they occur to you. Then paste them into the scrapbook later." I couldn't quite believe I was saying this. Never mind the crass commercialism of my suggestion; I was not normally a purveyor of good cheer. Still, I was thinking of Tiffany's mandate for inspiring future generations, and couldn't help but think there was something to all that, even if it was sort of corny. And anyway, if you were going to go to all this trouble to document your life, wasn't it better to make it seem happy? Why record misery? Having had a mother who was inclined to do the latter, I felt qualified to offer this advice.

"That's a good idea," said Nancy. "Do you think I really should?"

"Absolutely. And do you know what would be great?"

She looked up at me, her eyes wide, waiting to hear what would be great.

"Some rainbow bold-tipped pens."

"I have some," she said, disappointed. She seemed to have a lot of faith that the Memories, Inc. product line could really improve her life.

My eye skimmed the supply list as I spoke. "We have a special on cases for the pens. It allows you to store them horizontally, for a longer life span, but you can stand them up when you are working, to make it easier to reach." I was reading this from the blurb just below the price: $25.99.

"You're right," said Nancy. "I have no place to store my pens and they're always getting lost."

"I'll take one of those, too," said Madeline. "But I also need the pens. I'd like the thin-tipped pens."

"Would anyone else like anything before I tally up the supplies?"

Carolyn called me over to consult on a page she was working on commemorating her mother's eightieth birthday. I thought for a moment, then suggested a "Remarkable Rite of Passage" packet that I noticed was a new product on offer. I didn't know what that meant, but had to think an eightieth birthday counted as a remarkable rite of passage. Carolyn evidently agreed.

There was another rush of orders as I was asked to consult each participant's page-in-progress. Elly's sister was getting married, she explained, and she wanted to make her an album, so I suggested she order one Magical Wedding Album and one pack of Magical Wedding Stickers, as well as a block sheet of Magical Love Quotes. I talked Rita into ordering a Memories, Inc. Power Scrapping Pack. Nancy wanted five additional albums, at thirty dollars a pop, because she was suddenly inspired to make a separate journal for each vacation she had taken with her family these last few years. Joyce asked for two additional albums and an entire stockpile of standard supplies, opining that she would be reimbursed by the city of Rockville for her work. My tax dollars, I couldn't help but think, coming full circle, back into my wallet.

Tiffany had some of these things in her storage room, but most of them had to be ordered, and it took more than an hour to complete the paperwork. As I sat with a calculator, collecting checks, Tiffany's son Aaron walked in from school. He asked me to make him a snack and help him with some math homework.

It was four-thirty by the time I succeeded in seeing everyone to the door. On her way out, Nancy Reisman pulled me aside to thank me for the advice. I couldn't remember what it was I might have said, but she insisted I had really been helpful and wondered if I would like to have coffee with her one morning. Carolyn smiled sympathetically as Nancy scrawled her phone number on the back of a lavender triangle border and pressed it into my hand.

As I was pulling out of the driveway I remembered Joyce's pictures, and went running back inside. Something about these photos was bugging me, and I couldn't let it go. Maybe the spot was not a thumb, or even a speck of dirt, but a figure of some sort. Whatever it was, it appeared to be lifting off, floating just above the store, hovering beside the sign.

Could that have been an old loafer of mine sticking out of the blurry patch above? The speck seemed to not quite belong in the picture and yet there it was, bound by forces beyond its control: family and a sense of duty, not to mention a just-arrived shipment of bunk beds on the loading dock, waiting to be logged in and tagged.

9

TOM RAPPED on my window as I idled at the intersection a few blocks from the store. He shook a Starbucks cup in my direction and I could hear the coins rattle inside. I knew only a few sketchy facts about this raggedy man, gleaned over the years while waiting for the light to turn green. He had lost his job as an insurance broker in the early 1990s; his wife had left him; he had a couple of grown kids, somewhere; and gin was his beverage of choice. The sign around his neck identified him as a Vietnam vet, but when I asked about the war he said he still couldn't talk about it. I tried to be generous, but since I passed his way several times a day it seemed unfair that he proposition me at every red light. We discussed this once, and Tom acknowledged that would amount to a pretty high toll. If I gave him twenty dollars at the start of each week he'd give me a pass, he said. I told him that was extortion, that I'd give him money when I could. We had achieved a playful if uneasy détente, one that allowed me to feel less guilty on the occasions I chose to keep my window up.

Justin had no idea that the homeless man and I had made private arrangements, however, and he started to lecture me when I waved Tom away. He said something about how we comfortable middle-class people thought only of ourselves. I considered disdain for the bourgeoisie, and one's parents, by proxy, a healthy phase of development for a teenager, but a lecture from my son on this particular subject touched a nerve. I could go head to head with any aid worker on poverty, famine, and indifference to the plight of those less fortunate. That had been my childhood, in a nutshell. I didn't want to get into this with Justin, so I rolled the window down and stuck a dollar in the cup. Tom winked at me and waved as the light turned green.

My right ankle had been tender for a few weeks, but it was not until I sat that afternoon in rush-hour traffic that I made the connection. It seemed I had contracted a case of repetitive stress syndrome from driving around in circles all day. A sliver of pain shot up through my leg whenever I pushed down on the accelerator pedal.

Certainly I couldn't complain about this to Justin. He would have been happy to drive, although he did not seem to be in a huge rush to get his license, especially since he had Mike to chauffer him around in a far nicer vehicle than he was likely to ever get his hands on. He had his learner's permit and would be eligible to take his road test just as soon as we spent the requisite number of hours with him behind the wheel. But the few times I had taken him out had been truly terrifying. He wound up on our lawn once, when he miscalculated the turning ratio into our driveway, and knocked down a small tree. I decided I didn't have the right constitution for the job, and ceded this area of parenting to Leon, who said in turn that he would take him driving as soon as he got new tires on the Explorer. Our lives sometimes seemed like one long, circuitous act of procrastination.

The strip mall with Tuxedo Land was just ahead, and I considered popping in to return Leon's suit from the WZOP dinner, but couldn't bear the thought of waiting to make a left turn at the busy intersection even if delaying its return meant paying a late fee. I wondered how many actual hours of my life had been spent sitting behind a steering wheel. Months? Years? It was possible *this* was where I was aging. One too-long red light and I'd be old.

This was the same patch of strip mall where we'd had a family picnic the past Fourth of July, in the shadow of the blinking neon signs for Galaxy of Batteries and Sink and Faucet World. There had been a terror alert downtown, so we avoided the Mall. We had brought Enrique with us—our family's small nod at patriotism and the repair of Cuban-American relations. But two minutes into the fireworks, Enrique had to go to the bathroom, possibly the result of the vat of soda Leon had bought each of us, whether we wanted one or not.

We had trouble finding an open store for Enrique to pee. I urged him to urinate against a wall, but this must have been something discouraged in his proper diplomat family because he refused, so we continued searching for an open shop, wandering three blocks up the Pike toward an illuminated Taco Bell. By the time we'd accomplished our task, the fireworks were over.

At first I thought I was hallucinating when I saw Delia lying on the enormous faux rosewood table, capable of seating fourteen. "Agricultural Estate," it was clumsily named, a cheap knockoff of Crate and Barrel's more popular "Plantation" table. We had a glut of these tables because a dozen orders had fallen through when the shipment from the Philippines was inexplicably lost at sea, arriving six weeks late. Delia was wearing a bikini top, with a striped beach towel wrapped around her waist. Sunglasses were propped on top of her head. She skimmed through a magazine while Uncle Seymour fussed with floor lamps, dragging them over from the lighting display area and plugging them into every available outlet to better illuminate this shocking display of Delia.

"I don't know," I heard Leon say from behind me. I turned to see him frowning, deep in thought, his arms crossed against his chest. "I don't really think this is working. I mean, it's a dining-room table, and you look like you're doing a pool ad or something. I think we're on the wrong track." Despite this spot-on assessment, he snapped a bunch of pictures with a disposable camera, then walked around to the other side of the table. As he brought the lens to his eye, he noticed us. I cringed, expecting to be reprimanded for our late arrival.

"Oh hey, Janie, Justin. I didn't even hear you come in." He sounded surprisingly upbeat. "Before I forget to tell you, some crazy woman, Tiffany I think, was trying to reach you earlier. I gave her your cell phone number. She said something about some checks."

"My cell phone is lost," I reminded him, squinting as the flash of the camera went off.

I expected him to pick a fight about this, too. But he didn't. This would have been good, except that the thing distracting him from picking a fight with me was Delia.

"What do you think, Janie?" he asked, motioning toward Delia, as if asking what I thought of a choice of typescript for letterhead. "What do *you* think, Justin?" Justin stood behind me, looking anxious.

"This is kinda weird, Dad. It looks like the set of a porno movie. What's going on?"

"Oh. Hi, you guys!" Delia chirped, before Leon could answer. She swung her long, thick legs over the side of the table and sat up. Her bikini was certainly patriotic: red and blue stars and stripes with white polka dots. It did not go well with the pink-and-white striped towel, but all the same I was grateful that she had been modest enough to at least partially shroud herself. Part of me wanted to run and hide in the back office, but part of me wanted to absorb as much of Delia as possible to get a better fix on who she was.

Whoever Delia was, she did not have the body of a swimsuit model. She was well endowed on top, for sure, but her lower half—or what I could see of it—was too thick, too awkwardly proportioned, to be clad in a skimpy bathing suit.

"What are you doing here?" she asked cheerfully.

"I work here," I snapped. I'd been waiting years for something to push me officially over the edge, and here it was: Delia in a bikini.

"Janie . . . relax, would you?" said Leon. "All she meant was that she thought you weren't coming in this afternoon. We didn't know where you were. But we're glad you're here. We could really use your input," he said, walking toward me with a newspaper that was open to a full-page ad for Ethan Allen. This had clearly been the inspiration for this current tableau; it featured an elegant model leaning against a dining-room table. The chief difference being that the model in the Ethan Allen ad was dressed as if she might properly belong in a dining room, eating a meal or serving dinner. Something about her having clothes on leant it the element of class that we seemed to be lacking.

Uncle Seymour picked up Leon's camera and began snapping pictures. He took a picture of me, hands on my hips, scowling. A photo for the scrapbook to inspire future generations to work hard in school and stay clear of the family furniture business, perhaps.

"So you're thinking of doing some print advertising?"

"Not print. Television . . . You know," Leon said, still holding the newspaper, "one thing Ethan Allen does that I think works really well is they write these nice descriptions of their furniture. They make up cute little stories. Like listen to this: *'Design a Dream: This Swedish Home bedroom was inspired by comely cottages and enchanting gardens. But if you love the Orient, or wish for the magic of Paris to grace your doorstep, we can make that happen, too . . .'*

"What do you think of that, Janie? Isn't that clever? Do you think you could do something like that for us? You're a good writer."

"Yes, that's brilliant," I replied flatly. "Very compelling." Just what I've always dreamed of doing, writing fiction about furniture.

"Wait, did you really say *television*?" I asked. I must have misheard him. We could not afford television any more than we could afford the house we were living in, or the tuition checks we'd been writing.

"Cable television. Local access. That's the future, Janie. I am telling you, after that WZOP dinner I am through dealing with those people. What an insult that whole night was, being seated at a table full of housewives! And besides, those ads were not effective anyway. No one listens to WZOP."

That was not technically true. More than 400,000 people listened to WZOP. Plus I had just been listening to the station as I drove to the store. I'd heard an advertisement for something called "Focus Factor." It was a brain support supplement. I didn't know what a brain support supplement was, exactly, but it sounded like a good thing. I wanted to jot down the telephone number and learn more, but by the time I found a pen I had forgotten the last four digits. My own listening habits aside, WZOP was the number-one station in the Washington, D.C. metropolitan region now that it had exclusive Washington Redskins broadcasting rights. Our problem was simply that not a lot of potential furniture shoppers listened between the hours of midnight and 5:00 A.M.

"So what we have to do is make a commercial," Leon continued. "Luckily Delia's got a friend in Queens who is in the video business—he has his own production company—and will make us a demo for free." I hesitated to think what sort of video production business Delia's friend might have in Queens, particularly given Justin's earlier observation. Equally disturbing was the question of how it was that Justin knew what the set of a porno movie looked like.

"Did it ever occur to you that the seating arrangement might have been intended to flatter you?" I asked. "I mean, who knows, it might have been an honor for these women to be seated next to you!" Leon did seem to brighten ever so slightly at the thought of being a celebrity dinner guest, the center of attention at the table. I didn't know why I was defending WZOP. I was the one who had been lobbying to sever our agreement for years, yet suddenly any form of advertising that did not involve Delia in a bikini seemed desirable.

"All the same, Janie, I think it may be time to rethink our advertising strategy. You've been saying that for years. So I'm listening to you!"

"Great. I'm all for change. But local access television? What do you mean, exactly? Who watches these channels?" More flashing ensued. Uncle Seymour was now getting the angle from behind, while Delia leaned on an elbow, flipping through her magazine.

"I don't know yet. I've got to pull some demographic figures together and identify the right market. They are offering super-low rates on the Spanish-language channel right now."

"The one that runs those saucy soap operas all day?" Delia in a bikini suddenly made a lot more sense.

"How are you coming with the patio furniture, darling?" Delia asked, adjusting the strap on her bathing suit while Uncle Seymour stared lecherously. "I'm asking 'cause my friend, the one in Queens, he said he could shoot a promo for that, too, while we're up there. It would just be a demo, of course, 'cause we don't have the actual furniture yet. But we could get a feel for it."

"I haven't gotten too far," I said, pretending to be on board with the program. My plan, insofar as I had one, was to be wandering the streets of Puerto Rico in a wide-brimmed straw hat well before the patio furniture scheme reached fruition. Still, I wanted to remain involved in this conversation, in part because it was my chief source of interaction with Delia. But I was also intrigued to have learned that Fitzgerald's father had been a failed wicker furniture salesman, and couldn't help but wonder if there was some cosmic significance to this coincidence.

"I've read through *Gatsby*," I continued, "and all I've found are a couple of wicker settees . . ."

"Wicker settees are good."

"Yes. And I'm going to start *Tender Is the Night*, but . . ."

"That's a nice name. Very poetic."

"Yes, it's from a poem by Keats. Anyway, I read it a few years ago. I remember that they were out on the beach on the French Riviera and they didn't have much furniture. They spread out mats and blankets on the sand. There were a lot of umbrellas. But none of that is technically furniture . . ."

"Umbrellas are good. Wicker settees and umbrellas. It's a start . . . Honey," she said, now addressing Uncle Seymour. "Could you scratch my back, right here? I don't know why my skin is so dry. You know, actually, maybe if I rub some of this oil in it would help," she said, picking up a bottle of coconut oil that was positioned beside her, meant as a prop for the ad.

Seymour didn't appear to hear any of this, because otherwise he surely would have jumped at the opportunity to slather her in oil.

I felt acutely uncomfortable standing there, fully dressed like some bookish prude.

"You know, hon . . . I've just had an idea!" Delia jumped off the table and approached me. She was somehow frightening in her bikini, massive and muscular, like Wonder Woman. She had on her pink Pumas again. The sneakers had cushions on the bottom that lent the optical effect of her being springy, adding to the superhero mystique. Even Justin took a step back.

"What's that?" I asked as calmly as I could.

"Why don't you forget all the reading. I didn't mean to make you do all that work, like you're back in high school." Her phone began to ring from her bag, which was over by the cash register. She stared at it, thinking, then chose to ignore it. "Wait a minute," she said, her forefinger in the air. "What was that first book you mentioned?"

"*Gatsby?*"

"*The Great Gatsby?*"

"Yes. *The Great Gatsby.*" Given that this had been her idea in the first place, I had assumed she was somewhat literary-minded. Now I wondered how she had thought this up at all.

"Wasn't that made into a movie with Robert Redford?"

"I think so. That sounds right. I saw it ages ago."

Justin listened in apparent disbelief.

"So just watch the movie. Look at the furniture. I mean, who cares what Fitzgerald actually had to *say* about patio furniture. As I explained to you before, we're just going for an 'aura' thing."

"That's a good thought, Delia," Leon agreed. Then, to me, he said, "Why don't you go to Blockbuster. You can get something and watch it tonight. We're leaving anyway, so it will give you something to do. You and Justin can watch together. 'Cause as far as I'm concerned he's to stay with you every minute until he cuts out this Goth business."

Justin and I looked at each other again, a brief sympathetic exchange.

It occurred to me that this might be a good time to kill my husband; I could probably get a reduced sentence, on account of these extenuating circumstances, of being driven off the brink of sanity by the thought of him traveling to Queens with a flirty superhero in a stars-and-stripes bikini. I still had Roger Josephs Jr.'s card in my wallet. No case was unwinnable, he'd said.

"I was saying, why don't you go rent the movie at Block-buster . . ."

"I heard you!" I snapped so loudly that even Uncle Seymour turned to look at me.

"Oh. Sorry. I misunderstood," he said, taking a step back. Now he seemed afraid. Sweetly innocent in his astonishment. I hadn't noticed until then that we actually had a few customers in the store; two of them turned to look at me. Leon walked over and put his arm around me, steering me toward a quiet nook at the back of the store.

"You are acting very strangely. Is something wrong?" Then he leaned over and whispered a question in my ear. "Are you menstruating?"

Menstruating? After all these years of living with a person with a female reproductive system, could he not find a more elegant word? I decided not to give him the pleasure of an answer. I was, in fact, menstruating, but that was very much beside the point.

"Where are you going?" I asked, my voice trembling.

"I told you. Queens. Well, we're not going to stay in Queens. I'm going to look at some patio furniture showrooms in Wee-hawken first, and I'll just stay there. I've actually asked one of our vendors to put together a few samples. Then we'll go out on Saturday and talk to the friend in Queens. I think we'll also visit a couple of other manufacturers in case we do launch our own line."

"You are going away with Delia for the weekend," I said, recapping as calmly as possible.

"Yes. But not *with* Delia. You've got it all wrong. Why don't you come? We can look at samples together."

"You know I can't come. We've got Justin. I'm not leaving him alone, especially given what's going on in his life . . ."

"Of course you wouldn't leave him. Bring Justin. It will be fun! A little family getaway. Janie, believe me, we're going to jump-start this patio furniture scheme. That's all there is to this."

He sounded so sincere. Why, then, did I find it impossible to believe him? Delia walked by and whispered something to him. Before she walked away, she'd patted him on the back. Oh, yeah, that was why I had trouble believing him. *Delia.* Her existence in our furniture store was messing with my head.

"I don't really see us all going to Weehawken, Leon. You, me, Justin, and Delia. I just don't see it. I don't know, how would we all get there? Where would we all stay?"

"That's no problem. I'm driving."

"In *your* car? That doesn't seem like a great idea."

"Oh, I meant to tell you, good news! Delia took care of the tires for me."

"What do you mean?" It was maddening to think she had taken the car in for him. This was something Leon had been promising to do for more than a year. We had agreed this was his responsibility, and now he'd delegated the job to Delia, like she was his personal assistant. Or a second wife.

"She said she used to have a job at a gas station. She knows how to change tires and do an alignment."

"Delia is an auto mechanic in her spare time?" I asked, incredulous.

"You know, Janie, I don't know what's wrong with you lately. It's like you are mad at me all the time. Everything I do is wrong."

"Maybe Delia—" I stopped myself midsentence. *Maybe Delia what?* I didn't want to be small-minded and sexist, but how many women knew how to change and align tires? I thought back to that moment, digging through her purse, finding Andrew Ryder's license. I thought that maybe . . . maybe Delia was . . . a *man?* But that made no sense, particularly given the amount of time she had been spending with my husband lately. And if there was some possibility that her gender was in ques-

tion, and if she and Leon were . . . and even if they weren't, and
Leon was . . . No. . . . That was impossible. I was surely over-
thinking this. My mind shut down at this point, and I was glad
Leon had cut me off.

"Leave Delia out of this," he scolded.

"You don't even know what I was going to say."

"You know, Delia seems to care about this store more than
you do. This is your store, too. You ought to be even half as
interested in its survival as Delia."

"Oh, and I suppose I ought to be out there changing your
fucking tires, too." I had just said "fuck," possibly for the first
time in my life. This was definitely not good.

"Is that what this is about? Are you upset that she's trying to
help me out? There are worse things a woman could be doing
than changing tires," Leon said.

Were there worse things? It was bad enough that Delia was
around all the time, bubbly and full of good ideas. But the fact
that she had changed his tires had me irrationally depressed.

Leon softened his tone. "Look, Jane, let it go. You are overre-
acting. I'll be back on Monday or Tuesday. Everything will be
fine. And if you want to come this weekend, that's fine too. We'll
let Seymour take care of the store."

This was a crutch of a proposal, used far too often, usually in
the midst of an argument. Seymour could *not* take care of the
store (we had tried that once, and when we returned from a long
weekend two homeless people were living in a mock bedroom
ensemble), but enough bad things had been said already to keep
me seething all weekend and I was running out of fight. And
anyway, maybe Leon was right—this drama today might well
have been nothing but a little hormone adjustment. But then I
sometimes wondered if these patches of edginess, of feeling
murderous and insane, were really when a person could see
things most clearly, could understand that all of the crap she puts

up with the rest of the month was the real problem. Month after month after month.

"This patio furniture thing is going to be huge, Janie. Just you wait and see. We'll pay off our debt. We'll start over again."

If Delia had not reappeared by his side just then, I might have been reassured by these words. I couldn't seem to get a grip on this, and it still seemed the best solution was for one of us to just quietly disappear.

Part Two

Two hundred a month is worse than nothing. Let's sell all the bonds and put the thirty thousand dollars in the bank—and if we lose the case we can live in Italy for three years, and then just die.

The Beautiful and Damned, F. SCOTT FITZGERALD

~

10

WITHIN MINUTES of my plotting the rough coordinates of Leon's destination, it began to rain. Forecasters predicted an entire week of precipitation, which was good. The latest thinking was that the manhole-cover explosions still plaguing the area were related to the unusual patch of hot, dry weather that had left the region close to drought. There were other theories, as well: the FBI was investigating rumors that the explosions were the work of terrorist cells, although no one offered any explanation as to why they would be mucking around in our sewer system with so many more compelling targets nearby.

One tabloid blamed the recurring manhole blasts on aliens. I didn't believe in the existence of aliens, or at least not in their ability, or inclination, to visit us on a routine basis. And anyway, the same question still applied: couldn't aliens and terrorists alike find more effective, or at least higher-profile, things to do with their resources?

Since Justin and I would be spending the entire weekend at the store, the weather didn't much matter. Uncle Seymour was going to be in Philadelphia on Saturday, attending the funeral of a childhood friend, and he said he might stay overnight. I didn't learn of Seymour's plan until Leon and Delia had left. Now I wondered whether Leon was bluffing, if he had proposed Justin and I come with him knowing leaving Seymour in charge was not just a judgment call, but a real impossibility.

Anyway, there were worse ways to spend a weekend than in the store. Given the forecast, it was bound to be quiet. Foul weather kept people away from stand-alone discount furniture stores on Rockville Pike—or at least I could say with some certainty that it kept them away from ours.

We used to have more freedom than this, a bit of distance from the store when we needed it. That was because we used to have help. Once there had been a rotating cast of characters who worked part time, some of them quite loyal. There had been Marta from Bolivia, for instance, who had stayed with us for about three years. She spoke very little English but was nonetheless one of the most productive salespeople we had ever seen. Leon maintained that as long as we didn't ask to see her green card, we couldn't be held liable if it turned out that she was illegal. Since we had paid Marta in cash and she had been deliberately vague about her personal life, we didn't know where to begin looking for her when she simply stopped showing up one day. Her cousin, Ignacio, still drove the delivery truck for us three times a week in the evenings, but he claimed to have no idea what had become of her. He grew agitated whenever we asked, and we finally decided that either they were not really family or there were other issues that we didn't want to probe too deeply.

There had also been Mrs. Wong, a physicist from Beijing, who had followed her daughter, Mei, to the United States while she attended law school at George Washington. She had also been a great help in the store, but when she graduated, they both packed up and moved to Seattle, where Mei was offered a job in the legal department of Microsoft. That had been disappointing—not only because we valued Mrs. Wong's help, but because she had invited me to visit her in China someday. I had fantasized about accepting her offer, maybe taking a long walk one afternoon and getting lost, making a new home for myself in Tibet. We talked about hiring replacements for these people, someone to at least liberate us from the store on weekends, but then we talked about a lot of things.

So Leon and Delia were going to be wherever it was they were going and Justin and I would have a quiet weekend together at the store. Part of me believed Leon's assertion that he was going with Delia, but not *with* her, a subtle difference in pronunciation that had huge implications. But part of me did not believe him. It was easy enough to see the attraction. Assuming, of course, that her tire-changing prowess was not indicative of that other thing that I decided to forget about, effective immediately. Who wouldn't want to be with Delightful Delia when the alternative was me? Not only was I the very antithesis of delightful, but I couldn't change a tire, never mind align a set of them.

A small part of me refused to believe our marriage was doomed even if I kept actively fantasizing about its demise. I could not imagine Leon walking away from his family any more than I could see him switching sports team allegiances. Yet things did change, incrementally. He was already contemplating infidelity to WZOP, after all. And who could blame him for wanting to escape? He had even more reasons than I did to want to run away. Certainly no one had suggested that *I* might have killed a bunch of coeds and stuffed them under a barn. I hardly thought he was a serial killer, but I did hold him responsible, in a way that I was increasingly having trouble repressing, for having attracted these problems with the megalomaniacal expansion of the store.

The trouble began shortly after Leon and Delia left. Justin and I locked up the store at 7 P.M., after we disassembled the makeshift porno set. Since we were under orders to stay together, I thought we would make the best of things and have dinner at our favorite Italian restaurant. We could turn his punishment into something positive, to try and reconnect. Before money concerns intruded, we used to eat there a couple of times a month, sometimes bringing Mike with us. The waiters all knew Justin, and they still brought him complimentary Shirley Temples with extra cherries and umbrellas even though he had stopped asking for these about six years earlier. But Justin said he didn't want Italian food. I suggested three other restaurants, but he rejected each one. This was especially frustrating since I was willing to do just about anything, to drive any distance, to accommodate him.

"Do you want to eat dinner at all?" I asked as we idled in the parking lot outside the store. I didn't want to leave until we had a destination: U-turns could be labor intensive, particularly on a Friday night, in the rain, at the tail-end of rush hour.

He shrugged his shoulders.

"Is that a 'yes' or a 'no'?"

He shrugged his shoulders again. They were bony knobs beneath his T-shirt, sticking up like broomsticks.

I took a deep breath. I was hungry and tired and it had been too long a day, but I was determined not to lash out at him. "How about Hamburger Hamlet?" That used to be his favorite place, years ago. I'd never liked it, but offered it up as a conciliatory measure.

"I don't eat meat," he said.

"I'm sure they have other things. Since when don't you eat meat?" That seemed like a detail I would have noticed, being the family provider of food.

He shrugged his shoulders again, and I was grateful that Leon was gone because he would not have had much patience for this conversation.

"Should we just go home, then? I probably have something in the freezer. Or, here's an idea, I'll make us some omelets."

"I don't eat eggs."

"You don't eat eggs? *Who doesn't eat eggs?*" The van's motor was running and the windshield wipers were set to the highest speed, batting the water around aggressively.

"Vegans don't eat eggs. I've decided to become a vegan."

"A *vegan*?" I had never heard of anyone becoming a vegan without first mentioning, even in passing, some general ambivalence about meat. Even then, one would assume that conventional vegetarianism would be a steppingstone along the way. Was it biologically possible to go from ordering steaks medium rare and enjoying quarter-pounders with cheese to quitting meat cold turkey without experiencing any withdrawal symptoms? I fumbled for something to say, wanting to sound supportive, but it was hard to mask my gut feeling that he was already too thin to be eliminating entire food groups from his diet.

"What do vegans actually eat?" I asked.

"Lots of things. Vegetables, fruits, grains."

"I'm guessing not fish?"

A stony stare served as his answer.

"I'm just asking. I know there are lots of different kinds of vegetarians and I thought that maybe some ate fish."

"If they ate fish they wouldn't be vegetarians. Anyway, ever since that fishing trip with Dad I haven't been eating fish."

"My mistake." I had sort of forgotten about that family fishing trip a few years earlier. Forgotten was too mild a word, actually; that was one Sunday outing I had tried to *obliterate* from memory. There would be no page in a scrapbook commemorating the summer day a few years ago when we went out on the Chesapeake Bay with Chandler and his now ex-wife in their speedboat. I had accidentally left my hat in the car, and wound up with sun poisoning on my nose. Chandler's wife had brought her cell phone and spent most of the time in the boat talking to a friend (or, in hindsight, her lover— Chandler's former law partner), complaining whenever we drifted into a patch of bay that caused her to lose her signal.

Now I remembered what had made the day especially awful: Justin insisted Leon throw back every fish he caught. He couldn't bear to watch them thrashing around on the end of the hook, their pathetic little fish mouths tragically sucking in air. Leon grudgingly agreed to liberate a few, tossing them back in the water maimed. But he still brought home three striped bass and cooked them on the grill that night. I had not quite made the connection between that outing and a refusal on Justin's part to eat fish.

"What if I make *you* dinner?" Justin asked, and he actually smiled for the first time all day. I felt bad that the first thing to occur to me was that this was going to involve yet another trip to the grocery store.

"Can you wait a minute? I saw a recipe online," he said. "I'm going to just run back inside and print it out."

I turned off the motor and handed him the keys. "Don't forget to turn the alarm off," I reminded him, "and turn it back on when you come out." I sighed and closed my eyes, listening to the rain. Sometimes I didn't feel up to this task. I was too old, too tired, and too cranky, and wondered if someone would just shoot me, like an old racehorse.

I opened the van door when I saw him waving to get my attention.

"Don't get mad," he shouted from the front steps, "but I just wanted to warn you that I'm not going to eat any dairy products, either. Have you seen how they treat lactating cows?"

"No, but I can imagine. Especially given the way they treat lactating women."

As he walked away, my mind drifted back to the coffin in the garage, and I thought then that maybe I needed some sort of manual to help raise my son. I didn't understand the whole Goth relationship to death, and now, improbably, to life.

What were we going to eat tonight, then? I had asked with as much Delia-like enthusiasm as I could muster as we approached the supermarket. All of the carts were gone from the front of the store, indicating the likelihood of complete chaos inside. This happened every time they predicted a bad stretch of weather in the Washington area—people panicked and stocked up on toilet paper. Checkout lines were about ten people deep.

I had already been there that morning and was not thrilled to be back. I was such a frequent customer that several of the checkers knew my name, and I knew theirs, as well. Just that morning, Toby, now working aisle five, had complimented me on my deft ability to self-scan groceries. "Most people have problems keying in the fruit, Mrs. Kramer," he'd said. "But not you. And you're great with the bakery items, too. You could be a professional." I'd blushed at the praise. Kudos were few and far between in the domestic arena, arguably the place where they were needed the most.

"Soybean patties with brown bean gravy," Justin said, and when he smiled a huge dimple emerged on his cheek in the same spot as Leon's. For one delusional moment I actually thought it was the sweet dimple that was attracting the stares of fellow shoppers, that they too were marveling at the whole miracle of reproduction, wondering whether dimples were dominant or recessive traits. But then I realized it was probably the gelled hair standing straight up, or the baggy black jeans with the chain hanging from a belt loop, or maybe just the five protrusions of metal on his otherwise adorable face.

Justin and I had weathered so much so gracefully as mother and son—we had lived through at least two school years marred by petty, aggravating teachers; an entire summer trying to neutralize the taunts of bullies at the neighborhood YMCA camp; a horrid case of the chicken pox and countless viral flus; a wide variety of alarming hairstyles; two infected piercings; not to mention recent demoralizing family interactions, and now a suspension from school. I operated on the theory that there were enough problems in life to manage without creating new ones, and had therefore deliberately let the battles about food go. I never stayed awake at night fretting about my baby's nursing intake; I refrained from ramming spoonfuls of unwanted beets down his throat; and I never inflicted rules about finishing everything at dinner. It seemed unfair, then, that when Justin and I finally had our first truly significant falling-out after all these years of peaceful coexistence, it would involve a soyburger.

Justin was not necessarily a bad cook—he was just overly ambitious and working with less-than-appetizing ingredients as well as a difficult recipe. The soybeans were supposed to have soaked in the refrigerator overnight. There was the additional problem of our aged food processor, which had been given to us as a wedding present and was on its last legs, its blades dull and its motor sluggish, a possible metaphor for the marriage itself.

There was also gravy to prepare. It was getting late. I was hungry and could not really contemplate making pecan gravy from scratch, so I began to dig through the pantry, looking for a shortcut.

"Is it okay if we use this?" I held a jar of Boston Market gravy aloft, hopeful.

"Are you crazy?" Justin asked.

We both froze. It was a simple question, the sort asked every day in households around the world when a mother made a suggestion that a child thought was stupid. But in our family, the word "crazy" had added significance. No one ever said so explicitly, but I knew there was a fear that I might follow in the footsteps of my mother, start obsessively writing bad poetry, then mutilate pictures of myself and drive the car off a cliff. I'd overheard Justin talking to Mike not too long ago, wondering whether craziness was something one inherited. Justin had observed that I had just turned forty one, the same age my mother had been when she died. Mike had joked that they should be careful getting in the car with me. It took a lot of self-restraint not to go into the room and try to defend myself, but it seemed more useful to just keep listening.

I then heard Justin wonder aloud whether my cousin, whose disappearance had become almost mythological in our family, might have been the one sending anthrax through the mail. That was an interesting idea, one that had not previously occurred to me.

I walked away at that point, uneasy from having heard too much already. But I was not entirely without a sense of humor about this, and besides, I had no intention of driving my car off a cliff. Suicide, not to mention murder, which was what the death of my mother technically amounted to, was a horror no matter what the circumstances, and yet there was at least something sort of tragically romantic about driving off a cliff on a winding road in Nepal. Suicide in a white minivan in the suburbs had less of a ring to it. Not to mention that it would mean abandoning my son, something I would never consider no matter how trapped I felt, how low I sunk. Unlike my mother, I could still see the bright side to things. Maybe I longed for a different sort of life, but in this one I got . . . free furniture. And the suburbs were not all bad. There was ample parking, for example, and good public schools, even if we were too stupid to take advantage of them. There were shopping malls and super-size grocery stores and multi-screen movie theaters. Increasingly, there was ethnic food galore. And now there was this scrap-booking thing, an amusing distraction that offered the possibil-ity, however unlikely, of financial reward.

"What exactly is so crazy about Boston Market gravy?" I asked.

He grabbed the jar from me and began to read the contents.

My brain was not yet programmed to catch the sorts of key words offensive to vegans, and it took me a minute to identify the problem. This was chicken gravy. Chicken gravy contained . . . chicken. Hence it had no place on the menu of a vegan meal. I put the jar down and went over to the food processor to rinse it out for the next phase of preparation.

The kitchen was a complete mess by the end of the two-hour ordeal, the result of the food processor turning on when the plastic top was not in place. I knew that I should have been encouraging my son's interest in cooking, but it was after 9 P.M. by the time the unappetizing dinner was ready, and I was close to losing my composure.

Still, I understood that this was an important night. We needed to talk to at least remember that we generally got along well despite the tension swirling around us. I set the table in the dining room and lit candles in an effort to be celebratory of Justin's culinary endeavors. This was a room we didn't make much use of; the last time we'd turned on the lights had possi-bly been Thanksgiving. One of the bulbs in the chandelier was burnt out, and an elaborate spider web linked two of the crystal arms. We sat across from one another at the oblong table.

Justin was not very talkative, providing one-word replies to my string of meaningless, chatty questions. This sort of brood-ing was unlike him. Until these last few days he had seemed to exist on a mostly even keel, his embrace of Goth notwithstand-ing. I was unsteady navigating the arcs of male moodiness even though I had lived with a member of the species for close to twenty years. Leon's cycles were almost as predictable as mine, although his typically had to do with the arrival of bank statements. But I didn't know what was going on with Justin that evening, and I was afraid of setting him off by saying the wrong thing.

Certainly I didn't comment on the soyburgers being close to inedible. I ground them into the smallest bits possible, then swallowed politely, trying not to think about what effect this would have on either my digestive system or that crumbling filling I'd been ignoring. The sound of chewing filled in most of the awkward, silent gaps.

"So, what did Mike's dad say about his car? Is he in trouble?" This might have seemed like a topic likely to lead us onto unsafe ground, but Justin and I freely discussed Mike's family situation, and his father's evident lack of concern for his two sons. I presumed Justin would agree that Mike getting in trouble would actually be a *good* thing, in the sense that it would at least show that his dad cared.

Justin shrugged his shoulders and chewed some more. It took a few minutes before he could swallow. "He said it would be a good opportunity to go to New York. He said it was really convenient, because he was expecting some big delivery of a sculpture or something in his new apartment, and he couldn't be there, and it was too valuable to just have the super open the door, and his girlfriend had to be in London for a commercial— she's a model or an actress or something—and so he said it would be great if we could go."

"What do you mean?" I asked, my voice cracking slightly. Surely I had just misunderstood. Was I more upset by the outrageous proposal that our suspended sons take a holiday, or by the casual mention that Mike's father had a girlfriend?

"I mean, we'd go this weekend. I was going to ask you tonight. It works out really well, too, because there's a group we wanted to see—Mike knows the guitarist from some camp he used to go to. They've got a few gigs next week in the West Village. I figured you wouldn't care since we can't go to school anyway."

"You can't go to school because you've been *suspended* from school. Not because you are on vacation."

"I know that, Mom, but it's so stupid. I'm mean, come on . . . It's not like we did anything that wrong."

"I agree with you, it's not that big of a deal. But rules are rules, and you should obey them even if you disagree with them."

I noticed that the wallpaper—a ghoulish mélange of peacocks and hunters with rifles that some former owner of our house had chosen—was starting to peel from the corner behind where Justin sat.

The phone rang before Justin could offer a counterargument, but neither one of us moved to answer. There was no one I especially wanted to talk to, but Justin still had a social life and I was surprised that he didn't race to pick it up. From upstairs, where the answering machine sat on a low table in the hallway, we could hear Leon's voice being broadcast, but could not really make out his words. It seemed a horrible thing to do, to just sit there with the tacit understanding that neither one of us wanted to speak to him.

"What's up with that patio furniture woman?" Justin asked, after the machine became silent. Since we were clearly on the verge of having a fight about New York, I was happy to talk about something else. Even Delia.

"What do you mean?" I tried to sound oblivious to the possible implications of his question. My eye caught again on the sticking-out piece of wallpaper, and I wondered how difficult it would be to strip it off. How had I lived with this all these years? This room needed brightening. It was not bad, architecturally speaking. High ceilings, a built-in china nook, nice molding. Pale yellow walls would look good.

"There's something kind of weird about her, don't you think?"

I shrugged my shoulders. Yes! I wanted to scream. Incredibly weird. A fourteen-year-old-in-the-body-of-a-forty-year-old-who-could-align-tires weird. But I did not. This seemed like the wrong sort of conversation to have with my son.

"Why is she always hanging around?"

"She and Dad have . . . a scheme. A patio furniture scheme."

"A patio furniture scheme? Whatever *that* means."

"She's a patio furniture saleswoman, Justin. She has an idea about the store carrying a new line of furniture. She and Dad want me to work on it, too. That's all. There's nothing else to it. Don't go thinking the worst of people for no reason." This seemed like the sort of thing a good mother ought to say, even if she didn't believe it herself.

He spit out a piece of soyburger before speaking again. "I think there's something weird going on. But no one really cares what I think. Everyone treats me like I'm a criminal or something. Did you know that Dad asked me if I was taking money from the cash register? Like I would steal from my own family! I think it's her. I think maybe she's stealing money. I think there's something fucked up about her." He blew out the candles for no particular reason.

"Please don't say *fuck*. I hate that word. I had no idea your father asked you that."

"Just tell me one thing: was money disappearing before she showed up?"

I wasn't completely sure. It was possible that money had been slowly oozing out of the register for years, but it was only lately, with the convergence of many bad events and with our finances sliding dangerously into irreconcilable debt, that either of us had begun paying close attention to the details. Such a small percentage of our business was transacted in cash that it had never seemed to matter.

"I really don't know, Justin. But I don't think it's fair to blame Delia for something that awful without any evidence."

"Okay. I'll find some evidence. Maybe I'll go into the store right now and start digging around."

"Now? It's pouring rain. Absolutely not. You're supposed to stay here with me, remember what your father said?"

"I don't see my father here, do you?"

"Finish your dinner," I said. "You're too thin as it is. I don't really think this vegan thing is good for you. You need a normal diet."

"I did finish my dinner. And don't tell me what's normal. Just cause you want to eat dead animals doesn't mean that I have to."

I bristled; dead animals made me think of the bones behind the store. This was really starting to be a problem.

"Look, Justin, I understand why you are upset. Really I do, because I'm upset myself. There's a lot going on that your father and I need to sort through. He doesn't really think you are stealing money. He said the same thing to me. He accused me of *embezzlement!* But he doesn't mean it that way—he just says whatever pops into his head sometimes. He loves you, Justin. He even wants you to run the store someday!" I was also prone to saying whatever stupid thing popped into my head. The last thing Justin wanted was to contemplate running the store.

He stood up from the table and accidentally banged it with his hip, causing it to tilt to one side. A water glass slid to the floor and smashed, and for the first time in his sixteen years he gave me a look that I did not like. An angry, chilling glare, the sort he must have given to the woman on Rockville Pike that had caused her to summon the police and claim that she had just met Satan.

When Justin walked outside into the pouring rain, slamming the door behind him, I felt a sudden stabbing pain. We were not door-slamming people. True, we occasionally said regrettable things to one another, but we didn't physically display our anger. What Justin had just done constituted a provocative break in protocol.

As I prepared to go dashing after my son, I found myself seized by an entirely unexpected pang of regret about our long-gone dog. At least he had always been on my side. And he would have been useful in trailing Justin. But then, given his orthopedic history, it was likely that his hip would have dislocated mid-chase and then I would have been in the position of having to transport a wet, ninety-pound, crippled dog. That had happened once, and I'd had to ask some neighbors to help lift him into a little red wagon so that I could pull him home.

Although I had complained about it bitterly at the time, dog-walking had in fact been one of my few social activities—strolling around the block, saying "hi" to neighbors, feigning an interest in other people's pets. But really it was dishonest of me to wax nostalgic. The dog had created a font of guilt not dissimilar to the one inspired by my husband: the vet always insisted that the dog's hip problems were aggravated by his weight, and then would look at me accusingly. I never really understood this. He was a big dog. He carried a lot of bulk. Why was I constantly being made to feel responsible for the metabolism of everyone around me?

·   ·   ·

Justin disappeared rather quickly into the night. Maybe it was because he was dressed in black. Or maybe it was because it was raining so hard it was difficult to see. I called his name over and over, but the wind had begun to rage so loudly that my voice was barely audible. Although I had donned the neon yellow poncho hanging by the door, the rain slashed in sideways through the hood and I was already wet by the time I reached the Cuban family's driveway. I could see them through the window, standing in their kitchen. Carmen, the mother, was talking on the phone. Enrique was sitting at the table, eating. The diplomat father was reading the newspaper. They looked like any family through the window, their activities so clichéd as to be worthy of a sitcom. *The Cubans,* Fridays at ten, on ABC. They had a colorful windsock hanging from the front porch that was getting quite a workout in the storm. I wasn't sure why this struck me as odd. Shouldn't representatives of communist countries be allowed to enjoy decorative ornaments? Did Fidel Castro have a position on windsocks?

Our block was long, which was not surprising given that our neighborhood's chief claim to fame, aside from obscenely large houses, was football-field-size lots. Owning property in our zip code was supposed to mean you were living the American dream, but sometimes it made me want to pull the *Marx-Engels Reader* off the shelf and review instructions on how to redistribute some of this wealth. One neighbor had just built a regulation-size basketball court inside her house for her son's twelfth birthday. Three people on our block had recently installed movie theaters in their basements. Then there were those of us who would soon need to take up a collection to help pay our mortgage.

Although most of the houses were set far back, there was an inviting orange glow from behind each curtain, and I could practically feel the warmth emanating from inside. I didn't know all the people on our block but had a general idea who lived behind each fence. I knew our immediate neighbors, of course: the Cubans to our left, and the man whose wife had gone missing on the right. On the other side of the Cubans' property lived a young, sporty family with two convertibles—despite having a couple of little kids, they had not yet bought a minivan. Perhaps I should have been contemplating a separation from my own van, looking into buying some sort of midlife-crisis sports car that would put us even further in debt. Two doors down from the Cubans was the residence of another young family, this one with dot-com money—or perhaps that was with *former* dot-com money, because their lawn had recently sprung a "for sale" sign. They also had a folksy "welcome" sign hanging on the fence in the shape of a swan; underneath it was a notice from the alarm company that the perimeter of the property was wired to send electric shocks to trespassers. The house beyond that was occupied by an Egyptian orthodontist and her surgeon husband. I knew nothing much about these people beyond the random glimpse I'd catch from time to time, the faux friendly waves we'd exchange in passing. I'd stopped waving at the neighbor directly behind us, however, ever since he'd put the sign on his lawn opposing our expansion.

A lack of familiarity with several of my neighbors did not keep me from feeling envious as I walked past their grand houses with their freshly mulched flower beds, almost all of them sprouting seasonally appropriate pansies. One sensed that behind each door lurked a happy family with tasteful furniture. I imagined that I could even smell freshly baked bread emanating from their ovens, but suspected that was really an olfactory hallucination resulting from an excessive longing to be living other people's lives, even if I found their flamboyant displays of wealth distasteful.

I continued shouting Justin's name. A rough gust of wind

blew my hood off and caused me to lose my footing. The weather seemed to be turning dangerous, a thought confirmed by the sight of a giant, old magnolia tree lying across an intersection just two blocks from our house with electrical wires draped across the branches. No one with a brain in her head would be out walking right now, and in fact no one was, except for me and maybe my son.

After going home and changing into dry clothes, I got in the van and drove to the store. Traffic lights were out at a couple of key intersections and when I pulled into the lot, it appeared the power was out at the store, as well. There were well over one hundred spaces to choose from, but I pulled in tight next to Delia's Lexus, the only other vehicle parked in our lot. When I swung open the door to my van, it scraped noisily against the Lexus's passenger side. I bent over to inspect the damage and thought I detected a large gash on the otherwise shiny silver exterior, but it was too dark to tell. Anyway, she had no business leaving her car parked in our lot while she went away. This was private property! Signs clearly warned that the lot was for shoppers only, that violators would be towed. A little scratch was the least of her problems: she was lucky I didn't call the two thug brothers who worked on contract for us, disappearing cars at two hundred dollars a pop.

I went into the store and called Justin's name, spooked. Walking through the showroom with a flashlight turned up no sign of my son, but I did see a mouse scamper across the floor. Frantic, I drove to Mike's house, which took some doing with all the trees littering the roadway, but no one was there. Or at least no one answered the door. I then surveyed every possible route Justin might have taken to walk from the house to the store, from the store to Mike's, and alternatively, from the house to Mike's. Finally I gave up and went home.

I considered putting in a call to the police, but knew they'd only laugh at me. A teenager missing for a few hours on a Friday night? Hardly a cause for concern. Who was calling, they would ask. Oh, Mrs. Kramer! The woman married to Mr. Kramer? Mr. Kramer—the guy with those bones behind his store? Funny, we just wrote up a report involving a Justin Kramer. Any relation?

With that thought in mind I decided to continue my own investigative work. No one answered the phone at Mike's house, and I left messages at all of the other homes I could think of, including Brett's and Zondra's. Neither one of them was home. "Probably at the movies" was the best answer Zondra's mother could provide. "She loves movies, goes almost every night. She sees the same ones over and over," she said. I did not volunteer that this seemed improbable, that from what I had observed of her daughter it was more likely she was downtown scoring heroin than apprenticing as a film critic. But then, I'd read in the paper that our local movie theater was quite the thriving drug bazaar, the most reliable place to buy ecstasy, among other things, so perhaps she *was* at the movies, after all. Zondra was another troubled presence in our lives. Justin had known her since first grade, when she was a precious little girl with braided pigtails adorned with ribbons. Her father had died in an automobile accident—it was widely known that he had been drunk, and had killed a pedestrian before veering into a tree; shortly thereafter Zondra dyed her hair green and stopped going to school. As with many of Justin's friends, I was torn between wanting to help her and wanting to keep her away from my son. Even if she was a bad influence, she was only one of many, and I tried to at least stuff her with food when she visited.

The phone was tucked under my chin as I spoke to Zondra's mother and without quite realizing what I was doing, I began to tug at the loose bit of wallpaper in the dining room. It had been worrying me like a hangnail and it came off easily, in one neat strip. The feeling was oddly satisfying, and I began to tear at another piece. This one stuck halfway down the wall, then made a ragged tear in the middle of a peacock's plume. I dialed Mike's number again and let it ring and ring as I continued to mutilate my walls, reaching into the buffet and pulling out a cake server, which was useful in prying the paper from behind. After what must have been a hundred rings, I set the phone down on the table where the dirty dishes still sat and picked up a piece of cold, hard soyburger, chewing for a long while as I surveyed my demolition work.

I fetched a sharp knife from the kitchen drawer and attempted to scrape away patches of the stuck-on wall paper. A large chunk of plaster fell out of the wall, a hunter with a rifle poised on his shoulder still stuck to it. Leon was going to have a fit. The thought of Leon reminded me of . . . Leon. I had forgotten about his phone call, and went upstairs to listen to his message.

Passing through the front hallway, I saw a figure hovering in front of our house and was momentarily filled with relief. Justin? I was ready to run back out into the rain to throw my arms around him. But it wasn't him; just some poor sucker walking a dog. A burst of wind turned his umbrella inside out.

There were two messages on the answering machine. Perhaps Leon had called again while I was out in the rain. Now I wanted to talk to him. I didn't expect that he would have any helpful thoughts on Justin's whereabouts, but at least we could commiserate about his disappearance. For better or worse, maybe this was the crisis that we'd been waiting for, something to help clarify the long drift. Maybe good could come from bad; this might unite us in a mission to get our son pointed in the right direction again.

I rewound the tape and listened. Against the backdrop of sirens wailing, he claimed to be calling from the New Jersey

Turnpike. He gave me an unnecessarily detailed report on traffic and weather conditions before going on at length about more ideas for patio furniture. "This is going to turn us around, Janie," he said again. "You'll see. Things will be just like they were before."

He didn't say before what, exactly. But simply hearing his voice unleashed a complicated range of emotions including but not limited to love, hate, rage, sympathy, and admittedly even a little bit of longing. He was like a little boy when he got this excited. It was sweet that he wanted my approval, wanted me to share his vision for the patio furniture scheme. I had an image of Justin bounding off the school bus, proudly displaying an art project or a science experiment that hadn't quite worked. They blurred together like that sometimes, father and son, because, of course, they were very much alike, even if they were frequently at odds. And I couldn't love one without loving the other, even if they had both abandoned me.

Was this inability to sustain anger an unavoidable consequence of having cohabitated for such an extended length of time that we'd rubbed off on each other, like our laundry? After all these years of washing our whites with our darks, everything had started to bleed together. Part of me wanted Leon to vanish and part of me wanted him to come rushing home. I blamed him for our son's behavior, but I wanted him to come back to set things right. I had hoped he would disappear off some random exit on the Turnpike; now I was desperate to know which rest stop he was calling from.

His next sentence helped restore my equilibrium. "Oh, wait, Janie," he said. "I meant to tell you that I put those entertainment centers on sale tomorrow—you know, the ones that just came in, the huge Plexiglas sectionals. There's a WZOP ad running at 2 and again at 3 A.M., so hopefully we'll get some action on them tomorrow. You'll need to put a notice on the marquee.

Maybe do it tonight, if you have a chance. Hope you guys are good. My cell is low on batteries so I'm going to turn it off, but I'll call you when I stop somewhere for the night. Ciao!"

"Ciao?" That had to be Delia's influence. Leon was a straight-forward "goodbye" sort of person. I listened again, wondering if I could hear her in the background. But all I could make out were the sounds of a horn honking and sirens.

I pressed the "play" button to hear the next message. It was Leon again. "Janie . . . It just occurred to me that if it's raining as hard down there as it is up here you might want to check the basement."

Check for flooding in the basement. Put the sale sign up on the marquee. I could see myself standing on the top rung of the ladder in the pouring rain, felled by a lightning strike, or maybe blown away by gusting winds. Alternatively, I could go down-stairs and drown in the basement. At least these all seemed like fitting ways to go.

11

THE FACT that I had no one to call when my husband and son were AWOL and my basement had begun to flood seemed like one more sign of personal failure. What had happened to my friends over the years? What had become of the life, or at least the fragments of a life, that I once had outside of family and furniture?

I could barely recall the last time I went out to lunch, or did something fun with a person who was not a member of my family. The most recent non-work-related social outing I could recollect was lunch with Gina. We had known each other since high school, when we both lived in Panama. We'd never had much in common apart from circumstance and language, but that was enough for us to bond in a classroom full of local kids who spoke only rapid-fire Spanish.

Gina had never married, had no children, and worked as a receptionist at a tanning salon in D.C. After dinner at our house once she'd quipped that she was now certain she did not want a family. She quickly apologized, and claimed that she'd meant something else entirely. But I think she meant what she said: her taste of my life that evening scared her off domesticity even though we had all been on our best behavior.

The lunch date was about a year ago. I remembered staring at each other over sushi in a dimly lit, half-empty Japanese restau-

rant. Gina had gone on at length about her guru and the spiritual
retreat she was about to attend while I picked apart a California
roll, wondering if it was too soon to ask for the check. She kept
peering deep into my eyes as if there was something there,
something more to Jane Kramer than met the eye. But there
wasn't. Not anymore. Or at least not along the lines of what she
wanted to find. We kept in touch because it was more awkward
not to, but we never scheduled another lunch.

Anyway, the hole I felt in my emotional life did not seem the
sort that would be filled by having a best girlfriend—someone
to chat on the phone with, someone who dropped in unan-
nounced and sometimes borrowed clothes, someone I might
trek to Bed Bath and Beyond with when she needed new cut-
lery. Yet I did envy women I observed in the neighborhood who
seemed to have bonded as in the old 1950s sitcoms, their front
doors always open, their kids and dogs running between the
yards. I imagined the young mothers sipping coffee in one another's kitchens, discussing teachers and pediatricians and what
to cook for dinner. They were probably lawyers—my admittedly unscientific survey had established that *all* the young
women in our neighborhood were lawyers—but that certainly
didn't mean they were discussing penal code reform or what
cases were pending on the Supreme Court docket, because in
my experience some toxic combination of suburbia, motherhood, and too many trips to the dry cleaner numbed the minds
of even the most intelligent stay-at-home mothers.

At least the session at Tiffany's had forced me out of my shell
for a few hours, and that was probably a good thing. Still, even if
I was able to put up a good front as a cheerful memory consultant, it was hard to imagine that translating into any meaningful
relationships. Nancy Reisman may have given me her phone
number, but I couldn't see calling her to ask for help moving
boxes out of my basement, for example. Nor could I imagine

calling Rita and crying on her paint-splattered shoulder, even if she did strike me as a nurturing, understanding sort of person.

Sometime after 2 A.M., Mike Stahl finally answered his phone. I had been hitting the redial button on and off for a couple of hours, and was so startled when he actually picked up that I had to pause for a moment to remember what I wanted. Yes, Justin was there, he said, but he was asleep. I made Mike wake him—I wanted to hear his voice to be sure this was true. Perhaps because Justin was too groggy to protest, I managed to extract an apology as well as an assurance that he would stay put until I picked him up the next day.

I should have been able to go to sleep after learning he was safe, but my mind kept racing. I replayed the scene in my mind, freezing on the moment he walked out, wondering if I could have steered our conversation toward a better outcome. I had this sick, sinking feeling that we had just turned a corner far more worrisome than was foreshadowed by any piercing or hair dyeing or eyeliner wearing. That had all been fine—if not my personal ideal of how I wanted my son to present himself to the world—because we were still in synch. But slamming a door and disappearing in the night was not all right. It was personal.

No sooner did I manage to talk myself down, however, than I began fretting about Delia's car, wondering how badly I might have scratched that gorgeous exterior. The answer to that would have to wait until sunrise.

I decided to make use of some of this nervous energy by dragging boxes of photographs up from the damp basement. The sump pump had blown a fuse, but that was at least something I knew how to fix, and fortunately the little bit of standing water had not caused any significant damage. There was one box in the back of the closet that was stuck, wedged in at an awkward angle, and I couldn't pry it loose. The handwriting on the side was unfamiliar—possibly in another language, although I couldn't tell for sure since the ink was smeared. But clearly it did not contain family photographs. I wondered if the box had been left behind by the former owner of the house, who had been somewhat haphazard in his final spot-check of closets. Maybe it included intriguing documents of international importance. I found a screwdriver and made a ragged tear through the duct tape that held the lid, then stuck my hand inside. I felt a plastic frame, then another frame, and then started to laugh.

The box held evidence of our demise.

I recalled in detail the night that I had stayed up late to wait for Leon after inventory-taking a couple of years before the renovation. There were tax issues, he had said, and I hadn't asked him to elaborate. Inventory was an annual event, a week spent categorizing and rearranging, refreshing stock and engaging in a little spring cleaning. At the end of these sessions I would have to reorient myself in the store because the changes were so extensive. I imagined the taking of inventory was something every family-owned furniture store did on a regular basis to prepare for tax season, but it was possible there was something more sinister going on—sofas that had been sitting idle for months, resisting movement despite massive markdowns, went away, never to be seen again. They were erased from the ledger and ceased to exist, as if some sort of an ethnic cleansing of furniture had just taken place. I would ask about these items, odd bits of furniture that I had grown attached to, had begun to root for like older orphans waiting for adoption, like Seymour's Super Bowl Special reclining chairs. Answers were typically vague. One year I was told that Samuel had donated certain items to his synagogue; another year one of our part-time employees was said to have bought them at a discount. The last time I'd inquired about the fate of a particularly hideous floral armchair Leon had looked at me as though I'd had a sudden onset of Alzheimer's disease, and said he had no idea what I was talking about.

Although his answers made no sense, I didn't push too hard: this was my own version of not asking to see the green cards of employees. My name was not on the ownership papers back then, so I liked to believe that I would not be the one serving jail time if some sort of genuine tax evasion was really going on.

On that particular night of disconnect, Leon had said he'd be home at ten. After Justin had gone to sleep, I'd taken a long perfumed bath and poured myself a glass of wine, then dimmed the lights in the bedroom to wait for him. By eleven he had not returned. I called him at the store, but there was no answer. There was no Delia to be paranoid about back then, but we had a different sort of problem: Leon had been spending an inordinate amount of time with an architect whose name sounded like a Spanish wine—Julio Gris. They were drawing up plans that would keep us grounded here forever at the same time that I was dreaming of a way to leave. I figured Leon had decided to meet Julio for a drink after work to go over the latest set of blueprints. I was getting cold in the ridiculous frilly ensemble I had donned, so I put on ratty old flannel pajamas and fell asleep watching the news.

Leon finally walked in after midnight and dropped a box on the floor in the front hallway. The thud that echoed up the stairs woke me. Then he stomped back down the stairs into the garage and retrieved a second box from the back of his car. By then the dog was awake, and moments later, so was Justin. Patch seemed to think it was morning, and he ran out the garage door, which Leon had forgotten to close.

As I descended the stairs to find the dog I noticed that the house still smelled like the lasagna I had made for dinner, which might have been an appetizing aroma hours earlier when the table was set and we were hungry, but which now hung in the air like bad breath. I meant to give Leon some sort of subtle signal that would indicate my earlier amorous intentions, but when we spoke, what spilled from my lips were more like words of war.

In the morning I was tired and crabby and when I asked Leon about the contents of the boxes in the front hallway, he heard it as yet another criticism. The sour mood in the house seemed fitting given what was inside the boxes: dozens of small watercolors by an artist named Lena Min. Samuel had met Lena Min on a trip to Vietnam a few years earlier. He'd been quite taken with her, and had commissioned about a hundred paintings, which was probably more than Lena could have reasonably expected to sell in a lifetime. They were mostly portraits of peasant women on rice paddies in various stages of repose, their arms slightly too long, their hats disproportionate to the size of their bodies. It seemed clear that there must have been something about Lena other than her prowess with a paintbrush that had attracted Samuel to her work. So far as I knew, we hadn't sold a single one of her paintings, ever. And that morning nearly all of them had come to a final resting place in our front hallway.

I watched Leon root around in the kitchen drawers, looking for picture hooks. I didn't have the energy for a fight, so I took the dog for a long walk instead. When I returned about an hour later, a dozen of the paintings were hanging on the walls. The others went into the basement closet along with the souvenirs from some of my own thwarted ambitions. And so began another week in the annals of deteriorating marital relations.

Even from afar, from across the dining room with its chewed-up wall paper, one could tell that things were not quite right in our house apart from the issues of poor interior design and bad drainage. The power had gone out in the wee hours of Saturday morning, and until a shaft of Monday-morning sunlight illuminated the pictures I had set out on the kitchen floor to dry, I had never really appreciated the overall visual effect of what my mother had done. It looked as if some sort of scissor-wielding maniac (a disgruntled former Memories, Inc. consultant, perhaps) had broken into our house and attacked the photo album.

Spread out on the floor were yellowing photographs set across the backdrop of dozens of exotic locales. In one picture, a little girl smiled, holding the hand of her rugged, bearded father. The father had his arm around a woman with silky dark hair. She was slim and wore a sleeveless dress—batik, from Indonesia. She held a straw pocketbook out of which stuck the top of a newspaper. She was lovely. So incredibly lovely—a vision of young motherhood, until you looked more closely and realized that this was nothing but an illusion. Perhaps she was lovely and perhaps she was not. It was difficult to tell, because her face had been sliced out of every single picture with surgical precision.

My mother *was* lovely, for the record, but her beauty didn't seem to do her much good. She was sturdy on the outside—family legend had it that she had walked a mile while in labor to give birth to me in a bamboo hut with the aid of an Indonesian midwife. (My father had been off on a fundraising mission in New York at the time. Why he had been away that close to her delivery date was a question I didn't think to ask until I had my own child, and by then there was no one left to answer it.) She climbed mountains and drank the water in the developing world straight from the tap and never once got sick. It was her psyche that was fragile as glass. Since I only knew her for a selective fragment of her life, it was impossible for me to separate cause from effect. Was it the weight of the world that finally crushed her, or was it the weightlessness of travel that kept her alive? It was hard to imagine her in my world of bills and laundry and tedious obligation, and yet I knew it was also these things that kept me grounded. Another reason why I couldn't drive my van

off a cliff was because there was a load of wet towels in the
washer and who would ever think to stick them in the dryer?

I continued sorting through another box of photos. Some of
the prints were stuck together and I had to separate them carefully. For better or worse, all the photographs of me had faces,
and I wondered if perhaps my mother wasn't on to something,
choosing to destroy all evidence of aging before she departed. In
one picture I could almost see a wrinkle forming and was mentally transported to another episode of disconnect. I had taken
Justin to New Hampshire for a soccer tournament that summer
and we had spent the week sleeping on air mattresses in a
friend's living room. I had just been nodding off when Justin
crept over to the corner where I was lying in the cramped room
and began to rummage through my pocketbook, looking for
something—gum, or maybe Tylenol, my cell phone, perhaps. I
could hear my car keys jangling in the bag, coins rattling in the
change purse. I rolled over and looked up and was momentarily
stunned by the height of the figure towering over me. I felt old
and small, and this tall boy, a man-child, loomed above me. That
was what I was thinking, full of pride and self-pity, as he rum-
maged through my bag and found a disposable camera, then
snapped three pictures of me in my pajamas while I yelled at
him to stop. He had captured me perfectly, it now seemed: an
aging shrew, lying low to the ground, in a messy state of mind.

But there was really another reason that I remembered that
night well. Just before inflating my air mattress and unrolling
my sleeping bag, I had called Leon. Even from a distance I had
felt his attention wane as I ran through a perhaps too detailed
description of our day. Maybe he didn't need to hear about the
egg salad sandwich that had made me sick, or the anecdote about
how I ended up in the wrong lane at the tollbooth on the Massa-
chusetts Turnpike without exact change and a truck driver had
given me the finger. As I heard myself rambling on, I began to

wonder if I hadn't detected a certain lack of enthusiasm on his end upon hearing my voice on the phone in the first place.

This registered as either another moment of sudden clarity or extreme paranoia. What did it mean when your spouse was no longer happy to hear your voice on the telephone? Then I had heard something else on the line. Chewing. He was eating. Something crunchy and noisy. A pretzel? Maybe he was eating because he was not interested in what I had to say. Or maybe he was not interested because he was eating. Maybe he had just been hungry.

There were hundreds more photographs, the decades all mixed up, with color prints from just last year mixed in with fading, yellowing shots of great-great grandparents. What they had in common after being briefly saturated was curled edges. Several hundred dollars' worth of scrapbooking supplies were waterlogged as well, and the irony of this was not lost on me. Perhaps I had potential as a Memories, Inc. consultant, but I was clearly a failure when it came to preserving my own family memories. Probably this was not that unusual. I'd heard of cleaning ladies with filthy houses, and of divorced marriage counselors, so maybe this was par for the course. It might be part of my destiny to be a furniture store owner with shoddy furniture, and a memory consultant with photographs in active stages of decay.

I kept meaning to get up, to get on with my day, to take a shower and change clothes, but something kept me glued to this spot on the floor, lost in memories. The cup of coffee beside me had grown cold at least an hour before. This was like some mental jigsaw that would be finished if I could just find a few missing pieces. There was something decidedly odd, almost sacrilegious, about the juxtaposition of these two very different lives. There were the bright color prints of my current family: Halloween, Christmas, various birthdays. There were more batches of soccer pictures (jerseys in red, yellow, teal, copper—spring and fall for ten years, twenty seasons of soccer in all). There were pictures of the dog as a puppy with Leon's shoe in his mouth. There we were on a family trip to northern California, posing beside a statue in Golden Gate Park about five years earlier, before we started to bleed money.

I saw a picture of the Olde Towne Diner, which used to be just a few blocks from the store. It had since been razed, made into a parking lot for a movie theater. I used to eat at the diner all the time. It was the sight of a memorable if scarring lunch. Justin had been about six years old, and we had gone out with Uncle Seymour for a sandwich. When it came time to pay the bill, I realized I had no cash. In keeping with its quaint name and the overall eighteenth-century feel of the place, the restaurant did not take credit cards, which may have been part of the reason it went out of business within the year. I left Justin and Seymour at the booth while I dashed just next door to the cash machine. When I returned a few minutes later, they were gone.

I worried, but I didn't completely panic. Seymour could seem batty sometimes, but he wasn't without basic common sense. Then again, he had no real experience with small boys, and I couldn't be certain he would be able to keep Justin from dashing into traffic, or from wandering out of sight. I called the store, to no avail. After an hour spent looking for them I called the store again. This time Leon suggested I try Seymour's apartment, which was in fact where they were, contentedly watching cartoons with the volume turned up full blast.

"Why did you leave the restaurant?" I demanded.

"We waited and waited, and then we thought you were just going to leave us there on Rockville Pike forever," cried Justin, which would have been funny had it not inspired in me immediate feelings of failure. How could they have thought even for a moment that I would have done such a thing? Was that the reason he had embraced Goth? Become a vegan? Run off in the rain? And worse, isn't that precisely what had happened? Here we all were, years later, still waiting on Rockville Pike.

"Why didn't you call Dad?" I asked.

Justin shrugged his shoulders.

Perhaps, like a small animal, he could sense things I could not: impending storms, earthquakes, parental discontent.

"Jane, why don't you sit down. Watch some television with us," Seymour shouted. "I'll get you some doughnuts."

"No, thanks. I've got to get back to the store. You guys should probably come, too."

"Glazed or with sprinkles?" he asked.

I looked down at the coffee table and saw a nearly empty box of doughnuts. It appeared they had begun with a dozen and eaten ten. I asked for a glass of milk and then sat down with them and polished off the lot.

I put down the diner photograph and picked up a photo of the village children I used to toss balls with. My mother was standing behind me, again without a face, and I panicked. I needed to separate these pictures. I had the sudden irrational fear that one life would contaminate the other, and that it was entirely possible the process might already have begun. I quickly sorted the pictures, slapping them into piles. Ones With Faces. Ones Without. I was almost finished when I saw another photo from the same time period as the batch that Joyce Berger had brought to the Power Scrapping Session. There was the original façade of the store. The old street lights in front, the strip mall adjoined to the former Kramer's. There were Julio Gris and Leon standing together looking at blueprints. And there was that same weird speck in the background that seemed to be wearing my shoes, lifting off the ground like Dorothy, en route to Oz.

Sticking to the back roads, the drive to the store usually took about fifteen minutes. It could also take twice that long, depending on the time of day. The Pike would have been the better choice that morning, but until I set out I hadn't known that several more trees had fallen, blocking one of the key access roads. A brand-new BMW, still sporting dealer plates, was wedged under a tree just before the intersection of River and Falls roads. The car was completely crushed, and I shuddered, contemplating the fate of the driver. It took a full twenty minutes to extricate myself from the line of traffic that had formed to gawk at the accident. As soon as I turned around and made a quick right turn, I got stuck behind a Verizon truck, the driver of which was attending to a telephone pole stretched across the road. I was grateful to see the repair crews, since our own phone service had gone out sometime Saturday night, along with the electricity. This had forced me back into the basement to retrieve more items; the room was liable to begin flooding again if the sump pump sat idle too long.

By the time I arrived it was 10:30, half an hour after we were supposed to have opened the store. Uncle Seymour was back. For some reason he was not inside, but was sitting on the front steps. As I drew closer, I could see that he was with a young couple.

Seymour noticed my van approach. He struggled arthritically to his feet and came limping toward me. His greeting was effusive; he held me a bit too long in an embrace, as if more than a weekend had passed since we'd last seen one another.

"Jane, Jane, Jane," he said loudly, taking my hand. "Come meet our customers."

He pulled me toward a young couple seated under the awning. The sun was bursting through the clouds triumphantly, and it was already unbearably hot and muggy. Two mosquitoes vied for the same spot on my arm.

"This is Oda," Seymour said, leading me toward a pretty young woman with luminous wavy hair. She appeared to be about six months pregnant. "And this is her husband, One."

"*Juan*," said Juan, shaking my hand.

"Uncle Seymour, why are you out here? Why don't you take the customers inside?"

"I was afraid to open the door," he said. "The alarm, it's flashing. I didn't want to set it off."

I went over to the front door to inspect. I had attempted to open the store on Sunday, but when I arrived there was still no electricity. Oddly, Delia's car was no longer parked in our lot, and I couldn't imagine why that was. It was technically possible that it had been towed, but the two brothers we kept on contract had been warned to stay away unless summoned after one particularly aggressive Saturday afternoon when they had removed the cars of four customers who were still inside shopping.

Rattled, I had made the executive decision to stay closed. After using the store phone to call Justin, who had successfully worn me down into agreeing he could spend another night at Mike's, where at least they had power and hot water, I went back home, stared at the pictures on the kitchen floor for a few more minutes, and then spent the entire afternoon reading *The Beautiful and Damned*. I could have been putting photos in scrapbooks, of course, utilizing some of my slightly soggy supplies, but I could not seem to get motivated.

Instead, I had grown obsessed with the plight of Gloria, the heroine, wondering whether she would ever be able to afford the new gray squirrel coat she wanted. Whether she and her husband, Anthony, would ever be released from their endless bloodsucking lawyer bills. I knew what it was like to covet a new winter coat, although personally I would not choose to warm myself with the hides of a bunch of poor dead squirrels and anyway, I was far more resourceful than Gloria when it came to finding ways to pay for things we could not afford. I had read the entire book forgetting to look for references to patio furniture, and when I was finished all I could recall was a hammock. A hammock and a marriage in even worse shape than my own, although notably one that was salvaged in the end by the fortuitous arrival of a large chunk of change. Which was not to say there was a happy ending.

"It's okay, Seymour," I explained, examining the flashing lights. "The alarm just needs to be reset. When the electricity went out it got messed up."

Seymour nodded, but I could tell that he really didn't understand. He'd always been baffled by the alarm, offended by its very presence. We had the system installed after the renovation in order to receive a discount on our insurance policy. Uncle Seymour's preferred version of security might have involved Doberman pinschers, or men in armor stationed around the perimeter of the store, or a moat with alligators. I pushed the reset button and punched in the code and we all entered. It was still stifling inside: the fuse on the air conditioner had probably tripped when the power went out, and various lights were off kilter, the digital clocks all flashing. I busied myself going around the store, setting things right, while Uncle Seymour got straight to business with the customers. Evidently they had had plenty of time to chat in the parking lot, and they headed directly toward the entertainment centers.

"They heard our ad on WZOP, Jane," Seymour shouted to me as they walked by. The couple nodded, confirming this fact.

"I was up being sick last night," Oda stopped to explain. "I was having the bleeding. I thought I was losing this baby, and I was crying, crying, listening to the radio. Then I heard the ad for the entertainment center and a three-piece sectional sofa for only $500 and I thought, Dios Mio! This is a miracle. That is exactly how much money we wanted to spend and never in our dreams did we think we could get so much furniture for so little money! And then I went to tell Juan, and I had stopped bleeding!"

"Thank goodness," I said. "I'm so happy for you." She related this tale with such poignancy that I wondered for a moment whether we could use this as a testimonial on a WZOP infomercial. Kramer's furniture: The Power to Heal.

"I told Oda and One that I'm going to give them an additional discount since they were forced to wait outside for half an hour, okay, Jane?"

I frowned. We needed every last penny, but what could I say? It seemed to be a done deal anyway. The phone rang, but Uncle Seymour was busy with Oda and Juan, and I couldn't bring myself to answer it. The only person I cared to speak to was Justin, but he seemed unlikely to be awake this early—on days that he had no school he'd been known to sleep as late as 1 P.M.—and anyway I planned to drive over to Mike's to wrestle him home later in the day. I had not heard from Leon since Friday night. He had not returned messages left on his cell, and by now I was too furious to want to speak to him. I had spent an entire weekend alone in my house, with plenty of time to concoct fantasies about what he was up to with Delia.

The phone stopped ringing, then began again. Why wasn't the machine picking up? I headed toward the back office to check. On one desk, taking up half of the available surface space, was an archaic answering machine, a big black box that looked like the sort of contraption that might have been used to break codes on Soviet submarines. Various lights were flashing and I studied them, unsure what to do. I hit the "play message" button, doubtful that would really do the trick since the symphony of bleeps suggested something more complex would be required, but in fact the machine's creepy nasal voice informed me that there were ten new messages. Seven of them were collect calls, unable to go through since there was no one there to accept charges. One message was from Jerry Radnor, and although the name was familiar, it took me a few minutes to remember that he was the *Washington!* editor who needed new eyeglasses. He wanted to meet with me as soon as possible to talk about the store and discuss our new line of patio furniture, he said. Could I call him back and arrange a time to meet? I accidentally-on-purpose deleted his message. The next message was from the bank, and I felt an instant seizing up of my intestines. Could I please call Marsha in their security department? There had been an unusual amount of activity on our credit card. *No shit, Marsha.* My husband was off on a romantic tryst; these things can get expensive. This time, I hit the delete button deliberately. There was one last message, this one even worse than the one informing me that my husband was draining our bank account because it was the other person sucking us dry: Chandler Chandling. Urgent. Call him immediately on his cell at the following number.

I hit the delete button again and turned my attention to the computer. Either Justin had failed to turn it off or the erratic power surges had caused it to turn itself on. The screen saver was flashing, an amusing cartoon with talking armchairs that Justin had downloaded from who knows where. When I clicked the mouse, however, a long list of text appeared, evidently the result of a Google search. I saw a bunch of entries all bearing the name of Delia Ryder.

This was horrible. Justin must have been checking her out. I sat down at the desk and began to scroll down the list. This felt like a shameful thing to be doing, and the fact that I knew that everyone else did it, including my son, did not make me feel much better. There was not all that much to be learned about Delia Ryder, however, unless our Delia was a poet from Wales, or a former drum majorette from a marching band in Wichita. There were no Delia Ryders listed who happened to be patio furniture saleswomen from Pittsburgh.

I typed in the name *Andrew Ryder.* I was so intent on my research that I no longer even registered the ringing telephone as anything other than background noise.

Andrew Ryder turned out to be a pretty popular name. Captain of the wrestling team at some high school in Florida, owner of a chain of restaurants in the Midwest, a physician running for Congress in a small town in Maine, an ex-con from Sacramento, California. An ex-con? I scrolled back up to that entry, then slowly linked through to the Sacramento Police Department and the *Sacramento Bee.* Our Internet connection was always sluggish, but it was especially frustrating that morning, almost certainly because of the lingering effects of the storm. Two words of interest kept appearing: check forgery. Granted, check forgery was not quite the same thing as pinching cash from the till, but they were close cousins in the world of crime. There were dozens more entries, but this seemed a sick exercise, and I forced myself to cut it short.

I hadn't noticed until my eye wandered over to the paper tray that an e-mail to Justin was sitting there, as were a few discarded vegan recipes, probably printed out prior to our disastrous dinner Friday night. The e-mail was from his science teacher:

From: Wanda Vondenstaut
To: Justin Kramer
Subject: Science Lecture Notes
Understanding Objects at Rest
1. An object at rest remains at rest because it has inertia.
2. Inertia is the tendency of an object to resist change in motion.

3. To overcome inertia you need to apply some kind of force.
4. The amount of force you need to apply to move an object must be greater than the forces acting to keep the object at rest.
5. Some forces that cause objects at rest to move are: push and pull.

I read this over and over and over, then folded it in quarters and stuck it in my pocket. Later I would put it in my purse with Delia's makeup kit, part of the collection of small treasures I was gathering on this scavenger hunt of a life.

Seymour appeared at the door. He had brought Oda and Juan into the back office in a frank violation of store etiquette. This was like bringing a stranger into your bedroom, inviting him to sit down on the chair where you casually tossed your bra. The back office was meant to be a zone of privacy. Privacy from the public, at least, if not from family members one might occasionally wish to avoid.

"One and Oda just wanted to thank you," Seymour shouted, and I swiveled around in the desk chair, trying my best to be polite.

"No, thank *you*," I said in the saccharine tone reserved exclusively for Kramer's customers.

"This is a very nice thing," said Oda. "I will tell all my friends about this wonderful store. And this wonderful man—you will go to heaven!—giving us a free entertainment center. I cannot believe it. It is a miracle!"

Uncle Seymour looked down at his shoes. "There was a huge scratch on it, Jane, and one of the wheels was off. I thought we'd just have to return it to the manufacturer anyway, and she's going to have a baby and One just lost his job, isn't that right, One?"

Juan nodded shyly.

"Don't worry, Jane. We'll make it up. There will be a huge

rush on entertainment centers, you'll see! Samuel and Leon will never have to know. Isn't that right, Jane?"

"It's fine, Seymour," I said. There was nothing else to say. I stood up to shake hands with Juan and Oda and to wish them good luck with the baby. Then I ushered them to the front door, walking briskly to be sure they did not have time to fall in love with any additional pieces of furniture that Uncle Seymour might feel compelled to give them. Still, I understood his impulse—it was not every day that a customer professed to fall in love with a piece of furniture in our store; it was only natural to want to reward such enthusiasm.

To hear a second customer praise our merchandise on the very same day was disorienting, but just as I said goodbye to Juan and Oda I heard a familiar voice fawning over a console table. "Just look at the price on this! Fifty dollars! I could buy four of these for the price of one at Crate and Barrel. And it's not half-bad, really."

"Five, actually," I said, having done the math myself. "Crate and Barrel sells them for $250. And it's the same manufacturer, believe it or not." Still, I wasn't quite sure how to interpret such glee. Bargain-basement prices were obviously the cornerstone of our business, but I found the numbers embarrassing.

"Shall I ring this up for you, then?" I asked the customer from behind. She had short blond hair and was wearing sunglasses. It took me a minute to place her.

"Tiffany? Is that you? . . . What are you doing here? I like your haircut!" She was quite the chameleon, between her hair and her house.

"I've been trying to call you all weekend. Your phone is out of order. I need to ask you a favor," she said, seeming agitated. "I've got to go out of town."

"Another work emergency?"

"Yes. That same DEA case. I've got to dash off to Houston."

"And you have a Power Scrapping Session you want me to take over?"

"You did such a great job on Friday. Everyone loved you. I'm not just saying that—you sold twice as much as I ever do at one of those sessions, and a couple of people asked for you, especially. I just wondered if you could do it again."

This was flattering, even if I wasn't sure I believed her. "In truth this isn't a great time . . ." I began, but she quickly interrupted.

"Look, just do this one session for me—it's on Wednesday, and I'll do anything. How much more do you need for the cruise?"

"Jeez, about a zillion points. I've sold about $1,200 so far, I think." I didn't bother to explain that out of that, I'd ordered about $500 myself. It was possible that was normal memory consultant behavior, anyway—ordering your own supplies to puff up your sales records.

"I can help you get there more quickly. Sheri Turk, the founder, likes me. She'll help me give you the points you need. I'll call her as soon as I get back. That's how important this is to me. In fact," she said, reaching into her bag and pulling out a notebook and pen, "you can go ahead and log onto the website—www.scrapbookcruise.com—and see which cruise appeals to you. Just use my Memories, Inc. consultant ID number: 056554."

She was an odd fairy godmother, with a cruise at the tip of her wand. I didn't know Tiffany well, and couldn't say for sure, but it seemed like something might have been wrong. "Is everything all right?" I asked.

Instead of answering, she stared over my shoulder. I turned to see Uncle Seymour standing right behind me.

"Jane," he said. "Justin is on the phone. Why don't you go talk to him and let me help this lovely lady."

He then put his hand on Tiffany's shoulder. "Has anyone ever told you that you look just like Lauren Bacall? Except that her hair was longer and she smoked. Do you smoke? I don't mind if you do; I'm just asking. Would you like to take a look at our new entertainment centers? They are on special today. Lowest prices in town."

"Thanks, no," she replied. As I picked up the phone, I saw her politely trying to wriggle free of the arm Seymour had placed around her waist. "But definitely next time," she said.

I heard static; then the line went dead. I tried calling Mike's house again, but no one answered. I was at peak frustration level. With all these sophisticated forms of telecommunications, I seemed to be having an inordinately difficult time actually talking to anyone. Sending a letter on the pony express seemed more reliable.

"Jane, thanks a million." Tiffany said, when I returned. "I really owe you one. Here are the details. Did I mention it's at my house again? Same drill, except you'll need to bring the lunch this time. You don't mind, do you?"

"Hey, doll, are you sure about the entertainment centers?" Seymour asked again, before I could object to the catering request.

"Like I said, maybe next time," Tiffany reiterated, and Seymour smiled, as though he believed her.

12

OVER the past few summers random farm stands have begun
to dot the roads, turning up in church parking lots and at highway exits. Last week someone was selling fresh tomatoes, home-
made rhubarb jam, and sweet corn, six ears for a dollar, in the
parking lot outside Target. A security guard shooed him away—
he said the truck and portable picnic table were hogging parking
spaces. Another enterprising merchant already had pumpkins
on display, although there was something slightly off about their
color.

Driving along River Road toward the Stahls' estate, listening
to the crickets chirp, it was almost possible to pretend that we
lived in the country when in fact we were just minutes from
some of the worst sprawl outside of Los Angeles. This *was* once
the country, of course. Now it was an expensive patch of real
estate carved from the wreckage, obligatory green space on the
urban planner's map, set aside like a nature preserve: *And this is
where the rich people will live. If we paint quaint street signs and leave a
few roads unpaved, they can pretend it is a charming village.*

I turned off the radio and took a deep breath of the swampy
air. My eyes burned from an infusion of ragweed and whatever
else was in full bloom, the second wave of summer allergens,
the ones that always caught me by surprise.

Off to the left I passed a soccer field where Justin had practiced one season when he was in elementary school, the field where a Ford Taurus station wagon once caught on fire. There had been a new boy on the team that fall, memorable not just because his car went up in flames but also because before this incident, his mother used to sit alone in it during the hour-long practice. On a couple of occasions I had considered strolling over to her, identifying myself as a kindred spirit, but that was not the sort of impulse alienated soccer moms tended to act on. She was a sad-looking woman with dark rims under her eyes. She had four little children, including an infant whom she was nursing in her car that day. She had been adjusting her seat, searching for a more comfortable position in which to feed the baby, when the wiring that controlled the seat movement short-circuited. I had been sitting on a bench, reading, when I noticed smoke seeping from her window and ran toward her, shouting. She cleared her brood out of the backseat just in time. Someone with a cell phone called the fire department and within minutes, five fire trucks arrived to douse the vehicle, which by then had actually exploded. We never saw the little boy or his mother again. She didn't return messages inquiring about her son's status on the team, and we remained short a player the rest of the season. Station wagons blowing up on the soccer field seemed to me rich with metaphor about the hidden hazards of suburban life. I went on about this for several days until Leon couldn't stand it anymore. Tauruses were notably crappy cars, he said. There was no hidden symbolism. The only message was to not buy Fords. A message he had apparently forgotten by the following year, when he bought his Explorer.

The driver of the Jeep behind me flashed his lights and honked, and I realized I had just crossed the solid white line on the side of the road. I held up my hand to thank him for the warning. I was only going forty miles per hour, and this was just a little swerve, one that I would have corrected the minute my tires hit gravel. I was a good driver, safe and reliable behind the wheel, the veteran of many a carpool. But how easy it would be to drift off the road, to be lulled by the hypnotic chirping of crickets, or distracted by tomato farmers, to train your eyes on a pot of geraniums on someone's front porch and drive right through their white picket fence while preoccupied, thinking about a certain patio furniture saleswoman. Sometimes it seemed possible that was all my mother had done: she might have been admiring sheep in a pasture, or mentally composing poetry. Maybe all that really happened was she averted her eyes for a split second and took an accidental plunge, one that haunted me, as well as my son, and would hang like a dark cloud over my family for generations to come.

I pulled into the Stahls' long private driveway and parked in front of the middle house. This was where the butler resided and where visitors were meant to be received. The place had the feel of an English manor, or rather, *three* English manors. The ugly aluminum-covered walkways that connected the otherwise elegant structures ruined the desired effect, however, as did the appearance of a disheveled man at the door.

Even though Lord, the butler, was bedraggled-looking, he was still striking with his lively brown eyes and earthy good looks. With multiple loops through his left earlobe, two days' worth of stubble, and blue jeans with holes complemented by a stained T-shirt, he did not look very butler-like.

He stared at me, looking slightly impertinent, eyebrows arched, waiting for an explanation. "I'm Justin's mom," I said. "I want to talk to him . . . He needs to come home . . ." Lord just continued looking at me, inscrutable.

"Oh, right, yes, come on in," he said at last, sounding slightly bored. His accent was exotic and hard to place, vaguely Afro-Caribbean-British. I wasn't sure why he had invited me in, because his next words informed me that my visit was pointless. "I'm afraid they're already gone."

"Gone where?" Almost as soon as I stepped inside there was a loud thud, and the light fixture over our heads began to sway. It was a Prague-style crystal chandelier, the largest size manufactured so far as I knew, with some thirty bulbs, retailing for about $3,000. We had a reproduction at the store that we sold for about $250. It was a China Electrical Corp. special and it looked almost exactly the same, although the quality of the crystal, not to mention the wiring, left much to be desired. There were no follow-up thuds, nor any sounds to suggest that whatever had fallen was capable of righting itself again. Lord excused himself, taking the stairs two at a time and leaving me alone in the lobby. He was gone for a long time and I just stood there, not sure what to do. There was no furniture there to ogle, only a tall wrought-iron stand that held a vase of dead wildflowers, a couple of which had dropped to the floor.

I leaned against the banister on the stairs and began to rummage through my purse, hoping it might contain some sort of potential activity. The only semi-engaging item was the checkbook for the store, and I pulled it out, studying the deposit slip from that morning. I had stopped by the register on the way out just an hour or so earlier, intending to take any excess cash to the bank for deposit as well as check on our change-making ability on the off-chance that a customer with actual legal tender came shopping. While this was rare, it was not completely unheard of. There had been instances of people winning the quick-scratch lottery at the liquor store down the street, for example, then walking directly to Kramer's to buy a bed or a sofa and carrying it right out the front door, tying it on top of a car, or throwing it in the back of a truck. The most recent incident had involved an irate woman in curlers dragging her husband into the store and forcing him to unclench a sweaty fistful of bills in exchange for an area rug and two armchairs while they shouted at one another. There had been other large cash purchases over the years, and there was always something slightly suspect about them. One could only guess that a person walking around with a cache of hundred-dollar bills had either come from the race-track or had just sold a kilo of crack cocaine. One supposed, as well, that anyone with a more sophisticated criminal mind—someone involved in international arms smuggling or running an escort service, even—would be doing his furniture shopping somewhere slightly more upscale. It was an honest transaction on our end, at least: cash for furniture. It was none of our business where the money came from or where the furniture went. Our job was to be prepared should a lucrative cash sale come our way, and for that we simply needed to be able to break large bills, no questions asked.

In the till, however, had been more bad news. No one had walked in with a pile of cash, but someone had walked out with one. We were another $75 short. It was not a huge amount, but it was particularly disturbing because Delia was not around to blame.

"Sorry, didn't mean to leave you standing here like that," Lord said, returning after about fifteen minutes. "Madame just lost her balance again, and I've got to rush into the kitchen. I've got something in the oven."

"Madame?"

"Yeah. If you don't mind, follow me this way . . ." he said, opening one of the side doors. "They don't know if it's an inner ear thing or some sort of seizure thing. Whatever it is, the drinking doesn't help. She won't leave the house to get one of them fancy brain scans they keep wanting to do. The doctor, she comes here, but she can't bring the machine. And Madame won't go out. Now she wants me to get her a bottle of vodka. You don't happen to have one, do you? In your purse, or in your car?"

I tended to have just about one of everything in my bag, but happily I had not yet taken to toting around bottles of alcohol, and I hoped there wasn't something in my manner or appearance that suggested otherwise. "I have Tylenol," I offered.

Lord shook his head. "She's way beyond Tylenol," he said. "Really, she's tried every pill in the book."

"The poor woman!"

"Yeah, if you ask me, which no one does, mind you . . . I think they should just drag her out of here. Either check her into a hospital or throw her into detox. I've been saying that for a couple of years but they tell me to just put up or shut up and hey, the money's good and I'm waiting on my green card."

"So, she never leaves? Ever? Does anyone visit her?"

The butler just shook his head, no. "Mr. Stahl doesn't even go in there anymore. I'm the only one, except for the doctor, once in a while." He continued to lead me through a long, winding corridor. There were pictures of some of Mr. Stahl's achievements on the wall, including several pictures of the famous cloned rat.

"So remind me, what can I do for you?" Lord asked as we neared the end of the passageway.

"I just wanted to talk to Justin, actually. I think it would be best if he came home now. It must be starting to feel like he's moved in here!" I said, embarrassed. "Do you know when they'll be back, or where they went?"

"They're in New York. They left yesterday afternoon."

"That's impossible. I didn't give Justin permission to go . . .

I'm sure he would have called . . ." I felt dizzy. Things seemed to be spiraling out of my control. "He didn't have any clothes, or money," I said, still looking for reasons this might not be true.

"Not to worry. He took some of Mike's things. And Mr. Stahl said he'll just buy him what he needs."

"How could he have just gone off like that? Didn't Mr. Stahl even want to talk to me about this? He didn't have my permission to go," I repeated absurdly. "This is like kidnapping!"

Lord looked at me as if I were a lunatic. "Well actually, Mr. Stahl didn't go," he explained. "He's on his way to London. The boys drove themselves. They took Madame's car. She isn't going anywhere anytime soon. So there was technically no kidnapping involved."

"When will they be back? Do you know where they're staying, or how I can reach them?"

"They're at the Stahls' apartment. I'll have to find the number. I'm not sure where it is. The phone was just installed. I'm not completely certain that it's working yet."

He swung open a pair of French doors that led into an enormous, bright kitchen. A Sub-Zero freezer took up half of one wall; a Viking gas range sat beside it. A giant island in the middle of the room was outfitted in limestone, and another crystal chandelier hung overhead. An entire village could live in this kitchen, I couldn't help but think. There must have been a day when the elephant woman upstairs had planned to cook, or entertain, or at least descend the stairs and admire her culinary empire.

"If they call in, I'll tell Justin that his mum wants to talk to him. You did say you're his mum, right?" he asked.

"Yes, that's right. I'm his mother. Jane Kramer." Of course we had met before, but by now I had stopped expecting people to remember me.

"Yeah, that's what I thought!" said Lord. "You even look

alike." He seemed proud of this observation. He went over to the magnificent range and opened the oven. The smell of something yeasty hung in the air.

I slumped down on a stool, drained of momentum. My son was gone. My husband was gone. Even Delia was gone. Was this mere coincidence, or was I not being quite paranoid *enough*— perhaps the threesome had pre-arranged to meet in New York. Maybe no one had the nerve to tell me that they'd all had their fill of me and my bad attitude about furniture, about life in general. If I was now alone in the world, this lovely kitchen seemed like a good place to be, and Lord a seemingly decent companion. Besides, these dinner preparations were surely wasted on Mrs. Stahl. If she was drinking herself to death and regularly thudding to the floor, it seemed unlikely that she'd have much of an appetite.

"I'm making a vegan loaf," Lord reported. "The boys gave me the recipe. They're on some weird diet. Must be something wrong with them to want to eat stuff like this. This is what they give you in jail as a punishment. It's so heavy you could kill someone with it. I had already prepared it for tonight—I try to get some of the week's menu done ahead of time, but then they took off. I thought maybe I'd eat it, but I've changed my mind."

"Mike's eating this stuff, too?"

"Yeah, just started this week. Don't know what's wrong with him. You Americans are hard to figure out sometimes. Maybe you'd like to take it home with you? Otherwise, I'm just going to toss it."

"Thanks, that's really generous, but I don't think so." Then it occurred to me that I was on my own for dinner, and possibly for every meal for the rest of my life. Here was one less trip to the grocery store. "On second thought, why not? If I can't chew it, I'll use it as a murder weapon!" I was joking, of course, but Lord just stared at me strangely and I knew right away what was running through his head. Black comments like that always seemed to jog their memories. Yeah, *now* he remembered who I was. *Jane Kramer. The woman with bones behind her store.*

As awful as the vegan loaf looked and smelled, it reminded me that I had not yet eaten that day. Leon and I were really quite a pair: he couldn't stop eating, and I couldn't remember to feed myself. I knew I had to get back to the store—*always dutiful,* my tombstone will someday read—but I thought I'd keel over on the sales floor if I didn't stop and ingest something first, and Lord's creation was not quite what I had in mind. I stopped into the Starbucks closest to the store. My head was throbbing and I thought a jolt of caffeine might help.

A lone, wilted salad was all that remained from the lunch hour, but I took it and an iced latte and a newspaper over to a corner table. A young woman next to me had her laptop computer on the table and a stack of books piled high beside her. A man who looked like he was homeless was asleep on a chair, his head resting on the windowsill, a small plastic shopping bag clutched in his lap. I did a double take and realized it was my friend Tom, from the corner.

It was a relief to sit quietly and catch up on the news. I had become so caught up in my own petty problems the last couple of weeks that I hadn't realized the country was in another state of alert. I skimmed three separate stories on the front page about recently intercepted telephone calls, one of which alluded to a threat meant to be carried out that same day. I glanced at my watch. The day was almost over and so far as I knew, nothing unusual had happened. Perhaps there was something to be said for being uninformed.

In other, less dramatic, news, it appeared that the same judge assigned to our barn litigation was also set to rule on the "big box" case later that week. The two national retailers whose building permits had been denied three years earlier had resubmitted their applications. I was two-thirds of my way through the story and expected to run into a mention of our store any sentence, since these articles almost always referred to "The Kramer Blight," when someone tapped me on the shoulder. I had the absurd hope that it was Justin. Instead I saw a middle-aged man with a neat beard holding a tattered briefcase.

"Mrs. Kramer?" he asked. The voice was familiar. I knew I should have been able to place it, but I couldn't quite.

"Hi!" I said, bluffing recognition.

"I've been trying to call you all afternoon, but you were not in your store and your telephone at home has been disconnected."

"It wasn't disconnected," I said defensively. "It was probably just knocked out by the storm."

"We were going to talk about Pablo . . . ," he began, and I suddenly realized who he was, and recalled the whole French-speaking-Spanish-teacher thing. Then I thought in horror that Justin was in New York, and I wondered if his counselor had tracked me down just to catch me in the act of negligent parenting.

"Oh, right, of course," I said, and realized that it was Monday. Not just any Monday, but the particular Monday on which I had failed to visit my son's guidance counselor at one o'clock. He had probably already concluded that Justin's mother was a complete flake, likely the source of the problem altogether.

"It's been quite a day," I said, apologizing. "I tried to call you," I lied, "but as you know, our phone is out. All our phones are out and I'm so sorry, we were having some problems at work and . . . I also lost my cell phone." I said this last part a bit too enthusiastically, but was excited to be saying something that was true.

None of this really explained my failure to keep our appointment, however, a fact which I planned to just basically gloss over by continuing to blather.

"How is Justin doing?" Jean asked, sipping from his coffee cup. "We're expecting him back on Thursday, no?"

"Yes. Thursday." Would he be back from New York by Thursday, I wondered? "He's fine. He's okay, I guess. A little . . . I don't know . . . he's become a vegan, and there's a lot going on in our family right now," I said. None of this was especially shocking, yet it was much more than I'd meant to say.

"Yes, all the boys are becoming vegans this month. Maybe they are learning something in their science class that is disturbing? Not so many girls are not eating meat. I don't know what this is about, but I think it is probably just a phase. It's a rough age," he said kindly. "Especially for boys. But Pablo's a good kid. He'll grow out of all of this."

I could see a tall, striking woman approach from behind as he spoke, and she came up behind him and put her arms around his waist. "Hello, darling," she said, kissing him on the neck, seemingly oblivious to my presence.

"Oh, hi, Louisa," he replied. "This is Pablo's mother. Mrs. Kramer."

"Oh, *Pablo's* mother!" she exclaimed. This couldn't be good, that she knew about Pablo, but it was mildly comforting that they only seemed to know him by his Spanish alias.

"Mrs. Kramer, this is Louisa, my fiancée as of just this morning."

Louisa shook my hand. She was quite beautiful: tall and thin, with the most gorgeous hazel eyes I had ever seen. Her hand sported a small but sparkly diamond ring.

"Please, call me Jane," I said. "And congratulations on your engagement!"

I tried to sound enthusiastic. But really I was envious of this couple's prenuptial élan and cynical about its eventual outcome. I was also mortified that I had entertained even the briefest fantasy that Jean had been flirting with me on the telephone. I felt a flash of heat to my face—humiliation, or the sudden early onset of menopause.

Louisa and Jean both began to stare at something just behind me. It was my homeless friend, now awake, tapping me on the shoulder.

"Oh, hey," I said to him. "How are you doing? Tom, this is Louisa, and this is my son's Spanish teacher, and they have just become engaged!"

"Congratulations!" said Tom. "I used to be married but my wife left me. She kept the house and kids," he said in a monotone.

They all shook hands, Louisa somewhat reluctantly. I felt like quite the social butterfly there at Starbucks. I was no longer the woman sitting alone in the corner. I was the one who knew everyone, and was helping people network.

13

YOUR PHONE has been disconnected. It's a real pain in the
ass. I've been trying to track you down all day."

Chandler's complaints were blanketed by the *whoosh* of traffic
along Rockville Pike. He was perched on the front steps of the
store like a gargoyle, possibly scaring less affluent customers
away with his expensive haircut, his preppy pink shirt, and his
zillion-dollar wristwatch. I couldn't help but think that our legal
bills had helped pay for much of his ensemble.

"The phone isn't disconnected, our service just got knocked
out by the storm," I countered, beginning to wonder if this was
true. I flashed back to that unpaid telephone bill on the dining-
room table.

"That's what I thought at first, but when I tried to call you just
a few minutes ago, there was a recording that said it was *disconnected,* as opposed to *out of service.* There's a difference, you know.
I worked in the legal department of AT&T one summer when I
was in law school."

"Whatever. It's probably just a mistake."

From where I stood, Chandler was centered perfectly under
the awning, the letters KRAMER'S suspended just above his
head. He looked like he was posing for an advertisement, except
that he was all wrong for the part. For better or worse, our customers looked nothing like Chandler Chandling. I had a strange

vision of Chandler as the speck in the old photographs, and wondered if he ever felt trapped. I tried to picture him as some puffed-up version of himself—a Macy's Thanksgiving Day Chandler Chandling balloon floating high above Rockville. But then, he already was a puffed-up version of himself. Plus he didn't strike me as someone struggling to escape this life. He was the guy who knew how to make the most of it, who turned life upside down and shook it for every penny in order to make his time here more amusing.

Chandler dismissed the topic of our phone problems with a shrug of his shoulders and stood up, preening for a moment. He adjusted his tie, checked the point of contact where shirt met trouser, and smoothed his pant legs with his palm.

"Sorry, Jane," he said, "I didn't mean to greet you like that. Let's start over. " He kissed me on the cheek. He smelled of one of those manly colognes I found off-putting.

I led him inside the store, through the showroom, and into an empty office reserved for such meetings. He settled into a chair across from the desk where I stationed myself in an effort to look more authoritative. The sight of Chandler caused an actual burning sensation in my stomach. Of course there were many factors messing with my digestive tract: anxiety about Justin, my missing husband and his bouncy friend, plus that sad-looking salad I'd just eaten along with the coffee swilled too late in the day. And then I felt ill thinking about the check I had forgotten to write Chandler for his monthly retainer fee.

The monthly retainer fee was just one small aspect of the whole problem of Chandler Chandling: he charged us by the hour for every movement that he could claim had anything to do with our case. Even this unscheduled visit to our store was bound to set us back about $300. Last month he'd charged us $60 for his paralegal to make a phone call to the courthouse, then another $40 for her to stand in line at the post office to buy stamps to mail us the bill. I wondered whether some of the miscellaneous charges that showed up from time to time on his statements included the cost of his dry cleaning: clothes worn while working on *City of Rockville v. Kramer's Discount Furniture Depot Corp.,* a case he said would likely be dismissed on the grounds that the demolition permit we had been issued was, in fact, legitimate. Or maybe we were helping purchase and launder the clothes he wore for *State of Maryland v. Leon J. Kramer,* which was the case about the disinterment of bones, presumably the one requiring smarter, more frequently dry-cleaned, attire.

"To what do I owe the pleasure?" I asked. Before he had a chance to answer, Uncle Seymour came into the room and stood just inside the doorway, waving to get my attention.

"Yes, Seymour?" I said. He suddenly looked older and more frail than his seventy years, his eyes rheumy underneath his thick glasses. I was sorry that I had lost my temper with him earlier, after Juan and Oda had left the store. I had scolded him about bringing customers into the back office, and warned him to stop giving the furniture away for free. I presumed the sheepish look on his face meant he had come to inform me of a similar episode, another needy couple whose problems, and those of all their relatives, and perhaps even of their strife-torn countries, would be solved if only their family rooms were outfitted with new pine hutches they could not quite afford.

"There's nothing to do, Jane. I've done everything I could think of. I've vacuumed, I've dusted, I've counted the money in the cash register, I've had a nap. I've . . ."

I cut him off. Chandler didn't really need to know that business was so slow that we sometimes invented ways to stay occupied. "I've got something for you to do," I said, and actually I did. It was a little project I'd been saving for Justin, something to give him a kick, to remind him why it was he needed to do well in school and make a more stimulating life for himself. I excused myself and went into the adjoining office, where I retrieved a list. "Call these people, Seymour, and ask them about their unpaid bills."

Seymour smiled proudly as he turned and left the room. We could hear him read the names as well as the telephone numbers aloud as he walked down the hall.

"Something's come up," Chandler said after Seymour was gone. He had settled into one of the swivel chairs that faced the desk, and I realized in a panic that he had chosen the one with the unsteady back. Or had he? I stared at the two identical chairs and wasn't sure which was which. I hoped he didn't wiggle around too much; I imagined him falling off the chair and breaking his back. Could our own lawyer sue us? *Would* our own lawyer sue us? Of course he would.

Chandler, usually inscrutable, actually looked a bit rattled. His hairline appeared to have receded about an inch since I'd last seen him, which was only a few weeks ago, and he was perspiring through his Brooks Brothers shirt. I'd never found Chandler in any way attractive—he was too prim, too tightly wound, too serious, too close to Leon, and too integral a part of our problems generally—but today he looked almost sexy in his distress. I hadn't noticed until then that Delia had left a white cardigan sweater on the credenza behind where Chandler sat. Just beside the sweater was a pair of Leon's sunglasses. It was a completely meaningless juxtaposition but it irked me nonetheless, and also reminded me of the knick I had possibly made on Delia's now missing car. The knot in my stomach tightened. I tried to imagine what it might be like to have an affair with Chandler, just for revenge. I could leave my sweater by his reading glasses while we rolled around in bed. The fantasy held zero appeal. Perhaps he read my mind, because he realigned himself more prudishly, crossing his legs and folding his hands in his lap. Fortunately this did not require too much shifting of weight in the chair.

"The lab called this morning," he began, clearing his throat. "They found the bones."

"They found the bones?" I repeated in disbelief. This could be good news or it could be bad news, but unless our luck had changed all of a sudden, it was sure to be bad. "Where did they find them?"

"Turns out they were in the back of a squad car. They had slipped under the seat. The lieutenant's wife found them when she was looking for her kid's mitten or something."

"Yuck. How unpleasant." I'd had to stick my hand between seat cushions countless times in search of lost objects and had found myself retrieving all sorts of nasty items, from old bits of food to dirty socks. But I'd never pulled out anything as horrible as a bag of bones. "How could something so important just sort of slip between the seats?"

This was a rhetorical question, of course. Important things slipped between the seats all the time. Just like drivers fell asleep at the wheel, babies were left in hot cars to die, and hunters shot themselves cleaning their guns.

"So what this means is that they will have the final lab results by Wednesday or so," Chandler continued. "I'm just giving you the heads-up. No matter what they find, you can bet the press will be interested, so you might want to prepare some remarks for each possible outcome. In the meantime, I need to see Leon."

"He's not here."

"It's rather urgent, Jane. I need his signature."

"Leon's unavailable," I said. "But it's not really a problem. I can sign his name perfectly. I do it all the time." My eyes fixed on the objects behind his shoulder. *Still Life with Sweater and Sun Glasses.*

"Don't tell me that, Jane. You shouldn't be signing his name. You don't have power of attorney. He needs to sign." He uncrossed his legs and then crossed them in the other direction, shifting in his chair as I cringed, but mercifully it still did not collapse. It must have been the other chair that was broken.

"Well, I do. I sign his name all the time. I've been doing it for seventeen years. What is this we're signing, anyway? Can't you just file for an extension? Since when does the court give such short notice?"

"I admit this is a bit unusual," he said, clearing his throat.

"Well anyway, don't *you* have power of attorney, seeing as you're his attorney?" I wasn't sure how that worked.

"You're making this very difficult, Jane. I'm trying to spare you here . . . but see, the thing is, I don't really need his signature. I need his fingerprints. And a DNA sample. Court orders."

"*Why?* Why now?"

"I don't know, exactly, but now that they've found the bones and they're going forward on these tests, they want to match up some evidence. Another missing persons case just came to light. Young girl went missing a few weeks ago. Turns out she was last seen just a few blocks from here. Leaving Montgomery College, I think. No connection to Leon, of course, except everyone's jumping to conclusions . . ."

"It was a cow!" I protested, almost shouting. "I saw it myself. I know I'm not an expert, but it looked like the jaw of an animal to me. This is crazy . . . And besides, don't they need a warrant, or a subpoena, or something to get his fingerprints and DNA?"

"I'm afraid they've taken care of that already," he said quietly, shrinking back a bit, like he was afraid of me. I wondered where his real allegiance lay just now. Leon and Chandler were still great buddies in a back-slapping, sports-talking, guy sort of way, but they no longer played golf each weekend, and they hadn't gone fishing together in over a year. Perhaps the two of them should have paid closer attention to the advice about not mixing business and friendship.

"You shouldn't forge Leon's signature," he repeated, apropos of nothing. "It's a felony."

"Okay, Chandler. I get it," I snapped. "But that's besides the point. I'm not going to forge his DNA, am I?"

Chandler just stared at me. He scratched his neck, before replying, "It wouldn't really work because of the sex thing . . . I mean, I'm not an expert but I'm guessing his DNA would show up male." His nails left red stripes on his neck.

I stared back at him in disbelief. We paid this guy how much per hour?

"Anyway," he continued, "that's only part of the problem. The other problem is that regardless of the DNA thing and whose- ever goddamned bones those are, Anna Berger's lawyer just informed me that she's about to file a motion seeking repara- tions."

"Reparations for what?"

"For emotional distress stemming from the destruction of the barn."

"She's a therapist! Can't she just heal herself of this 'emo- tional distress?' This is all completely outrageous!" I said, rising from my chair. "The barn was crumbling. Literally crumbling. Termites were eating it. And anyway, it barely even qualified as a barn. It was practically a shack. Just big enough to stick a few horses inside. Anna Berger is causing *me* emotional distress."

"That's not a bad thought, Jane. We could counter-sue on that one. Leon and I had talked about filing for punitive damages. Here's the tough part, though. Anna has hooked up with a national group of historic preservationists. They are exception- ally well funded. They've won a number of similar suits around the country."

"It was a stupid little barn," I whined.

"They're like those animal rights activists," Chandler contin- ued, ignoring me. "In fact, some of them *are* animal rights activists. The president of this chapter was the past president of one of those radical groups that's always liberating animals from slaughterhouses, and they've got some of their membership involved as well."

"Great. Excellent. The thing is, we're broke anyway, so I'm not sure what they think they'll get from us. Maybe some furniture. We can't even afford to pay *you*, never mind them." I hadn't meant to say that last bit.

"Look, I know this sounds ridiculous—it *is* ridiculous—and probably the judge will laugh herself off her bench. But you never know, and we have to take it seriously because on the off-chance that this judge agrees with them, Leon could be in enormous trouble . . . I mean, he could be in enormous trouble anyway. But on the upside, this group has a reputation for filing nuisance suits just to jam up the system. The judge probably knows that. Still, this case is really in the spotlight right now, so we've got to be careful. When can I talk to Leon?"

"Excuse me, Jane?" Seymour asked in such a loud voice that Chandler and I were both startled. He always had trouble getting the volume on his hearing aid right, and was constantly bringing it in for repair. He was leaning against the door frame, holding the sheet of paper I had given him with the names of creditors. I had thought this activity would have kept him occupied for hours, possibly even for a couple of days.

"I'm not having much luck with these people, Jane," he said apologetically. "I'm afraid I'm not really very good at this. Is there something else I can do? Should I take the trash out?"

"That's a great idea, Seymour. Go ahead and take the trash out. And don't worry, you can finish this later."

"No, I'm done. I've gone through the entire list. These first people, Jane, they just can't pay. He lost his job, and his aunt is in the hospital with chest pains. They don't have health insurance, and they don't know what to do. The second people on the list did not speak a single word of English. I don't even know what language they were speaking—but we failed to communicate entirely. The third people, a little kid answered the phone and said her father is in jail and her mother went home to Florida because her grandmother is having surgery. I didn't ask who was watching him, and after I hung up I wondered if I should call back, or call the police or something. The fourth people . . . "

"Okay, thanks, Seymour," I said, cutting him off. "You did a great job. Thanks for trying."

"Great. I'll go take out the trash. Do you know where the extra garbage can liners are, Jane?"

I adored Seymour, but he could be exhausting. "I'll show you when I'm finished with this meeting, Seymour. Why don't you just relax for a while?"

"Don't worry, I'm just about to leave anyway," said Chandler, rising. Fortunately he was firmly planted on his feet when the back of the chair fell to the floor. We all just stopped and stared at it for a minute, but there was nothing to say.

"How's your kid?" Chandler asked as I escorted him to the front door. "I was sorry to hear about his problems. I just wanted to say that if you need me to do anything . . ."

"What problems?" I said lightly, as if we did not have a problem in the world. But what did Chandler know of our private, family problems? "How are *your* kids?" I asked, a cruel diversionary tactic. "I forget, how old are they now?"

"Blair is twelve. Tessa's nine. They live with Debbie. And the new baby. Bill's baby."

"Oh, I didn't realize they had a baby," I said, instantly feeling guilty for having brought this up. Shortly after Debbie had run off with Chandler's former law partner, a ruddy-faced man known to be an avid goose hunter, they had married. They had recently been featured in *Washington!* magazine in a spread on local power couples. (She ran a posh catering service.) In the photograph, Bill had been holding a goose upside down by its feet, and the photo caption said something not terribly witty about him killing game and her serving it for dinner to Washington's elite. The affair had contributed to Chandler's status not as only a divorcé, but as a sole practitioner.

"When I saw that story in the *Gazette* today I thought, poor Leon and Jane. Do they really need more problems? I figured you'd tell me if you needed me to represent you, but maybe you've got some other counsel on this one and hey, that's okay. No offense taken."

"What are you talking about? What story?"

"My God, Jane! You didn't know? Apparently there was some accident last week on Rockville Pike, some woman said she was the victim of a hit and run by two Satanists . . ."

"Oh, that!" I said, relieved. "Just a misunderstanding. But it was in the paper? Why do we need a lawyer? Did she press charges? It was just a fender bender, and the kids said it was her fault. Was there a picture?"

"No picture. Sorry, Jane, didn't mean to alarm you like that. It was actually just a little feature about kids leaving school at lunchtime. It didn't say anything about her pressing charges, I just figured maybe she had, or maybe . . . never mind . . . sorry. So, Jane, I've really got to go," he said, glancing at his watch. "Have Leon give me a call ASAP. And really, don't forget, no more forging!"

He winked at me as he said this, and I had a vision of myself hitting him on the head with the vegan loaf. I think I actually might have had it been within reach, and had our legal problems not been too complicated to contemplate the additional charge of assaulting our own lawyer.

.　　.　　.

It remained quiet in the store until closing, which was both a good thing and a bad thing. Selling furniture was useful as a device for earning money, and money was good for paying bills. But the absence of customers late that afternoon and into the early evening gave me time to catch up on paperwork, and this in turn seemed like a productive thing to do, something to take my mind off all the other bad problems. Besides, Chandler's visit, coupled with the phone bill debacle, were reminders that it was time for money day.

Money day was a close relative of laundry day, but with less chance of realizing an end as satisfying as clean clothes. Unlike the parsing of most domestic chores in our household, which with few exceptions continued to divide along traditional gender lines (except for yard work, which was a task neither one of us performed), we were fairly democratic about this one: the job of paying bills fell to the first one of us to panic, the first one to wake bathed in sweat in the middle of the night, seized by the realization (or really, the *recollection*) that we were hemorrhaging money, and that the moment was drawing near in which we would no longer be able to brush this rather significant problem aside. Soon there would be nothing else: money woes would engulf us completely and we would be buried alive in an avalanche of bounced checks and unpaid bills.

There was also a tacit understanding that whoever was doing the reviewing on any given money day would conclude that the other party was to blame. Me, for overspending generally; Leon, for his delusions of grandeur regarding the furniture trade. On this day, it always seemed obvious that money itself was the mother of all problems, not just in the world, but in our marriage, where the shortage had created emotional conditions akin to famine. Leon and I were undernourished, in a state of advanced marital starvation.

The most urgent problem was the phone. Assuming Chandler was right, which I feared he was, we had reached the critical stage of disconnection. This undoubtedly meant the problem was now compounded, like a cavity ignored so long it required a root canal. In addition to the overdue bill itself, there would likely be penalties: reconnection charges, a calling-in of deposits, the demand for new ones. It would also be more difficult to get through to the phone company given the high volume of calls they would surely be fielding after the storm. I took a deep breath. Sorting out our finances this month would require even more fortitude than usual.

Our main checking account was getting dangerously low. Obviously there were people in far worse shape than we were, people who could not afford to put food on the table. But this did not mitigate the fact that if we continued moving in this direction, we would lose our house in about a year.

Staring at the ledger for half an hour, occasionally using an eraser to shift decimals from one column to another, did nothing to improve the situation. The only way to fix this was to find more numbers to move into the "assets" column, but like unruly children, the integers refused to cooperate. I was not an especially strong numbers person, but I understood that the negative events that keep occurring in the "assets" column were definitely the source of the problem. In the face of monthly expenses like $1,800 electric bills (the store was enormous, a fortune to keep cool, particularly during a summer as hot as this one), my occasional overspending seemed really quite minor: $40 here, $50 there. Little things. Over the course of many years, perhaps, my expenditures might amount to an alarming sum, but month to month they were paltry, particularly when weighed against our two massive mortgages.

I had been trying hard since the embezzlement accusation to be more frugal, but already I had had a couple of small, regrettable shopping incidents. On my way to Tiffany's house on Friday, for example, I had stopped at the bank to deposit a cashier's check. I found a parking spot right in front of the bank, but I didn't have any change to feed the meter. I decided to take my chances. By the time I reached the teller's window some twenty minutes later I was certain there would be a $35 parking ticket on my windshield. Remarkably there was not. With the saved $35, I bought a T-shirt at one of my favorite shops, next door to the bank.

The other incident had occurred earlier that same morning, when most shoppers were still asleep, when even the people whose job it was to calculate credit card debt were probably still at home in bed. It was hard to be abstinent when temptation lurked at every corner, as it had that morning at Safeway. As I tossed my load of items onto the conveyer belt, something caught my eye. Nordstrom's gift cards! What were those doing at the grocery store? How terribly convenient this was if, say, one had a birthday party to attend and had forgotten to get a gift. No more last-minute dash to the mall, no need to apologize for a belated present. Just pop down to the neighborhood Safeway and pick up a gift certificate. And how terribly convenient this was to sneak in just a little bit of off-the-books shopping now and then. What was a $25 gift certificate tacked onto a grocery bill? Who would ever notice? Why not take two? Or four? Surely I'd saved more than that with my careful selection of bonus items, anyway. This was merely my reward for being a frugal shopper.

We could keep ourselves afloat for a while longer with another loan, as Leon had suggested. But this was a terrible solution. The more strategic move might be to go to Vegas and lay what was left of our savings on the craps table. Without some miraculous influx of cash, we were not going to be able to pay our two mortgages much longer, and no matter how many times I sharpened my pencils, I could not seem to land on a pretty solution. Visions of the bailiff showing up and putting a padlock on the front door woke me at night: I could see our furniture set out on the lawn, the once friendly Cubans staring through the window waving *adios,* muttering about how we had turned this otherwise proud street into a ghetto.

Which would be more embarrassing, being thrown out of our house, or having our furniture on public display? I'd heard other people describe bad dreams that had them standing up before crowds, naked. My own nightmares, no matter what the larger context, always involved furniture.

After a while, I made the following unremarkable determination: we needed to do something. Soon. Something drastic. This was not a new realization. We both knew we were on the verge of bankruptcy, but it was the sort of thing you could both know and pretend not to know, at least for a while. Eventually, of course, money problems would become more urgent, because if you no longer had a roof over your head—a place to eat and sleep—debt, like disease, got personal. I knew this, yet still felt strangely detached from the problem.

I found myself wondering how this would end, as though I were watching a movie. What if the people in the movie simply *moved into* the furniture store? There was a time, I reminded myself, when these characters actually found it *romantic* to hang out in the store after hours. I looked around and thought this would solve a lot of their problems and really, the place was so big they could fit quite comfortably. The boy could live in the room they had set aside for baby-sitting back when the husband had visions of becoming the next Ikea. They would have to repaint, however, as the defunct nursery was, in its present state, far too cheerful for him with its primary colors on the walls and the border of ducklings. Then again, perhaps waking up to the sight of little yellow ducklings might cure him of whatever it was he had. Visitors could sleep in the outer office, which would easily accommodate two beds. Jane could live in the back office, the place she was most comfortable, anyway. And Leon. He could sleep out on the sales floor somewhere with Delia, if Jane decided to permit them to stay. And she might, even though it would surely drive her mad, because this might well be a French film, the sort where the heroine pretends not to mind when her husband takes a lover.

But we weren't in a film. We were in financial hell. And a really large influx of money was the only way we'd be able to fix this. The only really large influx of money on the horizon was one that I could earn as a memory consultant, and that was a stretch. I didn't even want to do the math. Maybe I was off to a good start, but it was a far cry from pulling us out of debt. I retrieved the packet of testimonials from the desk drawer and stared at them. What I ought to do is forget about the stupid cruise and set my sights on the bigger prizes—try to be the sort of memory consultant who wins the million-dollar jackpot, then gets the company to pay her mortgage, give her the free car, and an all-expense-paid trip to World Company Headquarters in Salt Lake City.

Still, I couldn't resist turning on the computer to take a quick look at scrapbookcruise.com, where I was greeted with the friendly question, *"Ready to Crop 'n Cruise?"* The page was de-signed to look like a scrapbook itself, one with pictures of a cruise ship. An arrow instructed visitors to click on the words *Scrapping at Sea.* This led to a page offering a choice of several destinations including Mexico, Alaska, Hawaii, and Norway. All of the cruises had activities galore. Dizzying Dazzling Tags! was one workshop on offer. Another was called Sea Treasures, at which one would use shiny objects—beads, sequins, mirrors, and glitter—to create scrapbook pages with style and flair. I wondered if I'd be required to attend these workshops, if there were rules that demanded passengers be friendly and participate in activities for at least a few hours a day.

I needed to stop daydreaming. We were cutting the numbers uncomfortably close. It would have been helpful to know precisely how much money Leon had spent in the last couple of weeks. We did not share this sort of information generally; we just spent and spent and spent until the bank statement arrived at the beginning of the next cycle and then we'd have a fight. It may not have been the best of systems, but it had worked for us for years. Until now, when it suddenly seemed to be failing. I thought for a moment about Justin's tuition, about how much we would save by sending him to public school, where, in my opinion, he would get a perfectly decent education. But given how fragile he seemed just now, switching schools had to be the wrong solution.

The phone rang. It was Marsha again, from Bank of America, calling to verify certain charges to our Visa card. How weird was that? Had she read my mind? I asked her if she had ESP but she didn't understand my question, and seemed to think I was inquiring about a new form of checking. Listening to her read through an itemized list of our credit card charges was like standing in front of the mirror naked. I felt ashamed, although in truth I had not been too bad so far this month. I was guilty of a few inflated grocery store charges, and a check to Tiffany for more supplies, but it turned out it was really Leon who should have felt ashamed. I tried to remain calm when Marsha mentioned that $1,925 had been charged to the Plaza Hotel in New York, as had $7,565 at Tiffany's. Even more baffling: $545 at Niketown. *Niketown?* What was Niketown? I could barely muster an answer when Marsha asked whether the $542.86 charged to Victoria's Secret was legitimate. *Define legitimate,* I wanted to ask.

I needed to stay calm. This was nothing more than data. Just numbers and information. The first thing to do was take care of the most immediate problem. I pulled a random envelope from a thick stack that I had been saving for this very sort of emergency. Inside the envelope was a solicitation for an American Express blue card. That was a new one. I already had a gold card and a corporate silver card, and I used to have a green card. Now there was blue to add to our dazzling kaleidoscope of debt, conveniently pre-approved. All I had to do was dial the number at the bottom of the letter to activate it and God Bless America, within half an hour I had another line of credit and the phone bill was paid off, although it would take two to four days to get it reconnected given the backlog created by the storm.

In the meantime, I resolved to make more aggressive attempts to sell furniture, as well as follow up on Seymour's aborted efforts to call and harass our many overdue creditors. But first, it appeared that I needed to track down my wayward husband and take his credit card away, then haul him in for some swabbing and fingerprinting. After that, perhaps I'd murder him with a quick blow to the head with the deadly vegan loaf.

14

BESIDES the standard fare of sleep sofas, dining-room tables, rustic buffets, and Basque sideboards, the new Crate and Barrel Fall Collection catalog included a smattering of such eclectic items as an autumn berry garland (*a touch of nature for seasonal decorating*), clay roosters, and reproduction prints of Mark Rothko paintings. I wondered what Mark Rothko would make of his inclusion in the Crate and Barrel Fall Collection catalog. Would he be flattered, or might he find it slightly crass to be mass marketed this way? Probably one takes one's posthumous recognition in whatever form it comes.

With all these things to buy to warm the hearth, to distract from the onset of shortened days and dreary weather, the catalog was missing the one thing I was looking for: people. Unlike the Fjorki catalog, there were no people, happy or otherwise, in Crate and Barrel land, although there were occasional signs of life—someone had left a book and reading glasses on the claret chair, and there, by the mahogany Mission bed, were two glasses of wine. On a nearby drum table, a green olive floated apathetically in a martini glass. Cups of coffee were growing cold on just about every page, possibly left to sober up the people who planned to consume these cordials once they returned from wherever it was they had gone.

Although I coveted every stick of furniture, every piece of

stemware in the catalog, it otherwise failed to give me solace. And I needed solace, badly. Buying a train ticket and heading to New York to hunt down my wayward family was without a doubt the craziest thing I'd ever done. I had not slept at all the previous night and was in a daze, but the mental fog was not all bad—it at least took the edge off some otherwise unbearably stark problems.

I pulled another catalog from my overnight bag, consciously avoiding eye contact with the panhandler working Union Station that morning. The waiting area was jammed, and a tanned woman wearing all Lilly Pulitzer asked irritably whether I could move my bag off the adjoining chair so that she could sit down. An announcement was made over the loudspeaker: at 7 A.M. the schedule along the Northeast corridor was already off due to a door malfunction in Philadelphia. In a rare, magnanimous gesture, Amtrak would honor all tickets on the next train to arrive. Depending on which sort of train it was, this could be a small coup for those of us who had bought the cheap seats.

While the woman next to me looked over my shoulder, making me somewhat self-conscious about my low-brow selection of reading material, I leafed through the new Pottery Barn catalog. It featured pretty much the same items as Crate and Barrel, but at cheaper prices. Still, not as cheap as Kramer's. But it wasn't furniture I was after, it was people, and Pottery Barn land was also curiously uninhabited. At nearly 140 pages it contained only one human figure, and she had her back to the camera. This seemed like sheer bad luck, that when I most needed a face from which to draw inspiration—to remind me how to smile and hold my head high amidst endlessly compounding personal problems—I was given, instead, a faceless woman like my mother. This one was sipping from a coffee cup, staring at a clump of trees, and for all we knew she might well have been falling apart herself, weeping hot tears into her steaming mug.

Three more furniture catalogs were stuffed in the side pocket of my bag, but these were not going to sustain me either emotionally or intellectually for the three-and-a-half-hour train ride. A quick glance at my watch confirmed that I had about ten minutes to dash into the newsstand to get something more substantial to read. I offered my catalogs to the tanned woman, and she gratefully accepted.

Once in the shop, I was overwhelmed by the amount of choice. I picked up three paperbacks and surveyed the blurbs on the backs. I had not yet read either *The Divine Secrets of the Ya-Ya Sisterhood* or *The Red Tent* and was beginning to feel this was some sort of moral failing on my part, one that possibly explained why my life was a mess. Oh, if only it was that simple! As if my family might be any less dysfunctional if I had only joined a book group!

I struggled to keep the heavy bag that hung from my shoulder from accidentally knocking into the two men reading on either side of me. The sandy-haired man to my left looked familiar. I stared at him. I definitely knew him. Could he have been a fellow soccer dad? Or one of Justin's teachers? Maybe he was a movie star, one of those character actors whom everyone recognizes but no one can actually identify. But this was Washington D. C.; there were no movie stars or even character actors here—the only famous people were politicians. Perhaps he was a congressman. But he seemed more familiar than that, even though I couldn't place him. I had just about worked up the nerve to tap him on the shoulder when I realized that he was reading a pornographic magazine. Actually, *reading* would be the wrong word, because what he was doing was studying a picture of a naked woman. I looked more closely and saw that she was on the floor on her hands and knees with a collar around her neck, which was attached to a leather leash. Without really meaning to, I took a step toward the magazine. The man turned the page, and what was occurring on the next spread was really unspeakable, particularly given that we were standing at a public newsstand in a train station in our nation's capital very early in the morning. I let out a little noise, a gulp of astonishment, and this must have caused the man to notice me because he suddenly slapped shut the magazine and returned it to the shelf and headed toward the rack of business publications without so much as glancing in my direction.

Another magazine caught my eye as I turned away. There was something peculiar about the woman on the cover, although I couldn't say what it was that seemed so odd. It was probably a magazine for large women, plus-size women, completely commendable for featuring real women on the cover instead of skinny, teenage supermodels. Whatever it was, I would buy it just to show my open-mindedness, to applaud this bold venture in publishing. Yet I couldn't help but observe that this woman was really ugly. Could there be a magazine targeted to very ugly women? That seemed unlikely. I could now see that the magazine was called *Transitions*. A query on the cover asked the following question: *Are you stuck in the wrong life?*

Yes, I am! I silently screamed. I needed this magazine. I reached for it, but it was up high. I stood on my tip-toes, and even though I was wearing high heels, I still couldn't quite get it. A man reading a dominatrix magazine plucked it off the shelf and handed it to me, and I thanked him without making eye contact.

Just as I joined the long line to pay, an announcement was made that the train had arrived. I waited for the line to move, torn. I really needed this magazine, possibly more so than I needed this trip to New York. When a final boarding announcement was made and the line had not visibly moved, I simply turned and walked out with the magazine, pretending to be flustered, checking my watch and my ticket, feigning obliviousness to the fact that I had not actually paid, that I had just become, by definition, a *shoplifter*. A few more billable hours for Chandler Chandling, if I was caught. After walking out of the store I began to run, arriving only seconds before the heavy metal doors shut behind me and the train lurched forward.

I was surprised to see how completely packed the train was this early in the morning on a completely random weekday. Of course this was because of the supposed door malfunction in Philadelphia. I heard someone say that a woman had been trapped, and that she had to be rushed to the hospital with a crushed rib cage when the doors were finally pried open by the fire department. I walked through four cars, my bag occasionally whacking a passenger on the head as I muttered apologies, until I found a vacant seat. This would not have been my first choice: next to the window at a table of four, too close to the smelly, crowded café car, and riding in the backwards position, which was liable to make me ill if I thought about it.

The man in the aisle seat was forced to get up so that I could squeeze in, and while I was not one to read much significance into coincidence in this case I made an exception, because the man next to whom I would be sitting for three-plus hours, unless I was arrested at the next stop or he got off earlier, was the same man who'd been reading the magazine at the newsstand who might have been a congressman. I couldn't help but note how very attractive he was even as I inched away from him and leaned my head on the window, then closed my eyes to feign sleep to avoid having to make small talk. I feared I might blurt out something inappropriate about women on leashes generally not being a good thing.

"It's for work," I thought I heard the man say, but I refused to acknowledge him. I didn't want to talk to anyone, especially not some sexual pervert, and after a few minutes I was lulled into a lovely oblivion by the swaying of the train. I don't know how long I managed to sleep before he shook me awake.

"Look, I know you won't believe me and we both know it's none of your business anyway, but I don't want you to get the wrong impression," he said forcefully. He sounded angry, although a sweet southern drawl took the edge off his words.

I opened my eyes. I knew this man! Who was he?

"Do I know you?" I asked. Outside the window the country-side rolled by: cornfields, ramshackle houses with sheets hung on clotheslines, old barns that had just crossed over to the wrong side of the thin line that separated decrepit from quaint. Ditto for the haggard-looking horses that grazed in the fields and looked as if they had seen better days.

He misinterpreted my question, probably assuming I was try-ing to nip in the bud any conversation. "I'm sorry," he said. "I thought you were someone else." He then opened his newspa-per.

"No, I mean, I am who you think I am. I saw you in the news-stand . . . but it just seemed like we'd met somewhere else, before."

A cell phone rang, and the man sitting catty-corner from me, a balding, pasty, and otherwise nondescript man in a dark suit, fumbled agitatedly in his briefcase and retrieved it. A middle-aged Asian man wearing a golf shirt sat beside him. He held a video camera that was aimed out the window.

"Well I want to explain, regardless," said the man next to me. "I was reading the magazine for work. The woman . . . the one you saw . . . I think you know the one I mean . . . I represent her."

Another cell phone rang. Then another. A woman across the aisle was rescheduling an appointment to have her dog groomed. Someone else was speaking to her kid's teacher about a missing homework assignment. I found this somehow thrilling, all these phones ringing, everyone absorbed in the business of life. I knew that most people found this cell phone clamor annoying, but for those of us who spent our days in mostly silent furniture stores, it was actually quite invigorating. I thought about the opening scene of *The Music Man,* that song where everyone is talking at the same time on the train—*whaddaya talk, whaddaya talk, wahadddaya talk.* And then I remembered that the Music Man was a musical instrument salesman, and heard the man across from me talking about reeds and bows and rosin. Was my life some great Russian novel, full of heavy symbolism, just waiting to be interpreted and then translated into many languages?

I sat up and stared at my seatmate in amusement. "*Represent?*" My eyebrows arched in mock astonishment. "How much does she get for a spread like that? What's your slice? Must be a pretty lucrative business." I couldn't believe I was speaking quite this boldly to a stranger, even if he was somehow familiar.

"You're quite a feisty one, aren't you?" he asked, amused. "Presumptuous, too. I'm her lawyer, actually. Sorry to disappoint you, but I'm neither her agent nor her pimp, which is obviously what you are really driving at."

"I was not thinking anything of the sort," I lied. *Pimp* was exactly what I was thinking, not in a hugely judgmental way, just as a matter of fact. The music man began to stare at us as he held his cell phone to his ear, pretending to be occupied, but quite obviously listening to our conversation. I guessed the word "pimp" had piqued his interest. His seatmate didn't flinch, however, and he continued to point his video camera out the window.

"She's suing a radio station for invasion of privacy," he continued. "They gave her address away on some call-in show. Surely you heard about this. It was in all the papers."

"Invasion of privacy!" This seemed laughable. "Which part of her privacy was invaded, exactly?" As I spoke, batting away more lewd thoughts, something began to click. *Radio station, handsome lawyer, southern accent* . . . "Oh of course. I'm such an idiot. You're Roger Josephs Jr.! We just met, remember, at the WZOP dinner?"

He stiffened and ran his fingers through his hair nervously. "Sure . . ." I was guessing that he had no memory of our meeting, although sadly I had found it quite remarkable; no man had lavished that much attention on me, even if it had been completely insincere, in years.

"Well, that's not the radio station in question," he quickly interjected. "It's DC 95.1. Anyway, I've already said more than I should have. I really can't discuss this with you."

The conductor came by and I reached down to my lap, where I had tucked my ticket inside my magazine. Roger stared at me, which was making me nervous. Not only was this one of the most extensive social interactions I'd had in years, but there was a friskiness to our sparring that had me on edge.

"I had a client once who was a *fa'afafine,* so I get it. I'm cool," he said after the business of punching tickets was finished.

He gestured toward the magazine on my lap.

"What's a *fa'afafine?*"

"You know, a man who dresses up like a woman. In Samoa. It's quite common. Samoans are more broad-minded about these things than you'd expect. Especially given that they have such a macho reputation. My client had issues when he . . . she . . . got to the U.S. He got in trouble at work, using the women's bathroom. He was quite beautiful, really. You look pretty good, too. I hadn't realized at the dinner last week; you really dress up well. But now that I think about it, that was quite a gown you wore! I'm beginning to piece this all together."

"What are you talking about?"

"Transitions."

"What about it?"

"Surely you know what kind of magazine that is?"

"Not really," I said, flipping it open to the table of contents, then quickly realizing what sort of transitions were at issue. There were articles on subjects such as how to disguise beard stubble and catalog shopping for brassieres. It also featured an article on the difference between transsexuals and cross-dressers, and another one on hermaphrodites. So that was what it meant by proposing one might be stuck in the wrong life. They meant stuck in the wrong body, which was probably worse than being stuck in your husband's family furniture store.

"I bought it for the recipes!" I said absurdly, not sure whether *Transitions* even had recipes. "You don't actually think that I look like a man . . . a man dressed as a woman, do you?"

"Whatever," Roger said.

"What do you mean, *whatever*? Do you think you can talk to me like this just because of the magazine sitting on my lap? Or is it just that we've broken down all normal barriers of conversation given your line of work? Or your line of clients, I should say."

"I'm a lawyer. That doesn't usually break down a lot of barriers." The man across from us was eavesdropping intently, no longer even pretending to mind his own business.

"My client is an accountant. Modeling is just her sideline."

"What's the name of the agency that she works for?" the music man asked boldly. I wondered if the video camera had audio capability, and how strange this conversation would be unfolding out of context as footage of Aberdeen, Maryland, rolled across the screen.

Roger shot him an angry look.

"I think I might know her, that's all," he said defensively. "Professionally, of course. I'm just wondering if maybe she's my accountant."

It made me angry to think of this nosy little man entertaining sexual fantasies about his investment advisor. Whoever she was, she deserved better. She probably worked hard, trying to help his assets grow.

"You know, this is actually a private conversation," Roger said. "I need to discuss this here with my friend and colleague . . ." He looked at me, and it seemed to occur to him that he didn't remember my name.

"Jane," I offered. "Jane Kramer."

"Of course. I knew that. Jane Kramer," he repeated. "Jane the Memory Consultant. How are your lovely parents, by the way? How is Esther? She's such a character."

"They're my in-laws," I said, perhaps too emphatically. "And Esther is dead." I had some dim memory of having told him this the last time we met, but I didn't recall having mentioned my sideline in scrapbooking. I must have been the subject of discussion after my inelegant exit from the dinner. This was an alarming thought.

"Right, of course. I'm so sorry. I liked that Esther. She was a real fireball. And Sam, he's quite a sharp businessman. We could all learn a thing or two from him. How goes the world of furniture? That's a great store you've got there. I keep meaning to come in and buy something."

I laughed. I didn't really see that happening.

"Jane, listen, would you do me a quick favor?"

"Possibly," I said, still wary of him and his dirty magazine. "Depends what it is."

"It's a bit complicated to explain right now, but I see someone approaching and, well, would you mind pretending to be with me?"

I looked at him, confused. "Well, I *am* with you, actually."

Before I could protest he grabbed my hand and held it on top of the table, the force of which caused me to fall against him, my head landing on his shoulder. With my neck slightly twisted, it was not an entirely convincing position. Just then a young woman appeared at his side. Roger pretended not to notice her at first. He was saying something incomprehensible to me about planning our Christmas vacation to Capetown and asking whether I had confirmed the flights.

"Capetown?" I asked. "Wow! It's really gorgeous there."

He didn't reply. He moved even closer and I feared he was going to kiss me, but instead he picked up *Transitions* and flipped it over on my lap. The model on the back cover was not much more attractive than the one on the front—it looked like a Marine drill sergeant wearing fishnet pantyhose and a polka-dot dress.

"Roger?" a sweet-sounding voice asked. "Roger! I thought that was you. I haven't seen you in like, a hundred thousand years?"

"Hello?" he replied, cruelly.

"I'm Chloe?" she said. "We met in court?" I wondered what had transpired between the two of them to cause this conversation to take place in question form.

"Of course, Chloe whom I met in court. This is my, er . . . wife. Jane? Jane, this is Chloe . . . whom I met in court?" He began to twist my wedding ring around on my finger, pausing to admire the diamond inset as though he had picked it out himself. I was tempted to take it off and fling it out the window in some sort of double act of defiance. I was not married to this man, and the man to whom I *was* married had literally outgrown his own wedding band. How symbolic was that? He'd had it removed by a medical professional and never bothered to replace it. Now he had run off with a patio furniture saleswoman. So why did I continue to wear my own ring? A bad habit.

"Hi, Chloe," I said politely. I wasn't sure I really wanted to play this game, to be an accomplice in helping Roger extricate himself from whatever mess he'd gotten himself into with this too-young girl.

Chloe, a cute thing with short, cropped hair and a large crucifix around her neck that looked more like a fashion statement than an indication of any real religious preference, blushed. She couldn't stumble away quickly enough, and she tripped on her high platform sandals, then landed in a seat occupied by an elderly woman when the train suddenly swayed. "Bye, um, Mrs. Josephs," she said as she righted herself. "Nice to meet you."

"Pleasure," I said, and then I turned and glared at Roger as if I was truly an aggrieved spouse. "You've got quite a complicated little life."

"So do you," he said, picking the magazine up off my lap and opening it to a random page, from which he began to read aloud from an article entitled: "My Husband Is the Other Woman: A First Person Account":

"For years I thought my husband was having an affair. I'd find lipstick smudges on his clothes, strands of long dark hair in his car, charges from women's boutiques on our American Express bill. When I'd ask him about these, I'd hear nothing but denials. And then, one day when I was putting the laundry away, I noticed a bra underneath his boxers . . ."

"Okay, okay, okay! Enough," I pleaded. "I told you, I bought it for the recipes."

"It's not what you think," he said.

"What's not what I think?"

"Chloe."

"Of course not. It never is what you think. Let me guess—she's a client? Her privacy has been invaded?"

"You really have the wrong impression of me. I can see this is going to take a lot of work to turn you around."

"More work than usual?"

"There is no usual, you know. Chloe is an aberration. I don't really want to get into it. It was poor judgment. Jesus Christ, here she comes again . . ."

Roger leaned over and grabbed my hand again, which struck me as preposterous. I couldn't imagine there was a married couple in the world, not even one on their honeymoon, that would be sitting on a train holding hands. But then I remembered a train trip through England four years after we were married, when I had let my head rest on Leon's shoulder as we sat close, watching the English countryside roll by. Another passenger had brought a cat in a carrying case into our compartment, causing Leon to sneeze throughout much of the trip. The week had been romantic in its own way, marred only by the occasional phone call home to the martyred, baby-sitting Esther, who reported in too much detail Justin's every spoonful of cereal and consequent bowel movement. She also helpfully identified several flaws in both my housekeeping and child-rearing techniques.

Chloe passed by again and glared at Roger, but she kept going this time, wobbling a bit as she held a steaming cup of hot coffee without a lid. I hoped the train didn't do any more sudden lurching or some unwitting stranger was going to bear physical scars from Roger's sordid little affair.

"What are you going to do in New York, anyway?" Roger asked, letting go of my hand after she'd passed. "Let me guess. Something to do with your memory job."

"No, actually . . ."

"Something to do with furniture. Or no . . . something to do with drag queens . . ." He said this last bit like he was proud of himself for being so witty.

"Yes, that's more like it. The second thing."

"Wait, which was the second thing? Furniture, or drag queens?"

I shrugged my shoulders, not inclined to try and explain that I found his question to be obnoxious and that this supposed joke was stirring up disturbing thoughts of Andrew Ryder.

"Where do you stay in New York?" he asked, mercifully changing the subject.

I liked the way he phrased this question. It suggested that I was the sort of person who stayed in New York frequently. Who left her minivan behind to go somewhere, sometimes, besides the grocery store. Already I felt like I had pulled off some miraculous feat just by getting on this train, possibly even tricking people into thinking I was something other than a sub-clinically depressed hausfrau. I had dressed carefully, putting on my best black skirt and a tweed blazer, stockings, and shoes with high heels. I had even taken time to blow-dry my hair, and had then paused to apply Delia's lipstick, a shade to which I had become quite attached despite her admonition that it was not my color. Really I had begun to think that was precisely *why* I had become fond of it—it was not my color, and since I did not want to be me, Merry Mango *was* the right color. I had evidently been successful in my grooming if this handsome man sitting next to me mistook me for a person with a life. But then, this same nice-smelling man also seemed to think I might be a man in drag, which wasn't the effect I'd been aiming for.

"I thought I'd just wing it this time," I told Roger. "I've got some business at the Plaza this afternoon, but I might finish up in time to go home tonight. I brought a change of clothes just in case." This was not entirely true. I'd brought enough clothes to last a week, although we couldn't afford the expense and I needed to get back to the store.

It all depended on whether I could find Justin. Lord's information turned out to be sketchy at best. He'd given me a Manhattan phone number, but no one answered. I'd pleaded with him for an address and he kept promising to come up with one, but never did. I had called him four times, and tried everything from shouting to crying a pathetic mother's tears, but he was impervious. He said he couldn't find the address, couldn't reach Mr. Stahl, but he'd keep trying. All he knew was that the boys were somewhere in the West Village.

"And you? Where do *you* stay?" I asked.

"Me? I've got the keys to my sister's apartment in SoHo. She's in L.A. for a week."

"How convenient. Nice of her to let you stay there."

"I got her the apartment as part of her divorce settlement. I represented her. I wanted to get the apartment in Paris and the boat and cars, but all she wanted was custody of the kids and the New York apartment. Pity, eh? He was such a two-timing schmuck, it was a piece of cake."

"Really?" I asked, suddenly interested in Roger Josephs Jr. for reasons that went beyond his good looks. "I didn't realize you handled divorces." Considering the circumstances, divorce court could well be where I was headed, regardless of what it was that I really wanted.

"There's nothing I can't handle," he said with a cocky grin. He was unbelievably full of himself, yet there was something attractive about his confidence.

"Would you like to see it? It's really nice."

"What is?"

"The apartment. You could come up for a drink tonight. Say, about seven?"

I didn't know what to say, but the glimpse of Chloe waddling by on her crazy platform shoes again made me pretty sure I should say "no." Yet I wanted to say "yes," even though I wasn't completely sure what the attraction was, and what my own motivations were. Was it simply that he was not Leon? That in just the brief glimpse I'd had of him, he actually seemed the anti-Leon? But he was not really the anti-Leon, because it was already clear that while Roger Josephs Jr. was charming and successful and did not clutter sentences with the word "fuck," he came with his own set of complications. I speculated that the attraction had more to do with what *he* saw in *me*. He thought I was someone other than the boring person I had become. He saw me as the anti-Jane. That was probably the most seductive thing of all.

"You should see the furniture," he said.

"What furniture?"

"My sister's furniture. She's a decorator, and her furniture is spectacular. Come up and see it. She's just commissioned a few new pieces, all really weird stuff. It's from Norway. Or maybe Sweden."

"Maybe Iceland? Is it Fjorki?" I asked, excitedly.

"It could be. That sounds familiar, but I'm not sure of the name. In truth I don't much like it, but it's very trendy. I'm a conventional guy at heart, I guess, or at least I am when it comes to furniture." He handed me his card, and on the back he scribbled an address. "Seven o'clock, then?" he asked.

"I don't know, I'm just not sure if I can make it," I replied. But I was already justifying a visit to the apartment on business terms. I needed to see this Fjorki stuff. Plus SoHo was near the West Village, so I might accidentally pass his sister's apartment while wandering around downtown aimlessly, searching for my son.

"Great, then. I'll be waiting."

"I'll try, but really, I just don't know how this day will turn out."

"I'd really like it if you came. I have some things I'd like to talk to you about. I kind of feel like I need to have my memory consulted . . . I mean, nothing heavy or anything, but there's a few issues . . ."

"Look, I'm not a therapist. It's not like that . . . And I don't help people remember things they've forgotten, either. It's completely different . . ."

"I'll pay you whatever your going rate is."

"Seriously, that's not what I do. I don't think I can really help you."

"Don't worry. I think you can. And anyway, it will be fun. I'll make us some sort of colorful drinks. My sister has a blender."

I didn't say anything, nor did the man with the video camera. He continued to point it out the window into the darkness of Pennsylvania Station. He was still sitting, filming, as I left the train.

15

THE KEY words "Plaza Hotel" must have stimulated brain cells, dredging up bits of useless information. Sitting on a park bench, working up the nerve to walk across the street and actually *enter* the Plaza Hotel, I thought of Jordan Baker in one of my favorite scenes from *The Great Gatsby*. "I love New York on summer afternoons when everyone's away," she says. "There's something very sensuous about it—overripe, as if all sorts of funny fruits were going to fall into your hands." The characters are lolling around Tom and Daisy's house, where lacy white curtains billow in the wake of the fan while they complain about the weather. They are bored in only the way the idle rich can be bored; that is, people without household chores to perform, people with gardeners. The heat, the malaise, the tension, are all palpable. "What'll we do with ourselves this afternoon . . . and the day after that, and the next thirty years?" Daisy whines. The answer is, go to New York and hang out at the Plaza Hotel.

At this stage in life, Leon and I had more in common with Homer and Marge Simpson than with any of these posh characters. In my mind's eye, I did not see Leon sitting in an elegant armchair sipping cocktails and wearing a dapper suit, but rather propped up in bed in his underwear, his whites not quite white enough, his T-shirt fraying with age. In fact I imagined him actually *watching* the Simpsons, drinking beer from a can and laughing too loudly. There was a name for that now, for the idea of Homer Simpson drinking a beer watching Homer Simpson drinking a beer. Meta, they called it. They had a word for everything these days, except perhaps for the way I felt, so full of conflicting emotions, clashing motivations, and ill-defined desires. Surely Leon would disagree. "Fucked up," he would say, a pithy little phrase that summed it all up, useful for many different occasions. But of course that was *two* words, so I would argue that it didn't really count.

"Sensuous" had definitely not been the first word to leap to mind in the steamy subway station, although there was certainly a preponderance of overripe funny fruits, mostly of the sort I did not want to contemplate. It was still technically summer, but the city itself was in full September swing. As a consequence I was unable to hail a cab. The line that formed outside Pennsylvania Station was about thirty people deep, and I was too impatient to wait. I was also anxious to cease conversing with Roger Josephs Jr., from whom I was having trouble separating in part because Chloe was trailing him. I felt a tad sorry for Roger. Chloe was clearly more than he had bargained for. She seemed borderline psychotic, the sort of woman who, when spurned, would not stop at stalking. She would slash his tires, or stick a garden hose through his mailslot and turn on the water. Or maybe I was overdramatizing, possibly even projecting how I might behave should I be foolish enough to go down that path with the man.

I crossed over to Ninth Avenue in an effort to get away from them both, and realized I was walking in the wrong direction. Roger tried to point me the other way, calling me "dear" as he shouted across the street, but I was too embarrassed to acknowledge my error.

"See you at seven, then, darling," he shouted anyway. Chloe

stood a few feet from him. I could sense her fury intensifying even from a distance.

By the time I had circled as far as Hell's Kitchen, my feet were blistered from my heels, which were only marginally less ridiculous than Chloe's. Another problem was that the strap of my bag was cutting into my shoulder and my arm was beginning to tingle. My hair was damp with sweat and I had a long run in my stockings. It seemed grossly unfair that the one city in America where a woman wants to look fashionable is the one that most appropriately lends itself to hiking gear. In desperation, I finally asked someone to point me toward the subway. I ducked into the next station and bought a Metro Card, but my bag snared on the turnstile as I pushed through, and a hot blade of pain seared through my shoulder. By the time I'd walked across town and reached the Plaza Hotel I felt, and looked, as if I'd been beat up.

I collapsed on a bench across the street from the hotel and wiped away someone's half-eaten hot dog and a few pigeon droppings. The air was sticky and oppressive, pungent with horse manure. Sitting there for any great length of time did not seem likely to restore my equilibrium, and yet there was no place else I wished to be. I was losing my will. I had no desire to pursue the task that had brought me here, and now I wondered why I had come at all. What had I been thinking? What sort of outcome, happy or otherwise, could I have imagined there might be?

It had been rash of me to pack a bag and get on a train, and completely out of character. But after the front desk at the Plaza confirmed that Leon Kramer had indeed signed for the room, I had been too angry to sit around and await his return. I needed to find him to tell him about the bones, to inform him that there were now official demands for his DNA, but that was just an excuse. The point of my visit was to swing open the door to their Plaza suite and find Leon and Delia together so that I could . . . what? What, indeed?

And did I seriously think I would find my son by wandering aimlessly through the West Village? Of course not. Yet I couldn't sit home, waiting.

I sat on my bench, hungry and thirsty and exhausted. I could not will myself to move. I thought of the e-mail from Justin's science teacher: *Inertia is the tendency of an object to resist change in motion.* Jane Kramer on a park bench. An object at rest, like a piece of performance art. I was very good at this. Soon pigeons would come and perch on my shoulders. Perhaps this was the very state of mind that turned otherwise functional people into vagrants. Maybe half the homeless people in New York had simply paused on a bench midday to ponder a problem or two (bones beneath their barns, sluggish retail sector, etc.) and then, unable to find a solution, never got up again.

A group of tourists alit from a bus with Indiana license plates and swarmed the hawkers selling replicas of the World Trade Center and NYFD T-shirts. Two young mothers walked past, pushing strollers that looked like little SUVs, and I stared at them wistfully. Their children looked so sweet with their chubby cheeks, brightly colored toys hanging from the awnings. It wasn't that long ago I'd been pushing a stroller, getting stuck in doorways and knocking things off shelves in the supermarket. Had I been as young as these women? It seemed impossible.

Three separate carriage drivers approached to see whether I wanted a horse-and-buggy ride through the park, and each time I shook my head, "no." By the time the next one approached, breaking my otherwise enjoyable reverie of baby gazing, I snapped at him, which did the trick so effectively that I could only presume the hansoms had no desire to deal with contentious American women, and that until I opened my mouth they thought that I was a foreign tourist, one from a less affluent country where women routinely wore torn nylons, perhaps.

Inertia bred inertia. I wasn't sure if that was really another law of physics, but the longer I sat, the less inclined I was to go looking for missing family members. It was easy to get caught up in the rhythms of the city, even the annoying ones like the carriage drivers. I was tempted to forget my mission and just have a pleasant day on my own. I could buy a pair of walking shoes and go to a museum, or take a long walk through the park, maybe even see a play. New York had always felt forbidden, in part because Leon and I had been unable to find our way back here after a promising start so many years ago. But also because my father had always condemned it as a place of conspicuous consumption. I remembered visiting this same spot with him as a child once to engage in a protest. I don't recall the issue of the day, what we had chanted, or what was written on our signs. His work had been practical and secular. He had not been a missionary, he did not have strongly held political beliefs, but he had a fanatical streak all the same, as well as a host of unresolved issues, not the least of which involved being married to my mother.

After about thirty minutes of further procrastination, I made a bargain with myself. If I followed through with my mission I could go to Bloomingdale's and charge one hundred dollars on my new blue Amex. This did not include the purchase of shoes, which at this point really counted as more of a necessity than a luxury. There was something admittedly pathetic about needing to motivate myself with bribes at this stage of life, but I found it worked, and within minutes I had crossed Central Park South and was standing at the entrance to the Plaza Hotel.

I took a deep breath and paused to pull my hair back into a ponytail before making my way across the elegant lobby to the registration desk, where I planted myself before an intimidating blond clerk with otherworldly cheekbones. I had not really thought this through to its logical extreme, but forged ahead all the same.

"Good morning," I said purposefully. "My husband already checked in and I'm meeting him here. He said he'd leave a key at the desk for me."

She looked nonplussed. "Let me just see, Madame." She began to tap at her keyboard for at least two minutes, which seemed curious given that I had not yet provided her with any useful information. Fidgety, I took the elastic out of my hair and then put it back in again. Without looking up, she finally asked the obvious next question: "Name?"

"Kramer," I replied. "Leon Kramer . . . my husband, that is. I'm his wife. Jane. Jane Kramer. He had a meeting yesterday and I just came up from Washington; I'm supposed to meet him here because we have a dinner to go to tonight and I couldn't come until now because we didn't have . . . a baby-sitter." Why did I blather on like this? It only made me sound suspicious, when, in fact, this was not a *complete* lie. I *was* his wife.

She stopped typing and stared at me for a minute as if to say that this was about ten times more than she needed to know. "There's no note in the system," she said instead.

"What does that mean?"

"It means that typically when one guest wishes to have another guest let into a room we make a note of that and post it to our system. Your husband has not left a note. Have you tried ringing the room? Perhaps he is still in, which is why he has not left a note."

"Good idea," I replied even though this did not strike me as a very good idea. I had been trying to call him for twenty-four hours. If he had once answered the phone, or responded to a single one of my messages, I would not have bothered to come hunt him down in the first place.

"Can you ring the room for me?" I asked in the sweetest tone I could muster.

She looked back at me, still without expression. This was probably something she had learned at hotel training school under the heading of "pass no judgment." My request, regardless of the squirming that accompanied it, was probably one of the more benign things she was asked to do on any given day. She picked up the phone and dialed.

"Good morning, Mr. Kramer," she said.

I tried to hide my astonishment. He was in the room, answering the phone? This I had not expected. I thought I detected the slightest rolling of eyes above the stunning cheekbones, as if she was constantly forced to waste her time dealing with people like me who could not ever get their information straight. "Your wife is in the lobby," she said. Then, after a brief silence, "Very well, sir. Thank you."

"He said you should come up," she informed me, and before I could ask the next question, she spoke again. "Room 814." Then she smiled, displaying two rows of perfect white teeth, and returned to typing something into the computer screen. "Hang on!" she called as I began to turn away. "I need to see your ID."

"Of course." I fished my driver's license out of my wallet. She looked at it, looked at her computer screen again, then looked at me before nodding and handing the piece of laminated plastic back. I felt smugly satisfied at having passed this test, as if something more exciting had just happened than being confirmed to be myself.

My heart was racing at the prospect of what I was about to do, and I stood in the lobby for a few minutes, trying to collect myself, taking deep breaths. Cleansing breaths, they used to call

them in Lamaze class. Leon had come with me to those weekly
sessions, back in the days when we were in this together. Back in
the days when it was inconceivable that I might one day come to
hunt him down like a deranged wife, like a thwarted lover, like a
Chloe.

I watched as groups of busy people, including a Japanese del-
egation of some sort, came and went. A bunch of tourists
arrived, all wearing identical yellow T-shirts identifying them as
being from Sonoma, California, sponsored by, or possibly
employees of, a lumber company. I wished I could join them. I
imagined myself slipping into one of their yellow T-shirts and
climbing aboard their bus.

What was I playing at? This was wholly undignified. I was a
middle-aged woman, not Harriet the Spy. I had scraped myself
off the park bench only to go limp again in the lobby, but this
might have been a protective biological response, because probably the only sensible thing to do was to abort this mission now,
before I made a fool of myself. And yet I was already there, just
a few floors below my husband, and I had some legitimate, truly
urgent business. He had to stop charging things to our credit
card immediately; our lawyer needed his DNA; and our son was
missing. All I would do was knock on his door and deliver this
information. I took a step toward the elevator. I was still certain
that fate, or at least hotel security, would intervene.

Either no one really cared who roamed the hallways at the
Plaza, or I looked like I belonged, my shabby appearance
notwithstanding. I was practically sick with dread by the time I
reached Room 814. I set my bag down on the floor and stared at
the door for a minute, wary of the *Do Not Disturb* sign that hung
from the knob. I knocked hesitantly, but there was no answer. I
could hear the television on too loud. It was set to the sort of
earsplitting volume you might select if you wanted to camou-
flage other sounds, ones of the sort I preferred not to think

about. I knocked again, but knew no one would ever hear me given the blare from inside. I then kicked the door a few times with the heel of my shoe, still to no avail. I took my shoes off and left them outside the door like a bitch marking her territory and wandered down the hallway, looking for a maid to let me in. Predictably the maid was not authorized to grant me access, although she did make a phone call back down to the icy blonde, who must have radioed a security man, who arrived to find me sitting cross-legged on the floor, leaning against the door of Room 814, reading a magazine about cross-dressers that did not contain recipes. He checked my ID again and eyed me suspiciously before producing a pass key.

"Turn that noise down," he warned. "Someone is going to complain."

"Sorry! My husband is hard of hearing," I lied. Given the sorts of lies I'd been telling lately, this didn't feel like a big one, especially given that Seymour's deafness might have been genetic.

I stepped into the room and quickly shut the door, then raced to the television to adjust the volume. I couldn't quite believe I had pulled this off, even though, looking around the room, I had no idea what I had really accomplished. Where was Leon? I called his name, spooked. He had been in the room just a short time ago since he had answered the phone, but he was obviously not here now. An inspection of the closet and shower stall confirmed that he was not hiding.

Still, the room had the definite feel of having recently been inhabited. The bathroom mirror was foggy from a shower, and a room-service tray sat on the table. The coffee in the pitcher was still lukewarm. I sat down on the edge of the unmade bed and ate what was left of a croissant, staring at the television screen, which was tuned to some post–*Today Show* program. A group of women was sitting around a table talking about infertility. One of them was crying. She felt like a failure as a human being, she said, unable to perform this most basic human function: reproduction. Another woman nodded her head and she, too, began to cry. I reached into the breadbasket on the tray and pulled out a roll, then dug around for a knife and smeared it with a pat of butter. I wondered if I could still get pregnant. It was not impossible. Maybe that was all that was wrong with me and Leon: we needed more children. Why not have another baby? We had not deliberately decided to stop at one, but a second was not forthcoming and we had tacitly chosen to accept our fate. But these days anything was possible, and I was not *that* old. I imagined myself in my late fifties, attending back-to-school night, unable to climb to the third floor of the building that housed the high school. I'd seen these parents before and had privately laughed at them, huffing and puffing their way up the stairway, a few of them even leaning on canes. But now I understood where they were coming from, trying to ensure that their senior years would not be lonely.

The thought was like a slap in the face, and I set my roll down and turned off the television. The room was a mess, and I considered taking the sign off the door to invite in the maid. Thrown in the corner were a bunch of empty shopping bags, among them the signature robin's-egg-blue bag from Tiffany's, a larger bag from Niketown, and nearly a dozen other bags of various shapes and sizes from a wide variety of stores. Price tags lay on the floor, receipts were balled up and lying by the side of the trash can, obviously having missed the mark as someone tossed them carelessly toward the bin. I went over and picked up a scrap of paper. On it was the name of a manufacturer in Weehawken, New Jersey. *Wicker Wholesalers. Larry Hampden, mgr. Last exit before the Lincoln Tunnel, on the right, across from Denny's.* All of this was written in Leon's nearly illegible hand, which I had learned to decode after all these years.

The bed was unmade and wet towels were lying on the floor.

There were no clothes hanging in the closet, no sign of any luggage. In the bathroom, a couple of complimentary hotel toothbrushes sat by the sink, and I wondered whether one could scrape a DNA sample from the bristles. I picked them both up and held them at arm's length. They were still wet and caked with bits of toothpaste. I wrapped them in the plastic shower cap and stuck them in my bag.

I continued to scour the room. I found a cardboard tube, the remnant of a tampon, in the trash can. So much for my unthinkable theory about Delia. I dug around some more and found, to my absolute horror, a condom. Then I felt truly ill.

There was only one reason to have a condom that I was aware of. I held it up to the light. It was blue and ribbed and disgustingly sticky. Here was a DNA sample, for sure. I stuck it inside the shower cap with the toothbrushes. More souvenirs for the scavenger-hunt game of life. It occurred to me belatedly that I probably should have wrapped them separately. Now there would be saliva in the semen, or semen in the saliva, and then I realized that there might be anyway, which did little to improve my overall state of mind. I felt a slow seepage of energy, like someone had just pulled my plug.

Why had I done this to myself? The effect of this knowledge was so powerful, so confusing, so demoralizing, that I just wanted to cease thinking.

I pulled the curtains shut, turned off the light, and crawled into the bed. As I lay there I tried to get a whiff of Leon on the sheets, but I could not. What I got was a different smell, an unfamiliar blend of fragrances. When had I lost track of his scent? He used to smell a bit like furniture, really, a masculine scent that reminded me of leather armchairs. This seemed to me a terribly sad thing, that I didn't know how he smelled anymore. Had I simply grown so used to him that I'd stopped noticing? Or had we blended together aromatically? Maybe I, too, smelled like furniture, and that was why I could no longer distinguish our bouquets.

Now I couldn't recall the last time I had taken him in fully, had inhaled him without letting something—some critical observation about one little thing or another—cloud my senses.

16

PREPARATIONS to kick me out seemed to be moving into high gear, so I decided to cut my losses and leave before learning what mechanisms were employed at a fancy hotel for the removal of obstinate guests. By 4 P.M., I had been twice awakened by a man at the front desk with a snooty British accent, who called to advise me that it was well past checkout time and the room had only been paid for through that morning. The first time he called, I told him that I wished to keep the room for one more night. I had fallen into a delicious sleep, punctuated by a memorable flying dream that had me working as a CIA operative, gliding over Rockville Pike on some sort of reconnaissance mission. Anna Berger was gliding behind me, asking pointed questions about my mother. Then I got tangled like a kite in some tree branches behind the store. When I awoke and thought about it, I recalled that that particular tree, an enormous old oak that Justin used to climb, had been torn down to make way for the renovation.

The second time the man with the snooty British accent called, I was informed that the credit card on file would not go through. His accent seemed to grow a shade more pretentious with the delivery of this information. This should have been my first clue, but I was too groggy to grasp the significance. When he called yet again to say that my other credit card, the new blue

Amex, would not process, either, I began to see where he was going with this.

"Declined," I believe was the word he selected, a nice euphemism for "rejected," but it stung nonetheless.

This was not the first time in my life a credit card had been pronounced dead, which was why my policy was to have many lines of credit, an endless font of funds. Still, according to my quick mental calculations, neither one of those cards ought to have been refused. The one that Leon used to pay for the room drew directly off our main account. Even if we had drained all of our available cash flow, which seemed unlikely—his recent extravagances notwithstanding—there were supposed to be reserves in place to guard against this sort of thing. This was troubling and inconvenient, but I was not particularly worried. It was probably the hotel's mistake. Or maybe they were overbooked, and management just wanted us to go away. Whatever the reason, it didn't really matter—I had another credit card in my wallet, but I'd be damned if I was going to give the Plaza any more of my business after the way they had treated me.

I moved slowly, stepping into the shower, planning to fully exploit all available hotel amenities before leaving. The way my life was headed, who knew the next time I'd be able to groom in such luxurious surroundings? After bathing, I doused myself with complimentary moisturizer and wrapped myself in the soft terry-cloth robe while I dried my hair. I sat at the table with the room-service tray and ate every last morsel of the continental breakfast. I even drank the cold coffee in the thermos. I felt a small wave of panic—surely this could not be happening, *any* of this—but a glance inside my bag confirmed that the existence of the blue condom was no fantasy.

I didn't know what I was playing at. I was not going to find Justin without an address and anyway, I didn't really think that he was running away so much as skirting the issue of parental permission. He'd come home, probably even in time for school on Thursday, and when he did, what he would need was a sense of normalcy. This meant that I ought to go back and at least pretend to be a stable parent.

When there were no further resources to drain in the hotel room, I checked the schedule in my pocket and decided I would return on the six o'clock train. This would require getting to the station a bit early, since I had not purchased a ticket and it would presumably be crowded at rush hour. So much for my exciting day in New York. But then, at least I had spent a quiet afternoon in a comfortable hotel room, and that was a far better way to have passed the time than printing up invoices and tracking down creditors.

There was of course the option of not going home at all. Or at least disappearing for a few days, maybe going on a short, crazy bender. I could let Leon worry a bit, perhaps reflect on what he had done and how he had driven me away and how quickly living conditions would deteriorate in my absence, assuming he ever came home again, himself. There was probably something to be said for being irresponsible once in a while, but I just didn't have it in me. I was not a lot of fun. I envied people who could belt down a few drinks and laugh with strangers at a bar, who liked roller coasters, who were easily amused by sitcoms. I was pretty sure that whatever else she might be, Delia was this sort of person. I wondered if I ought to resolve to drink more, to visit amusement parks, to circle programs in my TV guide, to make more aggressive attempts to be more fun. But for now, all I wanted to do was go home. *Then* I would run away, share drinks with strangers, and watch more television. I was an organized person. I had a plan for my eventual disappearance, and I needed to stick to it.

· · ·

All lines are long; all traffic is bad; everything is more expensive than it ought to be. Acceptance of these simple facts of life did little to calm me as I stood in line after learning that the automated ticket machines were all down due to a computer malfunction. That should have been another one for the list of modern woes: computers break—all the time.

Halfway through the line, my chances of making the six o'clock train were rapidly diminishing. At least I had a shot at the 6:20. The lesbian couple in front of me kissed; the businessman behind me kept muttering obscenities about Amtrak under his breath; a blind woman with a guide dog shuffled forward in line without complaint; a baby somewhere started to wail. My head started to ache, a possible precursor to the fact that the worst was yet to come.

I made it to the front of the line at 5:52. If things went smoothly I could race to the track. Of course, that would mean I was not going to have time to stop at the newsstand and would squander another rare chunk of time in which to read. I still had *Transitions,* but I had moved past the point of wanting to know more. Now I wanted to know less. Less about everything. I wondered if there was a magazine for *that. Oblivion,* perhaps. I glanced at my watch again and, with a sense of déjà vu, thought that maybe I could pull off a quick dash to the newsstand and at least grab a paper. I could always do a repeat of the shoplifting performance that had worked so well before.

The clerk was wearing too much purple eye shadow. Finally I asked whether there was a problem. "Yes," she said simply, looking up from her computer monitor. Then she uttered that nasty word again: "declined." As in, your credit card has been . . .

I don't know why that quite obvious possibility had not occurred to me, given my track record that day, but I had allowed myself to think it was just a snotty Plaza-related thing. I offered to write a check, but the Amtrak lady actually laughed out loud, which surely must have been against company policy. Had I been in a position that afforded me any bargaining power, I might have pointed this out. Instead, I pulled all of the cash out of my wallet, but with exactly $41, I was $87 short. I was also, coincidentally, forty-one years old. What was the significance of *that*? I stood at the window a while longer, unwilling to forfeit my place in line. There had to be a solution. She asked if I had a AAA card, explaining that it would entitle me to a discount on the 6:20, which was also a less expensive train. I whipped it out of my wallet excitedly, but it didn't really help. I was still $23.80 short. If only my Safeway bonus card was of use, or my library card. Was she willing to barter for that free burrito I had earned at California Tortilla, or my membership in the bra-and-panty club at Hecht's? What about a sticky blue condom? She kept urging me to step aside, but I found it hard to move. Never in my adult life had my credit cards betrayed me.

Not yet panicked, I found an ATM near a newsstand and fed my card into the slot, but it was unceremoniously spit out, as was the next card I tried.

This would have been a useful time to have my cell phone, but it was long gone. Did they still have pay phones, I wondered? It had been ages since I'd noticed one; I didn't even know how much it cost to make a call anymore. I asked a police officer and was pointed toward a bank of phones hidden around a corner, but when I tried to call home I was informed by an operator that my calling card number was no longer authorized. This seemed like a good time to start getting paranoid, but I was still in deep denial, thinking this was all just part of a long run of ridiculously bad luck. I tried placing a collect call, but a recording informed me that my home number had been disconnected, another detail I'd managed to forget about for a few hours. I dialed the store and was so relieved to hear Uncle Seymour's voice that I almost started crying, but it turned out that he was either confused or couldn't hear the operator because he slammed the phone down with the admonition to please stop calling, as if I had been a solicitor offering to clean the gutters or consolidate debt, neither of which was a bad idea.

There was no place to sit in Pennsylvania Station, unless you were lucky enough to be holding the sort of expensive train ticket that would allow you access to the waiting area. Leaning against a wall, I watched the people watch the board that announced arrivals, suddenly envious of every last one of them with their train tickets and their wallets full of activated credit cards. An announcement was made that the 6:00 Metroliner to Washington had arrived and all of the lucky people who could pay for train tickets scurried to form a line, stepping over a homeless man who had chosen to take a nap just beside the gate. A billboard advertised vacation packages to California on board trains with names like Pacific Surfliner and Southwest Chief. How lovely it would be to drift between cities for a few days, falling asleep at night to the soothing rumble of the train.

Someone who looked like my mother passed by, carrying a newspaper and holding a briefcase, but I couldn't quite see her face. The hair was the same, as was her shape and size. Without thinking, in the grip of some weird biological impulse, I began to follow her, like a lost baby duckling. I needed to see this woman's face. Maybe it *was* my mother. This was absurd, of course. This woman was young, and my mother would have been in her sixties by now, had she lived—which she had not.

The mother apparition was speed-walking, and I had to jog to catch up. I overtook her just as she was about to enter the annex that led to the Long Island Railroad, and then I stopped short and turned around to glimpse her face. Our bodies collided, she dropped her newspaper, and then she yelled at me and called me a "stupid cow," which had a decidedly chilling effect. I apologized and stared at her, dumbstruck. She looked nothing at all like my mother—her nose was the wrong shape, her eyes were the wrong color, and she had a pronounced birthmark on her right cheek. I don't know why I found this surprising, given that my mother had been dead for twenty-two years. But something about her—possibly her brisk, efficient, scary manner—did remind me of Tiffany, and that reminded me that I had agreed to run a workshop the following afternoon. I had to get home, or I had to call Tiffany and cancel. But how could I explain my inability to get home without divulging my embarrassing credit card situation? I'd have to come up with some sort of lie. I'd been telling so many lies lately, I had not only become part of the problem Leon had so accurately identified, but was by now a certifiable and possibly contagious carrier of the affliction.

I headed back to the pay phone to attempt to call in my lie, it having occurred to me that it was still possible to use a pay phone the old-fashioned way, by sticking change into the slot. But when I finally got through to directory assistance, and then to Tiffany's house, a maid who did not speak much English answered the phone and told me to call back later. I tried the store again, but got the machine. It was only 6:30, but Seymour must have locked up early, and who could blame him?

Subtracting the long-distance phone calls I had just made, thirty-one dollars and eighty-five cents remained in my wallet, which suddenly seemed like a ridiculously small amount to have when traveling. Yet it would have sufficed to catch a cab or two and besides, this was New York City, with an ATM on every corner.

I dug around in my pockets again to see if there was any more change, and found instead a business card. It took me a couple of seconds to realize what it was, events of that morning already seeming like something from another lifetime.

Roger Josephs Jr. had lovely handwriting. He could have a second career as a calligrapher, I thought, imagining him working with some broad-tipped, jewel-toned pens. The address he had quickly scrawled on the back of a business card looked almost like a formal invitation. He had not written down a phone number, however, and since I didn't know his sister's name, there was no way to reach him. I would have to just show up. I hoped he remembered our supposed appointment, but suspected he might not. I got the impression that he did not have much short-term memory when it came to women. Perhaps this was the memory problem he wanted to consult me about.

Reluctant to part with any of my precious cash, and clueless about how the subways ran downtown, I just started walking. Maybe I would have a stroke of luck and would find Justin on the streets. I scanned the face of every skinny dark-haired youth I passed. I even tapped one promising figure on the shoulder, but when he turned around he was decidedly not Justin. Whoever he was, he did look like he could use a mother. After about ten blocks, I took off my awful shoes. Why had I not thought to stick a pair of sneakers in my bag? Now I was a barefoot woman in Manhattan. Was this progress from being a mere object at rest?

The more immediate question was what I would do if Roger was not there. There were a few options, all of them equally unattractive. It was possible that I had enough money for a bus home—I'd read about cheap buses that left in the wee hours of the morning from Chinatown, but I couldn't recall much more than that. I still had my aunt and uncle on Long Island, but I hadn't spoken to them in a few years and did not especially want to show up barefoot on their doorstep, in crisis. As a last resort I could go to a police station, where perhaps they would let me use the phone to make a more concentrated effort to get through to someone at home, but that seemed certain to prove humiliating. I remembered that wonderful children's book about the brother and sister who run away and hide in the Metropolitan Museum of Art: *From the Mixed-Up Files of Mrs. Basil E. Frank-wiler.* Now *there* was a good idea. I laughed out loud as it began to rain, thinking I was so not fun that my idea of fun would be to live alone in a museum.

The umbrella vendors who emerged from nowhere like ants at a picnic seemed vexed by my wetness, and by my lack of interest in doing anything about it. I was already soaked and feeling oddly euphoric, despite my throbbing head. Who needed an umbrella? Without meaning to, I dropped one of my shoes somewhere along the way, and when I realized it was gone I dropped its mate in the trash. After another couple of blocks I decided to get rid of my overnight bag, too, just to lighten my load.

I didn't know where I was going, exactly, but figured if I just kept heading south along Broadway it would eventually become SoHo. I began to play games with the traffic lights, seeing if I could get a rhythm going that would allow me to keep cruising. I played this game along Rockville Pike sometimes. Once I had made it all the way from the store into Georgetown without hitting a traffic light. Admittedly it had been late at night and there were few cars on the road. But the fact remained that I did not have to hit my brakes a single time. And to think I was doubting my ability to have fun!

The ink was beginning to bleed on my scrap of paper, so I hoped I had the right address when I finally approached what appeared to be a newly renovated apartment building, the ground floor occupied by a café. The façade was old and elegant, with much inlaid marble and fancy fluted columns. At the end of the block, just a few feet away, I noticed a bank of floodlights, then realized that the bottom of the street was closed. I wandered over to see what was going on and saw cameras. They were filming something, and I recognized the actress, although

I couldn't quite think of her name. She was one of the pretty prosecutors from some popular detective show—another person, like Tiffany, whose exciting career in law enforcement I had always envied, even if this one was just a television character. Someone yelled "cut" and she was instantly set upon by a team of attendants who brushed her hair and re-applied her makeup. How nice to be fussed over like that!

I turned back toward Roger's apartment and pushed the button next to 18P, then stood in front of the tiny camera, and was almost instantly buzzed in. A glance in the elevator's mirrored panels confirmed that I did not look like a very desirable visitor with my dripping, frizzing hair and my bare, dirty feet.

The elevator opened directly into a sitting room in the apartment where Roger stood, holding a phone to his ear. He took a step back in astonishment when he saw me. I couldn't tell if his surprise had to do with my disheveled appearance or if he had already forgotten he'd invited me.

"I've come to consult your memory," I announced.

He laughed and ushered me into the apartment. "Let me just finish this call," he said, putting his palm over the receiver. "I'll be right with you."

He parked me in a bright, modern room with a panoramic view of downtown. A set of chaise longues that looked like a cross between dentist chairs and dead polar bears flanked the window. Was *this* Fjorki furniture? It was certainly crazy enough, but it didn't look like anything I'd seen in the catalog. Maybe it was from an earlier issue, the Spring Collection. Or more likely winter, given the polar bear theme. I touched the upholstery hesitantly, not sure what to expect—a magic spark, an instant transformation? A bit of the white fur came off in my hand and I cringed. Was this the real thing? Dead polar bear? The thought was enough to make me want to become a vegan.

Roger was saying "yes" and then "no" into the telephone as he wandered into another room, then reappeared, handing me a towel and a glass with a windy stem that contained a blue cocktail of some sort. His gaze seemed to be indelicately directed toward a certain part of my anatomy.

I instinctively glanced down, then quickly wrapped the towel around myself. It was freezing in the apartment, I was soaking wet, and my shirt was too sheer. I wasn't sure what I was doing there, but even if my motives were not completely pure, I had not meant to be provocative. I was about to explain myself, but Roger had already drifted back toward the other part of the room and was writing notes on a legal pad, asking a variety of questions about a car accident.

I felt ridiculous standing there, so I began to wander around the apartment. In what appeared to be the master suite was the strangest bed I had ever seen—it was about six feet off the ground, and perched on dozens of silvery spokes as thin as twigs. The legs all sprouted from the middle of the bed, then fanned out, like the roots of a turnip. It seemed impossible that these frail-looking legs could support the frame, especially with the added weight of bodies. The ladder, made of the same material, looked nearly as fragile. Was this like the bed I had seen in the catalog? But nothing else in this apartment seemed to give the appearance of going anywhere, of being *simply transporting*. Perhaps I had simply imagined this whole Fjorki thing. That the first symptom of my mental collapse would involve hallucinating about furniture catalogs would not come as a surprise to anyone.

Over the dresser, but not quite touching it, were pictures, all suspended by silvery threads which ran from the ceiling. The photos were presumably of Roger's sister and her children. The two-timing schmuck of a husband whom Roger had taken to the bank in divorce proceedings did not make an appearance in any of the photographs, which was a pity, because I was curious to see what he looked like. For her part, Roger's sister looked rich. Maybe it was the severe angular haircut, or the preppy clothing. Or maybe it was the way she held her chin high, like she was either arrogant or just perpetually pissed off. She was neither attractive nor unattractive but she definitely looked like someone with a lot of attitude, which was perhaps what she was going for as a trendy decorator. It made me think for a moment that perhaps Kramer's furniture would have more allure if the owners tried a bit harder to spruce themselves up, to take themselves more seriously.

I put a hand on the back of a chair and looked at myself in the mirror. The effect was no different than it had been that day when the Fjorki catalog had first arrived. Something was still wrong. Maybe I'd just forgotten to smile? I tried again, flipping my hair back behind my shoulders, hoisting my sumptuous blue cocktail in the air. I even aped the Fjorki model's cool, confident grin. But I still looked like me, only more of a mess than usual.

A pencil-thin silver rod on the dresser appeared to be a telephone. I lifted it to inspect it and noticed that it featured buttons for two separate lines. I couldn't imagine Roger Josephs' wealthy sister would care about a long distance call to Maryland, so I punched in our home number again, which was of course still disconnected. And not surprisingly, the store remained closed. Then I called Leon's cell, even though he had not answered it in days. This time a woman picked up. It was definitely not Delia—it was someone more gruff-sounding, someone with a husky, raspy voice. When I asked for Leon, she promptly clicked off.

Enough, I told myself. My brain could process only so much bad information at once. Now I was batting away images of some biker chic Leon had possibly hooked up with. Someone in a leather jacket. Leon and Delia and a biker chic . . . I downed what was left of the blue cocktail in a single gulp and resumed wandering, inadvertently winding up back where I began. Roger was still on the phone, saying something about taking a deposition and getting photos sent from an insurance company. The room was beginning to sway and I felt queasy, but at least my headache was finally subsiding. Roger looked sexy standing there so purposefully, helping someone sue someone else. He approached me with the pitcher from the blender and refilled my glass.

I went back to the room with the not-quite-floating bed and leaned against the window. The Hudson was just barely visible between a couple of higher buildings to the west. This room was also rocking back and forth, and I braced myself against the windowsill. Off in the distance was a barge ship. I saw myself in the reflection, strangely superimposed against the vessel. I was drunk and seasick and I hadn't even left dry land.

Roger approached and stood behind me, setting his blue cocktail down on the windowsill next to mine. Here was a new juxtaposition of objects, surely more provocative than Delia and Leon's sweater-and-sunglasses still life. I was so lightheaded that I wondered if I had been drugged. Plus I felt that same sense of curious detachment I had experienced when studying our finances the day before, wondering, how will this end? As if the answer to the question was somehow out of my control. I flashed briefly on the toothbrushes and the condom in my pocketbook. How would *that* end?

Roger said something about pressing criminal charges, then tried unsuccessfully to wrap up the phone conversation with a variety of lame excuses. He even said he had a meeting with his memory consultant, who had traveled all the way from Washington to help him with a problem. I liked that. Evidently the person on the other end of the line liked that, too, because I heard Roger promise to pass his phone number on to me, to see if I could squeeze him in sometime.

I don't know what got into me, but buoyed by this new image of myself as a woman with a life, a woman on an important business trip to New York, stopping by her male friend's house for an early-evening cocktail (the sort of thing the pretty prosecutor on television might do), I turned around and kissed the King of the Litigation Bar. This was the first truly spontaneous action I could recall in years, short of getting on the train that morning, which was really more an act of twisted compulsion. His mouth tasted like the sweet blue cocktail. He seemed a bit surprised but did not protest, other than what was required to keep talking on the phone.

What had I just done? It felt all wrong, unfamiliar. He was too thin. Even his lips were too thin. There was nothing to latch onto. And yet, the kiss had been strangely invigorating, perhaps because it was not the sort of action typically undertaken by a woman paralyzed by inertia. I could see an old man walking his dog outside, eighteen floors below where I stood. A couple of kids in wet soccer jerseys headed into the building; a woman alit from a cab and retrieved about a dozen shopping bags from the trunk. A young couple with umbrellas ran into the street to flag the taxi but were too late. The television crew was loading equipment into trucks and I could see the pretty prosecutor under an umbrella, talking to a presumably fictitious police officer. Was Justin out there, somewhere? I wanted to shout his name. I hoped none of these people could see me, although there was nothing all that interesting to see. Just a wet middle-aged woman in a see-through shirt, sipping a blue beverage, contemplating infidelity for the first time in her life.

Roger rolled his eyes at the person on the other end of the line. He looked nonplussed. He did not look particularly like someone who had just been kissed by a woman who was married to another man. But then, that did not strike me as the sort of thing that would bother him.

He hung up the phone at last, and brushed his finger across my cheek. But instead of moving forward with the business of seduction, he asked me a question. "What do you think?"

"Of?"

"The furniture!"

"The furniture is extremely weird." My speech sounded slurred. Or maybe my speech was fine and my hearing was slurred.

"Yes, I told you you'd like it. My sister is a decorator. Did I tell you that?" Now he ran his fingers through my hair, thoroughly confusing me. Were we going to have sex, or a furniture consultation?

"You did. What is this called? This . . . style?"

"She's a Belgian minimalist. She's not actually Belgian herself, but she studied from some Belgian master. This is called sensualist modern, I think. Is this anything at all like what you carry at Kramer's?"

Surely it was the blue cocktail talking, because the word that came out of my mouth was, inexplicably, "yes."

"Really?" asked Roger. "That's quite a coincidence."

Why in God's name were we talking about our furniture? Why were we not kissing? How was it I was still vertical given how dizzy I was, how fast the room was spinning? I stared longingly at the not-quite-floating bed and thought I needed to climb into it. Instead, I managed to follow Roger into the kitchen, holding his hand. I think I asked him whether the kitchen was also Belgian minimalist sensualist modern, and I think he replied affirmatively.

All I remember for sure was that he refilled my glass with more blue liquid while he began to talk to me about his ex-wife. He had a recurring dream, he said, which contained a fuzzy image of her opening a door, smoking a cigarette, and saying something to him while pouring herself a drink. Each time he had this dream he woke up crying, and he didn't know why. He was blocking on something, he said. He was trying to get to some deeply repressed memory and he wondered if I had any advice. Did this dream hold the secret of why she had left him? He kept stroking my hair as he spoke and I wondered whether he was just trying to be helpful in untangling my messy locks, or whether this was foreplay. It had been so long since I'd been seduced that I didn't really remember how it worked.

I think that I began to answer him, but I don't remember anything I said. What I do remember is that I stood on my tiptoes to kiss him again, and then I collapsed. Strangely, as my knees were giving out, I had a pretty coherent thought. Not about his ex-wife, but about how it always bugged me when female characters in novels passed out drunk just when they were on the verge of engaging in questionable sexual behavior. This had always seemed to me a cop-out. But now I understood how it tended to happen. A certain amount of alcohol was required to get a woman like me into this predicament in the first place, and certainly a lot more than that was going to be required to take it the next step. But achieving just the right level of intoxication was a delicate, precise science. Too little and you wouldn't take the big leap, too much and you would wind up passed out on the floor. At least this was what I surmised when I awoke the next morning in the floating bed, alone.

My head was throbbing again, now even worse than before I had begun drinking. What registered was not pain, however, but embarrassment. Complete mortification.

I heard footsteps, the sound of a door closing, the ping of an elevator, and then crawled out of bed and down the wispy ladder. My wet clothes lay crumpled on the floor and I decided not to think about how they got there. A T-shirt of Roger's was strewn on a chair. I put it on, then followed the smell of coffee into the kitchen.

Roger's laptop computer sat on the table. I wandered over to it and pressed a few keys. His papers were piled beside it. I picked up one of the folders, then dropped it like a hot potato. It was that magazine again. The one he'd been reading at the train station, but a different issue. Did his client appear on these pages regularly, I wondered? I then picked up the phone and dialed home, thinking this would be somehow purifying. It was really just an exercise in diligence, because I assumed our line would still be disconnected. Much to my surprise, Justin answered the phone.

"You're home!" I cried, giddy with relief. I was so grateful he was safe that this seemed like the wrong time to start an argument about him running off.

"Where are you?" he asked. "Dad told me to track you down and I've been trying forever. Dad's at the hospital."

"The hospital? What are you talking about?"

"Grandpa. He's had a stroke."

I was staring out the window as we spoke, watching the morning rush-hour traffic creep by. People were on their way into work, children went off to school, life heaved onward, regardless of Samuel's condition.

"What happened?"

"He was on the airplane on his way home. The person next to him said he opened his tray table for dinner and then just slumped over."

"Oh my god . . . Poor Samuel . . . What do the doctors say?"

"It's not good, I think. He's unconscious, and he's on a ventilator."

"I'm coming home. I'll be there this afternoon. Tell dad, okay?"

"Okay. But where are you?" he asked for the second time. "Did you hear what happened to Dad?"

"No. What happened?" How much worse could this get?

"He was carjacked and robbed at gunpoint! There was an accident on the turnpike. They took his wallet. He and that Delia person spent the night at the police station in New Jersey trying to sort things out. He's been trying to call you for, like, two days."

I didn't completely follow this, but figured I'd concentrate on what seemed most urgent.

"Is Dad okay? The phone was out at home," I explained. "The storm. Anyway, where were *you*?"

Justin was just as adept at avoiding answers as I was. "Didn't you get my message?" he asked. "I left you a message. Dad's fine. He told me to call you and say that someone stole his wallet and he had to cancel all the credit cards. He asked me to go through all the drawers in the store, too, and cancel everything we could find a record of, just in case, cause he didn't actually know how many credit cards you had. How many *do* you have?"

Embarrassingly, I didn't know the answer to the credit card question offhand, so I continued our dance of avoidance. "I didn't get any message."

"I left like a dozen messages. On your cell. Isn't the number 301-936 . . ."

"I lost my cell phone, remember? Wait . . . was dad at the Plaza?"

"I have no idea."

"What about Delia?"

"What about Delia?"

"Where is she?"

"I don't know. Her purse was stolen, too, and she was really upset. Plus Dad said her son was sick. So maybe she went back to wherever it is she lives."

"Her son?"

"That's what he said."

It didn't occur to me to ask how Justin knew all this if he was in New York, himself. There was too much horrible news to process, and I let the details slide.

I heard the ring of the elevator, then Roger's already familiar footsteps. He walked in grinning and handed me a shopping bag from Barney's. I pulled out a silk blouse, a pair of what were surely going to be too-tight jeans, and pumps with very pointy toes. It was thoughtful of him to realize that I didn't have any dry clothes. Judging from his selection of garments, there was no question that he thought I was someone other than myself. If not an impressively successful businesswoman or the fictitious television prosecutor, or even just the anti-Jane, then Jennifer Lopez, perhaps.

I promised Justin I'd be home later in the day and hung up the phone.

"I need a favor," I said to Roger, wiping a tear from my eye.

"What's up?"

"My father-in-law has had a stroke. I need to get home right away, but I have no money. Leon's wallet was stolen and our credit cards have all been stopped. I need to borrow some money to get home."

"I'm so sorry," said Roger. "You've really got your hands full, eh?"

"Listen, Roger, I've never done anything like this before. I just want you to know that."

"Like what?"

"Like, last night . . . you know . . ."

"You mean the advice you gave me about Lucia?

Lucia? Who the hell was Lucia? Maybe he was confusing me with someone else. Perhaps last night had been a busy one for him.

"You're amazing, Jane. The way you drew all those connections, about my dream, about her opening doors and leaving me, about how the smoke was keeping me from seeing things clearly. Is it possible to talk to you more sometime? Maybe back in Washington? Once you've sorted out your own problems, of course. I feel like we've only pulled back the first layer of all this."

I didn't know what to say. All I remembered was kissing him.

"I told you, that's not really what I do."

"I know, I know. You sell furniture. So you didn't tell me, what do you think of her stuff?"

"I did tell you. It's weird."

"Do you think you might be interested?"

"In what?"

"In talking to my sister. She's always looking for new clients. She's trying to find U.S. outlets for some of these pieces."

"You mean, sell this kind of stuff at Kramer's?"

"Yeah. Remember, last night, you said it was just like what you carried in the store."

"I said that?"

"You did."

"You must have plied me with liquor to get me to say that," I said. "Is *that* why you invited me here?" I said this playfully.

"Of course not," he replied, walking toward me, touching my shoulder. He was so close I could smell his breath. I thought of the model in the Fjorki catalog again, about how happy she looked, and I wondered if it might just be Roger on the next page whom she was smiling at. I flipped my hair back like her again. Was there any possible equation in which sleeping with Roger Josephs Jr. might actually be the *right* answer? I couldn't think of one. I also couldn't think of a single reason why I might want another man in my life. I was having enough problems with the one I had. Not to mention that given the news I had just received about my father-in-law, this seemed an indelicate time to become an adulterer.

Still, I briefly fantasized about walking into next year's WZOP dinner on the dazzling Roger's arm, *Queen* of the Litigation Bar. But I was too much of a pragmatist to even enjoy the daydream. How different would it be, going with Roger? It would be no different at all, I decided, because it wasn't that I wanted a different man in my life. What I wanted was a different woman. A new Jane Kramer.

"I need to borrow some money," I reminded him again.

Roger took out a hundred-dollar bill and handed it to me. "You are a high-maintenance woman," he joked.

I gave him a peck on the cheek, letting my lips linger a few seconds too long, but he didn't notice. In fact he seemed completely blasé about what had just happened, which admittedly had not been much. Just another day in the life of the King of the Litigation Bar. You win some, you lose some.

Mostly he won, was my best guess.

17

A PROPERTY might be designated as historic if it could be identified with a person who had influenced society. Prior to his deification at his memorial service, no one would have denied Samuel Kramer had been a good man, a shrewd retailer, a steady contributor to a number of worthy causes, even a generous tipper in restaurants, but he had hardly changed the world.

Ditto for the proposition that Kramer's itself somehow exemplified the cultural, economic, social, political, or historic heritage of the county—another criterion for being deemed worthy of preservation. For years we had constantly been reminded that we were nothing but an ugly furniture store, an eyesore on an already afflicted landscape. Until all of a sudden, we no longer were.

More than two hundred people attended Samuel's memorial, among them many longtime Washingtonians who showed up to offer moving eulogies. They all seemed to have forgotten their recent gripe with Kramer's. One would have thought that Samuel Kramer had been a prince, that our store had been a palace, or possibly the palace clinic, dispensing free medicine to the poor. Suddenly it seemed Kramer's had been much more than the place to go for a good deal on sleep sofas to stick in the recreation room; in fact, in many a tribute the word "furniture" was not even mentioned. Kramer's was remembered in one speech as "a local institution that had left its mark on just about every household in the D.C. Metropolitan area." And Simon Wu, the owner of Cowboy Boot World, which was about a mile south of us on Rockville Pike, gushed that Samuel Kramer had been his role model ever since he'd been a kid, that he had "blazed a trail for other small business owners who had dreamed of one day building small empires." If Samuel had built an empire, it was very small indeed, although admittedly it was more expansive than that of Cowboy Boot World.

By the time the County Executive approached the microphone to lavish praise on the same store his office had spent years harassing, it was hard to keep a straight face. Leon squeezed my hand; even he was on the verge of laughing at his own father's funeral.

"A jewel in the crown of local business establishments," Jasper LaMott said before pronouncing Samuel Kramer to be Rockville's premier businessman, and the posthumous recipient of the just-created Rockville Lifetime Achievement Award. He called his passing "the end of an era" and then proposed—in what was meant to be a magnanimous gesture, but was really a misstatement of enormously stupid proportions, one that would merit a small item in the newspaper the following day and would come back to haunt him when he ran for reelection—that Kramer's be designated a historic property. Leon squeezed my hand hard as LaMott spoke. How he had managed to forget that we had been at the eye of the historic property storm on and off for three years was a question worth asking, and many did.

For a week or so, everyone was talking about Samuel Kramer, and about Kramer's Discount Furniture Depot. It seemed a pity that the store was closed for mourning, as this was the most positive buzz we'd had in years. There had even been a feature about Samuel on the evening news, with a grainy video of him in his younger days stretched out on one of his famous reclining chairs, smoking a cigar. It seemed there was some slyly ironic tinge to the story, as if the reporter was gently poking fun at Samuel's loud plaid jacket, as if he thought there was something slightly tacky about Samuel Kramer, himself. I got the definite feeling that this elegantly attired reporter was not the sort of man to have a Kramer's reclining chair in his Georgetown townhouse, or that if he did (in the maid's room, for example), he would have turned up his nose at the idea of getting Scotch Guard protection or signing up for the three-year warranty on moving parts.

There was an awful lot of hand-squeezing that week, and really nothing to do but squeeze back, to try to put aside thoughts of recent confusing marital events until a more suitable time. This was hard, particularly since Delia was at the memorial, impossible to miss in a busy black-and-white dress with zigzagging stripes. We had a lot of details to sort out, me and Leon and Delia, not the least of which was whose sticky condom was currently sitting inside a shower cap in a paper bag in the back of my bathroom closet, and why it was I still had it. Now it could provide a DNA sample for entirely different reasons, helpful in identifying the couple who had robbed and carjacked Leon and Delia. Handing my sticky souvenirs over to the police, however, would require explaining how I had come to possess such spectacular evidence. This, in turn, would involve a recitation of how I had chased my husband to New York and staked him out at the Plaza Hotel. This was not really a story I was prepared to share with my husband, never mind a judge.

When I first spotted Delia sitting in the back row at the memorial service, I had an entirely selfish thought. The service was not about me, but all the same, I couldn't help wondering what she was doing there, at *my* father-in-law's funeral. Couldn't she go and find some other furniture store to hang out in for a while? Yet in fairness, she had as much reason to be there as anyone else; more so, arguably, than Jasper LaMott and the hand-shaking, speech-writing drones from various county offices. At least she had actually known Samuel Kramer and, for better or worse, was a close friend of his son.

I tried to block on the subject of Delia. But the more I tried to stop thinking about her, the more she invaded my every thought. I couldn't stop staring at her, trying to determine what made her tick, and what she meant to my husband. All I knew for sure was that I wanted her out of our lives. But as long as she was there at the funeral and the week-long aftermath, she did serve a purpose. She was very helpful in the kitchen. Plus she distracted the eye, sucked up so much energy in the room that it allowed the rest of us to go about our business unnoticed. Even more usefully, she ingratiated herself with the extended Kramer family, which included about twenty-seven of Esther's nieces and nephews. She offered to drive them back and forth to their hotel, and even delivered a few of them to the airport.

While certain aspects of the week made a lasting impression, much of the time went by in a blur. There were funeral arrange-ments to be handled, which meant there were many checks to be written for many thousands of dollars, which would presum-ably be reimbursed once Samuel's estate was settled—not that this was the time to be thinking of money. As if money was something we could ever stop thinking about, given our cir-cumstances. Fortunately, the credit card company had agreed to take responsibility for the Plaza bill and the related shopping spree, so there were at least funds available to cover the fresh onslaught of expenses. There were relatives to sort out, beds to make, meals to prepare, and personalities to negotiate, not the least demanding of which was Leon's sister, Elaine. She stayed for eight long days, and while she was at our home she took it upon herself to try to talk several members of the funeral party into moving to Oregon and joining her religious fold. I learned only from overhearing her talking to the Cuban neighbors that her church had communal living arrangements. "Just like in Cuba," she enthused. The neighbors smiled politely and slinked away.

I considered Elaine mostly harmless, but was nonetheless alarmed the day that I found her talking to Justin. He was in an impressionable place. I didn't want her filling his head with extreme religion—not her version of it, anyway. Nor did I want to have to pursue him across the country, all the way to Oregon, especially having only just had him mercifully if mysteriously retrieved from New York.

While wandering around the house one afternoon, picking up paper plates and half-empty soda cans, then pausing to mop up a spilled glass of cranberry juice on the rug in the hallway, I spied Elaine sitting on the lima-bean-shaped sofa in our living room. Beside her, on the cushion, was a heaping slice of chocolate cake with gooey icing, edging slowly off the plate. I was not a compulsive housekeeper, but this potential stain concerned me because this was one of our very few nice pieces of furniture. The sofa was a sample that the manufacturer let us keep for ourselves because the gold fabric covering the armrests did not match the hue of the more yellowish material on the cushions. In a house full of reject furniture, mismatched members of the yellow family did not register as such a terribly egregious imperfection. I approached the couch and tried to be inconspicuous as I moved the plate to the coffee table. Elaine didn't seem to notice.

Assembled was an interesting trio: There was Delia, lounging voluptuously on one side of the sofa. She had her head cocked to the right, with one arm draped over the back of the couch, which caused the material on her dress to pull tight across the bodice. Sitting on the other end was my dowdy sister-in-law.

Poor Justin was wedged in the middle. He appeared acutely uncomfortable as he picked at the plate of food balanced on his lap. I observed almost gleefully that he was nibbling on a turkey sandwich, but knew better than to comment.

This struck me as a potentially combustible configuration: religious fanatic; moody, mercurial Goth/former vegan; and this endlessly enviably cheerful woman who was possibly intent on replacing me in both my marriage and my furniture store. I'd be damned if she was going to elbow her way into my son's life, as well.

I went over and sat on a nearby armchair angled slightly behind the couch, but still in partial view. I leaned back and crossed my legs and tried generally to appear as though I felt at home in my own home, which I did not. My house was full of strangers. Many of them were chatting merrily; some were smoking cigarettes, dousing the butts in half-empty drinks, or stubbing them into a long-suffering plant that Leon had given me for Valentine's Day years ago. There was a months-long patch where I had stopped watering it—a passive-aggressive reaction to the state of my marriage—but the scrappy thing kept clinging to life, and I finally gave in and revived it. Others were carelessly dropping bits of food on the floor. Few of them seemed to be behaving much like mourners.

No one seemed to notice me at first. I trained my eye on the far wall where a Lena Min watercolor hung, depicting a mis-shapen water buffalo grazing in front of a bamboo hut. Delia was recounting a story having to do with some wacky road trip she had once taken involving an overturned truck full of vegetables. At first I was only half-listening, figuring she was just regaling us with some self-indulgent adventure story from her crazy youth. When I realized she was talking about her recent road trip with Leon, however, I bolted upright.

"I've never been so scared in my life," she said, now leaning forward and scooping a handful of nuts from a bowl that rested beside the chocolate cake on the coffee table, an inoffensive hand-me-down from Samuel, nondescript save for the few bright bursts of permanent marker Justin had inflicted on it as a toddler. She popped a cashew into her mouth and chewed as she spoke. I hadn't noticed until then that her teeth were all capped, and felt a petty, unworthy sense of triumph at having spotted this imperfection.

"This guy was weaving in and out of lanes on the Turnpike. He was in this little red Porsche talking on his cell phone . . . He was a total menace. He nearly cut us off, then he zooms past. He must have pulled off at a rest stop for a while, because we saw him a second time, further north."

Through the door frame I saw Uncle Seymour standing in the dining room with a plate in his hand, eating a sandwich. He was surrounded by a small group of people I didn't recognize. The wallpaper was still in tatters, and little chunks of plaster fell to the floor periodically. I had cleaned up as best I could, but there had not been much time to ready the house for company. Anyway, I had done so much damage the night Justin disappeared that repairing the walls was now going to require the help of a professional.

"So then, in the right lane," Delia continued, "there's this rickety old truck full of vegetables. I could see carrots and lettuce and stuff poking out of the sides. It was like something you'd see in the twelfth century."

Justin leaned forward and I thought it was because he could not resist inquiring about this seemingly random reference to twelfth-century vehicular design, given that he was something of a closet history buff. But he only reached for his glass of water on the table.

"So then there comes the Porsche again! He cuts us off another time . . . slams into the little truck . . . there's smoke pouring out of the engine . . . the Porsche catches on fire, it's totaled really, the truck driver is pinned inside his car and the Porsche-driving asshole walks away without a scratch!"

"I wish you people would watch your language," my sister-in-law interjected in a complete monotone. "Especially in front of the boy."

We all stared at her, puzzled. Elaine was a woman of few words. Sometimes when she spoke she was razor-sharp; other times she seemed slightly off point, like she was distracted, having her own silent parallel conversation, possibly with God. I wondered whether she'd had any prolonged conversations with her foul-mouthed brother lately; if so, she would have learned that *asshole* was pretty low on our family's list of offensive vocabulary words. I also marveled that she had apparently forgotten her only nephew's name, referring to him as "the boy."

"It's Justin, Aunt Elaine," he said politely. "And I don't mind. I've heard it all before." He sounded so earnest it was possible to imagine him wearing an Eagle Scout uniform laden with shiny badges instead of baggy, ratty black cargo pants and a tie-dyed shirt. His only concession to the occasion was that he wore a black blazer purchased for a school concert the previous spring. Like a science project gone awry, he was growing so quickly that the jacket was already about a size too small. A streak of sunlight accented new purple streaks in his hair, which must have been applied the night before. Three tufts were molded into points that stood straight up.

"As I was saying," Delia continued, "this sonofabitch gets out of his car. Then his girlfriend emerges, with really bad highlights. She seems a bit dazed, looks around at all the food lying on the ground, picks up an onion, wipes it on her skirt, and sticks it in her mouth—I kid you not—then puts a bunch of carrots in her pocketbook. Meanwhile he comes over to our car and sticks a gun in my ear and tells us to get out. He took our wallets and he took the car and he drove it over the median strip and went the other way . . . He left us just standing there in the middle of the New Jersey Turnpike . . . Can you imagine?"

There was a moment of silence while we all tried to imagine this. Elaine even closed her eyes in an apparent attempt at visualization. Naturally I was imagining this, and other sorts of things, as well. My eyes scanned the room as I did my imagining. I saw Leon in the corner, talking to Simon Wu.

"So there was produce all over the road—it looked like a giant salad bowl!—plus they had to land a helicopter and medivac the truck driver to the hospital. I don't know what happened to him. It was awful. Leon and I just stood there for, like, two hours, before the police took us in to write up the report. Of course we had no phones or anything to start canceling our credit cards since they were both in the car, so this guy had a head start on his spending spree."

Justin leaned forward again to put his drink down, centering it on a yellow splotch, but this time he finally spoke. "I was going the other way, you know, and I saw that. I didn't realize what was going on, but I noticed the traffic backed up for miles. This was on Sunday, right?"

"Exactly, honey. Sunday, late in the afternoon."

"I'm kind of confused," I said, and they all looked in my direction, evidently noticing me for the first time.

"Hi, honey," said Delia. "Which part is confusing you, exactly?" she asked, sweetly concerned.

"The timing, for one thing. Justin left Sunday. You and Leon left Friday. This happened . . . when?"

Justin stared at me apprehensively. Evidently he thought I hadn't known about his little escapade. This was good for him.

I wanted him to think I was omniscient, even if I was almost certainly unaware of most of what went on in his life.

"I understand why you are confused, Jane," Delia said, sounding somewhat worried, herself. "We *did* leave on Friday, but we got sidetracked in Wilmington for a couple of days. We got back on the road Sunday afternoon. We were on our way into New York when this all happened."

This disclosure left many questions unanswered, and yet *sidetracked in Wilmington* was all that really registered.

"Who would want to steal Leon's car?" This was not high on my list of concerns, but it was one of several things that did not make any sense.

"Oh," said Delia apologetically, "you know, I had trouble with the alignment. Something wasn't quite right, so we left his car at a garage and took mine in the end. But the police called yesterday, actually. They found the car. It was left at a train station in Jersey, not too far from where this all occurred."

This part of the story was also full of holes, yet all I heard was that she had failed to successfully align Leon's tires. Another little imperfection, a piece of good news in a sea of bad.

"And Justin," I said in an even voice, "I'm just a little confused about your timetable."

"Mike is just such an asshole lately, Mom," he said nervously. "It's all really complicated."

"What's with you guys and all the cursing?" asked Elaine.

"That's not really cursing," Delia informed her.

"Well, just give me some clues, here," I said. "You drove to New York Sunday morning. You were on your way home already on Sunday evening?"

"We got in a fight on the way."

"About?"

He looked at me with big eyes, the boy equivalent of a dog

sticking his tail between his legs. "Mike's been dealing. Don't ask me why. It's not like he needs the money or anything . . ."

"*Drugs?*" Elaine shrieked, incredulous. No one bothered to answer her.

"Since when?"

"I don't know. I honestly didn't know until we were on the road, and he started making some calls about setting up some meeting in New York. Really, Mom, I didn't know what to do. I thought you would kill me no matter what. And Dad . . . forget it, there was no way I was going to tell him. So when we stopped for gas I bolted."

"How did you get home?" Elaine pressed.

"I caught a ride," he said in such a small voice that we barely heard him.

"What do you mean, *caught*?" This was none of Elaine's business and I really hated that she was hearing all this, but at least she was saving me from having to ask the tough questions. "Do you mean you *hitchhiked*? Haven't you read about that guy who's killed fourteen prostitutes in New Jersey?" she howled, failing to explain what connection this might have to Justin.

Either in an effort to get away from his aunt, or possibly in some intuitive move meant to ingratiate himself with me, Justin walked over and settled himself on the arm of my chair. One of the spikes on his head cut into my shoulder as he leaned into me like a little boy. I wondered how he had achieved this solid mass of hair. Was it was only gel, or something more permanent, like Crazy Glue or cement? I ran my fingers through his hair, marveling at the different textures.

"He had to hitchhike," said Delia, putting a hand on Elaine's shoulder like she was talking to a moron. "He knew he shouldn't but he felt he had no choice. Am I right, honey?" she asked Justin.

Justin nodded his head uncertainly. He seemed to understand that having Delia as his protector was not going to earn him any bonus points with me.

I thought these were a couple of the most preposterous stories I'd ever heard, but they turned out to be less astonishing than the one Delia would tell me just a couple of weeks later.

The crowd that surrounded Seymour had multiplied and was snaking through the doorway and into the living room, encroaching on our little chat, eventually ending it for good. Every time that I managed to catch a glimpse of Seymour during the week we sat shivah, he was flanked by people, the center of attention. At first I'd thought it was for the obvious reason that he was Samuel's brother, a natural figure to be collared by condolence payers. But then, as the week progressed and his group of well-wishers grew progressively larger, I realized that I rarely recognized the people he was talking to. One day, when I glimpsed a hugely pregnant woman among his hangers-on, I began to understand.

Oda? I didn't actually say her name out loud, although I might have if I'd been able to remember it. I did recall, however, her moving story about how our sale on entertainment centers had saved the life of her unborn child. With her was her husband and what appeared to be a few of their family members. They were huddled around Seymour, jockeying to get in closer, as if he were some sort of celebrity. Oda spotted me and gave me a warm hello.

I introduced her to Delia and Justin and Elaine. We chatted for a few minutes about her health and her due date and her new entertainment center, which she said fit in her apartment perfectly. And her television set fit perfectly inside the entertainment center. Miracle after miracle, she said in Spanish. Another small and illuminating miracle was the fact that she was able to buy a DVD player with the money Uncle Seymour had given her.

Having overheard a snippet of the conversation, another young woman came over and joined us, and she, too, began to rave about how this wonderful man at Kramer's had given her enough money to buy a wedding dress. Her cousin introduced herself and gushed about her new set of free dresser drawers. Uncle Seymour looked a bit nervous when he spotted me chatting with his friends, as well he should have. He must have fancied himself a sort of Robin Hood of furniture, giving to the poor, except that we were not as rich as Seymour seemed to think.

After my sister-in-law had been deposited at the airport, after the platters of chopped liver and corned beef and the endless trays of cookies had been put in plastic bags and stored in the freezer, after Delia had gone away, at least for a while, we reopened the store. Business was good for a few days; more money came in than went out for the first time in a long while, in part because I had pulled Seymour aside for a stern chat about leaving the money where he had found it. Customer complaints were down, a sale on office furniture was well attended, and Leon and I settled into a nice, easy rhythm even though we still had not had the conversation we were consciously avoiding. Justin went back to school, and one night I found him and Leon sitting on the couch watching a rerun of *Seinfeld* and laughing at the same inane joke. It may not have been the heart-to-heart talk that they needed to have, but it was something.

There was much to be said for this period of forced détente. After a week of pretending things were fine, the act we put on started to feel every bit as normal as our former state of hostile relations. I'd heard people say that one antidote to depression was to simply act like you were not depressed. That just going out and getting on with the routine business of life sometimes served as a cure in itself. I wondered if this same advice might hold true for a marriage in distress. Leon and I could just pretend we were not unhappy, and if the absence of anger and contempt and the cessation of constantly snapping at one another did not automatically constitute blissful marital relations, it at least provided a clean slate upon which to build.

I decided to try to simply be there for him for a while after his father's death, to be a reliable presence, a thing on which to lean. I would be an object at rest: a wife, like a sturdy piece of furniture.

By the time that Chandler Chandling dared to set foot in the store again, after a brief grace period following the funeral, we were at least standing on steady emotional ground. Which is not to say that Leon handled the request for DNA with particular grace. Nor to suggest that the "F" word did not return to his vocabulary after a brief absence, used in several ways that were quite possibly unique.

I accompanied Leon to the police station, and we went through the front door, holding our heads high. We were owners of a small business, with certain obligations to fulfill. Being fingerprinted, then scraped for DNA, was just another cost of doing business in the county these days.

18

TWO WEEKS into our precarious truce, I was still tiptoeing around my husband, trying my best to be a comfortable, practical armchair of a wife. I got up early each morning and made the coffee. I stopped buying sheet cakes and instead set out a breakfast spread that included fresh fruit and a selection of healthful cereals. I reactivated our *Washington Post* subscription and fetched the paper from the driveway after getting Justin off to school. I made a plan to start chipping away at some of our credit card debt, or to use our share of the inheritance—which was not a fortune, but was helpful nonetheless—to erase it entirely. I forced myself to drink an entire glass of wine with dinner each night and watch at least one hour of particularly mindless television. And I made Leon promise to stop cursing.

There was only one glitch in the improvement program, which was that Delia was still floating around in the background, a constant reminder that things were not really as unremarkable as they seemed. That the blue condom was not evidence of their coupling did not mean that no coupling had occurred, and in fact I was back to believing just the opposite was true. There was too much conspired giggling between the two of them about the ridiculous vegetable truck incident. I was sick of hearing about squashed cucumbers and bad highlights, and even though I was meant to be included in the hilarity, their

constant recounting of events started to make me bitter. I
wanted a chance to cross-examine the witnesses about that little
side trip to Wilmington. I wanted details about where their
nights had been spent. But I also just wanted this to go away. My
small epiphany in New York had made me believe it was possible to change my life without blowing it up. Before I could truly
move on, however, Delia needed to go back to wherever it was
she had come from.

There was a nice five-day patch in which Delia did not appear
at all. No one mentioned her name, and so far as I knew,
inquiries were not made as to her whereabouts. By day three of
no Delia, I tried on the idea that perhaps she had never really
existed at all. Maybe she had been nothing but a metaphor, a sort
of magical realist touch to our otherwise monotonous lives, as
inexplicable as Fjorki furniture and the floating speck in the
photographs. And if that speck was meant to be symbolic of . . .
what? a trapped soul trying to escape, a scratch on the camera's
lens, maybe a wayward eyelash, what was Delia? Happiness,
perhaps. An unadulterated, dumb, blind, puppy-frolicking-in-
the-snow sort of happiness. And maybe this was what I'd been
jealous of all along, that she was able to infect Leon with her
happiness.

But this was just me, musing. Because when Delia did show
up again, on day six, it was painfully clear that she was not some
impressionistic work of art, not some random stroke of color on
the dull canvas of our lives, but a busy, chattering, large, loud,
improbable, and—truth be told—annoying patio furniture sales-
person.

The only obvious change was that in her brief absence she
had acquired a headset for her cell phone, enabling her to more
effectively multi-task. She carried a white wicker settee and a
matching footrest as she walked through the front door, barking
directions to whomever it was she was talking to on the phone.

It sounded as though she was directing this other party to our store; I heard her say that they were just a few miles away. Then she set the wicker items down in front of me and smiled proudly.

All this fuss for *that,* I couldn't help but think. I could have bought the same thing on sale at Pier 1 without bothering to mine the collected works of F. Scott Fitzgerald for patio furniture references.

"I know it's nothing special," she said, "but what I thought is you might want to put little labels on it. Like this one could be named *Daisy*. Daisy was the Mia Farrow character in the movie. She was the one that Gatsby was still lusting after all these years later . . ." She still had her headset on, which made her look as if she was talking to someone else, like her colleagues at air traffic control.

Daisy. That was not a bad idea. I thought of the Fjorki catalog. I thought of the Ava chaise in Erin scarlet resting on Sadie driftwood. I felt that same pang of longing for a little girl in a flowery frock with a pretty name, or maybe just for a new piece of furniture. Delia looked at me strangely and I considered trying to explain that my emotional wiring seemed to be short-circuiting in middle age, but then decided against it.

"Have you seen the movie?" Delia asked.

"Years ago. But I've read the book several times."

"That movie really blew my mind." Her phone rang and she pulled it out of her pocket, checked the caller ID, and depressed a button. "No, no, you want to be heading north on Rockville Pike! Make a U-turn. I'm in an important business meeting, so just wait in the lot when you get here." Was it my imagination, or did she sound somehow less animated when addressing this party on the phone?

"What was it about the movie that blew your mind?" I asked. It was a decent movie, but not really a mind-blower, as I recalled. Delia settled herself onto the *Daisy* ottoman. I sat down in the settee, facing her. We both crossed our legs at the same exact time and giggled at the coincidence. Her legs were much longer than mine, and being so low to the ground, on the footrest, the slip-on sneaker she was wearing scraped the floor and fell off. We both stared down at the floor. My eye fixed on her bare foot. Her toes sported a cheerful shade of sparkly pink polish and yet that foot was a man's foot—big and hairy, despite the pedicure. It now seemed completely obvious that this man's foot was attached to a man's leg, although I couldn't say why that was, exactly, other than perhaps just power of association. Or maybe it was more than that: it was Andrew Ryder's driver's license; it was the summer job at the gas station that I had tried to be open-minded about; it was every article I had read in *Transitions* magazine; it was the realization that despite my largely successful efforts at denial, it was suddenly clear that Delia was almost too feminine to be female. She saw me staring at her foot. She stared at it too for a moment. Then she and I locked eyes.

She was about to say something when the door swung open and an elderly, overweight customer walked in leaning on a cane, sweating and wheezing. I jumped up to greet her and offered her a seat and a glass of water, since she looked like she might collapse and the ensuing lawsuit would require even further interaction with Chandler Chandling. She declined, but she did pause to lean on a desk for a moment to collect herself. Delia didn't move, and I felt obliged to explain to the customer that we were just testing out a new line of wicker furniture. I figured the woman's eyesight could not be so sharp as to spot the man's foot halfway across the room. But Delia was still something of a sight, sitting in stony silence in the middle of the sales floor.

After a few awkward moments, the old woman asked for Seymour. When I explained that he was not due in for another hour she scowled, checked her watch, and wandered off through the hallway that led to the kitchen tables. I told her to holler if she needed any help, but I knew she would not. She had come in looking for a Seymour special, and those were no longer on offer, at least not on my watch.

"That movie blew my mind," Delia continued, after the customer was a comfortable distance away, "because of the way that Jay Gatsby character was trying to be someone other than who he was. You know, he deliberately set out to be a different person. He changed his name from James Gatz, and he made a lot of money, and he bought fancy clothes and a big house, and he tried to forget about who he was before. And maybe *you,* Jane, you with your perfect life, might think that he made this choice deliberately, but the way I see it, he had no choice."

She put her head in her hands and began to cry. I sat there wishing I knew what to say.

"But when I saw the end," she continued, blowing her nose, "My god, Jane! When I saw the end and he died like that, I knew I couldn't do this anymore . . . I thought then, maybe I *do* have a choice, even if the whole situation is just impossible."

"Are we talking about what I think we're talking about?" I asked. It seemed like it might be useful to clarify, just in case I was wildly off the mark and we were really discussing something as mundane as wicker furniture salesmanship. While it seemed unlikely, there was always the outside possibility that she was a woman who happened to have big, hairy feet. I couldn't help but stare at her foot again. She stared at it, too, and began to rotate it in small circles, her toes pointed nicely, like a ballerina.

"I'm talking about what happened to Jay Gatsby. He was shot in . . ."

"I know he was shot. That's not what I mean."

"You know what I mean, Jane. I know you know."

"Gatz had to become Gatsby in order to get what he wanted. Is this what you mean?"

"Exactly, almost. It was not to *get* what he wanted. It was to *be* who he wanted. He was trapped in the wrong life. He wanted to be a glamorous man in a big house with a closet full of expensive shirts. But did he *have* to do that? Couldn't he have just been Gatz and *still* lived in a big house and bought himself a lot of fancy shirts? Don't you think that was possible, Jane?" She sounded almost desperate.

I didn't know the answer. I felt perhaps I should reread the book in this new light before commenting. This last time through, I'd only paid attention to the furniture. I wished we could speak about this in plain English, to say concrete things about men and women and their respective anatomies, and yet it was also a relief to be discussing this in language shrouded in metaphor.

"It's not for me to say," I replied at last. "But I do think it's possible to make the most of a situation, even if it feels all wrong. You can change your life without necessarily reinventing who you are. Or you can reinvent who you are and stay in the same life, I guess."

Delia began to cry again. I found this disturbing, that this beacon of happiness was not so happy, after all. I reached over and put my hand on top of hers, and she squeezed my hand back, hard. Then she leaned forward and hugged me.

"These goddamned hormones," she said after a minute, pulling away and blowing her nose. "I don't know how you cope. I really can't take it anymore!"

"It can be pretty bad," I agreed.

"I've been wanting this change for thirty years. This is all I could ever think about. It didn't matter that I had this life that was working okay. That my wife was supportive. That I've got a great kid. That I've got a successful business. I was like this Jimmy Gatz fellow. I had to be Gatsby."

I couldn't think of anything to say, so I squeezed her hand again. The skin was soft. I wondered what moisturizer she used.

"I knew that you knew, Jane. No one else seemed to suspect a thing but I knew that you knew. We're kindred spirits, in a way."

This was a troublesome thought, and yet she was sort of right. Maybe I knew but I couldn't bear to think it all through to its logical extent, especially given that it involved my husband in possibly unsavory ways. But kindred spirits? Maybe we were. Maybe this was part of the reason I had been so fixated on her.

"Anyway, I'm confessing this to you because I owe you an apology. See, because you and me are so similar is probably the reason we're attracted to the same sort of man. This wasn't the only furniture store I was experimenting with, you know. I went to several, all at least a hundred miles away from my home, just to see what kind of reaction I got. This was the only place I felt welcome, and comfortable, like I could be myself. Or rather, *Delia*. Leon was so excited about my ideas. And he didn't seem to suspect a thing. Not only did he accept me as a woman, but he actually seemed to find me attractive. You have no idea how much that means to me. Except that in the end . . . when push came to shove that night . . . I just couldn't deal with it. I've been married for twenty years. I don't think I could really be with anyone other than my wife, no matter how I end up, myself."

I took a step back toward a buffet, dizzy. I'd absorbed all this fairly shocking information about Delia being a man without flinching, but that something intimate had actually occurred between her and my husband was more than I could handle. Deep down I really thought that I had just been mean-spirited and somewhat paranoid in my take on all this.

"Plus, I didn't quite know what to tell Leon," she continued. "I mean, I'm just in transition. I didn't want to freak him out. Not that anything really happened, Jane. I hope you don't mind my telling you this. As I said, I feel like I can confide in you. No one else really knows except my wife . . . And my doctors, of course."

I rolled my head noncommittally. Did I mind? It didn't matter if I did. I needed to hear this even if what I really wanted to do was put my hands over my ears and give a long primordial scream. Leon's attraction to her had been real. My marriage really was quite possibly falling apart.

"So Leon still doesn't know?" I confirmed.

"No. And I don't know how to tell him."

"And you and Leon . . . what? What actually happened? What happened in Wilmington?" My voice quivered.

"Oh, Jane, it was humiliating. We got as far as Wilmington and his car starting making weird noises. I can't believe I'm telling you this . . . But then there was a really loud noise, and it turned out the back tire had actually fallen off . . . I've never made a very good man, see? I can't even change a tire properly, even though I worked at a gas station that one summer. I didn't fit in. Everyone always made fun of me for being so friendly and cheerful. The other guys at the garage thought I was gay. But I was never confused about that. I wasn't gay. I just wasn't supposed to be a man."

"Not all men are good with cars. Leon can't change a tire," I pointed out.

"Yes, well, I know that, now. We had to call AAA. And then it turned out all the tires were on incorrectly, so we left the car in Wilmington and I had to get mine, which I'd left behind at the store, and it was so embarrassing that I didn't want to tell you. That's why we weren't back on the road until Sunday. And then of course we had our next fiasco with the carjacking. The whole thing is a sign, I think."

I thought of asking her whether she'd noticed a gash on the side of her car, but decided against it. It hardly mattered now. "And you and Leon . . . are you in love or something?"

"No, Jane. I mean I could fall in love with him if things weren't so complicated, but he loves you, even if you make him miserable."

Was this supposed to make me feel better?

"I mean, I don't know," she continued. "Maybe something could have happened, but I'm not there yet myself. I'm still terrified of all this."

I found myself still staring at her foot while trying to splice this all together.

"I cancelled my electrolysis appointment," she said apologetically, nodding toward her hairy toes. "I'm in a transitional phase in my transition," she laughed. "I need to go home, is all I know. I need to be with my wife and decide what's next . . . I think part of this confusion is just the hormones messing with my head. The doctor said not too many people react as profoundly to the hormones as I did, in terms of my cup size. But you know, my mother was enormous and so is my sister and clearly my female side was just bursting to get out."

This was way too much information. And yet I wanted more and more and more.

"What did Leon say, exactly?"

"Say when?"

"When you said that he loved me but that I made him miserable."

"Those were his words exactly. Plus he said that he never envisioned himself stuck like this. Stuck in a store that was like a sinking ship. Stuck in such an unhappy marriage. He said that he was eating himself to death and you couldn't stop spending money and that he needed a way out."

"And were you the way out?"

"I don't know, honey. Like I said, I couldn't go there with him. I've got my own problems. But don't get me wrong. If I was going to go through with this, then I'd want someone like

Leon. I think he's amazing. He's so devoted to this store, and to his family, and he's having such a bad time of it with this bones business. But this just isn't right for me. Plus my wife needs me. She's having a worse time of it than any of us. Then, when I saw that movie, when I saw that poor, poor man die in his swimming pool just when he thought his happy ending was in sight, I realized that this just was bound to end badly, too.

"So I'm going back home now, Jane. But I did want to give you this settee, first, to get you guys started. Plus I brought a bunch more from my warehouse. It should be here by now." She walked over to the window. I looked out and saw a long white box truck in our lot.

"I'm going to give this first batch to you as a parting gift. It's all overstock anyway."

"You have a warehouse?"

I had forgotten about the customer until she came back through, sucking on an asthma inhaler. She made her way slowly across the showroom to the grandfather clock collection.

"Yes, honey. I'm into patio furniture, obviously. How do you think I know so much about the trade? We've got too much wicker this year anyway, so I'm happy to give it to you and I'll write it off—I'll just say it was a charitable contribution or that it burned up in a fire or something. It's sitting in the truck out there. Is it okay if I have them bring it in now?"

"Um, sure. Maybe put it downstairs? There's no room up here."

"Do you mind showing Rob, my driver, where you want it? I'm going to call him and tell him you are coming downstairs. Then I'll get out of the way. He doesn't actually know about the transition. And I don't really know what to say to Leon. Could you just tell him I came by and that my boy was sick or something? Tell him I had family issues and I'll be gone for a while."

"Sure," I said again, uncertainly.

"And Jane, I also wanted to tell you that I think this is a great idea. I think you and Leon can really make a go of this."

"It *is* a good idea," I said. "But it was *your* idea. You should really stick around to see it through."

"No," she said, "I need to go home now."

As she said this, she stood up and put her arms around me again. She smelled good, and her skin was surprisingly smooth, her complexion—the physical quality I most envied in her—astonishingly pale for a man, even one who was stuck midway between sexes. I considered asking her for some additional beauty tips. And then I thought about her observation that we were similar. That this was my soulmate, this man/woman weeping on my shoulder. I wrapped my arms around her and hugged her back, tight.

"If you are thinking you might not want to be a woman anymore, does that mean I can keep your makeup?" I asked playfully.

"I'm telling you, that lipstick is all wrong for you. You've really got to let me make you up sometime. But yes. It's all yours."

The customer wheezed her way back across the showroom and asked if it was okay if she sat down and rested on a red velvet sofa for a few minutes while she waited for Seymour to show up.

"Honey, you can stay all day," Delia replied.

EPILOGUE

THE FIRE occurred on Fitzgerald's birthday, a coincidence that was lost on me at the time. It had been just a few days after my revealing conversation with Delia. Later, when I had time to reflect, I remembered her presumably off-the-cuff remark about wicker furniture going up in flames. I wondered what had become of her, who she had really been. Surely the fire reference was meaningless, and she was the struggling, transitioning person she advertised herself to be, but there were times when I couldn't help but wonder about the results of the Google search Justin had done, on the ex-con from Sacramento.

It was another hot, dry day one year later when I went to the graveyard to meet Jerry Radnor, once anomalous September weather that was no longer breaking any records. A gentle breeze threatened to topple the stem of iris someone had left in an empty soda bottle atop the tombstone. Perhaps it was this same visitor who had thoughtfully left a box of safety matches beside a heart-shaped candle. I lit the wick, but the wind quickly blew out the flame.

Jerry had approached me at the WZOP dinner party a week earlier to explain that *Washington!* magazine wanted to do a

"Whither Rockville Pike" sort of feature for a special issue they were preparing on growth and economic development in the region. When Jerry tapped my shoulder I felt my heart leap, thinking it might have been Roger Josephs Jr. whom I had spied sitting two tables away. While I had no intention of pursuing things, I had nonetheless dressed carefully and hoped to see him, to catch an admiring glance from him, or at least make eye contact from across the room. I found myself staring at Roger Josephs Jr.'s cheesy ad in the newspaper sometimes, wondering what might have been.

As it happened, Roger Josephs Jr. did not come over to my table. When Leon was cornered by the new assistant to the advertising director as we tried to make our way out, I noticed Roger standing nearby and worked up the nerve to say hello. He stared at me blankly for a minute, trying to process who I was. Clearly he knew I was familiar, but he just couldn't place me. Maybe I was someone named Chloe? Maybe he wondered if I was a congresswoman for a moment or two. Whatever he thought, he summoned his impressive trial lawyer skills to fudge it until a light bulb went off. Then we talked about furniture and memory consulting for a while. He was still quite charming, but there was no particular sizzle to the conversation now that I had stopped hating my husband.

Prior to running into him at the dinner, Jerry Radnor had been pestering me about getting together since we'd met a year earlier, and I had successfully put him off until now. Each time he called his concept for the story seemed to change, but it was hard to blame him for that—Kramer's itself had been in constant flux. There were our multiple layers of controversy, followed by Samuel's death, and then the fire. Now the idea for the story was to focus on our patio furniture venture, and to tie this into a lengthier narrative about changes along, and the future of, the Pike. This was the sort of free publicity we could not really afford to pass on, even though I had a nearly allergic reaction to the idea of being the subject of an interview. And it seemed impossible to discuss our new venture without touching on a couple of related, more personal, topics that I had no intention of discussing with Jerry. He seemed to understand at least part of what lay behind my reluctance. It would be strictly about patio furniture, he kept promising, strictly business.

"No rehashing of the bones episode," I demanded. "And no questions about Tiffany Fleisher." Jerry pledged he'd leave both the bones and Tiffany Fleisher out of it, but I wasn't sure he really could. Even I had to admit these were the juiciest bits of the story.

Our patio furniture venture was set to launch in two weeks, and the article would come out shortly thereafter. This was a publicist's dream come true—a feature in a magazine with a circulation of 150,000, timed perfectly to our launch. When I started to get cold feet, Leon reminded me that we were in no position to be choosy about how we were going to attract customers, and we needed the money. In addition to expenses such as Leon's new car (the damage to the axle stemming from the flawed tire alignment was pronounced beyond repair), Justin had talked us into enrolling him in a local music conservatory for guitar lessons at $50 a pop. I had expected Leon to balk at the fee. Forking over large sums of money, no matter how worthy the cause, almost always made him clutch his heart—I didn't know if he was in actual physical pain or just struck sentimental—and start reminiscing about his hardscrabble upbringing. Either his propensity to embellish was growing to the point of forsaking any claims to reality or his memory was getting fuzzy, because his timing was increasingly off in these stories—it was hard to believe Samuel would not have purchased a car by the time Leon was old enough to be working behind a cash register, by which point his father would have been a well-established businessman.

At this rate, his stories would soon have him living in the days before supermarkets and refrigeration, gallantly hunting small game for dinner. I braced myself for the onslaught of one of these anecdotes when the conservatory registration form arrived, but strangely it was not forthcoming. Instead, Leon said he thought it was a good idea.

Washington! magazine had already run items about both the bones resolution and Tiffany Fleisher, so my refusal to address these subjects was not likely to have a profound impact on Jerry's reporting. Still, having been intimately involved with the two matters I might have been able to offer insight, or at least a fresh slant. Tiffany's arrest had made headlines, although were it not for her job as a federal prosecutor the story might have gone unnoticed—just another frustrated suburban housewife with a high-powered career, money troubles, and a cutting-edge psychological disorder having to do with obsessive-compulsive home renovation. Tiffany's big mistake was that she used her government-issued credit card to pay her contractor, and by the time that she was escorted from the Department of Justice in handcuffs she was close to a million dollars in debt. We didn't have much crime locally, but what little we did have tended to be interesting, and this one didn't disappoint in its multiple layers of scandal. By the end of the investigation Tiffany's maid had been implicated, as had her personal trainer. All of this was public knowledge, and on the surface appeared to have nothing to do with me, apart from the fact that I had taken over Tiffany Fleisher's Memories, Inc. franchise and had reinvested some of the proceeds in Kramer's Discount Furniture Depot, which was now operating under a new name: Fitzgerald's.

Tiffany's loss was my gain in another unforeseen way: with the blessing of Mrs. Sheryl Turk, founder of Memories, Inc., I had been awarded all of Tiffany's bonus cruise points. This was meant as hush money, an arrangement that was completely explicit. Evidently Mrs. Turk considered it bad for business to have it known that one of her highest-earning consultants had emotional problems, never mind that she had been indicted. She supplemented the points and essentially offered me the cruise with the understanding that I would keep quiet about Tiffany's problems. I was happy to comply, even before Mrs. Turk sweetened the deal by allowing me to bring a friend on the cruise.

This might have been a wasted perk were it not for the fact that I had actually *made* a friend. A few friends, even. Over the past few months I had begun to conduct biweekly Power Scrapping Sessions in my own home. My forced attempts at idle chatter had slowly, remarkably, turned into something more substantial. People began to call me at odd hours to consult on their albums. I had no idea what it was I said or did that made me an effective memory consultant, but perhaps it had to do with my genuine admiration for each of these small masterpieces.

Although I now had a Rolodex and an actual waiting list to attend my Power Scrapping Sessions, I had made no progress whatsoever in sorting through my own family photos, and I was beginning to take a peculiar sort of pride in this. It was not just laziness, or disorganization, or a lack of time that prevented me from getting organized. It was the knowledge that some memories are best left unconfronted, even by memory consultants.

When Nancy Reisman called and asked if I would join her and a couple of the other soccer-mom scrapbookers for lunch at a restaurant, I agreed. Really I went because I thought it would be good for business, but I found myself enjoying the easy conversation. We ate and talked about kids and schools, about real estate and college admissions, and admittedly we gossiped a bit about Tiffany. Nancy was still behaving like Nancy, but she managed to pull herself together long enough to appear coherent and ingest a salad now and then. She explained that the solution to her car fiasco was that she and her husband had swapped vehicles. She had repaired the windows and tires on the Navigator, but it still had streaks of orange spray paint and the stuffing was coming out of the seats she had slashed. She was saving up for further repairs, she explained nonchalantly, but in the meantime she felt she had the better deal, getting to drive the new car, even if it looked like a carnival wagon.

When it came time to pick a companion to accompany me on my cruise, I chose Leon. This had not been my original plan, of course, since part of the appeal of going to sea was to sail away from him. But I softened with his first apology, and melted with the second. He said he was embarrassed by his accusation that I might have been embezzling from the store, that he was just overwhelmed and frustrated by our dwindling resources and our multiplying legal problems. He added something about having been distracted by Delia and all her big ideas and that he'd gone slightly off his rocker for a while. He did not elaborate, and I didn't ask him to. While part of me wanted to needle him about Delia a bit more, to see if he had any clue about her true identity, I managed to refrain. I was happy to put the episode behind us, along with the metaphorical ashes of the burned-up store.

Which is not to suggest things were suddenly blissful. Leon agreed to go on the cruise reluctantly, after much grumbling about how there would be too much estrogen aboard, about how he didn't want to get sucked into any scrapbooking baloney. I received assurances from the Memories, Inc. travel agent that he would not be required to do any scrapbooking and could spend his time entirely as he chose. My own scrapbooking obligations were to be mercifully few, as well—only one mandatory Power Scrapping Session per day—and I otherwise planned to kick back and try to be a fun, happy person. And if that failed, as it no doubt would, then I would at least get some reading done.

Leon and I had our bags packed and were ready to sail away the following day for a brief break before the store reopened. Seymour agreed to stay in the house with Justin, although it was not clear who would be watching whom. It didn't much matter—now that Justin had his license he could take care of food concerns, and since he had stopped hanging out with Mike I felt less need to fret about him, generally. Plus, Justin had rejoined the soccer team—a healthy instinct, I thought. He scored three goals in the first game, possibly the result of being fired up after a brief argument with the referee, who insisted he remove his "jewelry" before playing. After some initial protests he relented, leaving his collection of metal studs in his gym bag on the sidelines.

So what, exactly, *did* I plan to tell Jerry Radnor? I would tell him that we had developed a new line of patio furniture based on the aura of the Fitzgeralds. Based on what sort of furniture F. Scott Fitzgerald might have been, had he in fact been a piece of patio furniture rather than a dead author buried here on Rockville Pike.

I would tell Jerry Radnor about our Daisy Buchanan Wicker Settee, about our Gloria Patch Hammock, about our Nicole Diver line of striped towels and umbrellas, and about our Amory Blaine rocking sea chair—a stretch based on a scene in which Amory, in *This Side of Paradise,* "seized a chair where he could watch the sea and feel the rock of it."

There were many more pieces of furniture I planned to tell Jerry Radnor about, most of them not actually derived from any patio furniture references in literature because, in fact, they are few and far between. This was possibly because Fitzgerald's father was a failed wicker furniture salesman, and this was his own version of a memory he did not want to confront. I would tell him about the Dick Diver divan, and I would tell him that if our launch was successful we planned to expand the line to include a set of Zelda furniture, maybe even some Scottie things for kids.

Jerry Radnor took notes as I spoke. We sat side by side on top of the grave. I had never shared this space with anyone before and TeeJay watched protectively, nodding to me from his wheelchair. The iris managed to stay upright in the bottle despite the wind. It would make a good picture, Jerry said. By the end of the day there would almost certainly be additional gifts—more flowers, maybe even a bottle of gin, I told him. Once someone had left a box of pencils and a pad of paper.

Jerry was more excited by this than I would have expected, or perhaps he was just good at his job. Either way, his enthusiasm was infectious, and I found myself opening up to him. It was hot, even though the trees provided a nice blanket of shade, and Jerry was perspiring heavily. I watched a drop of sweat slip off his forehead and onto the paper, smearing the ink.

He reiterated that this story brought together many themes of relevance to *Washington!* readers: the contentious subject of development along Rockville Pike, the presence of a dead celebrity in our midst, the launch of an exciting new local business, and the rehashing of a big news story—the fire.

This was undoubtedly his roundabout way of trying to trick me into talking about the bones. But he knew the story already. Everyone knew the story. So there was no real need for me to repeat that I was grateful the bones had been located and sent to the lab prior to the fire. No need to pretend, as I had already been forced to do countless times, that I'd been delighted to learn that our store sat atop hallowed ground. No need to say it had been a huge relief the bones turned up because otherwise there surely would have been speculation that Leon had torched his own property to cover up evidence. Evidence of what, exactly, no one would actually ever say, but surely it was images of dead coeds that danced through minds. The lab results came back the day after the fire, the first semi-good news we'd had in years. The bones were those of a cow *and* a human. The human bones were determined to date back to the late 1800s, possibly the shinbone of a slave, as well as some bits of ribs. The bovine bones were less impressively aged—DNA samples suggested the cow had keeled over sometime within the last twenty years, only coincidentally coming to rest near the remains of the possible slave.

This resolution, at least, gave Anna Berger something new to focus on. She leaped into action researching the story of the family of slaves who had lived out in the old barn. Within months she had pieced together a biography of young Natalie and Nataniel Johnson, the fourteen-year-old twins she determined belonged to the shinbone and the ribs. Nat and Nat's father had helped build the barn just prior to the outset of the Civil War; he'd been the slave of a tobacco farmer who had relocated to Rockville, Maryland, when his plantation went bankrupt. The twins' mother was killed in childbirth. Within six months, Anna had published a pamphlet, as well as a packet of Nat 'n Nat Johnson paper dolls, all of which were so preposterously rich in detail that even her historic preservation allies were rumored to be quietly discussing her credibility as a county representative.

The old barn was designated a historical property, the only problem being that it no longer existed. It was not just that the barn was gone, but there was a huge crater in the ground where the barn used to be, where the bones had presumably come from, where future bones might be found. Leon and I agreed—we were doing more and more of that lately, *agreeing*—that we would not get involved. If it became a historical property, so be it. If they wanted to build a replica barn and sell tickets to enter it and look at some imitation slave and cow bones, fine. It might be good for business.

Anyway, if the historic preservation people wanted to rebuild the barn they would first have to turn their attention to moving the gas line that had contributed to its demise. I was prepared to let Anna Berger fight that battle. I hadn't cared about the barn when it was standing, so I certainly didn't care about it now that it was gone.

Just a few feet from the gas line was the street, and in the street there was a manhole. And on that fateful day one year earlier, Anna Berger had organized a protest. The lab reports had just come back, and she had decided to hold a preemptive rally to oppose our plans to continue building an office. The framing had gone up months before, but the project had been stalled pending the outcome of forensics tests. One of the protestors had been smoking a cigarette, or so the fire department investigator believed. He must have tossed his still-lit butt in the general direction of the gas line, which ran underground and connected to the manhole, and this caused a minor explosion, which caused a minor fire, which quickly escalated when it ignited a shipment of mattresses sitting on the loading dock which turned out not to have been designed in accordance with fire safety standards. But that was another story entirely.

I'd been across the street at the graveyard, looking at the blue, cloudless sky, when I heard a bang. I thought of fireworks for a moment, but when I sat up I saw a giant fireball, then smoke. Within minutes, there were sirens. Three people suffered mild burns, but mercifully that was the extent of the human injuries. The building itself was not as fortunate. Only the front portion of the store was damaged, but insurance estimates and a return visit from Julio Gris confirmed that it would cost as much to fix as it would to tear it down and build a smaller, more cost-efficient structure. Given that the building had brought us nothing but heartache, we decided to opt for a fresh start.

If there was a winner in all of this it was, naturally, Chandler Chandling. He busied himself suing people on our behalf for the next year, and filled his own pockets with insurance money. He also wrestled reparations from Washington Gas, which denied responsibility for the explosion but preferred a quiet cash settlement to a lawsuit that would only draw attention to the fact that after a year of costly investigations, they were no closer to determining what was causing the manhole explosions. Our own not-insubstantial chunk of the settlement went toward erasing our credit card debt and rebuilding the store.

While I had begun the interview with a sense of dread, Jerry seemed entirely sympathetic, and by the end of our conversation I found myself unexpectedly warming to him. Not to him, exactly, since he was something of a cold if sweaty fish, but to his interest in our store and in the graveyard, which he seemed to genuinely appreciate. He repeated over and over that he simply could not believe that Scott and Zelda Fitzgerald were lying right here, in the midst of all this haphazard development. He started to say something about the hideous furniture store across the street—most people did—but he stopped himself. It was rude. Plus it was gone, anyway.

Since Jerry seemed to get it, I told him that I wanted to show him something. I took his hand and pulled him toward the southwest corner of the graveyard, where it jutted out onto Rockville Pike, catty-corner to the store. I was still startled each time I stared across the street and did not see the metallic façade that had once been our furniture store. There was a new Kramer's now, but it was inconspicuous; it no longer swallowed up the landscape, no longer hoarded all of the midday sun.

This particular corner of the graveyard hovered just above the chaos, offering a nearly panoramic view of endless, wondrous, traffic; of the nearby Metro station; of office buildings; fast-food restaurants; and the new parking garage under construction, just down the road.

I told Jerry to close his eyes and listen for a few minutes, to tell me what he thought he heard. We probably looking pretty odd, standing there—a white-haired man with perpetually broken eyeglasses, clutching a notebook and a pen, and a nondescript middle-aged woman, a memory consultant, owner of a new patio furniture store based on the aura of F. Scott Fitzgerald. We stood side by side, suspended just a few feet over Rockville Pike.

"What does it sound like?" I asked Jerry after a few minutes.

"It sounds like waves," he said. "It sounds just like the churning of a sea."

"Exactly."

Across the street I could see Leon beckoning to us from the parking lot. We walked to the store the long way, via the crosswalk, and Leon and I then showed Jerry around. He seemed to like the furniture. Later, a photographer arrived and took a bunch of pictures, mostly of the Daisy Wicker Settee. He also took a few of me and Leon in front of the store. We held hands. I flipped my hair back like the Fjorki model.

Did we look like people in a furniture catalog? Or like people in a Memories, Inc. album? Would we inspire future generations, or send them running for cover?

Dorothy Parker once said Scott and Zelda looked like they had just stepped out of the sun. I wondered what she would have said about me and Leon. It was a rhetorical question, of course. It seemed unlikely we would ever have crossed paths with such glamorous figures, unless, of course, they had needed cheap furniture.

ACKNOWLEDGMENTS

Thanks to Jennifer Finney Boylan, whose engaging memoir, *She's Not There,* inspired me to connect the Gatsby dots in the penultimate chapter. Thanks also to the folks at Peerless Rockville, who provided historical material and cheerfully answered questions.

Melanie Jackson and Marysue Rucci both helped shape this project from its inception, and I am grateful for their encouragement and support. Tara Parsons made things run smoothly. Valerie Strauss, Trustman Senger, Carl Lavin, and Jean Heilprin were insightful early readers. Ally, Emma, and Max kept me both grounded and aloft. And my beloved in-house editor, Steve Coll, saw me through many drafts while making life an adventure.

About the Author

Susan Coll's articles and reviews have appeared in the *International Herald Tribune*, *The Washington Post*, and the *Asian Wall Street Journal*. She lives in Maryland with the journalist and author Steve Coll and their three children.